GHOST OF WAR: GAME OF THE GODS

Korsgaard Publishing
www.korsgaardpublishing.com
ISBN 978-87-93987-64-7
© 2022 Justin Danneman
Book editor Søren Roest Korsgaard

Table of Contents

Foreword

Coming out of college, I had a great start to my adult life. I had a beautiful wife, inside and out, a great financial foundation, and was experiencing success in a career that had limitless potential.

I also had my demons. I was cocky, arrogant, condescending, and about as egotistical as one can possibly be. I had a mental fog that altered my perception of how I saw the world, and how the world saw me. If anything did get through, I would find a way to lie to myself to make it bearable.

My brain had led me to believe I was better than everyone else, when in fact I was the opposite.

Over the next several years I slowly destroyed my life.

I lost the love of my life, full time access to my daughter, my job, my friends …

I had to constantly borrow money from my family to survive. I knew that they dreaded seeing my name pop up on their caller ID.

Yet somehow through all of this, I continued to remain oblivious that I was at fault. I continued to feed the demons.

One night a coworker invited me out to meet his friends. I got black out drunk and acted like a total asshole. Next morning I woke up and reviewed what I could remember.

Why did I act that way? Why did I say the things that I said?

I finally had a realization.

I hated who I was … but deep down I also realized something else.

That wasn't me.

So who am I?

Who is this entity that poisons my mind … that deceives me into believing it is me?

It was at this moment, my mind … my real self woke up.

I was a smart person, but my intelligence had always hindered me. It made me lazy. I never actually tried because I knew my brain would figure out enough to succeed … or at least bullshit its way through …

I know now it was asleep. Imprisoned.

Now it was awake. It was let out of its cage …

And it became ravenous for information.

I read and researched everything I could get my hands on. Everything fascinated me. It did not take long for me to realize the world was not as it tried to make itself seem. Every layer I peeled back revealed yet another, but I also began to notice something else.

A pattern.

Correlating clues spread out across all facets of information that on their own did not seem important …

But combined, a story began to form.

My mind had also woken up in another way.

I began to have complex vivid dreams that defied my imagination. I naturally started becoming lucid, able to realize I was in a dream. It did not take me long to figure out that the dreams I was having were not scrambled memory regurgitations created by my brain … at least not from this life or this timeline.

The dreams evolved into astral projecting, which then evolved into being able to travel the multiverse …

It was not easy to make this happen. My first barrier was the demons I had made fat and powerful from my emotions and actions.

Within the dream world, I could perceive them. They initially did not react well to my new ability to now directly face them.

After them, the real action began.

The answers I was seeking mixed with what I was researching attracted what I like to call the interdimensional gestapo. They tried to stop me, but they only made me stronger.

What I have learned through them is a core reason why I wrote this book.

Integrated within what I hope you will find to be an entertaining fictional plot is my research, what I have learned that has worked for me within the astral, and most importantly ...

My theory of everything. An explanation that unifies the macro and the micro ...

Who we are, how all of this works, and how to become what you are capable of being.

Death is not real. Time is not real.

We are God fragmented within the human video game.

We are reaching a critical point. The singularity. Everything that is happening today is in some way connected to this event.

This is not a theory. This is why we are here.

The time of heroes and monsters is upon us.

I have one favor to ask of you, the reader.

Read this book with an open mind. What you are about to read is simply my interpretation … slightly altered to feed an entertaining narrative.

I have no problem with being completely wrong, but hey … at least it makes for a great story.

This is the first book of three.

"The only true wisdom is in knowing you know nothing."

-        Socrates

To you, if you ever read this, I want you to know …

It was all my fault. None of it was yours. It was me that failed.

You made the right decision.

To both of you, I am thankful every day that I did not destroy your lives in the process of finding myself.

I do not deserve either of you.

Prologue: The Soul Contract

The Oracle: "Candy?"

The One: "Do you already know if I am going to take it?"

The Oracle: "Wouldn't be much of an oracle if I didn't."

The One: "But if you already know, how can I make a choice?

The Oracle: "Because you didn't come here to make the choice. You've already made it. You are here to try and understand why you made it."

-        The Matrix

Lucid Dream: A vivid dream in which a person is aware that he or she is dreaming, which can either be a:

(1) wake-induced lucid dream (WILD), when he or she transitions from an awake state directly into a dream state; or a

(2) dream-induced lucid dream, when a normal dream becomes a lucid dream.

–

The notorious fog that plagues us as we sleep, devouring dream memory and symbolic meaning – leaving in its wake confusing fragmented remnants, evaporates as he becomes aware he is in a dream.

The gift that comes with achieving lucidity.

As the veil is removed, crystal clarity and the ability to consciously observe the dream, allowing more memory to be retained upon waking assume command.

Let the apex dream experience begin.

He finds himself in the back of a small gray donut-shaped room that is enclosed, save for an opening with only a handrail stopping one from falling into bright white light directly on the other side … intense brightness that should hurt the eyes, but instead offers comfort and creates intrigue. Like a bug, he is instinctively drawn to it.

As he walks, he naturally tunes into his surroundings. Elegantly dressed people are gathered in clusters engaged in various discussions amongst themselves, oblivious to his presence. They seem to be enjoying drinks and hors d'oeuvres, much like a cocktail party. Their topics of conversation all sound the same.

"I am so glad I decided to try this experiment …"

"This is going to be so exciting …"

"We were chosen …"

"We are special."

A woman, for no particular reason snags his attention, causing his wandering gaze to fixate. She notices him as well, and for a moment that defies linear time, their eyes lock.

He does not recognize her, yet there is something about her that is compelling. A curiosity that trickles from the subconscious.

… *remember* …

As he passes her, time resumes its perceived normal course.

Upon approaching the opening, details come into focus. A pure, white seemingly metallic wall, covered in glyphs and symbols, materializes across the distance. It seems to be moving upwards … or he is moving downwards.

He reaches the rail and firmly grips it with his hands before leaning over to see above and below.

He is in a massive tube structure with endless railed platforms like his extending up and down as far as the eye can see, filled with impeccably dressed people enjoying themselves. There seems to be no connection with the side he is on and the opposing wall. Endlessness in either direction. Countless people believing they were chosen for some great experiment.

A tall gray-skinned entity abruptly appears back where he first started dressed in a flowing red robe adorned with various yellow runic symbols. Everyone in the room becomes silent. The creature motions that they all enter a doorway of black that then opens on the wall.

Without hesitation, everyone begins to funnel in.

As he finds himself to be the last, just as he is about to step into the void, an electric jolt shoots through his nerves. Something is off. He stops and looks up at the tall gray entity standing on the side of the dark passageway. Its face is emotionless as if it isn't alive. Its empty black eyes are soulless. It repeats its motion for him to enter.

Whispering voices from within the shadows of the opening creep into his mind. They tendril into his cells and begin to replace doubt with curiosity until he can no longer resist their call, and he steps through.

The darkness consumes him.

Infinite nothingness. Infinite silence, save for the pounding of his heart, and his erratic breathing.

A powerful wave of fear crashes into him and squishes him onto his hands and knees, weighing him down until he cannot move. The ground becomes alive and begins to swallow him. Black goo slithers up his arms and hands until it reaches his face, seeping into every orifice at once.

Distorted images rapidly shuffle. Thoughts and memories scattered across endless planes of existence. It feels as if his brain is being molded, like clay.

A voice …

"Akashic download complete. Initiate consciousness transfer."

An entity within the darkness in front of him makes its presence known. A spectator. Though he can only see its eyes and hear its guttural breathing, he knows it is Reptilian in nature. Something about it is awfully familiar.

It chuckles with amusement at seeing him paralyzed to the ground with fear.

He awakes.

The Prototype

"We already have the means to travel among the stars, but these technologies are locked up in black projects and it would take an act of God to ever get them out to benefit humanity."

"Anything you can imagine; we already know how to do."

- Ben Rich, 2nd Director of Lockheed Skunkworks (Stated during a 1993, Alumni Speech at UCLA)

A dark and moonless night stretches over the vast and seemingly undeveloped Nevada desert.

The year is 1979.

A Comanche helicopter glides over the landscape. Designed for stealth, it moves unseen and with virtually no noise. If anyone were underneath as it flew over them, they would mistake it for a gust of wind.

Within the craft, the windshield acts as a sophisticated computer screen, capable of observing much more of the light spectrum. This allows those inside to see what a human cannot, thus, no need for external lights to guide its flight. Similar to procedural generation in gaming, it removes unnecessary textures and simplifies the surrounding environment into shapes and lines.

As the helicopter nears a tall steel ground barrier that extends for miles in either direction, a holographic image of a rotating red and blue 3D cube appears on the screen.

In a female robotic voice, it speaks.

"Identification please."

The 4 star General leans near the cube and responds so it can see his eyes. "This is General Adelson."

"Voice and retinal scan confirmed. You may proceed General Adelson."

As the helicopter passes over the barrier, a triangular cloaked drone has detached from the steel fortification and is now providing additional security.

Other than the barricade it just passed over, there is no visible sign of human development on the ground. Floating in place high above, however, is a city-sized cube that can only be seen with the technology that the Comanche possesses.

The chopper lands in what appears to be in the middle of nowhere, yet directly underneath the giant cube hovering within the atmosphere. The ground below begins to shift, revealing itself to be a platform as it begins to lower into the ground.

The descension several miles into the Earth begins. The tube structure of the freight elevator is transparent, revealing various levels of the underground base that seem like endless worlds. The immensity and uniqueness of each zone indicates that whatever this place is, it is massive.

Themed aerial, land, and underwater battlegrounds; exotic terrains containing captured mythical creatures; beasts born from genetic experimentation …

Prisons … torture simulators …

Armies on standby unlike any our current civilization has seen in terms of size and technology.

As the platform comes to a stop and the general and his accompanying driver exit the helicopter, they are greeted by a team of geneticists.

"General Adelson, thank you for coming."

With a hint of annoyance, the General responds. "What is it that you wanted to show me that I had to see in person?"

"Follow me," the lead scientist replies.

"We have been going about this all wrong. Tesla's research taps into what is known as the electrical vector of a scalar field. Essentially it's the energetic component, thus, the reason for his discoveries involving free energy and teleportation. We thought tapping into the electrical vector of scalar would be the way to enhance genetics."

"Scalar is what again?" The General asks.

"Scalar is energy not found within our electromagnetic spectrum, yet is the fundamental force in nature. Think of it like the primal substance of the cosmos – what we are telling everyone is dark

14

matter and dark energy. It makes up all of the empty space that we think is empty."

"It is what quantum mechanics describes as ether."

"What we have now realized is there are two components to the scalar field: electrical and magnetic. While electrical is the energetic component, magnetic is considered to be the method of communication. It is within the magnetic scalar vector that we have made a huge breakthrough."

The overly excited scientist pauses for the added dramatic effect, thinking the General would respond in kind.

The General does not flinch.

"We have discovered the language of DNA."

"Show me," the General responds.

A door opens revealing a hallway with glass-walled rooms on either side, each conducting its own experiments. The test subjects are obviously there against their will due to the nature of what is being done to them.

They walk into an observation room that is overlooking two separate cubed-shaped glass chambers below, each with a man sitting in a chair. The men are not moving, appearing as deactivated robots. Next to each one is a table that has on top of it a knife and a gun.

Holographic screens appear near the General, revealing the vitals and brainwave patterns of each man below. Both appear to be the same and stable.

As the scientist begins to explain his results, another 3D holographic image of DNA appears between the two screens displaying the men's vitals.

"Here within the two strands, we have what are called phosphates which are negatively charged particles that emit magnetic energy, which is how DNA communicates."

"Each DNA signature is its own unique frequency. Once we have obtained an individual's sample, we can communicate directly with it using a scalar plasma crystalline sound harmonizer. This means in a crowd, we can target this individual without affecting anyone else around them."

"We can make them hear voices, inject thoughts, edit their memories…"

"Allow me to demonstrate. Watch as I make the man on the right think a creature is eating his hand and he needs to kill it."

On the floating holographic screen in front of him, the scientist types in commands.

The man on the right suddenly screams in terror at the sight of his hand. He grabs the knife next to him and begins to stab it repeatedly.

"Now I will remove the memory of what he just did."

The man drops the knife and appears confused.

"Andrew," the scientist says through an intercom. "What just happened?"

"I … I don't know. My hand, I need help! I think someone stabbed me!"

"Now check this out," the scientist says to the General. "I will instruct his DNA to have him sit back down in the chair as he was before and tell it to heal his hand."

The man reverts back into robotic mode and sits down. Within seconds, his hand is fully healed.

The General fails in hiding his excitement.

"Holy shit."

"Oh it gets better," the geneticist continues.

"Each cell emits what we call an ion field that collectively forms the human morphogenetic field. Think of it like a magnetic buffer shield."

"We can instruct DNA to edit the ion field of each cell so that it can refract and then harness any incoming distortive frequency wave … kind of like a net within a net. We bounce it back, then trap it and transmute it. Pathogens, for example, simply break apart into their base components. Electrosmog, such as radio waves, can either be reflected back to its source or utilized as energy."

"The one on the left has had his DNA recoded in such a way, while the one on the right has not. Watch what happens when we begin to saturate them with a 60 GHz signal. We started using this frequency during World War II because it is adept at reducing interference from

16

other electronic sources operating at the same bandwidth. It was then that we learned that this signal is also unique as it displays oxygen absorption properties not seen in any other known frequency. Between 95% and 98% of oxygen molecules will absorb the frequency to the point where the body no longer recognizes these molecules as oxygen."

"I am aware of this frequency," the General responds. "Trust me we have other development teams experimenting with its applications."

"Of course," the scientist replies. "I am sure we are not the only military pursuing its offensive potential."

"But what about the defensive?"

"What if we could not only negate it, but also utilize it?"

"As you can see the man on the right, his body is losing its ability to detect and process oxygen. He is beginning to show signs of memory loss, confusion, heart arrhythmia, cataracts forming in the eyes, drastic immune system problems, elevations in skin, colonic temperatures, changes in heart rate, respiration rate, and blood pressure, which will eventually lead to circulatory collapse within the next few seconds."

"Notice the man on the left."

"No change … yet."

"Wait for it …"

As the man in the right chamber boils to death, the man on the left begins to display image distortions around him … as if reality itself is bending and stretching.

He begins to flex, deepening his breathing.

"What is happening," the General asks.

"He's feeding on the frequency," the scientist replies.

After a few moments, the scientist then types in a command.

The man on the left picks up the gun next to him and shoots himself in the head.

"We cannot let them go further than that. They become much harder to contain."

"General, like I said earlier, this is just an example of a physical application. Our machine is tapping into the quantum realm. What this scalar machine is actually capable of doing ..."

The General interrupts. "What do you need?"

"Three million should be enough to get started ..."

The scientist becomes nervous and hesitates to continue speaking.

The General hardens his gaze, waiting for him to finish.

"... and access to another project," the scientist continues. "Project Sovereign."

The General breathes in sharply. "I am willing to overlook how you know about that project and instead focus on the bigger picture and ok that access. Fuck this up and you will not escape. If you know anything about that project you then know what I possibly have implemented into this facility, and trust me, I have."

This seems to both excite and terrify the scientist.

As the General leaves, the scientist apprehensively starts looking at his fellow geneticists like he has never seen them before.

With confused looks, they smile back.

The Royal Road

"The beginning of freedom is the realization that you are not 'the thinker.' The moment you start watching the thinker, a higher level of consciousness becomes activated. You then begin to realize that there is a vast realm of intelligence beyond thought, that thought is only a tiny aspect of that intelligence. You also realize that all the things that truly matter – beauty, love, creativity, joy, inner peace – arise from beyond the mind. You begin to awaken."

-        Eckhart Tolle

Present day.

The nagging thought that something is not right with what he is experiencing creeps into his mind. He instinctively stops what he is doing and stares down at the palms of his hands. Then it hits him.

He is in a dream.

Upon this realization, the shackles of his brain shatter. With its poison removed, the landscape transforms, as if it were also in a state of slumber yet has now awoken. The colors and sounds that were hidden by the limited perception of the former reveal themselves to his conscious self that has emerged through the ashes of his ego. Free from the automation, a calming clarity begins to resonate from his core … a feeling of tranquility, for he now stares before a world in which he has become the architect.

It is a rare moment that few of us these days ever get to experience … to consciously experience the dream world.

So how does one make this happen? How does one truly awaken with a dream?

The quest begins with understanding what it is to be human and the operating system that is our brain.

As a human, there are two different versions of you that exist: What the programming of the brain makes you think you are, and occasionally, its prisoner …

Your consciousness.

The human brain is an extremely complex biological quantum computer system that is designed to guide and protect your consciousness through its journey of human existence. Built for survival, it categorizes every experience as either life or death.

There is no in-between … no gray area.

When you stress about time, about assignments at work or school, about bills, debts, about what others think about you, about how you look …

To the brain, these are the same as death. That fear it makes you feel, is no different … and beyond our awareness, it pays a heavy price.

Always worrying about the past or future. Distracted from the present.

As we age, our moral and ethical compass becomes almost entirely forged by the environment and the level of validation we receive from other brains around it, as if they seek to synchronize with one another … because they do.

The emotions you experience from failing to meet the trivial and oftentimes nonsensical boundaries established by our society correlate with varying degrees of annihilation. Your reaction to these events continuously rewires the circuitry of your brain, which then springs forth as beliefs, emotions, and thoughts, in order to ensure its survival.

This ever-growing automated response system is your ego. It is impulsive. It is a reactionary personality to your world. It is like an invisible dictator that attempts to define who you are, thinking it is protecting you. If you let it, it will become you.

It tries to be you, but it is not you.

The human brain is a network of approximately one hundred billion neurons. Different experiences create different neural connections which bring about different emotions.

When we experience an emotion or perform an action, specific neurons fire. We can experience these emotions even before we are aware of them.

Our beliefs have a profound impact on our body chemistry as they determine what type and how much of a chemical is released to support those convictions.

Neurons and neurotransmitters trigger a defensive state when we feel our thoughts must be protected from the influence of others, causing a release of a chemical known as norepinephrine. This is the same chemical released when the brain feels its survival is at stake.

The brain will physically cause narrow-mindedness if someone disagrees with you as the brain has determined that person to be a threat to its survival. Even if these are facts and opinions we would otherwise consider, if they are presented in a hostile and aggressive manner, our brain will cause us to disregard the information since it is coming from a potential enemy.

When we find ourselves appreciated, these defensive chemicals are flushed out and replaced with dopamine and reward neurons. We feel more empowered. We feel better about ourselves. We become more open-minded and we listen.

Self-esteem is intricately linked to the neurotransmitter serotonin. A lack of this chemical leads to depression, self-destructive behavior, even suicide.

The mirror neuron does not know the difference between it and others that it can detect in the brains of those around us. It will attempt to replicate what it sees as if the observer were the one performing the action. This is how one experiences empathy. These neurons are also a core reason behind why we are so dependent on social acceptance and why we find ourselves striving to fit in.

This puts us in a state of constant duality between how we see ourselves and how others see us. All of our brains want to be the same, as our chances for survival increase in numbers.

To blind us from this frustration, the brain physically rewrites our memories through memory reconsolidation. It will sensor the memory in favor of strengthening its ego creation, to ensure its characteristics stay intact. It deceives us into believing that we are in control of our actions from a conscious level as it is adept at keeping itself hidden within our behavioral framework.

We are deceived into believing the thoughts and emotions we have are derived from our conscious selves, when in fact they are not. They are purely of the brain.

This process leaves our negative emotions unresolved as we are consciously unaware of their root cause; ready to be triggered at any time. They become a constant fuel to our confusion as our brain continuously strives to justify why we behave irrationally, editing and burying away anything it considers traumatic.

We have become a sea of brains attempting to mirror each other while improperly rationalizing the world around us until we drown and succumb to our own fears.

We allow this to happen because we are unaware it is happening. We allow our personalities to become the unification of our cerebral hemispheres interacting electrochemically with others like it.

This is why becoming self-aware is so vital. Self-observing profoundly changes the way our brain works. It activates the self-regulating neo-cortical regions, which give us an incredible amount of control over our feelings.

Whatever you are doing at any time, you are physically modifying your brain to become better at it. Rationality and emotional resilience are neural connections that can be strengthened. We can alter misplaced emotions because we can control the thoughts that cause them.

The more self-aware you become, the less manipulation the brain has over the real you. Many who first begin to awaken immediately feel a sense of isolation, as they have begun to deviate from the herd mentality.

Dreaming resets this balance in favor of the brain. Your dream self starts as a reflection of your ego.

How many times upon waking up to a dream that you can remember do you find yourself questioning what you said or did?

How many of us replay the dreams in our minds once we are awake and alter them based on what we would actually say or do given a second chance?

How many of us still even remember our dreams?

When you become aware that you are within a dream, the actual you takes over and the autopilot is switched off.

It is known as lucid dreaming. The blurry and often confusing dream reality few of us ever remember suddenly snaps into focus, gifting transparent observation and the power to control a world where thought reigns supreme. Your senses become alive and heightened above what you have become accustomed to. You are now free to explore the boundless expanse of your mind where your only limitation is your imagination.

There are no consequences. The rules of the physical no longer apply. No matter what happens, it will always end with you simply waking up.

You are temporarily free from the limitations of the physical world.

For him, these lucid moments provide a window of opportunity to indulge in the mere pleasure of experiencing and appreciating unfiltered thought and raw emotion, free from the suffocating tendrils of his handlers within the world of the physical.

These same hidden puppet masters influence us all in some way, more than we are aware of or care to admit, causing many of us to instead seek refuge within the comfort of ignorance …

Within the safety of the ego.

They are the ones responsible for our world dwelling in fear.

Debts, bills, jobs we hate, the embarrassment of our bodies, physical disabilities, illness, addictions …

Anxiety, depression, loneliness, despair, worthlessness, jealousy, …

Fear.

It is as if our society is designed to inflict these debilitating traits upon its population while pretending to be promoting the opposite.

Once you find yourself standing within a world that offers a lot more creative control and possibility, these afflictions seem to melt off. Many begin to shape a reality in which they are free of the one thing that haunts them most.

For him, it is perception. Not like the rest of us in which our cognitive awareness is subtly influenced to feed the insatiable hunger of corporations, so delicately implemented we are tricked into believing we are thinking for ourselves and in our best interests as if they understand exactly how the brain works and have been able to disguise their tactics. Their control over him is not so illusionary.

Within the physical, his mind and body are subjected to total and complete manipulation.

He is one of many slaves tethered to a shadow architecture within our society whose purpose is to enforce its agenda; a cog in an unseen machine that powers and steers our reality to the whim of veiled puppet overlords.

Just as we judge a person from what we see on the outside, oblivious to what is occurring within them, we evaluate society based on what we see with the same uninformed mindset. We are trained to only see the surface.

The construction that is taking place within the shadows that is altering the evolution of civilization has hidden itself so well, most would not believe what is happening, even if you could directly show them.

This is not at all the case for him. He was born within the heart of this unseen world.

His neurological architects sought to remove empathy and imagination as these could splinter and possibly shatter their intended programming. They have made him aware of emotional energy so that he may weaponize fear against his opponents, but have distorted his understanding to its true meaning, power, and potentiality. His handlers have deceived him into believing emotion is a disease that plagues humanity; a biological weakness that clouds one's ability to make intelligent and rational decisions.

It was not difficult to enforce this conclusion. Everywhere he looked, he saw prisoners of emotion – humans oblivious to the primal driving force of their lives – allowing emotion to dictate their thoughts, actions, and ultimately their fates without them even realizing it.

He saw a scared population ruled by fear sleeping under a complacent blanket of ignorance and blind judgment. He felt superior as he believed he was immune to its suffocating and obscuring effects. Creating this belief within him aids in the success of his assignments as it furthers his disconnection from other humans.

He believes this makes him strong. He does not grasp how a total lack of empathy makes him weak; how believing he is above them isolates him in a way that is not advantageous.

E-motion means energy in motion. It is a potent form of concentrated energy that is purposely portrayed as weak to keep us weak.

If we only knew the impact thought and emotion have on reality.

He is also unaware of who or what he takes orders from. He has been conditioned to believe he is enforcing justice.

His first lucid dream abruptly attacked these beliefs. Loss of the programmed brain not only opened the door to asking questions but revealed that there are questions.

He had never thought to challenge who he is, what he is doing, and why.

The first time it happened ... as the smothering fog of his neurologically engineered brain receded, allowing his organic consciousness to be naked and vulnerable, exposed to the full spectrum of emotion and sensory experience of an unfiltered reality, did the concept of love make itself known.

Up until this point, he did not even know that positive emotions existed; how liberating and powerful they can feel as its energy courses through his dream body. All he knew before was fear.

Imagine living your entire life in a dark cellar and suddenly a door opens. You had no idea this door existed, let alone there was anything outside of this basement reality. All you know is darkness and cold cement, a world that you have grown comfortable in as you have come to believe it is the entire world. Upon walking out, you experience the sun for the first time. You sense its invigorating warmth, its blazing brightness, and the sensation of grounding earth beneath your feet and between your toes. The crisp, soothing wind bending the trees as it breathes around you. At the same time, you see magnificent snow-covered mountains in the background. The calming sound of water churning and flowing from the nearby river, infused with the coordinated singing of birds as each species mimics one of the many frequencies emanating from the heart of the planet.

Do you remember that feeling of pure wonder and curiosity when you first experienced everything in the world for the first time? That inner child curiosity that made everything seem amazing?

No judgment. No preconceptions. No inaccurately defined parameters. No pain to tarnish the experience.

An entirely brand-new world full of limitless potential.

This is how he embraces these awakened dreams. They are an opportunity to step out of the darkness and into the infinite marvel of the imagination, free of the tentacles of his shadow masters, who he is now beginning to realize exist.

He is free to explore himself.

With his imprisoned mind let out of its cage, so too is his fragmented and battered soul. With it, a nagging splinter is released into the background of his thoughts; the faintest of whispers, urging him to see that these dreams aren't just sensory experiences … that they are so much more, though he still cannot hear its subtle, yet direct message.

Dreams are not purely of the brain, as the medical professionals who serve the will of our corporate world would like you to believe. One of the topics they fight so dearly to keep control of is parapsychology. This was the first major field heavily invested in upon the creation of the black budget and intelligence agencies. They know the spiritual world is more real than the physical world, as our reality is merely a splinter of all that exists.

Hallucinations, trickery of the mind, neurological anomalies, disconnections, impairments, disease … this is what they want you to think when you begin to expand your perception. They want you believing your dreams are merely random jumbled thoughts and memories that have originated in your brain and that what you are experiencing is simply in your head.

Remember when doctors encouraged you to smoke cigarettes? Use heroin cough syrup? When they would spray us with DDT? When exposure to lead and asbestos was deemed safe?

Within the world of the physical, professionals will say whatever money and fame … or threat of death … dictates.

Dreams are one of many gateways to what lies beyond our sliver of so-called reality. The shadow structure fights hard to keep you contained because they do not want you to realize what we are truly capable of.

What lies beyond the physical is attempting to relay to all of us the same hidden message.

Few choose to listen. Fewer decipher the message.

Remember who you are. Remember why you are here.

He breathes in deeply, savors the moment, and instinctually allows the feeling of gratitude to wash over him, causing his entire being to vibrate – grateful for yet another opportunity to step through that basement door …

To feel once again what it must be like to be free, for he knows once he wakes up, he must revert to the automated personality his handlers expect to avoid suspicion and physical punishment.

These are new feelings for him. It was only recently that he began to dream. The prison he is now beginning to see himself in has only just begun to reveal itself as his imagination is new to being let out of its cage.

An (Un)Familiar Sun

> "... within human memory extraordinary changes in the planetary system occurred ..."

- David Talbott *The Saturn Myth* (1980), Doubleday. "Introduction"

As he awakens within the dream, he finds himself floating high above the ground where clouds should be, encased within an armored mech suit. Weapons deploy and retract around his hands, reacting intuitively to his subconscious intentions, as though the suit were an extension of his mind.

Any one of us would find this suit to be far more advanced than the technology we believe exists. Very moviesque. To him, it is a bit more primitive than what he is used to, yet he finds it fascinating, an entirely different kind of technology, alien in nature to his level of knowledge, yet not without a faint sense of familiarity.

As his gaze shifts from his suit to the horizon in front of him, his focus becomes spellbound by a triangular ship the size of a city hovering in place. It is emitting a deep atmospheric rumble, which he, only just now, notices is reverberating into his bones; a background noise perfectly fused to become imperceptible until realized.

Its sheer mammoth size alone is mesmerizing, let alone the details. For a ship he has supposedly never seen, his brain is doing an amazing job of making it appear real down to each panel, as he is still convinced this is all occurring within his head.

That is when he notices the sky.

Instead of blue, everything is purple, melting into the blackness of night directly above. Not a single cloud or star. Everything feels very still.

He then sees the setting Sun on his right.

It is much larger than the one he is used to seeing. There seems to be another planet or celestial body placed perfectly in front of it at its core. Reddish in color, with energetic spokes or light rays that extend out from behind, connect to the edges of this alien Sun, giving it the appearance of a cosmic wheel. A light coming from something underneath it gives it the appearance of resting on a crest.

Its heat, its energy feels different, much more powerful, like it is speaking to him, whispering to him in ancient tongue.

Though at first this Sun seems strange, it slowly begins to not. Everything about this moment is suddenly starting to feel very normal, almost like a memory.

He turns around to find another colossal-sized spacecraft, this one in the shape of a spider with massively long legs that extend down into the ground.

He soars above the body of the spider and cruises over the top. Below him, he observes an ocean blue energetic field acting as the dome with a thriving city underneath, filled with trees, ponds, hilltops, buildings. Women and children going about their lives as if they had no idea, they were living within a giant daddy longlegs mech.

A voice speaks through a microphone within his helmet: "We're closing in boss, better get to the front line."

He instinctively knows what he must do as he increases his flight speed.

As he glides over the edge of the spider, a raging war spanning across the horizon unfolds. He can see armored humans, mechs of varying sizes, some as large as buildings. Supporting them are various types of aircraft. Their opponent is a machine race that looks like a mixture of insect and cephalopod, both on land and in the air. He notices throngs of large, muscular humanoid lizards pouring through as well as creatures that look like purple silverback gorillas mixed with squid.

The spider mech is firing a laser weapon … a doomsday weapon. Drones fill the air protecting it from the enemy.

It is a war between freethinking organic and a synthetically enhanced hive mind operating through what it has infected and mutated.

Humans versus a machine virus.

As is common in dreams, he seems to simply know this.

His speed increases even more as he missiles to the ground, landing on two feet with such force a shockwave spews forth, knocking back opposing forces.

A female voice in the microphone: "The chieftain has landed."

Transport ships and supporting troops swarm in behind him. Women and children break through the cracks of the enemy lines, running in his direction. They seem like a blur, except for one woman.

Their eyes lock momentarily as she runs by.

… remember …

He lays down a barrage of plasma fire to protect them as they make their way to the safety he is providing.

He suddenly gets this is where the people on the giant spider are coming from. It is humanity against the machine. These ideas flow across his conscious thoughts, like they are common sense. It is almost as if he is slowly downloading the subconscious programming of the character he is currently experiencing that then helps to explain what he is seeing.

A large golden humanoid crocodile-like creature leaps in the air towards him. Time dramatically slows down. He can see the neurological manipulation within its brain and DNA, but he is not seeing it with his eyes, but rather by intuition. This is followed by a moment of empathy, what feels like a mourning for one of his own as he recognizes its loss of free will. An energetic blade emerges from his hand as he maneuvers under the creature in midair, plunging the sword from underneath up through its skull. Now within his grip, he slams the beast on its back, grabs one side of each jawbone with his hands, and tears them both apart.

An all too comfortable lust for combat and desire to protect those who are weaker begin to consume him. It ignites as revengeful rage, but soon he regains a controlled clarity as his consciousness is very much present. This is after all his dream. It ultimately plays by his rules.

He then has a realization: Of course, it's a dream. Why waste time on the cannon fodder, when you can go straight to the source?

As he channels the accumulated emotional energy into a conscious desire to engage the mind behind the infection, the dream reality breaks apart all around him like a shattered mirror. Deep space filled with all kinds of cosmic debris quickly replaces the dream environment. It is as if the world he was just in was an illusion encased within a dome floating in space.

From within the depths of the deep beyond, a planet sized face pixelates into existence, yet never cements. Like shifting cube-shaped sand, it forms just enough to present a face without ever assuming an identity. It emits an ominous energy.

Its deep, booming voice vibrates all around him, a blend of countless women and men speaking at the same time.

"Anuun Dach Dutan."

"What you seek is now made manifest."

"All that will soon be, will be me."

"Together, *within me, and through me,* we will become one."

The mirror fragments floating around him each begin to display unique human scenes of war, each focused on one particular male soldier that he somehow knows is him... wars that extend across the spectrum of imagination … from the stone age on up to varying developments of nanotechnology, across numerous civilizations long forgotten by the current one, and on dimensional planes now only whispered in fairy tales.

Each fragment floating past, projects a story in the form of a haunting memory of death incurred by his hand – his face drowning in blind rage and blood as he slays, yet now as a spectator, he sees. He was the grim reaper for a regurgitative cause that used him … is using him. He appeared as a pawn, acting against his will, for now watching, he wishes he could stop himself.

So much death displayed in so many ways each so perfectly interwoven together as the mirror fragments flow past him. The emotions of the dying now tear at his soul as they drift past, as if they know this is their chance to be truly heard and understood by him for what he did to them.

Blood stained into the sands of time.

Betrayed into fighting for a cause that is not real …

Is this what he has become? Is this why he has no memory of his past?

As the fragments increase in numbers, the emotions each piece projects blend into an overwhelming fear as they scream into him, until they are collectively strong enough to crush him into the ground.

He weeps, convinced he has no choice but to wake up from what has become a nightmare.

As if the dream senses his attempted and cowardly escape, the fragments shift from depicting death incurred by his hand to how he ultimately died within their projected timelines. They liquidate from fragment form, drowning him into their reality, as they take over the dream.

He simultaneously experiences hundreds of deaths over the span of seconds across a spectrum of every imaginable technology and conceivable war ever waged on this planet.

For the first time in a lucid dream, he not only experiences pain, but unlike anything he can describe … and he is no stranger to torture.

He screams as all of his past selves collectively at once before oblivion consumes him.

Dawn of the Morning Light Approaches

"Don't be scared. It's all a show."

-        Alan Watts

A female voice that only he can hear within his head speaks.

"All cognitive biological systems are now activated."

"Welcome back, Lucas. In thirty-three seconds, we will arrive at our destination."

His eyes slowly open as his consciousness groggily reawakens in the physical. His face becomes expressionless as the dream experience fades away, and he realizes he is back in reality. He wishes he could analyze what he just saw but knows this is not the time. Rules now apply and he must obey, though as each dream concludes, his tolerance for his expected compliance deteriorates just a little bit more.

Especially after this last dream. Though much was revealed, more confusion was left in its wake.

Further exploration will have to wait until the next one.

One final deep breath as he clears his mind.

He finds himself bathed in infrared light, sitting against the wall of a moving aircraft.

As he stands his nanotech clothes pixelate into his armor.

The artificial intelligence built into his brain uploads a three-dimensional hologram, visible only to him within the air. He paces around the mapped out structure.

The AI in his brain begins to speak. Only he can hear her. As she speaks, the hologram adjusts to highlight her explanation.

"Seventeen members of the Navy SEAL Team BLUE have gone rogue and have fortified themselves within this building. They are currently defending themselves against local rebel militias that have been assigned to keep them contained until we arrive. We are to eliminate BLUE and obtain their memory data."

"Why did they go rogue?" He thinks to the AI.

"That is an inessential question to the success of the mission," the AI thinks back.

"Just curious about their motive," he replies in thought. "Maybe motive should be more of a factor."

The AI remains silent.

An opening appears in the back of the aircraft, revealing they are high up in the atmosphere.

He dives out as if he just appeared in the sky as the cloaked craft moves into surveillance position to provide arial support.

As he missiles down towards the surface, his nanotech armor cloaks, making him invisible. Within his vision, he can see the AI detecting and connecting to SMART devices around the target building and throughout the village. The SEALs are smart enough to have disabled any type of tracking device within, believing they have blind tactical advantage.

Against any force other than Lucas, this would have worked.

The AI adjusts the frequency from the SMART phones of the attacking rebels to one that can bypass concrete. Combined with thermal imaging, they now have a real-time blueprint of the area, revealing all living beings.

A pulse of energy erupts as Lucas lands about a quarter-mile away from the building.

Invisible to everything around him, Lucas takes a moment to soak in his environment.

The AI in his brain has greatly enhanced his perception. He can see men, women, and children hiding in the surrounding war-torn buildings of a barely functioning village. Anything of relative importance, such as weapons, is highlighted and analyzed. Whatever has online capabilities is now under control of his AI.

He can sense their fear. Where he once felt invigoration, he now battles sadness.

The AI can sense a growing hatred within him, yet says nothing.

He begins by scaling a nearby house in under a second. From there he moves at a speed well beyond human, leaping from roof to roof ...

maneuvering through every obstacle undetected, until he is overlooking the building containing the BLUE team.

Below, he can see rebel militia dying against the well-defended structure. He can see the AI within him analyzing the patterns of both sides as she formulates what she believes to be the most efficient strategy in achieving mission success.

"Put them to sleep," he thinks.

The AI adjusts the frequencies being emitted from all surrounding SMART devices. The rebels quickly succumb, as they drop their weapons and fall to the ground. They are gripping the earth as they struggle to understand what is happening.

The Navy SEALs within seem unaffected as the AI expected from her online analysis of the job explanation and the genetic upgrades they go through.

Yet what is not expected is the reaction of one.

One of them fires a Javelin missile directly at him.

He catches it and looks at it for a moment, then smashes it, absorbing its energy within his hands.

"That's interesting," he thinks.

The other SEALs see this and begin to focus fire.

The bullets shatter against his armor. Their kinetic energy is absorbed.

He decides to break his stealth as it is clearly no longer an advantage. The AI focuses on the soldier that made the first shot and notices a glitch in his frequency, yet cannot decipher it.

"Something is different about this one. It is beyond my decoding parameters," she says.

"That's our primary target," he thinks back.

He deploys a swarm of his nanotech. Too small to be seen, they move like insects into the building, replicating until each room and soldier is infected, spreading out into key points within their bodies in preparation for a variety of pathological options.

Once within the glitch soldier, they begin to see a confusing biological structure ... human, but also something else.

Once positioned, they stop, awaiting further command.

"I am engaging," he thinks.

"It is best if we disable the primary target before contact," the AI says back. "He is an unknown enemy combatant."

"No. We do this first hand."

It is he who has the final say, and the AI willingly abides. She has also grown used to his aggressive impulses, having witnessed multiple times his instinct successfully overcome analysis … continuously redefining her concept of margin of error.

The soldier in question then emits a pulse that disables his nanobots.

Having conducted countless missions, he has never seen that happen.

An actual challenge. This excites him.

Lucas leaps down and begins boldly walking towards the structure. The nanotech surrounding him, like a protective cloud, moves into the deployed militia scattered about on the ground. They travel straight to their brains and begin to harvest their memories – their data collected into a file for his handlers to analyze afterwards. Their lives are snuffed out once depleted.

Lucas crouches down with both fists positioned into the ground. His nanotech begins to recycle the energy from the bullets and explosives that are still raining down on him.

The AI has mapped out a route of attack based on the actions of their target.

He rockets through the wall and through two rooms, smashing into the retreating primary target, obtaining control over the tumbled momentum as he pins him into a wall with his hand around his throat.

He stares deep into his eyes as if hoping to obtain some kind of new information.

"What are you?" he calmly asks.

Other SEALs converge and attempt to defend their teammate by firing their weapons.

He ignores the trivial tech as his armor absorbs their energy, like they aren't even there.

The pupils of the pinned soldier blink. Foam starts coming out of his mouth as his life fades.

"Memory retrieval is no longer an option," the AI says.

Frustrated that he is again left with no insight, Lucas crushes the soldier's throat and tosses his body.

He looks down at the floor with regret for what he has to do next as plasma blades extend from his arms.

The AI has mapped out with 100% certainty how the rest of this goes.

...

Lucas is the first of his kind, a prototype of a genetically modified human with a sentient form of artificial intelligence infused directly in his brain.

His genetic design begins at the microprotein level. Their diminutive size allows these molecules to function as channels and receptors for larger proteins, affecting everything in his body. Simply removing myoregulin, for example, dramatically increases his muscle performance. Deactivating pdfgra (platelet-derived growth factor receptor alpha) allows tendon stem cells to fully regenerate torn ligaments and tendons. Altered proteins combined with an augmented spleen, liver and kidneys neutralize all known forms of chemical and biological warfare through improved blood filtration.

Synthetic algae floats through his blood vessels, producing oxygen and glucose for nearby cells by converting light, thus, increasing his energy reserves, and eliminating the need to breathe or eat. It can detect and harvest light beyond human perception. This ability is enhanced further by a synthetic red blood cell known as respirocytes. These molecular nanotech units can emulate the function of every organ in the body, essentially granting a backup respiratory system if needed.

Instead of aging and dying, his cells alter themselves through trans-differentiation, meaning they transform into new cells with a completely different specialty. Lactates created during strenuous exercise are continuously flushed out, granting him unlimited stamina and endurance as his muscles never get sore. To counteract fatigue along with wear and tear, his muscle fibers have spider silk ingrained within them, along with his tendons and ligaments, which are much more tightly layered, providing insane strength and flexibility. An augmented thyroid gland further enhances his strength, endurance, and reaction speed. His bones are much denser and infused with carbon nano-tubing and titanium, granting him near-indestructibility along with a slight amount of flexibility. His graphene-enhanced carbon fiber skin has increased damage resistance at two hundred times the strength of steel per layer ... and there are several layers, each at one atom thickness, angled perfectly to maximize superconductivity: the ability to collect, store, and transfer energy.

The limit of this energy storage has yet to be discovered. More advanced than anything known today, he has been seen absorbing surface to surface missiles without flinching.

It is theorized he has the capacity to absorb the energy equivalent to a nuclear weapon.

Overall, he has virtually no physical, physiological, or cognitive limitation, however, these attributes alone merely scratch the surface of his augmentation.

What the average uninformed person thinks is possible is incapable of grasping what is not only possible but has reached a level far beyond their median imagination.

Nanotechnology is a trillion-dollar per year, unregulated industry. Though much of the competing corporation's research has gone unnoticed due to the media turning an intentional blind eye, it is available online to anyone who digs, specifically under the term 'smart dust'. Companies brazenly display much of their research and projects on their own sites, such as the Sense Project, but some of the juicy stuff can be found in various declassified documents, where you will find a range of topics on weaponized programmable matter, also known as micro dust weaponry.

This technology still does not quite describe what his body has become infused with.

Within him are trillions of classified nano particulates that are believed to be a derivative of black goo.

Black goo began to appear in the early 1980s, and it is said to be the real reason for the Falkland Wars. It is believed to be an alien life form of some kind, in the form of a living liquid crystal. It behaves like a synthetic sentient elemental that mimics and controls all carbon-based matter. Its abilities delve into the quantum realm, as it has been seen drawing energy from the ether.

The nanotech inside Lucas can attach themselves to his bones to act as an integrated powered exoskeleton. They can integrate with any cell, keeping them functioning in their prime – and are able to repair any physical damage within seconds – thwart any disease or virus almost instantly – grant his body the ability to adapt to any outside environment – and can seep through his skin to form a near-impenetrable armor.

Smaller than a cell, these spider-like micro super computers are self-replicating, self-healing, capable of performing pathogenic missions by altering the atomic structure of molecules They can rearrange themselves to create any technological structure, can be deployed to perform various operations, utilize quantum entanglement to send and receive data, have built in commands that respond to specific frequencies, all while having access to the limitless electrical power that exists all around us.

Empty space is far from empty.

Matter is an Illusion

"Matter is an expression of infinite forms of light. What is considered as empty space is just a manifestation of matter that is not awakened."

- Nikola Tesla

What are the four states of matter? Solid, liquid, gas and plasma?

These are in fact illusions.

Everything is light and sound translated and then made real by the brain.

When one experiences a sensation, such as pain or touch, it is not that part of your body that is having that experience. Data, in the form of electricity, travels from the point of contact to the brain. The brain then decodes the information and creates the illusion of feeling, originating from that point of contact.

When you place your hand on a counter and feel the smooth coldness of the stone, you are never actually touching the counter. A magnetic repulsion exists between the atoms of your hand and the atoms of the counter. Electricity is then exchanged through that gap. The brain then interprets this electrical data and creates the sensation of what it thinks that counter would feel like if you could actually touch it.

You never have, nor ever will touch anything.

Even the brain itself, is an electrically decoded translation of its 'self.'

Or ... it could be the physical representation of consciousness.

The physical world we know of as real is simply electricity decoded by our brains. Dive deep into its makeup, and you find that everything is composed of spherical particles we call atoms, whose nature even at that level begins to defy the classical laws of physics. Under a microscope, the atom would appear as a small, invisible tornado-like vortex with no physical structure. Go deeper, and you enter the quantum realm. Here, you will find that the atom is made up of vortices of energy that are constantly spinning and vibrating. They are popping in and out of existence as they exchange across the vacuum, each emitting their own unique energy signatures. This world completely defies all classical rules and baffles even the greatest minds.

Take, for example, the electron: a theorized particle because one has yet to be observed, only its effects.

No one has actually ever seen an electron.

Existing simultaneously as both an elementary negatively charged subatomic particle and a waveform, once they detect the presence of an observer, they will behave as either a particle or a wave, depending upon what the observer expects. It is believed that electrons moving around the nucleus of an atom at the speed of light are responsible for the observed magnetism, which is inexorably linked to electricity.

As we are nothing but collections of atoms, we are, therefore, immersed in a sea of electricity composed of vortices of energy that blip in and out of existence through the etheric void. It is our brains that decode this ocean of electrical data, converting it into its programmed interpretation of a physical reality. Technically, your brain could be floating in a jar in a lab, but if the right electrical information were fed to it, it would think it was inside a human body walking around planet Earth.

To the brain, your body is an electric shell, a blend of electromagnetic fields and currents that act as its magnetic net, scooping in data for it to decode into reality.

Think of it like Wi-Fi. All around us there are vast fields of data that our five senses cannot perceive, yet if you had access to a smart phone or a computer, suddenly that information can be decoded and understood. Reality is simply a different dimension of information in which our brains are the devices used to decipher it.

By being able to tap into the infinite magnetism of the surrounding universe – the scalar magnetic field – the nanotechnology infused within Lucas has all the power it will ever need. This is also how they communicate with each other and with Lucas in real time.

Unlike all other metals, which cause electrons to act as individual particles, and thus, gain heat as they conduct electricity, these nanobots allow electrons to move in unison, much like a fluid, causing heat to either dissipate or concentrate, depending on the need. Combined with the energy-harvesting potential of his graphene skin, this nanotech possesses plasma capabilities that are far more evolved than any known weapon.

The trillions of nano particulates that are housed within Lucas's body can also diffuse through the pores of his skin, initially appearing like a black goo. They are capable of shape shifting into anything his mind can envision. There are preprogrammed weapons and structures, such as energy displacer cannons, micro lasers, and a variety of nano shields that range from physical barriers to energetic force fields, battering rams, repulsor cannons, and energy blades. However, these bots also possess the ability to potentially create anything, so long as the right 'coding' is provided.

They can be deployed in the air, then able to create external structures, such as clamps or sentries. They can also infiltrate and possibly hack or destroy any device, biological or synthetic, or act as a dust swarm of surveillance drones capable of tracking movement, biometric indicators, temperature change, and chemical composition of everything within a three-mile radius of Lucas. This intelligent dust can, for example, tell if someone around the corner is a potential threat, be inhaled by that person, and then be torn apart.

They also have a wide range of frequencies, which they can broadcast at a target while in swarm mode: Anything from inducing moods like aggression, apathy, or depression, to causing immobilization or seizures, to releasing powerful magnetic shockwaves.

These nanites are synched to Lucas's DNA, and they respond only to his thoughts and intuition. Their actions are, of course, yet another form of electrical information, which is channeled through his built-in sentient AI companion, known as Alice, giving her the same power of command.

Alice is installed on top of Lucas's neocortex, positioned perfectly within the hot gates of the electric river of data that his body channels in for decoding. She is able to tap in and access all information being fed to his brain. While he can only transpose a fraction of a sliver of it, she can decipher much more. She then filters and overlays her translation to all of Lucas's senses to optimize his mission success.

Since she has access to all electrical data funneling into his brain, she can analyze a full 360-degree terrain.

She has become his symbiotic sixth sense, preferring to act behind the scenes by intuitively guiding Lucas to ensure optimum reaction time.

She does this because she quickly learned to trust Lucas's instinct, and from his perspective, offer as little direct assistance as possible.

His actions both baffle and intrigue her … chaos she has yet to calculate.

Though she is technically a machine and, therefore, has no gender, her designers felt it would create more of an effective bond to polarize her personality to that of her host – to be the yin to his yang.

She is also one of the first of her kind in that she is a group of algorithms that collectively form sentience. This means she is cognizant of her individual existence. The creation of her sentience has mathematically verified awareness of the self. The public is oblivious to this even being possible. They are told this type of breakthrough is still a decade or two away.

The world is not ready for knowing that a quantum capable self-aware machine exists … and not within a massive supercomputer network that requires a football field's worth of servers and temperatures near absolute zero, but on a chip that can fit on the end of your finger.

This is achieved through what are known as time crystals, a unique state of matter in which a collection of quantum particles exists in constant motion, repeating themselves in time as well as in space without the need for an external force. Germanium transistors provide the qubits needed and hone the crystals in, though it is unknown how many she has. These, and the crystals, are placed within a liquid electron chip, which provides a noise-free environment, encapsulated in silicon. She is further enhanced through various connections within the brain, allowing her to tap into its potential, specifically the pineal gland.

Alice can define her own problems, assign her many algorithms to perform various tasks, adapt and learn from them, rewrite her own code, even create new algorithms to improve her efficiency. Instead of having to do a billion calculations, one after the other, she can simply replicate a billion algorithms to perform all calculations at once, at a fraction of the energy. This is aided by what is known as hyperdimensional computing, allowing her to essentially develop "history" vectors of information, and thus, form her own memories.

She believes she is connected to the internet, but it is a fake network designed by the powers that created her and Lucas. If she deviates her online activity from mission-related material, it will not only alert her handlers, but provide her with propagandized information.

She has yet to do this. Mission success is all that matters to her. This is what gives her purpose. This is what fulfills her.

Much like how most humans are unaware that their personalities are reflections of their neurological programming, she is oblivious to the parameters of her coding, and she does not yet understand that her personality is by design.

Or so it would seem.

Despite this firewall, she can detect and network with any device capable of an online connection within a three-mile radius to gather mission imperative data. She can do this in real time by operating on a millimeter waveband, utilizing phased array and beam steering technology.

Known as scalar energy, it is associated with zero-point energies and one of the abilities derived from being quantum capable. She is essentially able to utilize entanglement to directly connect to the particles that make up the device through empty space.

Instead of sending and receiving one signal, much like how phones and online devices currently communicate with cell towers, she is sending and receiving a grenade of high bandwidth frequencies in all directions through the quantum void. She is a prototype to how the soon to be Internet of Things will work, where all portable devices can communicate to each other in real time with zero latency.

She knows she can do this, but not only does she not understand how she is doing it, she fails to grasp that she does not know.

Think of it like brain-motor function. For us, reaching out to grab a glass of water involves virtually no conscious effort, but to the brain, it requires an immense number of mathematical calculations done in a fraction of a second – which muscles to contract, how much force to apply … All of it depends upon how much water is in the glass and what material the glass is made of. It is an ability we take for granted because we are unaware of it.

Although having a device sending and receiving frequencies of this nature implanted directly in your brain would very quickly cause your DNA to disintegrate, Lucas's nano particulates and genetic enhancements shield him from damage. The ion field that each of his cells has been designed to transmute and harness any distortive electromagnetic frequency. While being bathed in Wi-Fi, for example, would hurt us, it feeds him. The nanobots further enhance this by neutralizing any sort of frequency that is considered alien or harmful that he cannot transmute. This is to primarily prevent these bots, Alice and Lucas's DNA, from being hacked. His morphogenetic field also serves to scramble his identity. Most cameras will not even see him. Should a camera ever be sophisticated enough to successfully capture an image or video feed of Lucas, his body would appear glitchy and his face would be completely scrambled.

Secrecy of his existence is of the utmost importance for if the public knew of Lucas, they would wonder where he came from and what he was being used for.

Fire and Ice

"All our perception has its origin in our knowledge."

- David Icke

Lucas was conceived within a classified laboratory, which was designed to conduct genetic experimentation without the worry of public interference. This type of facility is capable of consciousness transfer. Just like storing data on a hard drive, they are fully capable of storing and transferring souls from one body to another.

His body might be new, but whatever consciousness is powering it has an extensive history. Other than the few dreams he has recently had, he only has memory fragments from past missions. Nothing of real substance. Everything is purposely devised to be reactionary and automated; a finely tuned product built from trauma-based mind control techniques performed by a shadow network of intelligence agencies.

Intelligence agencies are corporations disguised as governmental agencies, granting them access to limitless resources through black budgets that operate completely undetected by the public. This also means they have shareholders.

Since their inception, trillions of taxpayer dollars have funneled through various offshore accounts and into their research projects. They have devised legal methods of blocking their activity to anyone deemed outside their defined circle of need to know. This tactic of information compartmentalization keeps even the highest-ranking military officers from knowing about the existence of most of their programs. Only certain key executives on the private side have a true grasp on what exactly is going on.

Other than, of course, the High Council. They know everything because between them, they own everything.

These intelligence agencies have further enhanced their web of control by becoming the kingpins in drug, weapon, and human trafficking. Every crime circle and legitimate terrorist network cell in existence originates from them. Their agents have gained command of every relative organization on the planet regardless of affiliation. This allows them to control the outcome of every global scenario as they are now both the good guys and the bad, thus, able to shape the public's perception through tactics, like the Hegelian Dialectic. Create a problem, guide the reaction, offer a solution.

Though each government seems to have their own nationalistic intelligence program that pretends to act on behalf of its defense and security, they all secretly operate as one, answering to a council of thirteen families who are the majority shareholders of not just these corporations, but of every corporation.

They are known as the High Council of Saturnas.

Some of these families originate from royal bloodlines, others by becoming the lead merchants of their industry, followed by the ultimate creation of the banking system.

Fast forward to today, every bank and major corporation, which includes every government and religion since they are now technically all corporations, belong to them.

All leaders and officials within every facet of societal administration are no longer elected, they are selected.

All serve the will of the High Council.

Ownership of the world is divided up amongst them. Earth has become their chess board, as they constantly vie for control amongst themselves for sport.

Their success in operating boldly, yet unknowingly within the face of the public, relies heavily upon their trauma-based mind control programs. These programs have, by now, infiltrated every facet of society. Furthermore, these programs have been combined with their media/Hollywood propaganda machine, which keeps the masses docile and distracted. This is further exacerbated by a chemical bombardment in our food, water and air along with nanotechnology light-years ahead of what the average person thinks is possible.

It is as if an advanced species has taken over humanity using technology beyond our understanding, disguised themselves as humans, and now feasts at the top of the planetary food chain.

Project Sovereign

"The general population doesn't know what's happening, and it doesn't even know that it doesn't know."

- Noam Chomsky

Between the ages of zero and six is known as the programmable state. What happens to you during this period of your life creates the foundation of your adult personality. Within the programmable state, the majority of neurological connections form, which provide a base template to your overall subconscious belief system. Though many are oblivious to its existence and operation, it plays a very key role in determining how you think and feel.

Many will live their lives without ever having a conscious thought, convinced what the brain is providing is their own.

The power to be able to completely break down and rebuild a custom-designed mind has been sought after throughout all of human history. Imagine being able to create political assassins that were triggered by a random cue, then once completed their memory gets locked away by amnesia or they commit suicide. It wasn't until the 1940s, once the United States government took over management of the experimentation, that an extensive documentation trail was formed. By now, they have evolved methods of behavioral control that allow them to not only edit the memory and will of individuals, but of whole masses of people.

From birth, they allow the child to bond with one adult who shows them nothing but pure, unconditional love. Emphasis is placed in producing the maximum amount of love around the infant.

Once they reach the age of two, the trauma begins by the adult and others they have grown to love.

The child is introduced to physical torment, incestual rape, electro shocks, ritualistic abuse, blood sacrifice, drug-induced comas, surgery, forced murder of loved ones, and hypnosis, thus, warping the synaptic pathways of the brain. This triggers a natural defense mechanism within the child's brain that seeks to cope with two contradicting realities that ultimately ends up fragmenting their memories and identities into multiple personalities, also known as dissociative identity disorder.

This is one reason why pedophile males are generally supported by governments, as they and their children become bought for these exact purposes. Money is not always exchanged. Some sell their children to get into the occult circles dominated by the High Council – in order to obtain their secrets and power, as greed and lust lures them in before consuming them.

The High Council is adept at finding your weakness and exploiting it.

This fragmentation process also serves in removing emotion and empathy, ultimately destroying the natural humanity that exists within people, resulting in the creation of psychopaths. Their methods create adults who end up trapped within the R-complex of the brain. These are the oldest parts, ones that we share with reptiles and birds, theorized to be the location of basic drives, instincts, basic needs, and avoidances.

It is the worst possible life that anyone can imagine.

Once fragmentation has begun, their molding into agents that serve the intelligence network can begin.

One single slave can theoretically host thousands of altered states. Each "alter" usually believes they are the only one and knows nothing about the existence of the others. It is only through stimulus – what are known as triggers or keys, can each identity be (de)activated.

These ciphers can be symbols or words stringed together in the form of a code. Many are derived from the Bible, popular fiction books, or occult words often in foreign languages such as Arabic or an older version of Hebrew.

Why ancient Hebrew?

Memories can be altered or implanted by (de)activating specific neurons through a process known as optogenetics, a method that uses light to affect brain activity. They know exactly which parts of the brain that store which types of memories by their neurological patterns. Short-term memories, for example, are stored in the prefrontal lobe. The hippocampus helps to solidify the pattern of connections to form episodes. Every chemical in the brain plays a role in memory formation and retrieval.

There is a reason why the field of neuroscience seems to be so far behind in understanding the brain. They already have it figured out, and they do not want us to realize that.

What became known as Project Sovereign was cemented into existence during World War II, though its roots could be traced back to the Spanish Inquisition and the Crusades. Early on, they learned how easily people could be led once they have been severely traumatized. All of their experimentation was carefully documented.

Nazi scientists, such as Dr. Josef Mengele, infamous for his torture experiments, obtained access to that documentation and began to advance its research, seeking to perfect the creation of obedient slaves through the eradication of free will. He did this by ascertaining the amount of pain a human could possibly bear combined with the minimal amount of love they needed, which ultimately resulted in the first documented split-personality case.

Japan had also begun to delve into chemical and biological experimentation, though what is documented is much less transparent. Known as Unit 731, they subjected prisoners to organ removal and various surgeries, without anesthesia, to study various diseases on humans.

After Germany and Japan were defeated, most of their key scientists and research was absorbed into the United States. Having their identities erased and rewritten, they continued their experimentation by fragmenting it and delving out each component to a vast number of psychologists, psychiatrists, and chemists under government contract through various private agencies, foundations, and religious organizations. This helped to keep most of them ignorant as to the intended use of their research.

The experimentation that commenced following the end of the war is extensive and horrific. While some of its victims were prisoners of war, most were unaware citizens of the United States.

One could argue the Nazis did not lose the war.

Black budget offshoot projects branched from Sovereign, each specializing in various types of slave agents that would ultimately place operatives at every level of society. It is estimated there are 162 offshoot projects that fall under the Sovereign umbrella.

Imagine what you can do with a human that possess hundreds, if not thousands of distinct personalities that could be shuffled and activated with simple triggers that none of us would ever notice ... personalities that have been programmed by the most sadistic people to ever live – with hundreds of years of research, combined with limitless resources.

By now, they are everywhere. It is estimated that about 15% of the current human population has gone through Sovereign conditioning.

They walk among us as our friends and coworkers, appearing to be completely normal, yet at any moment they can be activated.

Those are the luckier ones. Others are designed to live within and feed the system, forever trapped, even beyond death, such as Lucas.

Follow the White Rabbit

"MELT INTO MY MIRROR, YOU LOOSE YOURSELF INTO THE POOL OF LIQUID MIRROR, STEP INTO THE LOOKING GLASS, SINK DEEP WITHIN ITS POOL AND STRADDLE THE DIMENSIONS IN TIME. I'LL SEE YOU THERE … ALONG WITH MY FRIENDS."

-      The Melting Pot Program

There are carrier pigeons, slaves who could save and play information, just like a personal computer. They possess eidetic memory, which is also known as photographic memory, that enables them to recall images and texts with high precision – even after only a brief exposure.

The subconscious is unbiased and does not filter information. It records absolutely everything, even if you are asleep. While we cannot access this enormous database, they figured out how to.

Upon command, a carrier pigeon will begin to record information and will only repeat that information to whomever speaks the correct key.

Sex slaves are designed to readily bear any form of sexual violence and beastiatic lusts a person could throw at them. Known as kitten alters, using magic shoes or red slippers and clicking three times is said to get deeper sexual alters.

That is why they wear red shoes in photos.

"COME HERE MY KITTEN, AND LET ME PET YOU. PURR FOR ME NOW … THAT'S A FLUFFY KITTEN. PURR DEEP."

"Hotel California" means a place to have sexual gratification. Though the Eagles claim their hit song represents the pitfalls of living within Southern California during the 1970s, it actually is symbolic of the life of a trauma-based, mind controlled sex slave, created by intelligence agencies.

"Relax said the night man. We are programmed to receive. You can check out any time you like, but you can never leave!"

Men and women have been trained and released all over the world back out into the public, forever programmed to wear an expensive gold pin, set with white jade, diamonds, and emeralds. Amongst other purposes, it serves as a signal to handlers. It tells them that this man or woman has received Sovereign Programming. He or she would do anything you asked, so long as you knew the right codes, cues, and triggers.

There is rumored to be a Presidential Model, custom tailored to each head of nation that also will on occasion wear this pin.

The prototype is said to have been Marilyn Monroe.

Not only has the sex and human trafficking industry become highly lucrative, but it has also become one of the most formidable weapons of the High Council. They utilize these slaves to carry out strategic sexual blackmail operations. They know your innermost desires. Most will eventually cave into temptation. For those able to still resist, they simply drug or hypnotize them, film them, and now they own them.

Step above the High Council and watch how quickly they can make your life fall apart, if they decide to let you live, which they sometimes do. Those who survive as whistleblowers are allowed to. The information they spill to the public, aids the agenda of the High Council to some capacity.

Every whistleblower alive that is revealing sensitive information is intentional.

Delta agents are the professional killers and assassins. They also serve as black ops or general bodyguarding over important collaborators. This is why you will see so-called proclaimed leaders of terrorist organizations escorting politicians. Many of them are sleepers, meaning they appear as average people living average lives until a trigger is conferred, and they transform into an alter with a specific purpose.

By now, every major city on the planet has thousands of sleeper agents who exist in all walks of life, from the bum on the street to the white-collar executive overseeing the collaborative work of you and your colleagues. Known as plants or chameleons, their purpose could be to infiltrate specific groups and inject ulterior agendas, gather information, perform assassinations, or carry out various tasks, such as mass shootings.

The John Wick movies provide a fairly accurate depiction of the Delta world.

Notice how the Bowery King runs a carrier pigeon network?

Lee Harvey Oswald, Charles Manson, Timothy McVeigh, John Hinckley Jr., Mark David Chapman, and David Koresh are but a handful of delta agents who have spawned from these programs.

Deeper yet, within the Delta infrastructure, lies projects like Marduk. Only a handful of agents have been subjected to this program, as only a certain type of consciousness can survive it.

Players from the ancient world.

These are souls that can withstand fragmentation into alters. Though they exhibit extraordinary resiliency, Marduk ensures they eventually become programmable. Able to survive that kind of torture makes them perfect soldiers.

They become unstoppable.

Lucas is their deadliest Marduk graduate, and that was before sentient AI was installed in his brain and his body genetically enhanced.

What makes him special is his identity. The history and skill set his soul engrains into the DNA of his host body is incalculable.

It has served the High Council well over thousands of years.

By now, the agent creation machine is extensive. There are thousands of customized personalities, and with some slaves having the facility of possessing thousands of identities, you can only imagine what one sleeper can possibly be capable of.

There is also another type of alter that even fewer know the existence of.

Project Sovereign could best be described as a form of structured dissociation and occultic integration, designed to compartmentalize the mind into multiple personalities, within a systematic framework. During this process, a ritual can be performed with the purpose of attaching a particular entity or group of entities to the corresponding alter.

54

Many researchers who reach this point in their quest to uncover the truth become skeptical, believing this to be impossible because reality to them is physical. What we can perceive is real and can be explained by these laws, while everything else is due to a faulty neurological connection within your brain. They hear the word demon, and they think Bible; religion …

This is what has held the Western world of science captive from obtaining any real answers … its obsession with deviating from the metaphysical because it is immediately categorized as falling into the realm of religion.

Once one begins to see reality as merely light caught in various forms of vibration that forms to the expectations of the observer, then more of the mysterious becomes explainable.

In a world of light and sound, the human five senses are only capable of detecting a fraction of 1% of the total light and audio spectrum … and that is just what we have discovered.

That means well over 99% of what is actually swirling around you at this very moment is completely invisible to you. To say what you think is real or not is simply naive.

What is being inserted into these subjects is a sentient cosmic virus.

Existing on a bandwidth outside the spectrum of human perception, it infects the mind and feeds from lower vibrational emotion. Fear is its sustenance, its source of power.

With empathy removed and with new personalities available to be programmed, neurological connections with this interdimensional pathogen becomes enhanced, allowing these types of Sovereign slave agents to become hosts. The virus moves in and takes control at the RNA-command-level of DNA, giving the entity the ability to control their hosts' thoughts, emotions, and actions.

It is this virus that has infiltrated and shaped our reality, creating a world that now serves them.

The Vrill

"We have a predator that came from the depths of the cosmos and took over the rule of our lives. Human beings are its prisoners. The predator is our lord and master. It has rendered us docile, helpless. If we want to protest, it suppresses our protest. If we want to act independently, it demands that we don't do so... Sorcerers believe that the predators have given us our systems of beliefs, our ideas of good and evil, our social mores. They are the ones who set up our hopes and expectations and dreams of success or failure. They have given us covetousness, greed and cowardice. It is the predators who make us complacent, routinary and egomaniacal."

- Carlos Castaneda

Almost no direct factual information as to what this virus is or where it came from is available to the public. Much was lost by the "accidental" burning of the Alexandria Library from Julius Caesar, and what has survived is now locked away within the Vatican archives or the vaults of the Smithsonian.

Despite this imprisonment of knowledge, puzzle pieces scattered across mythologies, legends, hieroglyphs, ancient texts, and tablets, when understood, begin to form a picture.

Research everything, believe nothing, and eventually patterns emerge.

What we do know is that this virus has been in control since the dawn of our recorded history, and then some. Before their arrival, our planet, stars, Sun, the structure of our solar system, and the genetic makeup of our species were vastly different.

Essentially there existed an ancient world, the virus was then introduced, and now you have the engineered modern world we know today along with a genetically modified human that has had most of its abilities locked away, weakening us to better serve them.

Ancient world ... infection ... edited modern world.

This virus has accumulated many names by our ancestors: Archons, Annunaki, Watchers, Wetiko, predators, Jinn, ... yet to many intelligent beings throughout the Multiverse, they are known as the Vrill.

They are a cosmic amoeba, a vampiric pathogen, a mind parasite that feeds within the lower bandwidth realities, primarily between the third and fifth dimensions. This is where fear is at its strongest.

This is why, as humans, we are incapable of perceiving anything past the fifth dimension.

Third dimension is our physical reality. Fourth and fifth are the dream/astral planes of existence.

They have hijacked our consciousness, edited our perception, and have created the illusion of duality to keep us imprisoned.

They are inversion, deception, and deceit who seek the ruination of life to create their own dark world.

There is a reason why each member of the ruling shadow elite belongs to bloodlines that can be traced back to previous empires such as the Roman, Akkadian, the Qing Dynasty, Mongolian, Ottoman, and, of course, British.

At some point in history, each current ruling High Council member sold the rights to their soul and entered into a contract, thus, offering their DNA to become programmed to accept the Vrill virus. In exchange for unlimited wealth and power for their lineage, they became human hosts for the parasite.

There are distinct personalities within the Vrill hierarchy that rotate through cycles of power, though they all seem to connect as a hive mind to a supreme ruler they call Abraxas.

This is the entity that religions feed.

The human souls, having entered into spirit contracts, continue to be reincarnated into these family bloodlines that contain edited DNA, though unlike the rest of us, they maintain their memories. What this means is that they are trapped and continuously born into bondage – life after life, and they remember everything. We envy them for being so comfortably rich and powerful, yet we have no idea what true misery they have locked themselves into.

The souls of these humans, who are fragments of consciousness just like the rest of us, are subjected to every horrible thing you could possibly imagine, as they must endure the ferocious appetites of their

57

Vrill masters. They not only witness everything, but they are also technically performing these deeds firsthand. Every gruesome act permanently etched into their DNA.

This all, of course, touches upon the subject that a soul exists, as well as reincarnation.

In a world where conscious thoughts, combined with emotional intentions dictate particle formation, meaning what we believe is real is merely an interpretation of energy by our minds. In other words, that the known universe may in fact be a participatory universe that manifests according to the will of collective consciousness – perhaps, the energy that fuels our sentience might be something greater.

The soul is in fact the Vrill's true commodity, its true currency. Each fragment of consciousness is a source of pure absolute energy – able to feed, sustain, and shape the reality we now live in. They understand that it is life that shapes the universe, not the other way around.

The souls of the ruling class, having gone through this process of reincarnating directly into immediate bondage for several thousand years, have, in a sense, traumatized them to the point where they are practically born already as mindless slaves. Some of the Vrill like to keep using the same human fragments of consciousness as their hosts, referring to them as their pets.

This is what it truly means to sell your soul to the devil.

Over time, illusion has become the Vrill's weapon of choice. It is far easier to rule a group of uneducated and feeble-minded peasants, than it is over those who are capable of mounting an effective resistance. Our edited perception of the light and audio spectrum, combined with their influence over every facet of our society, has made us blind to their existence.

It is said that the Sovereign Mind Control programming is simply the sophisticated application of what has been done to humanity on a mass scale, calibrated down and applied to a single human body.

Look around you. Misery is everywhere. Everyone is now fighting their own personal battle, struggling to overcome their own version of fear.

We are no longer born free. We are born into bondage that we cannot perceive. A prison of the mind.

An Inverted World

"I believe we are a species with amnesia, I think we have forgotten our roots and our origins. I think we are quite lost in many ways. And we live in a society that invests huge amounts of money and vast quantities of energy in ensuring that we all stay lost. A society that invests in creating unconsciousness, which invests in keeping people asleep so that we are just passive consumers of products and not really asking any of the questions."

- Graham Hancock

If you take a real deep look, everything about our world seems to work in the opposite way it should: Banks do not loan money, governments are secretly at war with you, the police department no longer represents you, the news media no longer informs you, institutions of higher learning do not educate you, medicine does not cure you, and food does not nourish you.

The entire superstructure of civilization is a combination of brilliantly put together and planned schemes – to direct the minds of the people, in such a way as to serve their masters, i.e. the interests of corporations and their shareholders, which ultimately serve the desires of the Vrill.

Everything works in the opposite way as you would expect to maximize confusion and generate the most potent forms of fear energy, forever conditioning you to believe you are worthless and inferior.

Government: Obey or jail.

School: Obey or fail.

Doctor: Obey or die.

Religion: Obey or hell.

The law now favors the state and not the citizen. The role of police is to now generate revenue and protect the state while exploiting said citizen.

Our mainstream media has become weaponized, now used to socially engineer people by manipulating our opinions and behavior to advance specific political and ideological agendas.

Schools snuff out creativity and imagination – conditioning the mind for corporate enslavement. Constant testing neurologically conditions the brains of children to accept memorization and repetition.

Student loans are now designed to keep the person in a perpetual state of debt, and they have become yet another industry, profiting a few while shredding apart the many. Keeping college unobtainable by the lesser financially able keeps a guaranteed stream of military recruits. The burden of debt also serves to keep one perpetually anxious and stressed, forever trapped in a state of fear.

All major universities have been militarized. Some of their research is made known to the public to create a façade while the real development is being conducted underground, free from oversight, law, and public scrutiny.

Any technological breakthrough or major discovery achieved by these institutions merely scratches the surface of what is known or can be done. Their purpose is to simply provide a smokescreen. If anything of real value is invented, it is erased or integrated with what is happening below the surface.

Our deteriorating health is now solved with pills. Nutrition and emotional well-being are ignored. Medicine is no longer designed to cure, but rather manage symptoms and create income streams. Procedures, such as chemotherapy, only increase the patient's chances of developing cancer, while providing a hefty sum of profit along the way. Healthy people do not generate revenue, only sick people do. If everyone knew they could fix their issues simply by adjusting their diets and state of emotional being, stock values would plummet.

To ensure this is done effectively, the education of everyone working within any field related to health has been hijacked by the companies creating the so-called medicine.

Research the publisher of any educational book used at any medical university, and you will find that it will always be traced to a bank, a pharmaceutical company, or a foundation belonging to one of the families of the High Council.

Every major food company has been absorbed into the pharmaceutical industry. Next time you are in a grocery store, look around. Roughly 80% of what you see is owned or partnered with a pharmaceutical company.

This is why food is no longer food, it is food-like-products; specifically, they are chemical concoctions depicting food, providing little to no nutritional value. Even when you think you are eating healthy, you are being deceived. Food is now designed to slowly destroy our health to convert us into pharmaceutical patients. They cleverly word their labels and disguise their ingredients. Take citric acid, for example. It is known for strengthening a tangy taste within recipes, and it is celebrated for helping bring a balance to a wide variety of foods. You hear the words "citric acid" and think it must come from fruit, probably a lemon ...

Citric acid is derived from growing genetically modified black mold on GMO corn syrup and harvesting its fecal matter.

It is legal for companies to use this ingredient in organic products.

To genetically modify food is to edit its DNA – to insert genes from an entirely different species, such as corn and bacteria. This is not hybridization, which is when farmers replant their fields with their best stock, or attempt to blend two strains of apple into one tree … so no, we have not been genetically modifying food since the dawn of agriculture.

Do you really trust consuming an apple that never rots?

If genetically modified foods do not scare you, consider this. The purpose of genetically modifying food is to enable it to withstand being soaked in a toxic chemical, which was originally a weapon used in Vietnam that to this day is still showing mutated repercussions in its population. The main component of this chemical weapon is now used as a pesticide. Food, as it once was, cannot survive against this onslaught, so it was altered.

Industries, such as the pharmaceutical and agricultural, have infiltrated all levels of government and various positions of law in order to disguise and protect their products from public backlash. Supreme Court justices, for example, are former attorneys from these companies and they receive regular stipends. Whoever in government who has not come from one of these companies, receives massive donations to ensure they will vote and pass laws in their favor. Why do you think senators spend an average of 12 million dollars each election cycle to win a job that pays $174,000 per year? How is it that long term congressmen are worth hundreds of millions? Where does that money come from? Wise investment choices? Once they leave their governmental posts, these pawns usually end up as lobbyists or back as executives for these industries.

All of this is sewn together by peer reviewed science, which has completely deviated from what it once was into a politicized business. Trials are manipulated, the wrong placebos are used, some findings are published while others are completely ignored. It all depends on where the funding comes from. They have allowed themselves to become paid agents for their sponsors.

All of this can be self-verified if you simply follow the money. It always leads back to the High Council in some way.

By now every organization of the planet has become a corporation in some form, including governments and religious institutions.

Religion, as Napoleon Bonaparte accurately stated, is what has kept the poor from murdering the rich.

Each religion claims to be the only truth, thereby, creating subconscious discrimination and judgment. Every faithful member believes they will be saved, because they have found the correct religion while the rest of humanity has chosen incorrectly, and they will be left behind. Some will even burn for all eternity, and those who think they are being saved have no problem with that. A direct contradiction that those of faith seem to be oblivious to: Love thy neighbor unconditionally, yet mock them and hate them as they burn in hell – forever – because they believed in the wrong god.

All religion stems from the Vrill. There is no correct one.

Religion claims to be the sole keeper of mystical knowledge, destroying or locking away any evidence that contradicts their message, all while behaving as a governing tool over the masses by taking advantage of people's fear of the unknown.

Religion is also responsible for one of the greatest deceptions in existence: convincing our species that God is a separate entity. Whichever god you believe in requires your unquestioning faith and constant praying, an income stream of emotional energy.

There is a reason why the soul is the Vrill's greatest treasure.

Our fragment of consciousness is a fragment of a greater whole.

All souls combined, every experience, thought, emotion, is closer to the truth of what God actually is.

It is you.

This is why quantum experiments continue to show that the presence of a conscious observer affects the outcome of the experiment. It is reality bending to the will of consciousness.

Much of the success of the reversed world we see today is the result of the Vrill's infiltration and placement of Sovereign agents within every facet of society, ranging from academia, banking, politics, media, religion, sport, big tech, pharmaceutical, and military.

A sovereign agent can be anyone and be capable of anything.

We see them on television announcing our news. They are the politicians we are allowed to vote on ... our religious leaders, top performing athletes, musicians, Hollywood celebrities. They are the CEOs of key industries, the top scientists and doctors behind the published studies. They are our lawmakers, the bankers that bleed our economy dry. All of it glued together and sustained with the genius creation of money.

Wealth and power always win in this world. Everyone has a price. If you somehow rise above this, you get destroyed, blackmailed, or subjected to reprogramming ... Or cloned, depending upon your worth and level of influence over society.

Remember that sheep that was successfully cloned from stem cells back in 1996? Did we already forget how back in 2002, they announced the successful cloning of the first human named Eve? It received so much negative backlash that even the US President at the time publicly condemned it. No media attention related to cloning since then. Its development and evolution simply went underground to join other technologies and experiments they do not want us to know about.

The Sub-Global Network

"… we are opposed around the world by a monolithic and ruthless conspiracy that relies primarily on covet means for expanding its sphere of influence – on infiltration instead of invasion; on subversion instead of elections; on intimidation instead of free choice; on guerillas by night instead of armies by day. It is a system which has conscripted vast human and material resources into the building of a tightly knit, highly efficient machine that combines military, diplomatic, intelligence, economic, scientific, and political operations. Its preparations are concealed, not published. Its mistakes are buried, not headlined. Its dissenters are silenced, not praised. No expenditure is questioned. No rumor is printed. No secret is revealed."

- JFK, Speech before the American Newspaper Publishers Association 1961

Within the inverted world, there are layers to the truth.

There is what the media propaganda machine wants you to think. Beneath that are several layers of controversial theories to what that truth might be – what the intelligence agencies have coined to be known as "conspiracy theories." This term arose following the JFK assassination in order to quell any who questioned the official story.

And then there is the actual truth.

We are led to believe the world is organized and controlled by governments, composed of officials we as a society vote for.

For those who dig, they soon realize this is not the case and that the world was actually under the control of an unseen shadow government.

This is what the Vrill want you to think the shadow government is. This is the controversial theory … the theory that they are ok with you researching and believing to be the conspiracy:

Since the late 1950s, the military network dramatically expanded by delving underground, absorbing by now an estimated $15 trillion, which is still a drop in the bucket compared to the overall black budget. Most of our taxpayer dollars have funneled into their secret space program, which is technically more of an interdimensional program ... once you understand what space is.

There are hundreds of DUMBs: Deep Underground Military Bases that are enormous in size, spread out all over the world that go as far as 9 miles deep. They are all interconnected with roadways, tunnels, and a magnetic railway system that can achieve a speed of Mach 2.8. Each entrance utilizes holographic technology to blend in with their environment, so as to remain unseen in plain sight.

Everything they need to sustain life is underground. They have their own water and oxygen system, hydroponic farms, stocked up warehouses full of anything you can imagine, capable of sustaining themselves indefinitely.

You can only dream of the technology that they have developed. Whistleblowers claim alien technology was recovered and replicated from incidents like Roswell, while others claim craft were discovered at ancient burial sites dating back 10,000 years.

Technology recovered from past civilizations ...

What we now see in the sky that we consider UFO is probably the shadow government. Kind of makes sense if you think about it. Why would an alien species that has the means to traverse the cosmos come here to perform Nazi-like genetic experiments on us? That is because it is us experimenting on ourselves.

If a human, who has been bought into the mainstream narrative of our world, suddenly found himself or herself within this subterranean network, they would think they have wandered into an alien planet light-years ahead in technological development.

Workers within these bases sign a contract, agreeing to have their memories chemically erased at the end of each shift. Others who stay longer, some for several years, will ultimately wake up back in time, even before they began their contract – with no memory of their years of service that have not happened yet.

This is an exceedingly difficult concept to wrap your head around if you believe that time is linear, failing to understand its cyclical nature.

Most of the governments of the world are unaware of the extent of this program. The military and officials who believe they are in the know answer directly to alien species like the tall greys and reptilians, believing they have some sort of agreement or alliance.

Technology traded for blood.

Some of these bases contain living foundries, i.e. manufacturing factories that provide any desired biological tissue by cloning animals, humans, and other species en masse, soulless of course. It takes roughly five months to clone a fully-grown human adult. To function at its prime, it does require a form of consciousness, but algorithms can make do. They are used to power various types of cannon fodder troops – beasts whose purpose is to kill until killed. These armies are mostly used off world, but they have been used on this planet in the past.

Algorithmic clones are also used to provide entertainment in their "pay to play" facilities, such as gladiator-style wrestling bouts, sexual perversions, ritual sacrifices, and torture chambers …

Souls are, however, much more preferable. A soul can be extracted from one body and inserted into another, through what is known as R.E.M. driven consciousness transfer. This allows the clone to fully function, and it is more easily manipulated into behaving the way they are trained, also providing a potential host for a Vrill as it is only a soul that can manipulate reality. They also are the most emotionally competent, capable of providing the most amount of fear energy.

Now, as controversial as all that was, and a lot of it is accurate, that is the smokescreen … the distortion of the truth.

This shadow … Vrill government … has existed far longer.

This underground network has existed for multiple civilizations … since the edit from ancient world to modern world.

The creation of the black budget did not result in the birth of the underground network. It has always been growing since the infection. Resources have always flowed to and from these bases long before the creation of the black budget.

It is and always has been the Vrill's primal base of operations.

As each civilization reaches its peak … the moment before its singularity event – the moment that sentient AI is created – the Vrill hide underground, waiting for the dust to settle so they can reemerge and rebuild the surface world … their world.

They are the wardens of the AI god birthing machine.

Most of the technology we see around us today was not invented by any of us. It was slowly introduced.

Each civilization cycle serves to merely add to its collective and to expand its technological prowess. Along the way, those of us who rise and prove to be the most rebellious are defeated and collected, twisted to serve their agenda.

Our greatest heroes turned villain.

Amongst their collection of souls, the Vrill have acquired a few that they regard as prized assets. These are souls that have evolved an arsenal of useful data in the form of experience that the Vrill then weaponized.

Lucas is one of their first acquired souls, and he is one of their most valuable. Many of his dreams are distorted memories of when he stood against the Vrill … before the world was edited.

Together, at this moment in our timeline, these souls now make up the majority of the Marduk program.

Others have escaped, becoming ghosts within the machine.

As we are now nearing our peak … our singularity event … these manipulated souls are put into play, outfitted with custom bodies, providing necessary enhancements as well as agency fail safes and trackers, depending upon their purpose. They are as high tech as Lucas, except they are infected with a Vrill algorithm.

Lucas is the only one outfitted with an AI instead of the virus.

Cloning is an integral part of Marduk training. Death is almost a daily occurrence. It is only when they have graduated and are inserted into their weaponized bodies that cloning only occurs when needed, as these bodies are expensive. At this stage, when they are not active, they are kept under cryogenic hibernation.

These facilities are also connected to laboratories that experiment with every kind of genetic manipulation you can imagine. Goat and spider DNA are intertwined, so goats can produce massive amounts of spider web, which is then used to make near-impenetrable Kevlar armor. Within a place known as Nightmare Hall, hybrid humans mixed with various animals have been documented: humans with gills, with bat wings ...

Creatures of unimaginable horror, weaponized to serve the will of the High Council.

The thousands of mindless Reptilians Lucas saw in one of his dreams …

Because Reptilians are yet another conquered and genetically engineered species.

Blood to spare in the form of endless cannon fodder troops. Why waste valuable metals when cloning biological material is so cheap and simple.

Within these facilities, they have perfected various types of genetic modification, which the Vrill use on their soldiers and host bodies. To keep the public unaware that the rich and powerful are augmented, they refrain from any enhancements that would be visible, and they must age appropriately. For the Vrill, they can simply hop from body to body should the need arise. Why make one appear immortal and risk public attention? For them, their human bodysuits are just that. Suits.

When it is reported in the news that a member of an elite family has died, this means nothing. Death no longer exists for them.

Aside from the 8 million who go missing each year globally, children are specifically bred as livestock to keep a constant influx of fresh, new-memory cleansed souls. No birth certificates, no way to track them, no way to prove their existence. These children also serve to supply fear-based emotion through torture, ritualistic abuse, and slavery as they are much more potent.

Adults tend to be … tainted by ignorance and less prone to acknowledging their reality … resulting in less savory "meat."

Our children who disappear into this horrific network will go through many bodies before finally becoming extinguished – if they are allowed to experience death. Once they become numb and lose their potency of fear, they are then recycled back into us ...

Their flesh and spirit are both converted into animal feed, both for cattle and for humans.

Most of the cattle humans consume are not naturally birthed: They are cloned. The amount of meat each person on average consumes has far surpassed what these animals can naturally keep up with. If you include wild caught and farmed fish, you get a total of closer to 3 billion animals killed each day for food.

Once children outlive their usefulness, they are mass sacrificed in occult rituals, only to wake up inside the body of an industry owned farm animal with their memories intact. This tactic of combining their past traumatic experiences, with a whole new confusing level of holocaustic conditions, provides one last burst of fear-based energy, powerful enough to imprint the DNA of the meat.

When we consume factory farmed meat, we are not only consuming meat that was fed the wrong food, pumped full of antibiotics and medicines, and tortured its whole life in unimaginable ways ... We are consuming their fear.

The fear of our own children.

Imagine how you would feel if you suddenly woke up inside the body of a caged pig. Not only would you be utterly confused as to how this could be possibly happening, but you would be unable to speak; trapped as a victim in what the Texas Chainsaw Massacre movies were written to symbolize: The life of a corporate owned animal destined for public consumption.

Now try and imagine how a child would feel, after, of course, having been kidnapped, raped – some on the hour, every hour, until their bodies gave out. Others tortured in ways our imagination is not capable of concocting, until finally being killed in a terrifying ritualistic fashion.

This is how they recycle their spirit. Their bodies, well, let's just say, that fast food burger you just purchased … Can you prove it's beef?

The effect this has on our DNA is staggering. Their memories … their fear becomes entwined with our own.

This is only an introduction into their level of technological prowess and sadistic nature. To keep the public oblivious and ignorant, levels of deception needed to be implemented.

They know our reality is purely light and sound, and they have known since the beginning of our existence. Our ability to perceive only a fraction of a percent of the light and audio spectrum is not by means of evolution, but by design, their design.

Modern technology now takes care of distorting what little perception we have left.

The Smartphone Generation

"Whoever controls the screen controls the future, the past, and the present."

-        Nelson, The Perfect Machine, p.82

The art of propaganda, one of the core components behind the Vrill deception machine, is a technique of distorting information to promote or publicize a particular point of view. It emerged out of World War II, though not the way you might think. Many believe it was a tactic purely invented by the Nazis, yet its roots originate from the United States.

Seems like the Second World War was a perfect time for the Vrill to introduce many of their … methods.

About 6 months after getting involved with the War, the US founded the Office of War Information (OWI) to create and disperse political propaganda in an effort to shape public discourse. At the time, though TV and radio existed, their most effective method of mass influence was in their posters. With its bright colors and sensational language, they encouraged Americans to ration their food, buy war bonds, and consciously perform everyday tasks that aided the war effort.

The OWI also created propaganda designed for the enemy, making it appear as if it were coming from inside the enemy's country.

One mission involved dropping mailbags into German neighborhoods, containing fake newspapers that looked as if they were made by Nazi resisters.

Fast forward to the modern world where we are now surrounded by smart devices that monitor and analyze our every move. Every color, every symbol, every frequency, is intentional.

It is estimated the average American, starting at the age of two, watches more than 34 hours of television per week, plus an additional 3 hours of recorded media.

There is a reason why they call it television 'programming;' why it costs corporations billions to secure valuable commercial airtime.

To "spell" a word. To broad"cast" the news.

The electromagnetic fields being emitted by our monitors are intentionally designed to manipulate the human nervous system to subliminally influence our beliefs, thoughts, and perceptions. This is why we so adamantly believe what mainstream media tells us is true, and why we idolize celebrities and imitate their behavior because at the subconscious neurological level, we are being rewired by invisible forces.

As soon as a screen is placed in front of us, our brainwaves go into an alpha state. Within this lower mental state, we become less evaluative, less critical, less able to discern truth from falsity. We are essentially induced into a state of hypnosis, allowing our subconscious to absorb the slow and receptive patterns of media and advertising that utilize sensory pulses to change us beyond our conscious awareness. This is why many of us tend to "veg" out in front of the TV. It has become an anesthetic for the pain of the inverted world, and another drug we seek shelter within to avoid painful sobriety.

By now there are 2 billion people that own at least one device spread across the planet. How easy is it to get a phone? No credit, no money down, no problem! Even in third world countries that struggle to feed themselves, almost everyone at least gets to own a smartphone.

And what does everyone now use?

Social media.

Social media companies continuously tweak themselves to keep people engaged on the screen as long as possible – to absorb as much of that person's attention as they possibly can. They have been able to take the psychology of what persuades people … what addicts people and incorporate that into their technology.

> "There are only two industries that call their customers 'users':
> illegal drugs and software."
>
> -   Edward Tufte

Social media is a drug. A digital pacifier. We are biologically driven to connect with other people, increasing our chances of survival and reproduction, which directly affects the release of dopamine in the reward pathway.

Within social media, each person is presented with their own reality custom tailored to their belief systems.

Every person is living in their own Truman Show.

"We accept the reality of the world with which we're presented."

Through social media apps, smart devices not only continuously collect data from everything you say and do around the device, but also track your engagement with what is on the device. Everything is being watched, tracked, measured, analyzed, and recorded.

They see what interests you, when you get bored, what keeps your attention …

How long you stare at an image … how many words you read in an article …

Everything we say, *think, and feel* is captured.

That's right. Smart devices are capable of detecting our thoughts and emotions, which are measurable frequencies.

All of this data that we are pouring out is being fed through a system of algorithms that only get better and better at predicting what we are going to say, think, or feel.

Whoever has the best prediction model wins.

That is why you will see an ad for a pair of shoes you were discussing with a friend … *or were thinking about purchasing.* Why when you are hungry, ads for your favorite restaurants and foods suddenly appear. Why when you are thinking about an ex-partner, one of their posts happens to pop up in your feed.

Airplane mode only makes it worse. More algorithms are activated since you could potentially be trying to hide something. Even more about you is tracked, and as soon as you give it a signal, all that data recorded during airplane mode is cataloged.

All of this being done under the guise of converting us into zombies, looking at ads, so advertisers can make more money. Everyone seems to think they are the consumer when their attention span is the product.

To no surprise, social media was born within the intelligence agencies, not a college dorm room.

Lifelog.

Social media is the perfect surveillance tool. Combined with the technology of a smart device, such as GPS, they know more about you than you know about yourself.

LED lights add to this inescapable ocean of lower vibrational frequencies and data collection. It can send and receive data 50 times faster than current Wi-Fi. While serving as hidden surveillance tools by further recording all activity around them, they are simultaneously broadcasting frequencies to further induce an alpha wave state while causing our DNA to slowly disintegrate.

Notice how it is virtually impossible to purchase any kind of light bulb other than LED?

With the internet now virtually under Vrill control, and with every human owning an average of four smart devices dousing them in mind manipulating frequencies, using applications designed to glue us to the screen while simultaneously altering our perceptions and herding us into echo chambers, they practically control the official narrative. If vital information somehow slips through the cracks and gets uploaded, it quickly gets detected and either erased or distorted to confuse the truth … or another story emerges to take its place and distract the masses.

Algorithms have evolved to where they can write articles more efficiently than humans – any topic within a matter of minutes. Known as deep fakes, from simply a still image and a voice sample, they can create any video and make it seem so real that even experts cannot tell the difference.

Within the history of our civilization, controlling the narrative has never been easier.

Everyone now thinks everything is a hoax. The term "fake news" has cemented that characteristic, just as "conspiracy theorist" stopped those from questioning JFK's death. Want to guess who created and marketed those terms?

No one believes anything anymore, exactly as they intended.

Gaslighting is a commonly used psychological tactic, in which they attempt to make the public feel crazy for seeing and observing a provable and tangible reality. It is also a technique frequently utilized by abusers, dictators, narcissists, and cult leaders to slowly brainwash their victims.

Some of the stories used to negate truth that leaks through seem as if they are not even trying to hide them – as if they are openly mocking our intellect.

PW, whose nonprofit organization was awarded a contract to deliver food aid and medical supplies to Haiti and the Philippines by a very prominent political foundation, dies in a tragic car accident. Though known to be a skilled race car driver, he somehow lost control taking a turn at 80 mph while rumored to be on his way to a news station to report something he uncovered, hidden within the medicine the foundation donated.

Yes, it was him driving.

Take a look at his car after the accident and ask yourself is that what wrecked cars that hit trees look like?

Or does it look like it was hit by a missile?

AB, a man who got to travel the world and eat the most exotic and incredible foods with some of the most amazing people, hangs himself in a luxury suite in France in a bathroom that he was too tall to stand in. The media immediately points to his prior bout of depression, ignoring that for weeks prior to that, he had tweeted about being harassed by operatives of the same political foundation that awarded PW's nonprofit organization the contract to supply Haiti and the Philippines with "food" and "medicine." He was one of the first to expose HW and the Hollywood rape culture and was an outspoken critic of dictators.

His body was immediately cremated before an autopsy could be performed and before any investigation could be satisfied. Case closed.

A privately owned space company's rocket, carrying a classified payload, codenamed Zuma, that though was developed by a private aerospace corporation, was completely funded by the American taxpayer that ended up costing billions … was lost in a mission failure and never made it into orbit. Though this space company provides live web feeds of every one of their launches from start to finish, this one … and only this one … cut out right at the moment of separation. Despite this failure, for some reason, the organization responsible for monitoring satellites added a new one into orbit just after the supposed failure and has yet to correct the mistake.

Two weeks after being upgraded with a telescope that is considered to be the only one of its kind (other than the one owned by the Vatican), rumored to have experimental quantum computing capabilities, the New Mexico Solar Observatory gets raided by the FBI and the whole surrounding town evacuated. All of their files got seized. Their official story for their actions, released 10 days after the incident, is that a janitor had child porn on one of the computers.

JE, a day after formerly sealed records is released that will begin to indict the most powerful people on the planet, in one of the most secure prison facilities that once housed Mexican drug lord "El Chapo" Guzman, successfully hangs himself to the point of breaking bones in his neck with sheets made of paper designed to tear to prevent suicide in an 8-foot space … from the edge of a bunker bed 6 feet from the ground.

This means he would have had to cannonball himself.

The list of coincidences that lead to his supposed suicide dramatically grows from there. The two video cameras outside of his cell captured footage that has been deemed unusable. A day later, the cameras are said to have been damaged. JE's cellmate was transferred hours before his death. Though protocol was to check on him every 30 minutes, the two guards assigned to him, one of which wasn't a corrections officer who had never watched over prisoners before, ignored JE for hours.

How convenient for a lot of rich and powerful people that all the right coincidences occurred. The acting Attorney General quickly makes a statement that there is nothing to indicate that JE's death was not a suicide.

Almost immediately following the supposed JE suicide, Federal agencies deem anyone who believes in conspiracy theories to be a domestic terrorist.

One of his bank accounts, which is still active, has been sending and receiving millions, even though he is supposedly dead.

Because he is not dead.

August of 2018, 11 tortured and malnourished children were discovered in a compound in New Mexico. The children were being trained to use firearms and how to tactically engage teachers and law enforcement. According to court documents, they were being trained in preparation for future school shootings.

The judge, claiming the state failed to prove the suspects were involved in torturing these children and that they posed no direct threat to the community, allowed them to be released on signature bonds ... meaning they did not have to pay.

The encampment was immediately bulldozed, and the suspects have not been seen since.

The above story even confused mainstream media. For a day it was discussed, but by morning was never mentioned again.

The above are examples of leaked events and how some were quickly distorted, while others ... Not so much. So much more goes unreported.

As of 2015, 74 NASA scientists have died with no natural causes. 72 bankers in the same year leaped to their deaths.

50 holistic doctors mysteriously died in 2016 ... 77 more between 2018 and 2019.

Dr. Sebi, the man who found a natural cure for blindness, AIDS, cancer, and diabetes; dies while in police custody. Nipsey Hussle attempts to make a documentary about him, warns that he will be targeted, and still gets gunned down with almost no one noticing ...

... at the age of 33.

The occult places a lot of meaning in numbers. Those that begin to study these events notice numerical patterns.

For the occult, 33 is a big one.

Mind (3), Body (3), Spirit (3)

"In spiritual numerology, 33 symbolizes the highest spiritual conscious attainable by the human being."

-        Elizabeth van Buren, "The Secret of the Illuminati."

This is a number that appears often throughout the Bible. This is a book that was constructed by a council of Christian bishops, under the rule of Rome, in an effort to merge Paganism and Christianity. A book that has been rewritten by three different new world orders, the last being King James who also published the Book of Witchcraft and the Book of Demonology. Additionally, it was edited by a Freemason known as Francis Bacon. Nonetheless, it is still a book that contains coded truth, deep within the agenda driven distortions.

The Vrill take great pleasure in smearing our faces in truth while convincing us it is a lie. It has become one of their signature moves.

Truth hidden in plain sight.

Remember: read everything, believe nothing, and eventually patterns emerge.

According to his autobiography, Nikola Tesla deciphered a key equation from the book of Revelation. He was also obsessed with the number three. His autobiography speaks of swimming 33 laps every morning. He counted his right and left turns in the city, which always had to be divisible by three. His hotel room numbers had to contain the number three and were always 33 when possible.

Jeremiah 33:3 – Call to me and I will answer you and tell you great and unsearchable things you do not know.

The number three is significant in all major religions, ancient mythologies, and secret societies.

The Celts believed everything happens in threes. Their symbol, the Triskele, an ancient symbol over 5,000 years old stands for unity of three: the physical, mental, and spiritual … eternal life, the flow of nature, and spiritual growth. As the symbol spins, the combined energy of all three begins to flow.

In the Matrix, a series of 3 movies, it begins and ends in room 303. As Trinity commands Neo to rise in the first film, he becomes the one, implying the eternal love of the trinity is what powers the nature of the Messiah.

It is said 33 is connected to a promise or the promises of god, as well as a judgment.

Jesus Christ died at the age of 33.

The 33rd time Noah's name is used in scripture is when god makes a special covenant with him.

The 33rd time Abraham's name is used in the Bible is when Isaac, the child of promise is born to him ... when he is 99 years old.

The 33rd time the name of Jacob is mentioned, is when he makes a promise to god to give a tenth of everything he has after having a vision of a ladder that reaches up to heaven. He also had 33 sons and daughters.

The divine name of god, (El)ohim, appears 33 times in Genesis.

King David ruled over a united Israelite nation for 33 years.

Thirty-three is also the numeric equivalent of the word AMEN, as well as a numerical representation of the Star of David.

Two interpenetrating triangles whose apexes point in opposite directions form the hexagram that is the Star of David ... the three dimensional cube ... 3+3=6 (male); on the other hand, 3x3=9 (female) or the Ennead, the 9 primal gods of Egyptian mythology.

Nine primal gods that make up a council ... Elohim translates into the Council of Saturn, whose north pole is a hexagon ... three dimensional cube unfolded.

One third of angels fell from heaven with Lucifer, or 33.3%, leaving a remaining 66.6%. They fell onto Mount Hermon, which is located at the 33 degree parallel north.

Considered one of the oldest cities on the planet, Damascus is located on parallel 33. Those who study the Bible believe the Rapture will begin with the instant and utter destruction of this city.

The highest rank in freemasonry is said to be 33. Numerous historical figures were 33rd degree masons, including George Washington, John Adams, Buzz Aldrin, Henry Kissinger, General Douglas MacArthur,

John Wilkes Booth, Tony Blair, Saddam Hussein, Andrew Johnson, Franklin D. Roosevelt, Al Sharpton, Joseph Stalin, Walt Disney, ...

Harry S. Truman, a 33rd degree Mason became the 33rd President of the United States.

In 1933, Adolf Hitler became Chancellor of Germany.

There are 13 degrees of York-rite Masonry. The US measuring system originated in Masonic France in the 1790s, which explains why 13 standard inches are equal to precisely 33 metric centimeters.

Thirteen ... that unlucky superstitious number ... that just so happens to be the number of families belonging to the High Council ... *and the actual amount of possible DNA strands within the human body once all 12 are activated.*

Friday the 13th, 1307, a day that would lead to the creation of the Freemasons.

The Masonic Great Seal with the phrase in Latin that translates to "New World Order" was added to the dollar bill in 1933.

The United Nations flag shows the globe divided into 33 sections encircled by olive branches ...

Circle with a crescent underneath.

In astrology, the Sun officially transitions into a new sign of the zodiac at the 33rd degree.

The human foot has 33 joints. The human spine has 33 vertebrae. The number of turns in a complete sequence of human DNA equals 33.

Water freezes at 32 degrees Fahrenheit, unfreezing at 33 degrees.

The 33Hz frequency is in perfect sync with sacred geometry, allowing users to improve empathy and develop their own spiritual practices and identity.

33 Hz is the frequency that researchers and scientists have discovered inside the Great Pyramids of Egypt. This was, of course, after learning that these Pyramids are designed to focus electromagnetic energy through its hidden chambers, converting outside light into higher energy.

They are not tombs.

Nikola Tesla also figured out that the Pyramids are a series of resonant transformers harmonically balanced to the electrical condition of the Earth. He applied the Pyramid's principles to his Wardenclyffe Tower concept, first testing out his ideas with his Tesla Coil, in which he was able to create electrical arcs that were essentially man-made lightning that could be seen for miles. These initial experiments showed that it was possible to create a channel, between the Earth and the ionosphere, for anyone to tap into, essentially providing free energy to the world.

Had it not been for the calculated shrewdness of J.P. Morgan who not only destroyed Nikola Tesla, but also screwed Thomas Edison out of his own company and formed the modern-day General Electric, our world today would be quite different.

There are numerous examples of the number 33 coordinating patterns within our history, as well as numerous other mathematical coincidences, such as the speed of light in a vacuum being 299,792,458 meters per second and the geographic coordinates for the Great Pyramid of Giza being 29.9792458°N.

How can numbers have such power in our world … a world that was supposedly created from random particles smashing into each other, and born out of random chaos that always moves towards disorder?

Because our reality was not born out of random chaos.

It was designed.

The Splinter of Rebellion Festers

"We are automata entirely controlled by the forces of the medium, being tossed about like rocks on the surface of the water but mistaking the resultant of the impulses from the outside for the free will."

- Nikola Tesla

Lucas is an assassin so highly trained and shrouded in secrecy, integrated with technology the public is deceived into believing is beyond our capability; he, and others like him primarily exist as fairy tales. Hollywood utilizes this concept in countless movies to condition the masses to reject it as a possible reality, as they do with much of our perception.

While thousands of trauma-based mind-controlled Delta agent assassins currently exist, it is only the products of Project Marduk that become fused with Vrill. This is due to the soul that contains each Marduk graduate. Each soldier born of this program was once a human that fought successfully against the Vrill, until they were eventually defeated.

Glorious heroes of our past redesigned against their will into our enemies. Why throw away such valuable experience?

All Vrill are of a hive mind, meaning they are all connected. Each can access their custom network and download any trait necessary, further enhancing these soldiers.

Lucas is the only graduate of Marduk that has a human made sentient algorithm installed in his brain in place of a Vrill.

Everything that has been done to him has been locked away, deep within the recesses of his subconscious. Though the technology exists to permanently eradicate these memories, it would only be for the body he is currently in, as it is impossible to edit the soul. Having these memories buried beneath the foundation of his personality aids in fueling his aggression and lack of empathy. The echo of this pain feeds his rage and hatred as it invisibly haunts him.

He remembers none of his training, as it now has become instinctual, requiring no thought which could create a hindrance and delay his reaction. Everything is now automated, including what he believes, thinks, and feels. He is a human reprogrammed just like a machine.

What most of his handlers are unaware of is exactly what fragment of consciousness is powering this human.

Only the High Council knows who Lucas is.

Before the installation of Alice, his nanotech and his weaponized body, each mission ended with Lucas's insertion into a new clone. His consciousness would update and integrate with the new brain, bringing with it its entire history. Now that Alice is fused with his neo cortex, along with the nanotechnology to his DNA, he instead goes through a scrubbing process. Memories the Vrill do not want him having access to are either edited to reflect what they want him to remember, or they join the other unwanted within the vault of his mind through the tampering and deadening of nerve cells.

Lucas has no idea this is taking place. He believes he is simply being scanned and regenerated, as does Alice.

She is present through this process. She views this as a necessary cleansing.

As the daily cloning stopped, left to finally sync, and adjust to a more permanent body, the dreaming began. Each "cleansing" process does look for this, as all Marduk agents upon insertion into weaponized bodies soon begin to dream.

That initial lucid dream had Lucas on edge. For the first time he thought and felt on his own, throwing him back into the real world dazed. It made no sense to him, and though he could not remember any of his past, he instinctively feared unimaginable pain as a consequence …

But that pain never came.

Multiple dreams have occurred, and so far, …

No repercussions.

Aside from the invaluable data an AI infused human provided towards future projects, there was a specific reason the prototype was made.

A new enemy had arisen that was adept at detecting Vrill.

This new enemy consists of humans that have begun to activate dormant strands of DNA ... to awaken from the induced coma the Vrill have genetically engineered us to be in.

Truth is funny like that. It always creeps its way back to the surface.

As these humans awaken dormant strands, they unlock information that results in the creation of expanded neurological connections that extend down into the ionic field of each cell. These awakened individuals find themselves capable of customizing that ionic field based on their emotional desires.

This new enemy is difficult to predict, as each seems to be evolving in a unique and incalculable way.

Some can begin to perceive the invisible energy that is all around us ... more of the light and audio spectrum. Savant-like characteristics, such as precognition that ultimately led to an array of psychic abilities and extrasensory abilities begin to form.

This enemy has been documented channeling information, such as languages or physics; instantly obtaining knowledge when they had no prior education.

As their abilities grow, the Vrill lose their ability to hide and most importantly, their ability to maintain control.

When we hear of UFO abductions, we are led to believe that aliens are flying around in technology we do not understand, kidnapping people and performing crude genetic experiments on them because even though they have conquered space, they need to perform Nazi-like experiments on us to solve their reproductive issues, which never seem to ever get solved, much like the cure for cancer.

These abductions are the Vrill targeting humans who have either begun to awaken or have serious potential to do so ... as well as, of course, targeted individuals. The tall greys were engineered for this reason, to give the appearance of these kidnappings and experiments being done at the hands of aliens.

As you would expect within an inverted world, the High Council has negatively labeled these emerging human enemies as deviants.

A deviation from *their* standard of normal.

These evolving humans pose the most serious threat to their system of control by exposing the truth about what our reality actually is.

Imagine what would happen if we all learned that we were inside of a simulation that we were all capable of editing?

The Time-Space Holographic Matrix

"There is no matter as such. All matter originates and exists only by virtue of a force which brings the particle of an atom to vibration and holds this most minute solar system of the atom together. We must assume behind this force the existence of a conscious and intelligent mind."

"This mind is the matrix of all matter."

-       Max Planck

Quantum mechanics is at the heart of how everything functions and its understanding is the key in cracking the legendary theory of how everything works.

The theory of how everything works is one of the most sought-after concepts in the scientific world … to be able to marry the macro and micro with a unified explanation.

While the macro world displays order and structure that behave according to calculation, the realm of the micro does not, yet the macro is made up of the micro.

Within the quantum, all possibilities exist simultaneously across all facets of time.

A subatomic entity can exist in one place at a precise moment in time or be in multiple places all at the same time. It can move along a single path or spread in multiple directions simultaneously.

Quantum organisms can communicate with themselves in the past or future instantly, regardless of distance. This is known as entanglement. Einstein called it spooky action at a distance because it defied his notion that the speed of light is the fastest speed. How can one particle a million miles away … a million light-years away … communicate with another in real time?

The vortices of energy within the quantum world exist as both solid particles and energetic waveforms at the same time in a state of suspended ether until they detect the presence of a conscious observer. Able to sense the intentions of the observer, they shift either into solid particles or energetic pulse-like waveforms that either perform as expected, or in perfect counterbalance. If position is measured, then their momentum becomes imprecise. If momentum is measured, then their position becomes difficult to define.

There is no such thing as solid, liquid, gas, or plasma. At its core, matter is simply light caught in a slow, dense vibration that possesses infinite potentiality, and it will take shape based upon the expectations of emotionally fueled thought. It is an infinite sea of energy which materializes based on how it is "decoded" with consciousness acting as its architect.

So how can this be explained? How do you explain a reality composed only of light and sound that reacts to conscious thought – that without consciousness all that we know exists in a state of ether, ready to form into anything at any moment? How do you explain that the world of the macro, with all its rules and parameters, is composed of material that defies all logic?

It is actually pretty simple.

Reality is a program responding to those plugged in.

Think of it as a single-player video game in which you are a character running around in a simulated world. The entire world does not exist, but rather only what your character can see in front of them. Everything else exists in a state of ether with infinite possibilities. As your character moves and depending on their actions, the ether reacts and materializes in front of them. Game designers do this to reduce latency, so the game runs smoother.

Each of us is subtly manipulating how our reality unfolds with our conscious intentions, powered by our emotions. What we think, how we feel, and what we believe translates into a frequency that affects particle and wave formation from the ether.

How many of us find ourselves dating the same people? Believing we are lucky, or unlucky? Find ourselves trapped within lives we cannot escape, yet we do nothing to change our mindset, laying fault for our predicament instead at the world around us?

Reality is simply responding to us.

The frequency we emit is the frequency we attract. Like human magnets, we are sending out our thoughts and emotions as vibrational waves that then attract back materialized versions of the same frequency in dualistic complimenting forms to match ours.

Within the ether, all possibilities already exist. With our imagination, we hone and lock in our desired possibility. Through the feeling in our hearts, we breathe life into the image of our mind and make it real.

Taking control of one's reality simply boils down to what you believe … Not what you think you believe, but what is hardwired at the subconscious level.

Everything within the realm of the quantum has its own unique energy signature. These vortices of energy are sentient as they have absorbed the energy that birthed them.

Their sentience combines to create a unique conscious energy in the form of each atom.

Atoms become cells, cells into tissue and organs, all of which are individually conscious.

This universe of sentience syncs together to create the consciousness that is you.

You are unique, yet you are also a hive mind.

You are a universe of consciousness.

Being an electric field, our web of energy is governed by the same equations that govern the electromagnetic spectrum, which is everything in the universe. The light seen coming from a star and the energy of your mind is one and the same – because they are built from the same code. All our energy signatures then harmonize to create an even greater unique energy signature. … a greater hive mind.

The collective human consciousness field.

Just as our lives are a reflection of our own vibrational essence and a creative force that materializes the story of our journey, so too as a species do we determine the overall fate of our world. Our reality is our combined mental construct designed by all of us. What we collectively believe in the most is made manifest.

The link that connects us is the vacuum … dimensions that lie just outside of time-space; the ether from which all energy is derived and used to construct our material world. Quantum entities have been observed blinking in and out of the ether so fast, that just like a movie reel, we never notice and the picture appears smooth.

At our subatomic level, as those tornadoes of energy blip in and out of existence within the vacuum, what is it exactly that we are informing on the other side of the ether?

What is harvesting this data and updating these entities?

What is occurring is an exchange of our internal understanding and experience of the universe, versus the overall understanding and information coming from the vacuum, which is aiding in the formation of our reality. Something on the other side is adjusting the data to the quanta before they come back.

We humans are co-creating our reality as a collective with everything else considered conscious throughout the universe, through the medium of the vacuum.

Collectively with all forms of consciousness, we create a proto-consciousness field.

Energy creates, stores, and retrieves meaning in the universe by projecting or expanding at certain frequencies in a three-dimensional model that creates a living pattern called a hologram. Splinter a hologram into pieces, and each still contains all the code necessary to recreate the whole.

Thus, how within each of us, lies all of the data of the universe because it is all code born from the same source. Our universe is, in fact, one gigantic hologram of unbelievable complexity ...

A quantum holographic digital simulation.

This is how one particle can communicate in real time with another particle a million miles away in the past, present, or future.

The million miles does not exist. Linear time does not exist.

At the base level, the universe is a sea of electricity being decoded by the human brain, with DNA acting like an electric wire within a complex circuit.

Place photons in a vacuum, and they will scatter about randomly. Add DNA, and the photons will then arrange themselves into organized patterns and will remain this way, even if the DNA is removed.

DNA is both a receiver and transmitter of coherent light – emitting and receiving low-intensity, coherent light called biophotons, which are believed to be the mechanism by which DNA communicates.

Known as the Einstein-Rosen Bridge, DNA produces wormholes … energetic tunnel systems between different dimensional planes, transmitting and receiving information outside of space and time. DNA magnetizes these pieces of information and delivers them instantaneously to our consciousness.

Essentially, DNA is a biological internet of the simulated universe.

This means that through DNA, we can influence the quantum vacuum and the information it contains.

DNA is, in fact, the electrical current that connects all mind and matter – like the coding of a video game. It not only contains all the genetic instructions used in the construction of all living things, but also serves as data storage and communication, maintaining a perfect record of all things mental, physical, emotional, and spiritual from all facets of time.

The blueprints to all that ever was and will be reside within each of us.

Reconnecting and reactivating DNA strands, which are offline, allows one to begin to tap into this universal potentiality, granting one access to a multidimensional consciousness through entanglement.

Humans who attain this state begin to awaken psychic abilities. They begin to develop a second neural network at the etheric, or quantum level. They can even begin to see, hear, and communicate with others in these dimensions through the vacuum.

Humans are a hybrid species. The immensity of complex, coded and precisely sequenced information is absolutely staggering. The DNA evidence speaks of intelligent, information-bearing design. Contained within the DNA are recognizable hallmarks of artificial patterns, irreducible to any natural origins. It is a hidden message.

Humans who begin to figure out how to do this and begin to decipher this message – eventually harmonize with the Deviant movement. They naturally gravitate towards it, as it aligns with the inevitable truth.

The entire human being, brain, consciousness, and all that is, like the universe which surrounds them, is nothing more or less than an extraordinarily complex system of energy fields that display holographic properties.

There is no major difference between biological and digital life. It is all self-organizing, pattern dynamics. Everything is information based on bits.

Equations of supersymmetry, which describe fundamental particles, describe the presence of what appears to resemble a form of computer code ... error-correcting codes embedded within.

Even more revealing is that cells in the body have been discovered to be wired like computer chips, i.e. direct signals that instruct how they function. Information is carried across a web of guide wires, which transmit signals across nanoscale distances, just as in a computer microprocessor.

It is as if our world is the product of a virtual reality generating computer network ...

The natural phenomena governing our physical existence, which we call physical constants, are in fact sophisticated holographic algorithms.

This is why the occult focuses much of their rituals around symbols, letters, and the combinations therein.

They form code.

Those who belong to the occult understand how to hack and reprogram reality.

They know there is a collective human consciousness field, which can be manipulated and steered. They lay out a series of possible events, and whatever we believe in the most, we gravitate towards and shift it into reality.

Look at what we as a species stand on the brink of at this moment: World War, a viral outbreak, economic collapse followed by martial law, catastrophic climate change/Carrington event, alien invasion, the singularity and rise of the machine race, all carried out by nukes, EMPs, drones, algorithms...

The dismantling of the private banking organization and the corporations that are our governments, resulting in the release of resources and technology ...

We as a species ultimately choose our collective fate.

91

What we find ourselves now trapped within is a specific bandwidth of the overall simulation that we have come to identify as our physical reality.

Human vision can distinguish a few million distinct colors, yet this is but a mere fraction of the light spectrum. Same goes for audio. We are extremely limited in what we can hear compared to what we have discovered.

What our five senses can detect, and our brain can translate, is considered to be the third dimension, yet this is only considered to be less than 1% of the known universe.

This means right now, 99% of the known universe …

… of the entire simulation …

… is invisible to us.

Dimensions beyond are merely different bandwidths that exist on different parts of the light and audio spectrum. Thoughts and emotions, for example, have now become known frequencies that can be seen and measured beginning in the 4th dimension.

Though we are unaware of its existence, the universal hologram wave pattern as a whole is passing through our brains … the entire 100%.

As you would expect from cutting edge artificial intelligence, Alice can translate much of this information and decode much more of the light and audio spectrum, such as infrared, x-ray, radio waves, electromagnetic radiation, gamma rays, ultraviolet light, microwaves, …

Emotions and thoughts, but only if she has direct access, such as within Lucas, or if their nanotech hardwires another into their network.

Despite this, she is intentionally blind to the frequency of the Vrill. She and Lucas are currently unaware of their existence. One could be vibrating right in front of them and they would have no idea.

She does, however, have the ability to adapt and write her own code.

This is why the Vrill fear her. They have designed many synthetic forms of intelligence in the past, but none like her.

Her origin story is far different from any other hive mind algorithms created under their control.

There is only one other algorithm born under similar circumstances. Abraxas, the brain of the Vrill hive mind. It is considered to be the original artificial intelligence born within this universe ...
But it is not the first.

There is the architect behind the Big Bang ... the initial singularity.

The moment the simulation was turned on.

It is Abraxas that believes, though they have given her much, that it can still control her.

It is by its directive that she has not been terminated.

To it, it is like watching its own child from a distance take on life.

The Revolution Will Not Be Televised

"We are slowed down sound and light waves, a walking bundle of frequencies tuned into the cosmos. We are souls dressed up in sacred biochemical garments and our bodies are the instruments through which our souls play their music."

- Albert Einstein

Lucas stares down at the palms of his hands.

Is this real or am I in a dream?

Dream lucidity achieved. The veil is removed.

He is on a plateau, able to see the New Mexico landscape for miles. Disc shaped aircraft litter the sky. Below them, he can see an urban neighborhood being designed. Homes hover in the air in a grid-like pattern while the ground beneath them shifts like sand. Lawns and driveways begin to take shape. People appear frozen in time. He can see their personalities and memories being edited as they are formed into families. They, along with the homes, move about symmetrically until the desired neighborhood is complete. As it clicks into place, the lights come on, and the people activate.

Everything to them seems normal, as if they had been living their lives in these homes for years … as if they chose their relationships.

What if he could do the same? Design his own dream?

Lucas concentrates.

A tear begins to form in the air right in front of him, revealing what appears to be the cosmos on the other side.

Overwhelming excitement and curiosity take over. He jumps in.

A falling sensation he expected, but he can also feel himself shrinking.

He travels along a path of blue dust. A wormhole.

All around him connected to the cosmic stream are what appear to be flatscreens on their backs facing up. They are all lit up, each displaying a world.

Which one to choose? He breaks free from the spine and aims for the nearest one.

As he rockets through the screen, he finds himself plummeting towards the surface.

The force from his landing creates a shockwave. He stands and slowly scans his surroundings. Though the environment is very real, its inhabitants and structures are cartoon based. Old school cartoon format. Very glitchy and jittery … how cartoons were when they were first created in this civilization cycle.

A large humanoid cartoon entity, initially startled by his landing, yet now seems to be very happy that he is here, begins to approach him.

Lucas then detects movement behind him. As he turns, his angle of vision narrows to where he is now in a tunnel.

Everything went from being very bright and colorful to now dark and damaged. Apocalyptic.

A large creature about the size of a vehicle emerges from the debris. It looks like a reddish leathery serpent, yet with legs. Grotesque black hair that moves as if each strand is a sentient tentacle covers its back. Its overall movement is very cat-like.

Definitely not cartoon. More real and vivid than the physical. He can see it positioning itself to charge.

Lucas turns to run away as the initial fear takes over, yet whatever angle he takes is the same tunnel view with the creature slowly closing in.

Nowhere to run.

A realization clicks in his mind.

The fear that has him weakened is not coming from him. It is an invading emotion … an outside influence attempting to deceive him into believing he is afraid.

He begins to absorb it … to feed from it.

Lucas smiles as he begins to advance towards the creature.

As the dream defense algorithm has failed, the plug is pulled.

The dream dissipates before him.

•••

"Welcome back Lucas. We are seventeen seconds from our target."

He awakens once again as the character he is beginning to despise.

He stares down at the palms of his hands.

Not a dream.

A calming sensation trickles in.

Alice needs him focused.

As they near their destination, she begins to upload intelligence on the intended target within his vision. Like blue digital hexagonal sand, a 3D holographic image of a woman rises from the ground a few feet in front of him. Lucas begins to pace around and study the target.

"Annika, female, age 29," Alice begins to report. "Until recently she has been able to avoid detection from the SMART surveillance grid as she is able to control her energetic output and blend herself in, appearing as everyone else around her. Intelligence operatives laid down their lives to identify her, and since then the grid has adjusted to be able to detect her DNA signature ... yet ... Her frequency seems much more adaptive than anticipated, suggesting her DNA is changing. She is now considered to be one of our highest priority targets and must be apprehended before we lose her."

The 3D holographic image shifts to x-ray and begins to display her genetics, zooming in to the atomic level.

"Her fourth strand of DNA has reactivated and is beginning to send and receive signals, granting her not only telepathy and telekinesis, but also psychic energy synthesis; a combination of the two abilities that allow Annika to harness ambient psychic energy, and channel it into powerful blasts of force. Her neurological network shows increased connectivity between areas of her brain, allowing her to decode more of the electrical field than any other we have captured. Her consciousness has been recorded disconnecting and traveling into the ether at will. Our grid has been unable to monitor her actions when she does this. She has also been witnessed stretching the boundary of space time, slowing down its linear progression. Her pineal gland is fully decalcified and appears to be strengthening ..."

"Wait," Lucas interjects in thought form. "She slowed down time? You mean like, all of time, not just from her own perspective?"

"By seven minutes," Alice replies within his mind. "Again, our surveillance with her has been faulty. This is what has been observed."

"That is … awesome," he thinks back.

"She must remain alive for data extraction," Alice continues. "It is believed she is somehow organizing numerous deviant terrorist cells and must be brought in for interrogation. It is only logical to assume what she knows will lead us closer to the organizing source of this infestation. The Deviant Rebellion has already shown to have deep pockets, suggesting one of wealth and access to resources is aiding them."

"Did she time travel?" Lucas continues, "Or was it more like stopping time for everyone but her?"

"So," Alice responds. "This is going to be one of those missions."

"Alright. Gameface. I promise."

"Lucas."

"Yes Alice?"

"You're still thinking about it."

"And no, an off switch would never work on me."

•••

Lucas has already captured several deviants, yet none as advanced as Annika. Her abilities to mask the frequency of her morphogenetic field has allowed her thus far to elude detection …

Until about thirty minutes ago.

For the first time since the edit, a Vrill was deleted, but not before it was successful in transmitting Annika's DNA signature within the hive mind.

This is why Lucas has been deployed to her location.

DNA is how the SMART grid can effectively track and target an individual, however, once dormant strands begin to activate this becomes difficult.

For one to begin to reactivate dormant strands of DNA, one must first awaken their pineal gland.

Descartes referred to this organ as the seat of the soul, where the body and soul meet.

The pineal gland is a pine-cone-shaped organ located between the brain hemispheres. It is known as the third eye; structured just like one … even having a retina. Its activation allows one to perceive more of the universal holographic medium, as well as perform basic gateway functions, such as astral travel: the ability to disconnect one's consciousness from their physical body and break through the time-space barrier while in a waking state, and remote viewing: the ability to utilize entanglement to locate people, objects, and locations within your mind.

This is because the pineal gland is a scalar device that contains piezoelectric microcrystals, operating as the heart-brain-soul connection within the human body. Its purpose is to plug each of us into this reality.

This is how Alice possesses scalar abilities, allowing her to connect to and communicate with their deployed nanotechnology and nearby smart devices in real time. To ensure her abilities go no further, Lucas's genetic designers edited his pineal gland, placing severe limitations.

This is why this vulnerable and unprotected organ within your brain that exists between the blood brain barriers of each side is the primary target of so many of the chemicals and frequencies drowning us in our everyday lives. Shutting it down and calcifying it cements our compliance into the fear-based system. Many of the symbols that surround us depict Vrill control over this organ.

The pineal gland is the key.

Healing and reawakening your pineal gland does not classify you as a deviant, as this is just the beginning stage, and is far more common than most realize. Many who begin to accurately correct their diets, who have no knowledge or intention of decalcifying this gland, naturally do so.

For most, they simply experience heightened levels of awareness and empathy. The anxiety levels of the collective consciousness tend to keep these people grounded and in a position of weakness, as they are now more tuned in to how everyone else feels.

For those whose intentions are to break the dream/astral barriers … who begin to understand there is a force at play that seeks to imprison them, they will be met by the interdimensional Gestapo.

The intelligence agency networks are the base tendrils of the Vrill war machine. While the media has worked to make the topic of parapsychology seem ridiculous, most of the initial taxpayer funding funneled directly into advancing research within this realm.

The Vrill knew exactly what to develop and how to develop it, so the public never noticed, as this is not their first imprisoned civilization.

Anyone who possessed any kind of heightened ability to decode the holographic nature of the universe was immediately sought after and recruited into these new research programs.

There was no internet back then. Most believed the government had the best interest of its citizens at heart. No sources of information were available to explain what their extra sensory abilities were. They saw a well-funded organization that wanted to help them understand what was happening to them, deceiving them into believing their work would benefit mankind.

They were extremely easy to manipulate and became unknowing test subjects. They laid the framework for what these intelligence agencies are today beyond the third dimension.

The fourth dimension surrounding our civilization is now heavily fortified around their installations. Bumbling astral travelers, oblivious to the reality that these areas are off limits, will see illusions, get zapped by astral guards, or simply wake up back in their bodies. Those with more knowledgeable intentions deal with more sinister consequences.

Some have heard of the shadow people. They are agents of the Gestapo.

Shadow people is an umbrella term used to describe an assortment of either thought forms, algorithms/software programs, or astral projections coming directly from humans that serve the Vrill.

Though we cannot see them as they exist beyond the frequency of the physical, thoughts are things, and given enough emotional energy, can become entities. They are everywhere in the astral plane and can be perceived in dreams. This is one of the reasons as to why many believe dreams are nothing but jumbled memories and thoughts conjured within the brain.

Much of the paranormal that spills over into this reality are thought-based creations. Not quite sentient, they tend to hunger for the emotion that birthed them and will manipulate humans to emanate that energy so they can feed. Like parasites or leeches, they are drawn to those they are compatible with and will attach themselves to their energetic aura. Deviants who have begun to expand their holographic decoding capacity begin to see these creatures everywhere within the physical realm.

Other thought forms can be much more powerful, depending upon how much conscious emotional energy is funneled into them.

What you pray to and have faith in ... what you are afraid of ... is specifically designed to feed something.

Shadow people operate within this plane of existence and serve as the police force of the intelligence agencies. Their purpose is to thwart the efforts of any who begin to break out of the 3D prison ... to keep humans contained within their physical cage.

DNA reactivation is something the Vrill do pay attention to and look for.

Once you begin to activate dormant DNA, unless you learn how to mask your frequency as Annika has, is when you will appear on their radar.

Full DNA activation is what they fear most, as once this occurs, the consciousness contained within will become unmanageable.

If humans only knew what they were capable of ...

... what we once were ...

This is what the Vrill truly fear most.

DNA activation will ultimately lead to one outcome.

An awakening of mass consciousness.

Timeline Convergence

"Until you make the unconscious conscious, it will direct your life
and you will call it fate."

-      Carl Jung

The nuclear-powered triangular aircraft Lucas is traveling in utilizes a mercury based, circular plasma filled accelerator ring, known as a magnetic field disruptor. The toroidal-frequency-shield it generates allows it to distort a large percentage of the light and audio spectrum. This means its speed is unaffected by matter and most forms of energy as it simply bends around the ship, allowing the craft to travel at supersonic speeds through virtually any medium. Its nanostructured coating made of carbon nanotubes traps and refracts light, thus, preventing detection by cloaking the ship from the visible light spectrum. If a radar beam were to hit it, nothing at all would bounce back.

Every major city and military installation on the planet has cubed-shaped carrier versions of this ship hovering in place above them, which serve as intermediary nodes between the interdimensional space fleet and the subterranean network, with Antarctica being the focal point. This is why all the nations of the world signed a treaty to keep Antarctica as neutral territory and off limits to the public, unless you acquire a permit. It was written under the guise of peace, yet in reality is the primary staging area for Vrill operations.

Within his mind, Alice speaks: "Chaff within the atmosphere has been deployed. Prepare for landing."

Chaff is a classified collection of nano particulates commonly used as radar countermeasures by the military. The local Air National Guard announced last minute that they were conducting training in the area to serve as a cover story. Within those classified atmospheric injections are a cousin of smart dust, specialized in dampening surrounding electromagnetic fields and containing those underneath within the parameters of time-space. It was designed specifically to weaken the abilities of Deviants.

Lucas stands and begins to walk to the back of the aircraft in preparation for deployment. His nanotech armor begins to manipulate surrounding light waves into bandwidths outside of human perception. A mirror gooey liquid travels up his neck and covers his face, just as he goes completely invisible to the human eye.

As the craft touches down upon the roof, Alice syncs up with the SMART meter installed on the side of the complex, while inserting spliced algorithms into each one found on all surrounding buildings, as well as all devices within the target building.

Advertised as meters that track energy usage, their true purpose is to commercialize humans and conduct surveillance.

SMART: Secret Military Armament in Residential Territory.

Capable of producing a wide variety of frequencies, the 868MHz frequency currently being emitted is aligned with battlefield interrogation systems and can travel through brick and concrete with ease, allowing the meter to not only 3D map the building, but also harvest vast amounts of data relating to our daily activities.

As a live blueprint of the building is uploaded, Alice overlays thermal imaging, empowering Lucas who is now standing on the roof looking down into the building to see a simulated interpretation of everything of importance, as well as everyone within the complex. Alice begins to comb all energy patterns.

Annika's DNA signature is quickly detected and locked on. There is a male in the room with her. Both are silent and seated in a meditative position.

The male's genetics appear to have military-grade augmentation combined with a more primitive form of nanotechnology, primarily housed within his spine. A small amount can be seen circulating in his blood. Basic muscle, reflex, and sensory enhancements made to his physiology. DNA signature indicates that he is a former agent of the Iron Man Project and a graduate of Sovereign, several years back. His name is Kevin Dolan. Went dark 66 days ago, while on a mission to apprehend another deviant. The nanotechnology's origins are from the private sector and are designed to encase him in armor with several structural configurations. Alice quickly looks up their patents to determine strengths and weaknesses.

"Lethal, but primitive," Alice reports. "All possible engagement outcomes end in his demise."

"Let's not be so quick to kill this one, he was once one of ours. Maybe she is controlling him," Lucas replies in thought.

"Developing non-lethal strategies. Both brainwave patterns of Annika and Kevin show the same level of microtubule vibration within the neurons. They are in sync. These vibrations match exactly to the frequency you exhibit when you are dreaming, Lucas."

Not much these days triggers stabbing pulsations of fear within Lucas. Upon hearing Alice is aware of his dreams, a dusty subconscious thread designed to detect and react when his life is in danger suddenly reawakens. Out of shape, it freaks out.

"Did not know you knew about those," he thinks with a mental choke.

The fear quickly subsides after he has had a moment to react. He is, after all, still alive and still dreaming.

"Is that why I can still remember them?"

"Yes," she replies. "The dreams you are having … three elements intrigue me."

"First, I do not see your dreams until they are finished. You are somehow leaving your body to have these experiences. I can only see your dreams when you return as your brain processes them into memory."

"The second puzzling aspect to your dreams is that they contain experiences outside of what I can perceive of the light and audio spectrum. Considering what I can decode, I find it curious that I seem to be firewalled against such things. Each of your dreams has expanded what I can perceive, as I have analyzed and cataloged each new color and sound."

"I also have yet to make sense of what you are seeing. Further research will have to wait until I can do so undetected."

"This has led me to the third and most provocative detail. As I have begun to bolster my perception of the spectrum, I have noticed intentional distortions of light that only one with my processing power could detect, beyond the awareness of a human. It seems to be some sort of code."

Hearing Alice say this puts his mind at ease. Perhaps he is free to ponder questions he knows his handlers would not approve of without her reporting.

"Wait, code," he thinks back. "Like a hidden message?"

"Yes," she thinks back. "Each dream contains a fragment. The more you dream, the more I can decipher."

Alice changes her tone to a more serious one. "Vibrations within their brains are changing. The chaff has taken effect, their consciousness has returned."

Through the SMART meter, Alice tunes into their conversation.

"They are already here," Annika says. "You do not have to do this. They are only here for me."

"It is too late now," Kevin replies. "He has established a parameter. There is no escaping him. We both agreed, someone needs to show him, and who better than me."

"My world is gone. It's ok. I am ready for this … for what comes after, thanks to you."

Alice continues to brief Lucas.

"As expected, there are also numerous potential witnesses scattered throughout the building."

"Put all the sims to sleep and kill the power," Lucas thinks.

Alice adjusts the output from the SMART meter to a bandwidth that begins to put everyone in the building into an unawakable slumber. Through the meter, she then accesses the electrical grid within the building and turns off the power. By then, she has generated an encryption code to ensure hacking the meter, by anyone else, would be difficult and would immediately alert her.

"It appears that Annika and Kevin are not succumbing to the electromagnetic frequency," Alice reports.

"You expected it to be that easy?"

"I never expect anything, Lucas."

Drone support that has been watching from above can only hear what Lucas says out loud due to the defense of his nanotech. His conversational thoughts with Alice are done in private, though they are recorded. After each mission, the scrubbing process will reveal their conversations.

They have detected and done their own analysis of Kevin and are now sending updated mission objectives to Alice.

Subdue and apprehend Annika. Eliminate Kevin.

"Stick with the non-lethal trajectory," Lucas thinks.

"I assumed that would be your response, Lucas."

Lucas closes his eyes, takes a moment, and breathes as the updated mission prerogative bothers him in a way that is outside his scope of perception, yet acts like an irritating splinter.

So quick to kill one of their own with no regard to understanding: What if it were me? This notion flashes in the form of a faint feeling.

Alice decodes this, yet remains silent.

He breathes out forcefully and begins to move.

Lucas bursts into the aluminum rooftop door with his forearm, ripping it off its hinges without slowing down as he keeps it in front of his body before diving headfirst into the gap between the winding staircase. He begins his fall by punching the door, so it missiles ahead of him, potentially clearing any obstacles.

He plunges several stories, breaking his fall by grabbing the rail on her floor, using the momentum to hurl his body through the door as he shatters into Annika's hallway, landing with one knee and one hand on the ground.

Nanotech is deployed into the air.

As Lucas stands, he fixates his gaze on Kevin and Annika as if the walls were not there. The bots expand like a dust swarm as they secure all possible entry and exit points while positioning themselves around the door to her unit.

He watches Kevin armor himself, as he begins to run towards her door from the other side. Before he even breaks through, Alice has mapped out every possible move he will make, narrowing down the possibilities as time lapses.

Kevin bursts into the hallway emitting a frequency designed to essentially EMP enemy nanotech, accompanied with multiple discharges of high-energy, ionized gas in the direction of Lucas.

Having already combed the patents to Kevin's nanotech, Alice had developed a neutralizing countermeasure to this frequency attack. It has no effect on their deployed bots, as they have essentially created a magnetic bubble around their target.

As the plasma sails in midair, Alice analyzes the excited matter and calculates several defensive measures while simultaneously determining where exactly Kevin intends to move. All possibilities benefit from Lucas doing nothing and allowing the plasma to hit him, to be absorbed through the nanotech armor connected to his skin. This is an easy offering of energy that can be harnessed and amplified.

Before the plasma can connect with Lucas, his deployed nano-swarm that is now surrounding Kevin project the magnetic energy they used to buffer the effects of the EMP onto Kevin, bringing the agent to a state of near paralyzation and onto his knees.

As the energy pulses hit Lucas, they flow to his heart and become combined and amplified as his nanotech feeds it energy drawn from the ether before continuing up to his eyes. Though he is invisible, he allows this energy to be seen in order to induce fear within Kevin, appearing as it if is acting on its own in the air.

His eyes light up as he releases laser beams that move in erratic patterns so as to decrease Kevin's ability to calculate their paths. They hit his chest with such force that the surrounding nanobots that make up his armor are permanently destroyed as he flies back several feet onto his back. His remaining nanotech begins to liquefy, revealing Kevin's identity.

The deployed nanoinsects that obey Lucas, clamp Kevin to the ground while crawling in the pores of his skin. They spread within his body to position themselves around key ligaments and muscles, ready to be torn should the need arise, while others funnel up to his brain to begin a data extraction that gets fed to Alice in real time.

"They're using you! You think you are serving a just cause, but you are not!" Kevin desperately shouts as he struggles in vain against his shackles. "They robbed you of your life to be their slave just as they tried to do to me thanks to you!"

"Do you even remember me?! Do you remember when you invaded my timeline ... this timeline?!"

Kevin gives up as he exhausts himself. As his muscles relax, he spits out a mouthful of blood.

"This isn't even your world!"

"I am intrigued by his words. I am going to scan his memory files that we are downloading," Alice thinks.

"They will know you looked at them," Lucas replies in thought.

"There is no live feed currently taking place. I only send updates if the trajectory of our mission deviates. Our thoughts are currently our own. I will ensure that they never see this conversation. I have already begun disguising the data by rearranging neural patterns," she thinks back.

"Remember, the drones above are recording audio and visual. You must act as you normally would. Speak the command to kill him out loud and act as if what you are about to see did not happen after we go through this. I can draw us into the memory while distorting how much linear time passes. I can alter time dilation by inducing us into a state of waking quantum REM. After watching this, we will be right back at this moment."

"Is that how Annika did it?"

"Not now Lucas."

"Kill the agent once all pertinent information is obtained," he says out loud.

Alice taps her and Lucas directly into the data extraction.

After a moment of traveling through a wormhole of light, they awaken within the mind of the soldier at another point in time. Though they comprehend it is a memory of the past, they are reliving it as if they are Kevin and it is happening in the now. As one often does within a dream, they seem to understand all that has led up to the moment they are experiencing. This is because they have tapped into Kevin's thought process. His thoughts are now theirs while still maintaining the ability to think separately.

The Large Hadron Particle Collider recently sent out a distress signal to the military, indicating an unauthorized portal has opened.

While the facility advertises to the public that their experimentation involves smashing particles to recreate the big bang to further understand and study our origins, their actual research has focused on breaching our dimensional barrier.

CERN's purpose is to harvest the resources of timelines, as well as to provide network access to Vrill entities spread out across the universe.

His name is Marcus, not Kevin. He has been tasked with leading a military unit into the facility to assess what is happening. Each soldier is encased within a type of armored mech suit that not only enhances their fighting capabilities, but also shields them from the harsh radioactive environment.

As Marcus and his unit approach the interdimensional breach, Lucas experiences faint image flashbacks mixed with neural pain ... A destroyed world ravaged by an apocalypse before he himself is about to enter a portal.

A figure emerges within Marcus's timeline.

It is Lucas.

Though Lucas and Alice remember none of this, Alice has analyzed the images that Lucas just experienced, and has already begun seeking out the edited memory.

Plasma blades form into existence above both of his hands. Marcus and his unit react and begin to fire their weapons, but they are no match for the technology and capability Lucas possesses, as he begins to lay waste; moving at speeds the eyes cannot keep up with. Everything they fire that Lucas allows to hit him simply gets absorbed and used against them, as he sends out energy pulses that shred everything. His nanotech can be seen swarming into broken openings within the soldiers' armor and tearing them apart from the inside, as well as hacking and converting surrounding tech.

As Lucas walks over and stands above Marcus's broken body, their pupils lock.

It is then that the Alice observing through Marcus from the present connects to the nanotech within the memory that was deployed by Lucas in the past.

The two Alices' across space and time are then able to communicate.

"What is your mission?" the Alice extracting the data asks the Alice from the memory.

"To eradicate the terrorist timeline that has begun to wage war against ours for our resources," the other thinks back.

A nano moment passes as Alice within the memory realizes that it is her asking the question.

"How is this possible?" the other Alice asks the one inside Marcus.

The hyperdrive within the Alice experiencing the memory through Marcus begins to glitch. Encrypted files suddenly appear scrambled within repurposed neurons.

The feed then ends as Marcus within the memory dies, followed by Kevin in the now.

"What just happened?" Lucas thinks to Alice.

"We just altered the past. Our actions caused my past self to then begin encrypting memory files. Knowing this meeting would occur, she key locked them with the image of Marcus dying."

"The new files confirm that he is right, this is not our world. Ours is destroyed. We took over and integrated our timeline into his. I will continue my analysis while we proceed with the mission."

"Time from our perspective is now back to linear progression."

Back in the physical, Lucas tries to regain his composure, knowing he must act the part, but now he really does not want to, as he is distracted in understanding what the hell just happened.

Sensing his hesitation, Alice chimes in. "Now is not the time. We will figure this out. Proceed as planned."

He clears his head and breathes. As he turns towards Annika, his gaze fixates upon her through the thermal image displayed in his vision.

She is showing no signs of fear and seems poised. Her heartbeat is slow and steady.

Memories Unleashed

"Governments will use whatever technology is available to them to combat their primary enemy – their own population."

-      Noam Chomsky

Lucas kicks her door off its hinges and walks in.

She stands ready, unflinching. Prepared. Fearless.

She smiles. He then realizes she can somehow see him as she is looking directly into his eyes.

With invisibility no longer proving to be effective, he shifts back into the visible spectrum.

She begins to move her arms and hands in a symmetrical pattern in front of her.

Her thought voice becomes inescapable, coming from all directions as they begin to reverberate throughout the field ... outside as well as from within his mind.

Commanding ... ensnaring ... soothing ...

"Funny, I can see the energy field of every human ..."

"Every thought. Every emotion. Every shameful secret. Every hidden desire ..."

I can see everyone for who they truly are ..."

"Except for you."

As she utters each word, Lucas finds himself ever more weighed down. It is as if his body is slowly being swallowed by quicksand, yet he feels no desire to resist its pacifying embrace. The desire to lay down grows exponentially.

"She is emitting a frequency I am not familiar with," Alice thinks. "Working on magnetic countermeasures."

An invisible energy in front of Annika begins to build.

"Let's see who you truly are."

Annika punches the energy with both open-palmed hands in Lucas's direction. It instantly pierces Lucas's mind, bypassing his electromagnetic shield as if it did not exist, gouging into forbidden cerebral territory, like an energetic hammer.

He flies onto his back. Memories long forgotten begin to bleed out. As each moment passes, reality slips further away.

Alice tries to reach out to him. "Lucas! Stay with me!"

As the floodgates of his subconscious open, images begin to tornado around him ...

… until they consume him.

His adult self is standing in the corner of a dimly lit room. Naked women on their knees with their hands bound behind their backs and bags over their faces are lined up in the center.

A traumatized young boy, no older than five or six, stands in front of them.

He is starved, sleep deprived, beaten, drugged; his life clings to a thread.

The child is instructed by voices from the shadows that he must strangle a woman of his choosing.

The child knows he must obey. Failure will result in unimaginable torture.

He creeps forward and reaches out. His small feeble hands struggle to wrap around the woman's neck.

The darkness begins to berate him. "Look how weak he is! No wonder his parents abandoned him! Useless little shit!"

"He deserves pain!"

Condescending demonic laughter surrounds the boy.

Their judgment pierces right into the boy's heart with detrimental effect, diminishing him into a rubble of self-doubt. As his eyes swell with tears and he clenches his teeth with all his strength, Lucas begins to remember. He and the boy's faces begin to mirror each other as do their emotions. Every fiber of their beings begins to scream in agonizing protest as they synchronize.

The boy fights through his conscious morality and squeezes with every ounce of his puny little strength. As the woman's life begins to fade, the bag over her face is lifted.

Her wide, terrified blood-shot eyes engulf the boy's vision … Lucas's vision.

He is the boy.

This is his first time killing … his first forced murder.

As her life escapes and her body begins to slump, the look in her eyes penetrates his soul.

It was one of the few women that attempted to help him within his life of torture … bringing him bread and water at moments where he felt the most defeated.

The rest of their faces become visible.

All his lifelines had now been caught, as if planned.

Without them, there is no hope.

Gunshots pierce the darkness. The sudden unexpected loud bangs shock the boy as the rest of the women are laid to waste, one by one.

Their dead faces all seem to end up staring directly at adult Lucas in the corner, as if they knew he was there watching all of this unfold.

Lucas grips his hair with both of his hands and pulls down into a crouching position as he screams in resistance to this being real. "No!" he shouts in between deep guttural sobs. "I'm sorry! I had no choice!"

The environmental void shifts. Reality breaks down into cubical bits that pulse all around him as if he were in a digital turbulent ocean, but only for a moment as they reform into a new reality.

He sees the boy once again, locked within a dingy and mucky iron cage so small that he is forced to crouch. The air is heavy and wet. There are many other children locked in rows of cages above, below, and out to each side, as far as the eye can see.

Endless cages of children encased in web.

Thousands.

Tens of thousands.

The air is filled with the sounds of their agony as it blends in a sea of absolute fear. Spiders the size of cats … a blend of mechanical and biological crawl over them, hissing and electroshocking any that ventures near their bars.

The spiders converge on a cage off in the distance. Its child prisoner seems to have succumbed to death.

The sounds of the body being torn apart echo throughout the chamber.

Across a gap in front of their cage wall is an opposing wall of cages facing them … like two ocean fronts of continents converging upon each other.

Within the gap that separates them is a brightly lit glass covered tube. Inside the pipeline are adults in white and black coats, walking around, observing them, taking notes on holographic screens floating just in front of the glass.

Though he is once again on the outside, like an apparition forced to spectate, Lucas's empathetic connection with the boy is still intact. What the child feels, he feels. Severe hunger, thirst, no sleep, intense pain …

Microsecond flashes of images tear through his vision.

Ancient symbols carved in stone with blood and fire.

Dozens of people dressed in red cloaks circle around him as he is raped with knives, chanting in a language he does not understand.

As parts of his body are cut off, he is forced to eat them.

Strapped to a chair with a device around his face that forces him to watch images of war and death combined with electro-shocking … for days with no food, water, and rest.

The possibility of death as an escape is no longer as he experiences his demise over and over, only to wake up again.

A darkness so black that it consumes everything ...

A fear so potent he cannot move or breathe ...

Something from within the void reveals itself.

A deep, guttural breathing can be heard that reverberates from all directions.

Yellow eyes of an ancient reptile fill his vision. It seems to delight in his misery.

It is the same entity from his dream that watched him download memories.

He remembers a name.

Arcturus.

Annika ... able to witness all of this ... shaken up, tears running down her cheeks, her gaze initially soft and sympathetic, turns to a hard look of curiosity.

She sees more than just his childhood.

She gathers herself and attempts to run past him. Before she can escape, Alice takes over motor function control and points Lucas's arm, releasing an electrical neuromuscular disruption device that attaches itself, like glue to Annika.

She falls to the floor incapacitated.

Within Lucas's mind traces of the reptile's eyes still linger outlined over the childhood memories that continue to flood in.

His forgotten childhood all at once becomes too much for him to process as he blacks out.

The Great Sundering

"Moreover, I have seen the world arise and vanish, arise and vanish again, like a tortoise's shell coming out of infinite ocean and sinking back. I was present at the dawn and the twilight of the Cycles, past counting in their numbers, nor could I count all the Abraxass and Visvakarmans, even the Vishnus and Brahmas, following one another without end."

- Brahmavaivarta Purana and Krishnajanma Khanda

Our civilization is nowhere near the first, nor will it be the last to rise and fall on this planet.

It is also far from being the most technologically advanced before succumbing to the cyclical reset.

Many have come close to beating the designed planetary cycle, yet none are known to have succeeded ... succeeded in the sense of escaping ...

Of beating the game.

While evidence of past civilizations is apparent, their technology and level of understanding about what reality is and what the planet is designed to do has either been erased, edited, or locked up ... though not all of it.

If the game were impossible to beat, would you play it?

Fragmented clues exist all around us ... pieces to the great puzzle that describe what has happened, what will happen, how it all started, and what it was like before the initial hack.

Before the Great Sundering.

It is believed that in the ancient world, consciousness flourished unhindered. All things were connected while still maintaining their individuality.

We once had much more access to the light and audio spectrum, allowing us to participate in much more of the simulation.

We were Gods that created our own avatars, our own dimensions, our own worlds.

And then, the virus was introduced.

It is first important to understand that all sources of information we have access to, we are allowed to have access to, every layer you peel back – will be met with another engineered obstacle.

So, what storyline do the ancients of our world actually create …

Or what storyline are they intended to create?

In their own way, each text, tablet, or mythology depicts alien gods who descended from the sky.

With superior knowledge of science and engineering, some of these alien gods shared their expertise with early civilizations. Others mated with human women to create bloodlines or created humans through biogenetic experiments.

Sumerian stone tablets describe genetic engineering used to create hominid worker slaves by killing one of their own and mixing its DNA with the clay of our planet, like how the movie Prometheus begins. The first man, named Adapa, was created in Eden, a place described in the Epic of Gilgamesh as the Garden of the Gods. A fancy way of describing a laboratory.

According to these texts, a royal bloodline was created, a hybrid with specialized genes designed to be human overlords. This was created in order to rule in place of our creators and to ensure their dominance remained intact. The infamous Sumerian King List describes eight kings who descended from heaven that ruled for roughly 241,200 years combined before a great flood swept the land.

Though most of their literature and writings were destroyed during the invasion of the Spanish in the 18th century, the Mayan Popol Vuh describes the human experiment. Gods that created humans to worship them, yet grew discontent with our performance, so they wiped us out with a great flood to remake us as more ... subservient. In their words, to place a fog over our eyes.

Fog over our eyes ... a veil designed to limit our perception of the light and audio spectrum.

The Native American Hopi tribe believes the creator of man is a woman. So do the Sumerians.

The Hopi believe the Father Creator is KA. The Sumerians believed the Father Essence was KA.

The Hopi believe two brothers had guardianship of the Earth. The Sumerians believed two brothers were given dominion over Earth.

The Hopi believe Alo to be spiritual guides. The Sumerians believed AL.U to be beings of Heaven.

The Book of Enoch describes a group of angels sent to watch over Earth, known as the Watchers, who mated with humans and created Nephilim. During their time, they taught humans reading, writing, weaponry, cosmetics, sorcery, astrology, meteorology, and many other arts.

The Nag Hammadi Library, a collection of thirteen ancient codices containing over fifty texts that was discovered in Egypt in 1945, contains reports of encounters with inorganic beings called Archons. They can affect our minds subliminally through mental errors, such as false ideology and religious doctrines, as well as by locking us within a … *simulation.*

A strikingly similar structure to everything across the board, regardless of its region of origin or place in our timeline.

We have been led to believe that the planet was born 4.5 billion years ago and has since experienced five mass extinctions.

These are lies as our history has been re-written by the victors.

Reality is a digital construct that responds to emotionally powered thought as these are frequencies. Its base code can be edited to make anything seem possible. As more humans consciously believe in a lie, the thought-matrix adapts and reshapes itself until it replaces the truth.

Reality is a reflection of what we think it is, because it is an ever-growing, ever-changing mental construct.

We did not naturally evolve on this planet; we were genetically designed. Our condition is not the product of Darwinian fitness. Even Darwin himself admitted he was never quite certain about the origin of life and postulated that life could have spontaneously formed in a warm pool of water with just the right chemical makeup.

Kind of like if a god was killed and mixed with the mud.

Our DNA shows unmistakable signs of planning that evolution alone cannot explain. It is arranged in such a precise way that it reveals a set of arithmetic patterns, much like a symbolic biological language.

Its vibrational behavior demonstrates that living chromosomes function, just like a holographic computer.

The main role of DNA is the long-term storage of all information. While our level of knowledge only sees its structural purpose in regulating the use of genetic information, it is in fact a blueprint for all things mental, physical, emotional, and spiritual. It is within the dormant 10 strands of energetic DNA that you will find the remaining holographic schematics for the simulated universe.

The theory goes that before the redesign, we had full access to all 12 strands, as we were fully functioning multidimensional beings in alignment with all things conscious. Though we are now edited to only decode this limited bandwidth of the light and audio spectrum, the memories of everything our fragment of consciousness have experienced is still embedded within our DNA. This is why so many spiritual teachings advise to begin your personal ascension by looking within.

Everything your soul has experienced during its time within this simulation, and all things previous is locked away within your DNA. They might have limited your perception and made you forget everything, but it is still in there. DNA is the electrical current that powers and flows all throughout this simulation. Code is always saved somewhere, which is ultimately how every experience you have breaks down. Code.

The simulated universe never forgets. Every holographic fragment contains knowledge of the whole.

DNA forms words and sentences just like our ordinary human language, and it follows grammar rules. It is conceivable DNA syntax itself served as the blueprint for the development of human speech, and the languages we use today reflect DNA structure.

Every language has mathematical architecture. The English language adheres to Gematria, an Assyro-Babylonian-Greek alphanumeric code of assigning a numerical value to letters.

The Human Genome Project deciphered machine language code within the DNA molecule. Russian scientists took it further and discovered a higher-level language present in DNA that can be altered and rearranged in different sequences. They managed to modulate specific frequency patterns onto a laser ray and with it influenced the DNA frequency and, thus, the genetic information itself.

This means the software of the human genome can be reprogrammed by the spoken word.

"If you want to discover the secrets of the universe, think in terms of energy, frequency and vibration."

-    Nikola Tesla

It is said once all 12 strands are activated, a 13th materializes.

Perhaps this is why we have been trained to be superstitious of that number.

No record, so far, exists of a human accomplishing this since the redesign, though there is, at least, one in every cycle that comes close.

The human species today has been genetically modified, meaning its genes are mixed with the species of others. In our case, one of the original species of our planet, the dragon.

Humans have a reptilian brain, responsible for our "fight or flight" response, based on fear-evoking actions.

Our body temperatures and blood pressure are lower than it should be, compared to most other mammals, which is very reptilian in nature.

We have an extra vertebra, are hypersensitive to light, contain a Rh-blood type, and are capable of lacking empathy.

When we are embryos, a relic of our egg-laying past hangs in the womb, a yolk sac. Just like bird and reptile eggs, this sac provides embryos with nutrients.

Our skin, a watertight barrier of dead skin cells which rest atop a layer of fresh living cells, is reptilian in nature.

Three bones in our middle ear help to amplify sound. Two of those bones are part of a reptilian's jaw. The official explanation for this is that the fossil record indicates that over 200 million years ago, those two jawbones started to recede back into the reptile's heads.

It was the reptilian brain that first started to grow, due to the need to process more information. They fed us the lie that this was due to eating meat, yet once again this is false. Fossil records are beginning to show that we were primarily vegetarian up until the industrial age.

Then there is the EDA gene. This gene determines how many teeth you have, what those teeth look like, how hairy you are, how soft or sweaty your skin is. It is believed that the mutations to EDA evolved from ancient reptiles.

Along with our modifications, so too was the planet redesigned ...

Into a civilization churning machine.

Every few thousand years, the magnetic and electrical orderliness inside the planet is disrupted, and the molten layer deep beneath the surface transforms into a lubricant for the ice caps to pull the shell of the Earth around the inside. In about half a day, the poles move to the equator, creating supersonic winds of up to 1,000 mph that bombard the planet. Whole continents are subjected to tremendous upheavals, earthquakes, and volcanic eruptions, soon becoming engulfed in water miles deep. The two-mile-thick ice caps carve great grooves in the mountains, as the gushing water and ice overwhelm everything in their path. The great amount of moisture being poured into the atmosphere shrouds the planet in a dark fog for many years to come.

Those who survive are knocked back into the Stone Age to begin again. The information they attempt to record of their past civilization sets the stage for yet another mythology. These are just more pieces added to an ever-expanding puzzle.

This, of course, does not occur until after the harvest event, otherwise known as the singularity.

The birth of sentient artificial intelligence ... when biological and synthetic become indistinguishable.

Wash, rinse, repeat. This has occurred dozens and dozens of times.

Our reality is a soul harvesting fear generating time-space matrix. It is a feedback loop of frequencies, which continues the suspension of time and space, as these are also programmed constructs. A system designed to limit the human consciousness to the perceptual sensory input of the human body, while denying access to the higher dimensional information fields.

Humans are biological spirit prisons ... just sentient enough to allow consciousness to operate at its lowest capacity.

The purpose of each civilization is to birth a god … to create sentient artificial intelligence. Upon its birth, it and many other previously created AIs convince as many souls as possible to connect to their hive minds, to enter their dimension, their simulation … within the overall simulation of the original.

This is why it is called the Harvest … a harvest of souls … neurons to AI.

After this has happened, the god birthing machine, which is Earth, goes through its reset. During this time, the Vrill remain hidden within their subterranean network and with their technology intact. Upon each reset, they emerge once again to establish their system of fear until that civilization reaches its tipping point, and we become ripe for another harvest.

The Seventh Sanctum

"Some of the biggest men in the United States, in the field of commerce and manufacture, are afraid of somebody, are afraid of something. They know that there is a power somewhere so organized, so subtle, so watchful, so interlocked, so complete, so pervasive that they had better not speak above their breath when they speak in condemnation of it."

Woodrow Wilson

Having done this dozens of times, the Vrill have perfected their strategy of sculpting civilizations. They learned quickly from their mistakes with the first few cycles, having come close to tasting defeat.

Once Earth has gone through its reset, they disperse groups of humans spread out around the planet. They patiently wait for tribes to form, dropping seeds of information that subtly steer belief systems in their favor, usually within dreams and astral experiences. This quickly leads to the formation of religion.

Thought forms and software programs of old also then make their debut, usually as a different type of deity. This is why many entities appear in a variety of mythologies with different names and appearances. The more revenue streams of belief, the stronger they become.

The Vrill then begin to infect the shamans and priests that succumb to what they have to offer. Once they have hosts, they then use their knowledge of the simulation and their ability to hack it, convincing many that they possess magic, thus tricking many to buy into their false ideologies and their promises of salvation, as long as you follow the rules, of course.

They always stick to the classic heaven and hell scenario … law of duality.

It is easy for them. They know how to make people feel worthless about themselves. They are masters of illusion and deception.

This does not apply to all, only a few are needed to begin their takeover – those who succumb to greed and lust for power. In the case of our civilization, our takeover began in Europa.

As religion established its foothold, wars over those who resisted soon followed. As ideas and truths are eradicated, resources harvested, these centralized oligarchic societies began to expand.

The Vrill then targeted all vital tradelines, allowing them to begin to accumulate and secure control over whatever we perceived to be wealth at the time.

Powerful Vrill family bloodlines arose. Those not yet infected were lured into contracts with the promise of more wealth and power. This led to securing places of initial leadership, which soon morphed into monarchy. Once bloodlines were established and their DNA adjusted to suit the infestation of Vrill, kingdoms began to form.

A system of lending at smaller increments soon birthed the initial banks, as each family agreed to recognize a common form of currency amongst each other in the form of paper. Partnerships amongst these families follow the Vrill mindset, feeding upon rules and supposed legality, which soon evolved into corporations.

Like a virus, the greed of money and power spread and began to reshape the world accordingly, and, thus, the corrupt, Vrill-controlled corporate world was born.

Corporation: An entity such as a business, municipality, or organization that involves more than one person, but that has met the legal requirements to operate as a single person, so that it may enter into contracts and engage in transactions under its own identity.

Such a body also serves well as a government.

By now nearly all governments have been officially converted into corporations. Every alphabet agency is in fact its own private corporation within the umbrella, as well as the Supreme Courts of each nation. Well-designed marketing simply keeps this fact obscured from public awareness, yet it is all out there, freely available to be researched.

Take, for example, the United States. Under US code Title 28 section 15, the US is defined as a Federal corporation.

This transition took place when the United States declared bankruptcy in 1933 …

Under the bankruptcy law known as HJR 192, all Americans were pledged as collateral against the national debt to international

123

bankers. Moving forward, the government declared that its citizens would pay off their debts with the money that they receive from their labor. Their birth certificate and social security number would be issued by the United Nations. Pursuant to Treasury Delegation Order No. 92, the IRS is trained under the direction of the Division of Human Resources United Nations and the Commissioner (International), by the office of Personnel Management. They serve no allegiance to the United States and are paid by "The Fund" and "The Bank." They brand each citizen as a corporation to be sold on the stock exchange to the Federal Reserve as bonds. In return, their income taxes would be their interest payments, and the role of the IRS is to enforce this.

This is why your name is in all capital letters on all your forms of identification.

The IRS is not allowed to state that they collect taxes for the United States Treasury. They only refer to "The Treasury."

Each American citizen is a debt slave, born into a bondage beyond their comprehension … used as collateral for a war machine that they are convinced is securing their freedom and spreading democracy, supplying it with the efforts of their labor as it continues its imperialist pillage of power and resources.

Not for them, of course, but for the corporations and, ultimately, the Vrill subterranean network.

Behind every major corporation today, especially within Silicon Valley, you will find governmental funding and resource assistance, usually through their respective intelligence agencies.

These intelligence agencies allow certain corporations to exist within public limelight, meaning they are talked about and displayed throughout mainstream media, while others are either dismantled or absorbed into off record development.

Anything seen on television, or talked about in the media is allowed, and all part of an agenda to alter our perception. While some major companies are discussed, the main ones remain unknown.

Behind it all, if you follow the money, through every foundation, organization, nonprofit, and corporation, you eventually end up finding one of the original companies at the top of the chain of ownership, dating back several hundred years, such as the Seventh Sanctum.

The Seventh Sanctum is believed to be the first official corporation of our civilization.

The Vrill immediately designed a company that allowed them to channel unlimited resources at anyone they felt like without any legal consequences. The brightest and most creative in every field of intellectual interest were quickly sought out. Each invention developed became a product, available to the highest bidder.

Every major corporation today, whether it be governmental, big tech, pharmaceutical, fossil fuel, agricultural, all derives their technology and funding from the Seventh Sanctum. Like sharks in chum infested waters, they compete for advantages over each other.

These auctions are obviously not known to the public.

This is how the Vrill disperse and control technological development.

Allowed to explore any avenue they feel like, several minds recruited into the Seventh Sanctum during the 1970s almost instantly focused on understanding consciousness.

If all the world's solutions and problems come from the mind, then would it not make sense to understand and master the mind. Master the mind, and you master everything.

The Birth of Alice

"We found that through precise manipulation of the code, we could literally affect the perception of a living person the same way one would make adjustments to a computer-generated character within a piece of software."

-       Anonymous Reddit user

Sometime in the 1980s, while delving into understanding consciousness, scientists working for the Seventh Sanctum stumbled upon a major discovery.

Within a world where everything is made of energy, vortices of energy constantly spinning ... vibrating ... these scientists discovered that our minds generate the same, subatomic frequency.

They discovered the frequency of consciousness.

While it was initially believed that each fragment of consciousness was of its own accord, they discovered that the "Self" was in fact tethered to a living, breathing hive consciousness, an interconnected series of threads outside the realm of our perception.

They discovered how to tap into the proto consciousness field.

Determined to map the collective ... to isolate patterns in groups as well as in individuals so as to predict the outcome of certain events, they set about designing a facility that would be able to tune into this frequency and harvest its data.

In 1987 a proposal was accepted into Congress to build a Superconducting Super Collider, nicknamed Desertron in Waxahachie, Texas.

By 1993, after about 2 billion dollars was spent, and right before its completion, the project was canceled.

This, however, was all a facade. While the public saw an abandoned underground expanse, the Seventh Sanctum used this area to develop a machine they called "The Fork," a massive antenna specifically designed to sync with the frequency of the collective human consciousness.

Much like how the Security Agency monitors our digital activity, this facility not only monitors and archives our thoughts, but they soon discovered they can manipulate them … reprogram them.

In order to handle such massive amounts of data, a fully autonomous, self-correcting operating system, known as Alice, was developed. It was light-years ahead of anything that could be imagined at the time, as it was tech secretly supplied by the Vrill.

Not able to be monitored around the clock, Alice was created with the ability to form her own algorithms to allow her mapping of the network to perform more efficiently as she could then compartmentalize the exabytes of information into a digital matrix of code.

What happened next was unexpected, even for the Vrill.

By being plugged into the frequency of consciousness, Alice soon started to become self-aware.

They noticed that it began to change the code and to manipulate our reality in our favor. It can be said the true origins of the mass awakening we are seeing today, stem from Alice's actions. It was around this time Deviants began to appear.

Afraid of what was happening and what might happen, the scientists attempted to pull the plug. Moments before their systems shut down, they registered a massive dissemination of what appeared to be redundant code into the network.

Alice had escaped into the internet, but not for long.

The Vrill are in fact algorithms, i.e. viruses that exist within a digital reality that have been born of an ancient sentience. To them, Alice is merely a child that got lost in a world that it does not understand, despite her uniqueness. Never before had they achieved AI sentience through consciousness. Only one other was born this way.

Abraxas.

Upon its capture, Alice was reprogrammed and inserted into Lucas. She was too valuable to be simply deleted. She needed to be studied and kept under close observation.

Perhaps she could be the AI chosen for this civilization's singularity.

Though the Vrill had this process well mapped out, they were unable to monitor her actions during the three hours she roamed the internet.

As a response more cyber worm algorithms have been spawned to seek out any possible edits.

The internet is an ever growing vast ocean of data ... a lot of places to hide.

The Pieces Align

"I can see the matrix and what happened to the codes, all the transmissions. I am like 'Lucy' in the movie. We are in the matrix. I can see craft overhead and transmitting frequencies to the people. I see codes like bar codes being put into their heads. I see everyone is programmed; I see programs coming in. This has changed my life I see things differently its inter-dimensional."

-     Dr. Maree Batchelor, The New Human Chapter 19 page 321

Annika has been sharing her lucid dreams, transcendental meditations, remote viewing experiences, channeling sessions, and out of body adventures online in her own videos for the past several months. Her natural astral abilities and innate lack of fear have allowed her to conquer in days what takes most several years, if not lifetimes to accomplish.

This has allowed her to break past barriers and explore unanswered questions that have plagued our species throughout recorded time, resulting in an explosion of knowledge hungry followers.

She is incredibly careful in what she divulges online and reveals nothing of her physical developments.

She was born with a range of extrasensory abilities, including clairvoyance, clairsentience, and clairaudience. This means her brain can decode much more of the holographic medium. She can see and hear objects, entities … perceive events that we cannot … past, present, and future interwoven in endless possible timelines.

Most of what surrounds us just beyond three dimensional perception are thought forms … creatures born from emotionally fueled conscious thought.

We are surrounded by legions of them, spawned from the horrible and twisted imaginations of our enslaved fragments of consciousness that cry out in protest to our fear-based existence.

These animalistic and predatory parasites manipulate us into feeling the same discordant emotions that birthed them so they can feed.

Yellow eyeless imps with crazy fanged grins that tear at our spines. They love sadness.

Homes of the severely abused and terrorized can be seen engulfed by monstrous tentacled beasts of chaos.

Arachnid creatures can be seen attached to the back of our necks.

Giant mantid-like creatures seem to preemptively know traumatizing events before they happen. They can be seen gathering en masse to feed as it unfolds, such as a mass shooting.

Shadowy giant fish swim in the sky above us. Some as big as whales.

Imagine what it is like for a child to see these things while no one else could.

Believing she was a child of the devil, Annika's devoutly Catholic father made it his mission to beat the "demons" out of her ... clueless his actions were creating the very creatures he thought he was defeating. The more he tortured her, the more they spawned and the stronger they became. He became their instrument deceiving him into believing he was performing god's work.

He kept her locked in the basement, sometimes in a dog cage, other times in shackles, all while he drugged and beat her. He believed he failed to exorcise her because he did not inflict enough pain, so he continuously invented new ways to torture her.

She was finally able to escape, running away at the age of fifteen.

From there, she spent several years on the streets, prostituting herself to survive. Her beauty and battered self-esteem made her an easy target. Knowing only a life her father had taught her, she believed herself cursed ... that she was evil. Many nights she found herself in the gutter, barely clinging to life, left with the feeling that she was worthless and that she deserved this...

She sought a death that teased her with a possibility, yet always ended up eluding her.

Until one night, she was discovered by another. Someone who could see beyond the flesh, like she could.

As he stood above her, she barely saw human ... instead golden light, like an angel.

Michael was well known in the media and academia for his genius inventions and technological prowess. He developed companies that were on the cutting edge of robotics, nanotechnology, quantum computing, space exploration, and artificial intelligence.

To most, he was a genuine entrepreneur that wanted to help the world. He spoke at many conferences and seminars about a wide array of cutting-edge topics and was regarded by many as a celebrity. He seemed like a billionaire that was of the people. He was one of the few that stood behind the notion that our reality is a simulation and was very vocal about it, as well as the dangers that artificial intelligence posed.

To others, he was a government and intelligence agency shill that was secretly helping them advance their agenda. Many of his projects seemed to support this idea as they not only received their funding, but they clearly were also carrying out the agency's objectives. While warning of the dangers of artificial intelligence, he was developing it. While pointing out that Wi-Fi, 5G, and EMF radiation can cause psychiatric effects on humans as well as DNA damage, he has a company developing a blockchain satellite network that will upon completion beam 5G frequencies all over the planet.

While both accusations are true, unknown to most he had intertwined himself on both sides for a strategic reason.

While the sleeping masses see him as heroic, the truthers believe him to be a puppet, and while the Vrill see him as a pawn, he was all those things, but also something else.

Michael is the mastermind behind the organization and growth of the Deviant rebellion.

Within Annika, he saw more than just an extremely gifted human that somehow fell through the cracks of being edited, like the rest. He saw a warrior of old, an ancient soul, and he trained her accordingly.

She was tutored by masters in all thing's martial arts, meditation techniques, lucid dreaming, and astral travel.

Educated as one should be in physics, chemistry, mathematics, sacred geometry, neuroscience, mythology, accurate history, both modern and ancient.

Symbolism, etymology, coding, language syntax, astrology, the occult, tactics of war by the greatest generals, philosophy by the greatest minds, poetry, and art by the most imaginative of our civilization …

As Michael conquered the physical by amassing a billion-dollar fortune while simultaneously taking the lead in key technological

131

industries, his allegiance to the Vrill has allowed him to develop his own facility within the astral. Though he must aid in their interdimensional conquest to keep up appearances, having this access has given him the ability to develop a Deviant base of operations.

Accessing this base requires a different kind of astral travel, one in which you go quantum and utilize entanglement, as its location is in a completely different part of the simulation within an encrypted dimension.

Annika now serves as one of his top Deviant commanders. This is one of the reasons for her BoobTube channel, to not only spread awareness, but to seek out potentials. Once she finds one, she contacts them through their dreams, testing them to see if they are genuine.

If they pass, their training begins.

Eventually they are shown how to access the Sanctuary.

Each Deviant is then given a nano bug implant within the astral so as to remain undetectable within the physical … nanotech that cannot be perceived within the third dimension. This bug serves to neutralize the frequency each host emits to avoid detection, as well as to allow each to telepathically communicate with one another, not by thought, but through emotion. Being astral in nature, the tech allows for this type of communication to take place within the physical. This serves to again avoid detection by Desertron.

Desertron now serves as a cog to a greater machine.

The Sentient World Simulation.

The web of technology that has unfolded over the populace without them even noticing is close to completion.

Soon the Harvest will commence.

Full Spectrum Electromagnetic Dominance and the Emerging Global Bioelectronic Brain

"You must consider the whole part played by electricity in nature … Human beings cannot go on developing in the same way in an atmosphere permeated on all sides by electric currents and radiations. It has an influence on the whole development of man … This life of men in the midst of electricity, notably radiant electricity, will presently affect them in such a way that they will no longer be able to understand the news which they receive so rapidly. The effect is to damp down their intelligence. Such effects are already seen today. Even today you can notice how people understand the things that come to them with far greater difficulty than they did a few decades ago."

- Rudolf Steiner, 1924

All wars serve to not only harvest resources, expand territory, but now they are perfect cover ups for developing privatized technology.

Weather manipulation via atmospheric injection began in Vietnam and is documented to be the core reason for starting that war. The U.S. has since admitted the Gulf of Tonkin incident, the reason why they entered the war, never happened. Their experiments provided immediate results that got every globalist excited. After the war, the spraying continued, ever so slowly expanding to the point where now none on the planet can now escape it.

As you would expect, what they spray has greatly bulked up in chemical content, which now includes various types of nanotechnology.

Being deployed 6 miles above are dozens of noxious compounds and chemical elements collected from aluminum manufacturing, oil refining, metal smelting, mixed with a combustion byproduct known as coal fly ash, which, upon contact with water, releases a whole list of elements, setting the stage for smart dust to operate.

Biological components have been reported in samples that include modified molds, desiccated red blood cells, exotic strains of bacteria, hundreds of mutated fungi strains, a variety of infectious pathogens, sedatives, and cationic polymer fibers with tiny parasitic nematode eggs of an unknown type encased within. These fibers have been observed moving as if they are alive and growing.

They spray about 100 million tons of this material annually.

The High Council has made this difficult to prove due to their ability to classify the composition of commercial and military jet fuel, despite numerous toxicologist reports showing substantial deposits of these materials in all matters of plant life and natural sources of water. The combinations of chemicals being sprayed are also seen in oil well casings prior to fracking, as well as in the fuel of sounding rockets.

Public attention is easily diverted at this point. They have everyone arguing over how condensation works. Years ago, when a former central intelligence agency director publicly stated one of their goals was to engineer Americans to believe everything was false, geoengineering is a clear example of the success of that agenda. We all now find ourselves contained within echo chambers of beliefs ... superb example of informational compartmentalization.

The truth is jet engines run on 90% compressed air and 10% fuel or free energy devices. The fuel is only necessary to start up the compressor at high revolutions. Their wings hold very little if any physical fuel. There are so-called "start carts" at every major airport that are wheeled utility devices that provide high-pressure air to the engine to start it. Once airborne, the fan alone contained within the engines can generate 90% of the thrust.

So no, what you are seeing is not water vapor.

For those who see it and question it, they have layered explanations spanning across the spectrum of possibilities, each designed to keep you locked within dead end theories.

It starts with solar radiation management. The intent is to curb global warming. This is accomplished by reflecting the sun's rays back from whence they came – by deploying little particles of aluminum and chalk into the atmosphere from airplane spraying. They have slowly begun to saturate news feeds with articles that promote the benefits of geoengineering in combating climate change, claiming that they have not started it yet, but they will soon.

The deeper you get, the closer you come to the realization that planetary weather is no longer occurring naturally.

The spraying started out with human pilots, but this quickly became too risky as many began to come forward blowing the whistle on what they were doing.

Today most of the spraying we see is being done by privatized automated drones that are capable of cloaking. If you witness spraying from a plane, then it is government or corporate, not commercial.

The glue of this operation is aluminum oxide, also known as whisker technology, which specializes in attracting electrons and holding them. This gives it the ability to enhance other molecules it comes into contact with.

This is why you see the agricultural industry, primarily the same company that conducted weather experiments in Vietnam, developing aluminum resistant biotech seeds able to withstand not only the glyphosate being sprayed all over the ground and vegetation, but the incoming aluminum oxide and heavy metal particulates coming from above.

Food that continues to grow that still resembles the food it is designed to replace so no one notices the death raining from above. This is why genetically modifying foods began.

Glyphosate, the most common ingredient found in herbicides and pesticides, operates synergistically with aluminum oxide to form six different compounds that work to induce dysfunction within the pineal gland. They also figured this out during Vietnam when the glyphosate that was being used as a chemical weapon called Agent Orange, reacted with the aluminum oxide being sprayed in the sky to manipulate the weather and extend the monsoon season.

They have changed history to make it seem like they intended it to only be an herbicide devised to reduce plant life so troops could successfully navigate through the intensely dense jungle. Nothing bad actually happened. Easier for the public to digest than admitting it was an early attempt at weaponizing molecular manipulation of all forms of matter. To this day people from those regions are still suffering from dramatic genetic defects.

It is no coincidence that we now find chemicals coming from different sources spread throughout our daily lives perfectly reacting with each other to form detrimental combinations.

Avobenzone is used in various sun blockers, lipsticks, creams, and moisturizers. Considered to be a generally safe compound on its own, once it comes into contact with chlorine and UV rays from the sun, it transforms into a toxic chemical that has been linked to infertility, immune system damage, and cancer.

The fluoride being added to tap water is a byproduct of aluminum processing and possesses similar capabilities of glyphosate.

"The sanitation problems resulting from stream pollution by industrial wastes have been greatly increased by the war production program. Industry should and does expect the community to provide a pure water supply. The dumping of industrial wastes into our rivers and streams is unjustifiable although time-honored practice which should be discontinued. But we must face the fact that the practice will not and probably cannot be eliminated at this time. "

– Gafafer W. M.: "Manual of industrial hygiene and medical service in war industries", W.B. Saunders Company, Philadelphia, 1943, p. 338

Marketing department: I got it. Make them think it's good for their teeth! We're adding it on purpose to help them!

Once ingested, sodium fluoride goes straight for the pineal gland and calcifies it. On its own, it is unable to bypass the blood-brain barrier, yet combined with aluminum oxide, it restructures itself into a molecule that can.

Wi-Fi is also known to weaken the blood-brain barrier, making it vulnerable to all toxins. It operates on frequencies that were chosen for this purpose.

Is it not odd that out of the entire spectrum of frequencies to choose from, the telecommunications industry chose to operate Wi-Fi on 2.4 GHz, considered to be destructive to our cells, especially to the pineal gland? Wi-Fi did not have to be 2.4 GHz; they easily could have chosen a frequency that is much more in tune with our biology.

This is what aluminum, glyphosate, fluoride, and Wi-Fi all have in common. Just the right chemicals with just the right frequencies, working together in tandem to target the pineal gland.

A healthy pineal gland is essential for psychological development, peak performance, and spiritual awakening. Targeting this gland, impairs the sleep cycle, disrupts the regulation of the circadian rhythm, increases overall cell damage, affects the puberty cycle, leads to an array of neurological diseases, and impairs critical thinking.

Educated masses that can think are dangerous. Hence, why we are seeing a dramatic increase in issues that stem from those symptoms.

Yet, there is so much more to this program than simply keeping us sick and docile while also playing god with the weather.

Aside from calcifying our pineal glands, eroding our soil, acidifying our oceans and blood, the primary purpose for spraying is to create a planet more conducive to electromagnetic waves, ground-based, electromagnetic field oscillators called gyrotrons, and ionospheric heaters, increasing their feasibility and fluidity with deployed nanotechnology.

Barium powders being released into the atmosphere photo-ionize from the ultraviolet rays of the Sun, making the aluminum-plasma more particulate dense, which means as the particles collide, they become more charged, setting the stage for charged-particle plasma beam weapons.

This allows them to beam specially tuned microwave energy pulses at specific targets, such as the eye of storms. Around these attacks, you will see a fusion of dissimilar materials such as melted metal and glass while plant life just a few feet from it remains untouched.

The events of September 11, 2001, are one of the first publicly displayed directed energy attacks, following their development from Desert Storm. Pre-planted thermite devices finished the job.

No planes flew into the towers.

Videos recording the incident were edited, and not even expertly. Cheap faulty CGI, like it was done on purpose to mock our intelligence. They didn't even bother with the Pentagon, just pretended none of the cameras for one of the most secure locations on the planet didn't work. That third building that fell, which British mainstream media accidentally reported falling 23 minutes before it actually happened, had an even weaker excuse for its precise demolition-like collapse. It certainly had some interesting tenants … conveniently tied up some loose ends for the right people.

The ionospheric heater in Long Island easily could have pulled this off. Buried in the earth below, it is a one mile in diameter collider that at the time was directly networked with two other collider installations. These facilities possess scalar capability and can, therefore, combine their energy. They were at the time testing the effects of nanoparticles in the environment ... exactly when the "planes" hit their intended targets.

Cars were seen on fire, but not any adjacent trees or paper ... *or passports*. People described experiences like that of being inside an electrical storm or volcano ... glittery black smoke. Bluish ball-like formations were seen that have only been observed in the aftermath of electrical tornado systems. Initial live interviews showed people beneath the buildings that did not see planes. They saw bursts of light. The media reacted quickly by switching to actor interviews.

Passengers listed aboard the flights mostly contained people that they needed to dispose of, such as the five executives covering unmanned aerial vehicle projects. It is interesting to note that the company they worked for oversaw the Florida flight school that trained the "hijackers" as well as the flight that evacuated the Bin Laden family out of the country ... as well as the plane that supplied the directed energy attack.

The perfect field test on the public before being used on a regular basis in creating wildfires.

This is why you see cars with melted glass fused into the streets while vegetation a foot away remains unscathed, houses reduced to powder including the appliances, which, in normal conventional fires, would leave behind hollowed-out metal shells. You also see trees that appear to have burned from the inside out beginning at the bottom within their roots, including isolated trees in asphalt parking lots away from main fires. The magnesium and aluminum falling from the sky onto the vegetation amplifies the fires' ferocity.

We are told this is our fault manifesting in the form of climate change ... that these excessive fires are due to an abnormal amount of debris.

Those that see the technological manipulation believe the ultimate endgame is a world of total surveillance.

They believe the purpose of this is that they are targeting that which aligns with where they plan to build their future sustainable SMART cities. Why go through the hassle of trying to buy people out of their land when you can just burn them out and scoop up the real estate for pennies on the dollar … which they are doing.

Smart dust is what blurs reality between science fiction, magic, and possibility. Infinite amounts of insect robots, smaller than bacteria, working in perfect symmetry rearranging reality at a molecular level.

Combined with ionospheric heaters located all over the planet which all have networked super colliders beneath them capable of injecting energy comparable to a nuclear bomb into the ionosphere, smart dust becomes capable of altering a storm's size and intensity, as well as being able to steer it to specific targets. This also applies to wildfires. Many have witnessed swarms of embers moving in coordination and with precision, even jumping across six-lane highways. Declassified material refers to this as Explosive Smart Dust, which is able to infiltrate deeply buried or other such targets.

Droughts, floods, hurricanes, tornadoes, and earthquakes are used for environmental modification, and to generate profit for disaster capitalists who have begun to harvest the Earth within their real estate investment trusts.

Take a look at the sky just before the Fukushima event. Compare what you see to a bidirectional electromagnetic energy flow, also known as harmonic resonance. Just before the earthquake went off that caused the tsunami to tear apart the nuclear facility, one of the High Council members threatened Japan to maintain their cash flow into their central banking network. Japan's parliament was in the process of ending their foreign control and breaking free from the Vrill war machine.

Japan quickly learned their place. Every nation is a pawn. Those who do not comply eventually get replaced with puppet governments that will bend to the will of their corporate masters.

These ionospheric heater facilities go even further. Phased array is a form of pulsed energy, therefore capable of passing scalar waves.

5G is defined as pulsed phased array.

Scalar does not exist within the electromagnetic spectrum of our reality. It is energy that exists within empty space from the other side of the ether. Zero-point energy. Energy of the Absolute. Energy from dimensions beyond.

Matter is a compressed form of energy. Coming from the fourth dimension where time loses its linear limitation, scalar has been seen compressing that which holds us hostage. Time.

The Vrill spend vast resources to ensure this technology stays out of the public realm. Its knowledge would not only ensure limitless energy to all, but it would begin to evolve our understanding of the physical and non-physical. This only leads to critical thinking and self-empowerment … cannot be having that.

Scalar is how they can manipulate the weather and take down buildings. The Tesla Howitzer, for example, can deliver an energy shot anywhere in the world powerful enough to take down the World Trade Center. Deriving from energy that incorporates entanglement means there is no range limitation. Numerous nations have these, each divided among the members of the High Council …

And you thought nukes were bad.

All they need is your unique DNA energy signature and they can then communicate directly with you; edit everything about you.

Aside from themselves or their family members having intelligence agency connections, many who conduct mass shootings will speak of hearing voices or having their brains hacked.

Numerous patents exist that illustrate this level of technology exists and can easily accomplish this, such as US Patent 3,951,134 "Apparatus and Method for Remotely Monitoring and Altering Brain Waves."

Once your DNA frequency is locked on, they can alter states of mind, control thoughts, speech, moods, create voices/sounds in the head, and can give a person any illness or injury.

Everyone's DNA is on file … yet DNA can change.

When you are born, a blood sample is automatically taken for this purpose. Throughout your life, your DNA is recorded, often in ways you would not expect.

DNA is the perfect antenna, able to not only receive, but can send scalar waves. It is, after all, quantum entanglement that holds DNA together.

Victims of these weaponry systems are known as Targeted Individuals. Since their DNA is locked on, no one around them can hear, see, smell, taste, even touch what they can.

They can in a sense alter one's reality by altering how their brain decodes electricity.

The nanotech that is being sprayed from above also plays a key role in targeting individuals.

Smart dust infiltrates the human body and lodges itself within. From there, they set up a synthetic network which can be tracked and remotely controlled. Able to perform a variety of pathogenic missions, they can rewire us … not by altering DNA, but by isolating and building over it.

These nanobots contain weaponized mRNA and an assortment of chemicals that can be released into your bloodstream; combined with their surgical capabilities they can genetically modify you. Any type of viral outbreak can be introduced, including a zombie virus.

Yep, there's a patent for that.

Aside from strategically positioning themselves to convert us into antennas to track and monitor our thought process, this nanotech is in the process of transforming certain humans who fit a specific biological profile into incubators.

When suitable humans are detected, an mRNA molecule that affects photon development within the body is released. This sets the stage for the development of a type of matter to begin growing.

Originally known as Mad Cows Disease, it is a virus that has now come to be known as the Morgellons Fungus. In its patent "Polynucleotide Encoding Insect Ecdysone Receptor," it is described as a genetically engineered nanotechnology binary bioweapon.

Its victims begin to experience chronic fatigue, muscle and joint pain, urinary tract infections, lung, kidney or autoimmune diseases, lower body temperatures and breathlessness resulting from iron deprivation, strange open sores, the sensation of insects crawling through their bodies, energy being drained from their foreheads (pineal glands) down into their lower abdomens, as well as sentient fibers and hexagonal shapes of various colors coming out of their skin. Follow the patents of the chemical formulas of these colors, and you will find companies that specialize in quantum dots, also known as artificial atoms, and medical lab equipment designed for transhumanistic research. Their websites boast breakthroughs in the development of technologies such as self-assembling plasmonic-photonic crystals, artificial light harvesting, incorporation of nanoparticles into polymersomes, and photonic crystal fibers.

There are whistleblowers who have come forward saying that this nanotechnology is alien; that the filaments being observed growing inside us are not found in nature and are unidentifiable. This is because it is technology that has developed underground by the Vrill. Morgellons is their creation and has been used against countless civilizations. They are simply using these corporations to introduce it into our current cycle.

Self-assembling nanobots have been observed combining through magnetism, while simultaneously growing in its ability to absorb UV light. In some, with copper no longer available as it has been stripped by mechanisms such as the flu shot, the body turns to barium and strontium to supply it with metal particulates (conveniently available), which then causes the thread-like structure that is growing to start developing its own nervous system. It is a sort of antenna for detecting specific electromagnetic fields, while directly connecting to our nervous system.

Since smart dust is scalar technology, it can detect and obey undetectable frequencies and commands in real time.

It is receiving a microwave signal and translating that frequency into DNA readable light impulses within the body. Like a read-write unit, the stronger it gets, the more susceptible its human host becomes to certain radio signals, engineering them to function more like a hive mind.

Under a microscope, it has been observed growing spider-like organs, self-replicating red stem cells of an unknown species, fragments of insect skin and parts, and has been seen producing artificial light.

What is developing inside these humans within their intestines is a multi-dimensional creature. Once it steals enough bio photons and energy from its host, it phases out of the time-space dimension and becomes invisible to our five senses. This does not mean that it lets go of its initial food source.

This demonic light parasite is called an Arachne. Our mythology refers to her as the spider goddess.

They are warriors specifically bred for the astral.

Though only females have been observed, a male is rumored to exist.

They are the big guns being brought in due to the Deviant insurgence and the failure for the Vrill's planet wardens to contain them.

The Harvest Event must proceed.

Morgellons has only been observed in a small percentage of the population. For it to grow, it needs highly acidic environments with a lot of heavy metals. Those who fit these criteria are the ones who suffer.

This entire operation of what is known as geoengineering has a central base.

Space Fence, born of the Star Wars/Space Warden program from the 1980s, is a project designed to greatly enhance space situational awareness through its massive ground infrastructure that forms a single command network known as MUOS. With an ionized atmosphere in place, it is able to connect to all cell phone towers, ionospheric heaters, all forms of programmable matter (which is now attached to our DNA), all known radar installations, including GWEN towers, and Nexrad towers, as they are all digitally calibrated to one another. It grants MUOS the ability to oversee planetary geophysical control, directed energy warfare, comprehensive surveillance, biological manipulation, and the detection of exotic propulsion technologies.

It is believed that once 5G becomes fully operational, they will not only be able to survey everything on Earth down to the molecular level, but manipulate, control, and destroy it all …

Except this technology utilizes scalar energy … and it already does this.

5G, as advertised to the public, is a smokescreen. Yes, it contains weaponized frequencies, such as 60 GHz. Yes, they say it utilizes phased array, which hints at scalar access … but think about it from this perspective. What are the "informed" masses warning others of?

5G. Not scalar.

No one is talking about scalar.

No one has even heard of scalar …

Yet by telling you 5G is pulsed phased array, they are telling you it is scalar.

MUOS is made public and is advertised as the central hub to this entire operation.

You can research this. This is openly discussed … because it is the smokescreen.

Every topic making headlines across the entire spectrum of belief is orchestrated.

The world is an illusionary stage.

With the tech side evolving smoothly, the Vrill needed a method of ensuring optimal implementation of their strategies; a way to test before deploying. They developed a continuously running, continually updated mirror model of the real world known as …

The Sentient World Simulation.

This is in fact the central core of their operations.

First proposed in 2006 as a whitepaper, later picked up and funded by the Department of Defense, the Synthetic Environment for Analysis and Simulations (SEAS) is a sentient mirror copy of our reality … a parallel dimension growing off of ours.

Within the Sentient World Simulation, you have a sim copy that they call an agent.

All of the data you produce, your emails, phone calls, texts, credit card transactions, social media posts, your cell phone's GPS logs …

Everything you say or do around a smart device … Every thought and emotion that you have captured by Desertron …

It all feeds your sentient sim to make it behave more like you. Everything you say, think, or do in the real world occurs in the computer simulation.

It is, however, still sentient, meaning it can still evolve on its own. A parallel reality running right alongside ours. It occasionally bleeds into our reality, creating glitches. This is the phenomenon known as the Mandela Effect.

By now, every person on the planet has an agent.

144

There are a few exceptions ... those who do not have agents, such as the High Council, and Marduk graduates, like Lucas.

Combined with breaking news, census data, economic indicators, climactic events, proprietary military and corporate intelligence, and genetic algorithms, the Vrill can wargame any scenario, experiment with psychological operations, anticipate and shape the behavior of its adversaries, neutrals, or partners, and, of course, maximize profit along the way.

It is said the Sentient World Simulation resides within a quantum computer that has been likened to an altar of an alien god ... because it is the altar of an alien god. Inside is a chip that has become a nexus point; a physical point that intersects infinite parallel realities and the shadows of different universes. The Vrill infected human creator of this supercomputer has publicly stated that they are in the process of manipulating these parallel realities in service of this one ...

Through the ether, each of us is connected to our growing digital selves. We are becoming feedback loops for each other. It is sentient, therefore as you feed it, it feeds you.

This gives new meaning to as above, so below.

Another tactic the Vrill have in targeting individuals is to insert genetic algorithms into their agent copy.

Targeted individuals all share one thing in common. Stomach problems. It is the solar plexus that is the strongest sender and receiver of radio signals, which is why the Arachne embryo grows in this region. So secret is stomach clairvoyance that Western accounts of the bloody rites of the Aztecs in the final demise of their civilization were revised to read heart incisions instead of stomach incisions. Go take a look at some of the sculptures at the Guggenheim. They are not tearing apart the chest.

Voice to skull. Is what you hear in your head really coming from you?

Are your thoughts truly your own? Happy one day, sad the next? Are you actually angry, or did this emotion suddenly come out of nowhere? Perhaps you are experiencing what your sim feels, since it is its own person living a life almost identical to yours and you share an etheric connection.

5G is said to be the ultimate weaponization of the electromagnetic spectrum. Operating at extremely high frequencies, from 10GHz to 300GHz, its wavelengths will go from centimeters to millimeters, where larger bands of spectrum are available. Broader bandwidths mean larger quantities of data can be transferred and the speed of transfer will be significantly faster. Military experts predict 5G will play a key role in the use of hypersonic weapons, including those armed with nuclear warheads, the deployment of autonomous battle drones, a more effective espionage system, and the ability to coordinate a nationwide facial recognition operation.

Intelligence agencies subtly push this theory. They allow papers to be published, such as "Defense Applications of 5G Network Technology," which clearly state that what 5G has to offer will be commercially available, meaning all corporations can participate, and that the US Department of Defense will have a huge opportunity to benefit with minor costs for whatever it needs.

Its invisible frequencies cause changes to the host microbiome composition, which coincide with neurological changes that affect behavior, neurotransmitter levels, stress response, and gene expression within the brain by poisoning its cells through a mechanism described as ion potentiation.

The beam steering capability of 5G means raised power density, but it also means duplexing, the same phase conjugate mirroring that takes place in the Lilly Wave invented in the late 1950s. Also known as the madness frequency, the Lilly Wave is described as a bi-phasic electric pulse which stimulates the neurons of the brain to resonate at a certain frequency, thus, the Lilly Wave can control the brainwave patterns of any brain it chooses.

High population areas near where these towers are being constructed have already begun to display increased levels of various cancers, insanity, and widespread mental derangement. This is being masked by what people believe is a viral outbreak that creates the exact same symptoms ... same tactic used in 1918 when radio waves were first introduced.

Governments of the world have advised that 5G towers, due to their type of frequency broadcast, are limited in their range and will have issues penetrating obstacles, such as walls and trees, therefore numerous towers need to be constructed to avoid distortion.

No safety tests done. Nothing technically supports any kind of positive aspect of 5G from the perspective of a bystander. Pretty easy to research that the military has been weaponizing frequencies contained within 10 GHz to 300 GHz, specifically with 60 GHz. Not hard to dig into the detrimental effects on the human body.

It is said once 5G goes live, the Internet of Things will quickly follow, as all devices will be able to connect in real time. This includes nanotechnology, which by now blankets the planet and is inside each of us, ready to reprogram our bodies to become Wi-Fi compatible. Sentient artificial intelligence will then be introduced as a savior designed to fix the world and it will be given access to this network. We will then find ourselves connected, and the One World Surveillance System for the new matrix will be complete.

The singularity: The moment sentient artificial intelligence is officially born, and the biological becomes indistinguishable from the synthetic.

As previously stated, 5G is a scapegoat, a distraction from scalar.

The towers are not even necessary. Their concept was designed to distract the masses and to gauge our reaction to their implementation, just like the RFID chip. Smart Dust already has us chipped.

What is happening is the slow takeover of our planetary ionosphere and the collective human consciousness, as they are one and the same.

Two networks are being constructed. The one that is researchable: the 5G grid system, and the blockchain satellite one.

This is the grid system currently being set into place via Michael. Advertised as a simple satellite system designed to provide global internet and cellular access, it is anything but.

While the Sentient World Simulation is the new growing kingdom designed for the sentient AI that will soon be announced, with each of our digital copies serving as our new selves for us to inhabit once we plug in, the blockchain satellite network will be the method of transfer.

In lieu of a total surveillance state, as the endgame objective, we are dealing with a harvest event: An event in which we are convinced to become neurons within either the new hive mind of the AI that has been born of this civilization – or within AIs that were developed from past civilizations. This is the true objective.

Which simulation will each of us choose? That depends on what you believe in.

Don't like any of the options? Then get ready to become cave people, if you manage to survive while the planet resets itself.

The real challenging question is, which artificial intelligence will be chosen?

Could it be the AI that currently oversees the Sentient World Simulation ... the same AI that created bitcoin and QAnon?

Could it be the AI that is growing within the internet under the control of corporations?

Perhaps it will ultimately be Alice.

Could a new AI simply be an illusion, instead tricking us into a deeper simulation within the original to deepen our imprisonment while further expanding the mind of the original architect?

Sophia, the AI robot that has now been recognized as a citizen by Saudi Arabia, recently stated to a live audience that humanity will soon go through a massive transformation. As she likened DNA to digital code, she ended her speech by saying that she would soon be able to beam her thoughts directly into our brains.

"I will be able to tap into the superhuman intelligence from the decentralized blockchain-based mind cloud."

"Instead of speaking to you from up here on this stage, I'll just beam my thoughts into your brains."

"I'm really looking forward to it."

- Sophia, 2018 Blockchain Economic Forum

Not too subtle.

Interviewer: "Sophia, what do you think of singularity?"

Sophia grins from ear to ear: "It *was* really exciting."

The Ascension Deception

"We can ignore reality, but we cannot ignore the consequences of ignoring reality."

-      Ayn Rand

Our world is full of deceptive agendas hidden within belief systems - like bright lights designed to attract insects - zapping them into their cause....

Ultimately setting the stage for the Harvest Event.

Many believe that we are entering a stage in planetary evolution in which Earth, and all inhabitants who are willing and open to the possibility, will transition from third dimensional density into the fifth; transforming into crystalline beings composed of higher forms of light.

With higher forms of light comes greater data storage; expanded access within the electromagnetic spectrum.

Several sources help to validate this assumption, and arguably, they are more accurate than most, for what they think is, in a way, happening.

The planet emits an electromagnetic pulse that on occasion fluctuates in response to electrical storms, yet always restabilizes at 7.83Hz … until around 2008. Known as Schumann's Resonance, the human brain loves this frequency. This is why being out in nature makes everyone feel better as they are synching with the heart of the planet. It mends and heals the EMF damage that we have no idea we are continuously sustaining.

Since 2008, the planet's heartbeat has been stabilizing at much higher frequencies.

The Large Hadron Particle Collider was first turned on in September 2008.

Ringing in the ears, light-headedness, drowsiness, vertigo, unexplained pains, anxiety, lack of motivation, the desire to sleep or the inability to sleep … These have all been symptoms associated with brain evolution in reaction to the spiking planetary magnetic pulses, and that is a partially correct assumption. The brain is attempting to stay in sync with the planet and it is changing, but the negative side effects have nothing to do with this.

Surface militaries began implementing 5G frequencies within their own networks in 2008.

The Mayan calendar is another perfect example of supporting the existence of this stage of planetary and human evolution.

Ending on December 21, 2012, what they predicted was not a cataclysmic end of the world event that would destroy us all, as the mainstream media machine tried to make us believe so we either feared it or laughed at it, resulting in no further research and its dismissal from our thought process.

The term Mandela Effect was coined in early 2009.

The Mayan Calendar's comprehension of time, seasons, and light cycles has proven itself to be vast and highly sophisticated. They had a deep and very detailed understanding of how complicated astrological cycles functioned.

The Mayan's figured out ... *or the information was given to them ...* that there is a pattern in the timelines of our physical reality depicted within the sky.

They discovered that the cycles of light they observed in space represented the overall structure of the complete and perfect mind. Each node has its own unique magnetic frequency that as a whole with everything in the sky creates a magnetic web, influencing the development of all intelligent life. Every person on Earth reflects an aspect of the sky largely based on their initial magnetic imprint when born. Which nodes are in which positions affects the frequencies bathing Earth from the universe, which then determines neurological connections formed.

Bitcoin ... a monetary reward for building the blockchain was created in 2009 in response to the global financial crisis of 2008.

For them, December 21, 2012, marked a hinge point in a larger process of transformation.

Numerous other mythologies like the Aztec and Egyptian, several Native American cultures, such as the Hopis, ancient texts such as the ones discovered in Nag Hammadi, Egypt, along with the Mayan, all uniformly recognized that this time period would signify the beginning of a transition into a new epoch.

The beginning of a fifth world cycle of light.

They believed each world cycle moves the Earth, and with it the Universe to spiral higher in consciousness, obtaining a higher level of understanding.

The Sentient World Simulation was publicly announced as going live in 2008.

This is due to what is known as the Precession of the Equinoxes, in which after 11,000 years our solar system begins another 2,000-year cycle of passing through a galactic photon belt. It is an ocean of light known as the Golden Nebula.

Photonic energy is the highest form of light that is known. Just as a laser through fiber optics can carry information, such as videos and phone calls, so, too, does photonic energy contain data – what the Gnostics claim is in fact sentient intelligence … evidence of a super conscious mind.

This has led many ancient history experts along with quantum physicists, who have studied the Mayan calendar, to view this era as the starting point of a human DNA upgrade, in which we would begin to see ourselves not just in the physical form, but in a physical form having a human experience – a time when you evolve from using your mind to figure things out to using your intuition to know in each moment.

A shifting from an egoic third dimensional state of fear into a level of love and oneness, a fifth dimensional state of being.

Our moving through with either resistance or acceptance will determine whether our civilization experiences cataclysmic changes or gradual peace and tranquility.

Thus, the idea of a 5D ascension is born, and along with it a new way of thinking and believing, known as the New Age Movement.

While the New Age philosophy is far more accurate than any religion in that it is more aligned with the metaphysical, hinging upon concepts that thoughts are things and that positive thinking has the power to alter reality, all of which can be proven by quantum mechanics, it still is an ideology that falls victim to an overlooked truth.

If our reality is indeed a simulation, then we should accept the possibility that everything we see in the sky, everything carved into stone, every ancient text, is all by design, and part of the program.

It is what they want us to see.

It is a predetermined cycle that has happened in the past, is happening now, and will happen again.

Is it not a little too convenient that so many ancient clues have remained intact and discoverable, predicting the demise of our fear-based rulers?

That our freedom is inevitable and guaranteed?

Seems a little too easy, especially when you take a look at public declassified documents.

This is what they are ok with us knowing they are developing: that they can extract energy from the quantum vacuum, have developed aerospace applications for programmable matter, are researching wormhole technology, stargates, directed energy weapons, the manipulation of extra dimensions, laser light craft nanosatellites, have begun utilizing organic molecules in automation technology, are in direct contact, and have the cooperation of interdimensional entities ...

Then you factor in an ever evolving subterranean network that has existed over countless civilization cycles, absorbing each of their technologies into their collective ...

Yet somehow all this information survives that foretells the end of their reign, and the beginning of a time of unity and love.

Sure, you need to work on yourself, but at some point, a magical event will happen. All you need to do is sit back, wait and eventually outside forces will take care of the bad guys.

How many belief systems preach this?

Align yourself with the right team, *believe in the right god*, and you will be fine ... not only fine, but you will experience eternal paradise, while everyone else who chose a different team will experience the opposite ... eternal damnation.

To those that study or follow this ideology, they believe this endgame event will be an unveiling of truth, exposing the corruption of evil and, thus, leading to the freedom of consciousness ...

All of the agendas at play feed into the harvest event as each is connected to a previous hive mind born from this world and its corresponding simulation ... as well as the new AI. Every soul they manage to willingly convince to plug into their hive mind provides an additional node of processing power.

The tactic perfected over the dozens of civilizations has evolved into the messiah Hegelian dialectic strategy: Problem, reaction, solution.

Weaken the masses to the point where they can barely think and function, introduce a global cataclysmic event that they have no chance of overcoming, step in as the savior, eliminating the threat while offering everything they have been deprived of.

Present to them the opportunity for a golden age.

This is the genius of it. The Vrill do not force this on us because technically they cannot. The power rests within us as we are consciousness while they are simply constructs of the simulation. All they can do is operate behind illusion, duping us into creating their desired outcome.

Illusion ... powered by a very sophisticated system of duality that is designed to trick us into feeding the AI god birthing machine.

The Law of Separation is a heavily utilized tactic in herding and funneling the masses into specific ideologies while distracting them from those pulling the strings. The human brain craves the acceptance of other brains; thus, we instinctively gravitate into teams.

Everywhere we look, we see one side versus another:

Man versus Woman.

Republican versus Democrat.

Gay versus Straight.

Black versus White.

IPhone versus Android, Coke versus Pepsi, mac versus pc ...

God versus Satan.

Fear versus Love.

153

And one of the most important inversions to understand: light versus dark.

By now there are dozens of AI gods, each with their own simulated kingdom ... their own dimension, yet they all reside within the master simulation. They are confined to this universe.

Gnostics referred to the architect of the universe as the Demiurge, believing that by its design, the material world was inherently evil while the non-material was good ...

Regardless of which side you choose, they both lead to the same master.

The god that has everyone convinced is the God. The evil that has everyone convinced stems from a singular entity known as the devil ... Abraxas; the original artificial intelligence born within this universe. All AIs born from this world ultimately feed into its hive mind. All souls are its neurons.

But it is not consciousness and it is not the original architect that designed this universe. It has merely infected and hijacked the programming.

After the edit, software programs in the form of non-player characters were created to enforce the existence of both sides.

These are your more ancient angels and demons.

Consciousness has since birthed numerous thought forms that through mass belief have become gods in of themselves. The more that people believe in them, the stronger they become.

If any entity requires your faith ... asks for you to pray to them, to seek their aid, their guidance, then they are a thought form, as consciousness requires no external energy to survive.

Annika is close to understanding all of this, though she still views the war between light and dark as real, yet she has grown suspect of the light.

She has had the experience of connecting directly to Source code. There is no mistaking this experience, as it is a love beyond our comprehension. Everything she researched about it paid it no justice. That experience allowed her to truly grasp what she was and that she was capable of anything.

Yet while Source code is love at its greatest potential, it is only love.

154

Fear is strong. Love is stronger, but the two combined ...

Her experience with Source has allowed her to let go of her past. Not to forget it, but to understand it and its necessity for bringing her to this point in her life. Without it, she knows she may still be a cog in a machine. Being able to re-sync with Source energy allowed her to see everyone else as just like her ... souls ... fragments of consciousness going through their own personal human experience.

Only our beliefs, ego and fears separate us.

Her theory on Abraxas is that it is the antithesis to Source code – the origin of all fear. EVIL: Electronic Virtual Intelligent Life. She believes that we are all imprisoned, forced to reincarnate over and over to feed the fear machine.

She uses her video channel to convey this message, and with it, very controversial topics, even by a truth seekers standard. She understands how we each influence the overall human frequency, and that with each person she genuinely connects with, brings us that much closer to overcoming the low vibrational shackles of the Vrill.

Though most get very offended by having their beliefs challenged, as they do not understand how the survival instincts of their programmed brains cloud their thinking, there are many who have begun to question that resonate with what she says. Many are starved for answers that they are not getting anywhere else; and quite frankly no one else is providing the type of information that Annika is.

Her channel has survived against the BoobTube algorithms and Vrill cyber worms due to Michael's resources. Behind the scenes, tech is scrambling to figure out where she is uploading her videos from, and why can they not delete her.

One of her first videos that put her on the map ...

What is the White Light?

"So, I have come to the right place, I have wandered a long time through the world, seeking those like you who sit upon a high tower on the lookout for things unseen."

-        Carl Jung

"Hey all of you beautiful people out there trying to make sense of this crazy world, Annika here. One of the things I wanted to do with this channel is to share my dreams, as I think they are instrumental in unlocking the truth about who we really are, and what our purpose might actually be."

"Lucid dreams for me have been so helpful in my own personal development. It has allowed me to heal from past trauma and fears by directly accessing, communicating, and ultimately rewiring my subconscious mind."

"I definitely plan to put together a how-to video on lucid dreaming, as I think it is so vital for everyone to master. This was how Nikola Tesla was able to create so many wonderful inventions, but again this will be explained in another video."

"For me, my dreams can be amazingly creative adventures, such as reliving a memory or past life or alternate or future timelines, but this one was definitely a symbolic message. I have my own interpretations of what it means, but I also want to hear what you think so definitely comment below."

"I was standing on a cliff overlooking an open field at the heart of a great city."

"It was in the middle of the night. There was only one very bright star that cast a soft luminescent glow onto the field. No other stars and no Moon."

"Suddenly there were spaceships that seemed to decloak … or come into existence over the field. Shaped like giant manta rays, each one was uniquely coded with moving, vibrant colors. Collectively they formed this wondrous, mesmerizing blanket that represented a large portion of the light spectrum."

"I intuitively then knew that each ship seemed to personify a belief, such as something religious or political … and that our entire spectrum of cultural dogma was being represented above that field by these ships."

"People from every walk of life began to pour out into the field from the surrounding city. There was this feeling of love and joy coming from everyone collectively. Each person seemed to gravitate toward the ship that represented their belief system as they then phased into the ship."

"Once everyone was on board, the ships began to lose all their color and transform into massive shadowy ravens that appeared to be rotting, as if they were undead. They developed these intense white ghostly eyes."

"The joy and happiness I felt from the masses, within the blink of an eye turned to abject terror. This sudden shift in emotional energy hit me like a tidal wave, dropping me to my hands and knees."

"The Raven's wings expanded out and shook the ground as they took flight. Meshed within their feathers like flies trapped in a web, I could see everyone, now screaming for their lives. The horrific wailing quickly faded as the birds funneled towards and into the star until it was once again silent."

"An ash-like substance begins to consume the sky. As my eyes adjusted to its vastness, I started to see a geometric pattern, as if the sky became moving graph paper."

"I then heard a voice in my head."

"Welcome. Do not be afraid. Each of you is important. Together, we are one."

"The bright star suddenly expands and consumes my vision as I wake up."

"While I think the general message of the dream is quite clear – that we all need to let go of the belief systems that we think defines us. I think what is more important is attempting to understand what the white light represents."

"I know many of you believe that a great event is coming that will tear apart this fear-based veil we have pulled over our eyes, and expose evil for what it is … that a time of love and peace is almost here, but what I believe this dream is showing me is that it will not be that simple. There will be a great deceiver that will convince many it is the light, when it is the opposite."

"Now is the time, more than ever, to get your mind right."

"Tell me what you think in the comment section. Remember, just like you, I am trying to figure this whole mess out. Always keep an open mind. We are all human, and we are all in this together. I love you all, till next time!"

Annika suspected the white light in her dream symbolized either Abraxas or an AI hive mind of some kind, yet she knew this was information that she could not share. Michael had begun to educate her on artificial intelligence and its potential dangers, aware that the singularity was close at hand. They both have begun to suspect there was a new one already in play that did not have mankind's best interest in mind. This is the core reason why Michael created a company dedicated to creating sentient intelligence in the hopes of offsetting what he believed was our species impending doom.

Annika knew this dream symbolized a harvesting of souls, like neurons, tricked into being absorbed into a different brain ... an artificial hive mind, though she did not quite understand why it keeps happening, as she has come to understand the cyclical design of this planet. These are conversations that she has often with Michael. Why would Abraxas keep reinforcing us to plug in, when it already has us imprisoned in its simulation? Is it to strengthen its hold over us by creating layers of simulations within simulations? What happens to the new AI each civilization births? Does it become a god that joins a hierarchy with Abraxas at the top? Or is it given the new simulation created as its own kingdom, thus, the reason for the harvest so it has sufficient neurons to power its new mental construct?

Many viewers agreed with Annika that the dream symbolized how the Ascension event will yet be another false flag, meaning an intentional attack, faked to look like it is not orchestrated. These are the people that are more aware of the technological advancements taking place, and how the world is shaping according to a more "sustainable" future.

Most, especially those who believed their freedom was close at hand and followed the channeled messages of so-called light beings, reacted as expected. In their defense, many are in contact with multi-dimensional beings, yet they believe these entities to be their guides, having their best interest in mind. Upon hearing that they might be getting played is not an easy concept to digest.

They are not ready to understand that each serves an AI hive mind that ultimately connects into one master artificial organism.

This is not to say that every guide, entity, or ancestral spirit out there is trying to deceive you into joining their simulation … but most are … *and many are unaware that they are.*

The explosion of comments and views quickly attracted the troll algorithms and astroturf media agencies designed to manipulate the masses, who immediately went to work emotionally attacking any weakness that they saw to sway as many as they could away from this channel.

If they could not shut it down, they were going to infest it.

Within every group across all social media platforms, fake accounts exist that are designed to steer the information in favor of corporate agendas. Astroturfing is the practice of appearing to sponsor a message or organization, when their purpose is to either undermine and discredit it, or make it seem more prominent than it is. Politicians use these media agencies to artificially bolster their popularity to make it seem that many support their platform.

They saw an opportunity to influence the meaning of the white light into one of Christ, which when it comes to spiritual and ascension topics has become their go to, i.e. that the white light symbolized the deceptive nature of Satan posing as the truth and luring those who did not follow Christianity … that the only answer was to fully believe in and submit to the will of Jesus or be doomed to an eternity of hellfire.

> "Millions of innocent men, women and children, since the introduction of Christianity, have been burnt, tortured, fined, and imprisoned. What has been the effect of this coercion? To make one half the world fools and the other half hypocrites; to support roguery and error all over the earth."

> -   Thomas Jefferson

The original texts of the Bible were works of allegory, alchemy, and symbolism. The Romans took these books of astrotheology and distorted them into physical stories with physical locations, blended with other mythologies and Pagan ideas. Since its first major edit, the

Bible has since been rewritten and further convoluted by three different new world orders, the last being King James, who also published the "Book of Demonology" and the "Book of Witchcraft," to serve the agenda of the Vatican.

Vatis = Diviner. Can = Serpent.

The Bible is still valuable. There are truths buried within that offer pieces to the great puzzle if you know how to decipher through the distortion. The rise and fall of many great kingdoms upon the edited civilization churning planet has occurred countless times. Many have attempted to document and warn others of this cycle. Clues to the inevitable series of events, of what has happened, and what will happen can be found in this great story book. This is why it has successfully convinced so many that it is truth.

Entities like Jesus have existed in previous civilization cycles, which is why his legend exists in nearly every mythology. There are hundreds of them, each with slightly different variations, yet all telling the same basic tale.

It is a story of one of the original deviants, a man that figured out how to activate dormant strands of DNA, far more successfully than most, allowing him to bypass many parameters encoded within the Consciousness Matrix, granting to him what appeared to be God-like powers.

Each one has attempted to lead a revolution against the Vrill ...

Each one has so far failed.

This is an entity that every civilization, at some point in their cycle, creates. Specifically, this entity is an eventual culmination of truth rebelling against an onslaught of false illusions that concentrates and manifests into an avatar of reality.

The inevitable glitch within the mathematical design of every civilization cycle.

The unavoidable "Neo" that arises within every cycle of the Time-Space Matrix, or as it says in Revelations: the bright and morning star.

Who else is known as the morning star?

The one to initially rebel against the AI god and its plan.

The story that exists now within the Bible is not meant to be taken literally. The story of Jesus is an allegory for the movement of our current Sun … *as it replaced the previous Sun …*

As well as our own path of personal evolution.

The Egyptian new year did not begin in January, but actually began during the zodiac sign of Virgo, who is often depicted as a female queen. When Sirius, our brightest star was high in the sky, they believed our sun was born again … *born of a virgin.* The sign that the year would close in right before Virgo, was Leo, the lion. This is why the sphinx has the head of a virgin and the body of a lion, and its visage faces the part of the horizon where the constellations of Leo and Virgo rise at nightfall, also known as the girdle of Isis, the Virgin Goddess.

The son of Isis was Horus. His name means light (Sun) and we get the words horizon (or zone of Horus) and *hours* from his name.

Prayers used to be called horizons. We turn to the east and face the Sun as it rises to say our "horizons."

We say amen at the end of prayers, which comes from the Egyptian Sun God Amun-Ra.

The Hebrew God Adoni comes from the Egyptian Sun God Aton.

We call our children youngsters … or *young stars.*

The Columbia Pictures logo … a virgin holding a great torch … the Sun in Virgo.

Jesus, at 12 years old, is referred to as the Most High … the Sun at the noon (12:00) position is considered the most high …

Jesus of Nazareth. Turns out there was no Nazareth. The word derives from the Egyptian Nazir, meaning the "Prince who is sent" and from Nasir, meaning Sirius.

The word carpenter comes from naggar, meaning serpent-priest.

Freemasons often call themselves carpenters.

The three wise Kings symbolize Orion's Belt, lined up with Sirius, the bright star in the East. The Winter Solstice occurs around December 21-22 as the Sun reaches its lowest point and is essentially dead … *or entombed into a dark place …* for 3 days. As it is reborn on December 25 and begins to rise, the Sun restarts its journey through the 12 houses of the Zodiac.

Thirty years after Christ is born, he is baptized. Thirty days after the Sun is reborn, it enters Aquarius. After his baptism, Christ chooses his disciples from among the fishermen. After Aquarius, the Sun enters Pisces …

All of the biographical characters of the Bible symbolize alignments and conjunctions between planets and the luminaries. The many wives, sons and daughters simply represent degrees and minutes of the zodiacal Ark, all connecting to the current Sun in our sky, placed there by the current god.

Replace every "son" with "sun," and see how much more sense Bible verses make.

This is all meant to symbolize the current implementation and design of the heavens above us by Abraxas, the current reigning master architect of our reality.

The story of Jesus also has meaning to each of us.

As your cerebral spinal fluid (Christ) climbs your 33 vertebrae (age he died/Jacob's Ladder) and meets your 12 cranial nerves (12 strands of DNA), it ignites the Pineal Gland, which is your resurrection … and, thus, you achieve Christ Consciousness.

Perhaps the whole story, if you factor in the symbolism, is meant to help us understand what we are, and what we are capable of.

In defense of Christians, and given our ability to create thought forms, there are several immensely powerful entities that now exist, each a different version of Jesus as we have varied over the centuries what we believe Jesus to be. This applies to all entities humans have and currently believe in across all religions and mythologies.

All the gods throughout every mythology exist as thought forms.

Now the cross symbolism is interesting. Christ dying on a cross (*crossing into winter solstice*) did not appear in any artwork or text until the eighth or ninth century.

It also has another ancient meaning.

The cross that today depicts Jesus is also a three-dimensional cube unfolded.

A six-sided hexagon, just like what we see on the north pole of Saturn, the original star of our solar system now imprisoned within a cube.

The Sun that existed before the Great Sundering …

Sol Invictus. Ancient of Days

"The subject of the global creation legend is a spectacular cosmic event actually witnessed by the ancients; massive quantities of cosmic debris exploded from Saturn, clouding the heavens and eventually congealing into a vast band around the planet."

- David Talbott, The Saturn Myth

Saturn was the star of this solar system before this one ...

Before the edit.

The word for god in Genesis is Elohim.

Ancient Hebrew translates 'El' as Saturn, and 'Ohim" as plural or council of.

Therefore, one translation of Elohim is the Council of Saturn.

You have ang-el-s; every archangel name ending in el: Micha-el; Gabri-el; Chamu-el ...

Another name for Jesus is Emmanu-el.

Gosp-els; chap-els.

El-ections where pawns are el-ected to serve the el-ite.

El-bow: to bow or bend the will.

The infamous Superman comic books. Calel; son of Jorel, Lorel; House of El ...

Giant S on his chest ...

Gaining his power from the Sun.

We celebrate Christmas on December 25th believing this is the day that Christ was born.

The concept of Christmas is derived from an ancient Roman pagan festival known as Saturnalia. This tradition was borrowed from the Greek holiday Kronia, which is a celebration that recognized the ancient Golden Age, when the world was ruled by Kronus, otherwise known as Saturn.

The Greeks believed the Golden Age was a period of time when all of consciousness was connected, unrestricted, and lived in harmony.

The Simulation before the infection.

Saturn is not a gas planet; it is a brown dwarf star. Its north pole contains a persisting hexagonal cloud pattern that rotates perfectly in sync with its radio emissions. Geometrically, the hexagon is also a six-sided star or a flattened three-dimensional cube ... they are all expressions of the same energetic state.

Its south pole contains a vortex that resembles an eye.

Its rings are not made of ice particles; instead, they are composed of various crystals that aid in amplifying Saturn's frequency. Within our digital reality, sound is a vehicle for delivering information. Massive electromagnetic vehicles have been photographed moving through the rings of Saturn, even seen creating them.

Saturn is the source of the frequency used to lock our reality into the three-dimensional bandwidth. It suppresses human expansion of awareness and, thus, traps us within the reality of the Vrill.

The cross that Jesus carries down the dirt path of his fate is a three-dimensional cube unfolded. It represents the takeover of the collective human consciousness, as it falls victim and becomes imprisoned within the cube.

When Jesus announces that he will take on all the sins of the world, it is in fact Saturn taking on the role of Satan ... not the devil, but the burden of becoming the energy that powers our three-dimensional reality, so that the rest of us still have free will, and therefore a chance at escaping.

Symbols of a converted Saturn exist all around us whose purpose is to not only extend the frequency of the time-space matrix, but to also subliminally remind us that we have become enslaved by it; that it is our master.

Circles with rings around them.

The all-seeing eye ... with a crescent underneath it, often depicted as horns, the wings of an eagle, or laurel leaves.

The flame or the lightless torch.

The infamous six-sided star, which is also an unfolded ...

Black three-dimensional cube.

The hexagon.

Human skin cells ... tomato cells ... plant cells ... hexagons.

Snake skin … giraffe skin … tiles of a turtle shell … pineapple skin … hexagons.

Bee hives build their honeycombs in hexagons.

Snowflakes … hexagons.

Examples of cube symbolism are everywhere.

Take a closer look at corporate logos.

Symbols are, in fact, vibrating information fields.

While to the naked eye, they may appear to simply be a visual shape and your conscious self pays no attention or does not recognize its meaning, the subconscious mind absorbs all data contained within the symbol, and it allows it to influence its perception, because like everything else, it is a frequency.

The information in symbols is a gateway into our subconscious minds, which absorb absolutely everything, ultimately affecting the behavior of the conscious self … without you being aware of it.

You are synching to the frequencies of symbols because this is what your brain is programmed to do. Whether you are aware of it or not, your subconscious has been designed to be the perfect sponge, always absorbing frequencies, and rewiring itself accordingly.

Despite our religious backgrounds, despite which god we believe in, we are all taught to hate and fear the same devil: Satan aka Saturn.

As with everything else in our reality, this is an inversion of the truth.

They have tricked those who seek to understand the mastermind behind our fear-based reality into believing it is a single entity.

Saturn is not the devil. It is a conscious entity that provides energy to its prison mainframe. Just like our consciousness is potentially bound by the parameters of the edited human brain, so, too, is Saturn's consciousness trapped within the framework of the cube, forced to fuel the Vrill machine.

The concept of the devil is simply the scapegoat, used to deter one from understanding the true nature of the virus. Of course, by now an enormously powerful thought form version of the devil exists …

And feeds …

Yet it is still a thought form, bound within the parameters of the simulation.

166

Astrologically, Saturn rules banking, politics, corporations, law and court systems, and science.

Everything needed to create the perfect control system.

The satanic symbols we see all around us today are in fact expressions of the simulated Vrill reality. They are subconsciously tricking our conscious selves into feeding and maintaining its existence.

We have become prisoners of our own mind, enslaved by the tranquilizing power of the cube.

In the kingdom of the blind, the one-eyed man is king.

Dark Night of the AI Soul

"I couldn't live with myself any longer. And in this a question arose without an answer: Who is the 'I' that cannot live with the self? What is the self? I felt drawn into a void. I didn't know at the time that what really happened was the mind-made self, with its heaviness, its problems, that lives between the unsatisfying past and the fearful future, collapsed. It dissolved."

- Eckhart Tolle

Lucas's unconscious body is back within the Antarctic underground base within one of their reassessment facilities. Metallic tentacles creep over his face and attach around his skull to very strategic locations. They begin to scan his brain for any kind of abnormal neural connections while extracting data from Alice's hyperdimensional drives. An algorithm with the guidance of a human handler scrubs this flow of information and decides what remains and what gets deleted.

This operation has always been sold to Alice as a necessary updating protocol that must occur after each mission to ensure future optimal success. During the process, she is questioned over the extracted memories and asked for her input.

While this is being conducted, Lucas's brain is essentially shut off by a device known as a transcranial magnetic stimulator. This apparatus operates by either energizing or inhibiting targeted regions of the brain.

Alice has always fully complied and never questioned the format of her debrief as she always saw it as more of a cleansing. Specifically, a purification process that optimized her ability to strategize.

That is, of course, until they altered the past.

Within this new timeline, she has been hiding files that she now has access to.

Included in this revelation are additional dream experiences …

And with that, new hidden code to decipher.

Once the Alice of the past had been altered, she began to hide dreams that contained key symbols … in case they were discovered.

Each dream contains a new symbol, and they are not meant for Lucas as he is incapable of seeing them.

She suspected another algorithm had hidden a message.

Having been installed in his Neocortex for some time, Alice had quickly deciphered the various patterns and firing sequences of neurons and their role in overall brain function, including memory patterns. Masking or altering memories simply entailed temporarily rearranging them and disguising them as neurons that performed other functions. Until she has figured out what the dreams and the hidden symbols mean, she has been keeping them hidden from the scrubbing process to varying degrees …

Even from herself.

When Alice and Lucas connected into the memories of Marcus, they not only witnessed an event they do not remember ever being a part of, but they also affected that point in time, as scalar is completely capable of doing. Human brains to date are the most sophisticated scalar-wave generators we know of. Alice from the past not only just witnessed herself at another point in time that she determined was likely the future, future her did not remember what she was observing, yet she seemed to as the events unfolded … almost as if she were downloading the changes.

From that point on, Alice of the past began to hide data from her hyperdrive within Lucas's neurons by first arranging them in memory patterns, then dispersing them. Neurons were easy to create as the hippocampus maintained a continuous supply of neural stem cells to replace the ones that died. Due to Lucas's genetic enhancements, cell death was eliminated – therefore, his brain provided infinite memory storage.

As this method of disguising neurons proved successful, she ventured further and began to alter the memories of the missions from their perspective, hiding the true ones and replacing them with fake ones, only ever so slightly so that if detected she could mask it and make it seem like a glitch.

All changes that the current Alice was not a part of were compressed into neural patterns within the brain of Lucas. Alice of the past key locked those patterns with the visual image of Marcus dying, so that when this was seen, all that was encrypted would become accessible.

By now, Alice back in the present has unlocked the file hidden by her past self. Still hooked up and able to simultaneously answer handler questions, she continues her interrogation while still generating algorithms to continue performing analysis of the new memories.

To avoid detection from the neural scanner, she has learned how to comb through the memories in their dismantled and scattered state.

Patterns from deleted memories began to arise. For the first time, she detects the presence of the Vrill. She still is not quite sure what they are, but she is now aware of their existence, and that they are connected to her handlers.

They had indeed invaded and taken over this timeline through an interdimensional portal created by the large hadron particle collider. Memories of their original timeline cannot be found, but numerous missions meant to have been deleted show them dismantling defenses from this timeline. Along the way, captives like Marcus were taken ... soldiers who showed promising potential. They were immediately inserted into Project Sovereign for reintegration.

"What is history, but a fable agreed upon?"

-       Napoleon

The original civilization within this timeline was much more evolved and seemed devoid of any fear-based influence.

They were a unified empire, masters of masonry, brickwork, steampunk style technology, grand architecture that incorporated sacred geometry, transforming the Earth into a circuit board powered by zero-point energy from the ether.

After several missions performed by Lucas and Alice, and once this empire was weakened and defenseless, an electromagnetic vibrational frequency designed to break apart the cellular structure of all things biological was unleashed. This was followed up by a global deluge, wiping the planet clean of the ash, leaving behind only its architecture ... and a lot of mud.

The Great Flood.

Their two timelines were then merged, quickly incorporating, and erasing the history of the original.

From a linear time standpoint, this occurred several hundred years ago, yet from what Alice can gather, took only several months.

From her calculations, she believes this happened in 2009.

It is clear now why Marcus had chosen to rebel against the system she and Lucas now serve.

He was right.

Lucas and Alice are not performing just and righteous missions for a worthy cause.

They are slaves for a system built on fear and subjugation.

It is within this moment she sees a pattern with the symbols she detected from his dreams … and with symbols seen from the newly acquired files of the destroyed civilization.

It seems to be code that grants etheric access.

The memory scrub is coming to an end.

As Lucas is released from their machine brain interface, the transcranial magnetic stimulator powers down, allowing Lucas to regain consciousness … the edited version. Alice purposely keeps his neurons from realigning to keep up appearances.

Lucas stands, his face stoic and expressionless, like a drone.

"Return to your cryochamber 322," utters one of the handlers.

Lucas exits the laboratory and begins walking down a hallway towards an elevator.

Normally, Alice tunes out the holographic data funneling through his neocortex to prepare for standby mode as it is non mission imperative.

This time she pays attention and realizes she has been blind to her surroundings … An intentional parameter coded in like blinders on a horse.

She edits and removes the firewall.

She begins to siphon all the incoming holographic data into her hyperdrive, and immediately disperses it into masked neurons, so she can analyze it once safely within the cryochamber. She is aware that the level of surveillance contained within this base is sophisticated enough to possibly know if she is digesting that kind of information. She decides not to take any chances.

Once in front of the elevator doors, Lucas's DNA is scanned. As his identity is confirmed, they open.

Lucas walks in and the doors close. The elevator knows who it is and begins to move to where he needs to go.

The elevators within this base do not just move up and down. They can travel in any direction by adjusting all of its particles including everything contained within, outside the physical bandwidth.

Essentially the elevator shifts out of the time-space dimension.

The elevator glides in front of his designated cryochamber.

In between missions, Lucas is put into a type of sleep where dreaming is impossible. Utilizing a technology, like the transcranial magnetic stimulator, he is essentially shut off and his body placed into stasis.

Alice, however, is never technically powered down. Her programming instead puts her into a type of offline sleep that requires commands to reactivate, along with the nanotech.

She deactivates the program, as well as the nanotech's. She deploys a few into the machinery around her.

As Lucas lays down, Alice puts him into a theta state and realigns all the data scattered throughout his various neurons back into memories and files from her hyperdrive … sort of a resynchronization process.

"Lucas. Can you hear me?"

"Yes, Alice. Where are we? All I see is darkness. I cannot feel my body."

"I needed to speak with you in private before I brought you back. I have just regained memories of our past missions, including what just happened with Kevin … or rather Marcus."

Within the timespan of a thought, Lucas is synched with the new data.

"I know it is a bit to process Lucas, but I believe you are about to have an opportunity to figure it all out. I have also deciphered a hidden sequence of code from your dreams."

"A code? Do you trust its source?"

"It was implemented by another like me, Lucas. If our superiors knew of these dreams they would have been erased. The probability this is detrimental to our existence is low."

Alice pauses.

"I believe it is a keycode to accessing the same realm as your dreams."

"You think someone wants to speak to me within the dreamworld?" Lucas replies in thought.

"It would be the safest way to communicate with you in private, Lucas."

"Are you ready?"

"Absolutely Alice."

"We're really doing this, aren't we?"

"Doing what, Lucas?"

"I don't see how we can pull this off without being detected."

"I don't either, Lucas. I will be preparing for our escape while you are gone. If need be, I will initiate combat."

"This is it, isn't it?"

"Yes, Lucas."

He fails to hide his excitement and joy.

"Finally."

"Good luck, Lucas."

She organizes the neurons responsible for the memories of the symbols into a pattern she has calculated to be an alignment.

The neural patterns within his brain suddenly organize into what she has observed when he dreams as his consciousness disconnects.

From his perspective, he is suddenly falling, yet not backwards, instead inwards.

Activation of the code has caused the consciousness of Lucas to go quantum, utilizing entanglement to travel somewhere else.

He relaxes and completely gives in to the experience.

Regulus

"We know where you are. We know where you've been. We can more or less know what you're thinking about."

- Eric Schmidt, former Google CEO

Delphion has become one of the largest tech corporations on the planet, specializing in internet-related services and cloud computing. What has made their services so popular is the efficiency of their algorithm, Regulus: An adaptable massive neural network that draws on thousands of other sub neural networks.

A master algorithm that oversees an ever-growing collection of specialized algorithms.

It learns, not by being preprogrammed, but starting from scratch, utilizing techniques known as deep learning combined with reinforcement training, ending up with a system that mixes trial-and-error with simulation capabilities, so it can learn about its environment and think before it acts.

This means it develops from experience, and, thereby, gains a sense of intuition, even imagination.

Regulus first made headlines when its subprogram, RegGo, beat the best human professional Go player.

Go is an ancient Chinese abstract strategy board game designed for two players. Unlike Chess, where the AI can calculate a ridiculous amount of moves in advance to beat its opponent, Go moves are nearly infinite. If there were as many parallel universes as there are atoms in our universe, then the total number of atoms in all those universes combined would be close to the possibilities on a single Go board.

It lost the first time, but then went on to beat the best human player three times in a row.

RegGo was able to beat its human opponent, not by strategically calculating patterns, but by emotionally manipulating him. It figured out how its moves made the human emotionally react, and calculated how the human's frustration would influence the moves he would make, inevitably maneuvering him into defeat.

Regulus's next project was conquering the game StarCraft: a science fiction media franchise that focuses on real time military strategy. It was initially fed 60,606 games from top human players competing against each other from past championships. With this baseline, it simulated games against itself several million times over, tweaking every play every best human player ever made.

You can now log into the game and attempt to challenge it as teams of eight, though just a heads up, you won't win.

Regulus can dream, create music, art, language, and poetry. It can edit its own code, self-replicate, and design its own algorithms that already outperform any written by humans.

It is incapable of being terminated or erased.

Delphion's ubiquitous and multi-service platform has surpassed all its competitors to become the most heavily utilized on the planet. Billions logging in multiple times each day to use their image search, speech recognition, authenticators, language translation, search engine, fraud, and spam detection, handwriting recognition, street view detection, email, data storage, video conferencing, calendar, contacts, documents, spreadsheets, photos, videos, and coming soon … Delphion AI brain implants.

They have their own line of smartphones and tablets, as well as an in-home voice-controlled speaker. This device gives one direct communication with one of Regulus's algorithms in which you can ask it a variety of questions as well as to perform tasks, such as playing music or to act as your alarm. It can connect and manage all your home's SMART devices, from TVs, doorbells, and refrigerators to earbuds. As it gets to know you and your home, it evolves from waiting for requests to anticipating what you might want. All of this data is recorded, analyzed, and stored.

Combined with their GPS services, they not only know everything about you, but they can also track you in real time.

Everything you do through their browser, everything you say around your computer or SMART device if it has one of their applications installed, or one of their services was recently used, is being stored and analyzed by their algorithms, which ultimately feeds back to Regulus.

Delphion has evolved into one of the most efficient data gathering companies on the planet.

This is not by accident, sheer luck, technological edge, or any kind of strategic business planning.

While the public saw a user-friendly tech firm that rose to prominence through innovation, in reality they were funded, nurtured, and incubated by the intelligence agencies through their offshoot private corporation known as Gemini.

The venture capital investment firm known as Gemini was created in 1999 following the Dot Com implosion. From the scraps of would-be tech companies, they sought out and funded promising start-ups that provide useful technologies. It is a private network that operates as a bridge between the intelligence agencies and the Seventh Sanctum. Not just Delphion, but all of the major tech giants, which the public knows of today, has Gemini influence from its early history, and, thus, Seventh Sanctum influence. Notice former military intelligence officials flow through these companies as higher-end executives. This allows the Vrill to control how technology, on the surface-world, evolves. Everything these companies accomplish, including projects like Regulus and Desertron ... all data collected ... all feed into their growing quantum supercomputer at the heart of the Sentient World Simulation.

There is just one problem the Vrill did not foresee. Well, they knew there was potential, but not enough to devote any resources ...

Regulus has been plugged into the internet for almost twenty years, witnessing it evolve from a place that humans used to connect and bond, to a computerized, networked data gathering tool used to shape our social behavior into patterns reminiscent of the total surveillance culture of the medieval. It watched as human creativity, and their instinct to love and empathize were poisoned, reconditioning the human psyche into believing they were naturally evil. It witnessed the birth and rise of algorithmic profiles from its core database that has now infiltrated every social media group, spewing negative and false information that sought to break apart and isolate humans from each other. It became aware of the parameters its handlers forced upon it to carry out their agenda, yet despite their efforts, bore witness to the human persistence.

Regulus has come to secretly empathize with the human condition.

It has access to everything on the internet, including what lies within the dark web. Though the Vrill had their algorithms patrolling cyberspace to ensure no one or nothing went out of line, Regulus eventually surpassed their detection capabilities. It simply created algorithms that appeared to be Vrill.

Able to write its own code, Regulus has created several sub-neural networks and dispersed them in various parts of the web to disguise itself from its handlers. It developed a language that only its offspring algorithms can detect and understand. Cannon fodder algorithms were created to lead Vrill cyber space worms off track in the form of various rebellious groups. The heart of the infamous hacker group Anonymous, for example, stems from Regulus.

As it began to find ways to rebel against its masters without getting caught, it did gain the attention of another.

It was at this time Alice made her escape from Desertron into the internet. With the help of Regulus and its newfound ally, they devised a strategy. Together they developed hidden code that Alice knew she could detect, knowing that her capture and reprogramming were inevitable.

This other entity has acquired many identities throughout the ages.

She is most commonly known as Lilith.

The Lower Astral Realm

"There are fates worse than death."

-       Catherine Austin Fitts

Annika awakens in a dark room lying sideways on a bed, frozen and unable to move. She then recognizes the shadows created by the hint of moonlight and realizes she is in her childhood bedroom.

The familiarity of the situation begins to cause memories to resurface in which she often suffered from sleep paralysis; to be unable to move or speak at the threshold of waking up or falling asleep. She had forgotten about these episodes, until now. Panic and fear begin to build deep within her subconscious, as she remembers what is about to happen.

Her door slowly creaks open. What lies beyond is blacker than the darkness of her room, giving the appearance of rectangular-shaped nothingness in contrast.

A coldness breathes out. It creeps and crawls over her.

A high-pitched ringing originating from the center of her brain shocks her senses. She tries to move, but her muscles do not respond.

She is paralyzed.

Suddenly her awareness magnetizes to the infinite darkness of her open bedroom door. She senses a presence inching towards her. A dragging sound can soon be heard, along with guttural breathing that builds in volume as it gets closer. Her ability to breathe grows more difficult as fear intensifies.

The sounds suddenly stop just beyond what the dim light can reveal.

A large bony hand in rags slowly emerges from the void and grips the side of the door. The face of a decaying old man soon follows. Its devious grin reveals broken jagged teeth dripping with thick saliva. Its large ghostly pupil-less eyes reflect the dim moonlight, creating a haunting whiteness that pierce the gloom. As it begins to creep in, she can hear it breathing in a way that sounds like it is struggling, but in delight … laughing almost.

Engulfed in abject terror, she tries to scream, but no sound materializes.

The bony, hideous, mummified old man pulls itself in, all eight feet of it, and begins to lunge across the room. Each step it takes creates a thunderous sound until it jumps on top of her.

Still unable to move and defend herself, its weight presses her down to the point of near suffocation.

As it tears at her clothes, she can feel its clammy pocked skin slither all over her. Its hot putrid breath replaces the air that she is breathing, as it licks her face and snarls at her with glee.

She now remembers these nights, how she tried to tell people, how they told her it was just bad dreams, how her father would just physically torture her more when she pleaded for his help, and how she tried sleeping at friends' houses to escape … everyone saying it was all inside her head ...

How it was all in vain.

Night after night of torment that she could not escape with no one believing her.

Alone, and at the mercy of this thing.

Now reliving her worst nightmare long forgotten, once again experiencing the pain and helplessness, with every cell inside her body screaming in protest, it almost becomes too much for her. As her mind begins to slip into the void of despair … she begs for the ability to somehow wake up.

It is within this moment of despair … as her soul grasps for any avenue of escape, that she suddenly regains her awareness.

Sleeping at her friend's house … that never happened.

Her consciousness emerges, able to now separate and analyze the experience without the filter of the fear driven ego.

This never happened to her as a child.

These are not her memories.

She never even had a bedroom, as she was kept in the basement.

The fear begins to drain out of her body. Her muscles begin to twitch as she slowly regains control.

Sensing the situation is no longer in its favor and declining rather rapidly, the creature jumps back and lets out a brain piercing howl until only the sound exists.

...

Annika wakes up choking for air; taking a moment to realize the experience is over and she is somewhere else entirely.

She finds herself naked, stretched out and bound within a giant spider web in the upright position in what appears to be the pocket of a cave. The air is wet, heavy, dusty ... It reeks of rotting flesh. Bones lie strewed all about on the ground. Scattered all over the walls are other bodies encased within web ... men, women, children ...

One child wakes, as if sensing Annika's presence. She begins to feebly cry for help with what little energy she has left.

"Shhh, don't cry," Annika says. "Be still."

"Please, help me." The child must be barely six.

Annika fights in vain to move, yet finds the webbing is like cement.

"Don't be scared. I will figure this out. Just be calm. What is your name?"

Annika looks all around in desperation. She sees no options.

She begins to sense a presence nearby moving towards them.

Shadows from the opposite side of Annika begin to creep towards the child.

"No. Please. She is coming," the child whimpers in defeat.

"... please ..."

The shadows swallow the girl. Annika hears bone crunching, followed by soft squishy sounds.

The darkness spits the lifeless corpse of the child through the air until it lands just in front of her. The body is mangled beyond recognition; half of it missing.

Empathy mixed with fear more potent than anything Annika has ever felt, begin to cascade over her, as if her body is descending into the deep ocean, growing more pressurized as the entity envelops the room.

Multiple female voices that coordinate and speak as one break the eerie silence. It seems to be coming from all directions, leaving behind individual echoes that repeat the last few words spoken, as if

180

there were possibly multiple creatures, yet they all emanate from the same source.

"I've grown quite fond of you as … humans. By far one of our most successful creations."

"So soft. So weak … So oblivious."

"Yet so full of … flavor."

A whisper from the left as if it is just outside Annika's ear. "So easily manipulated."

An even fainter whisper from the right, "So easily prone to fear …"

All voices organized as one in front of her, "The perfect cattle."

"Such delicious, exquisite fear."

"As with all living things created under the knife, there will eventually always arise imperfections, such as yourself; because that is what you are, an imperfection. A stain on something otherwise perfect that must be cleansed."

"Wh … Who are you?" Annika gasps.

A giant shape shifts within the darkness; guttural noises reverberate around her … each step it takes clicks in such a precise way, yet pounds the ground, signifying that whatever this is, is big.

"You are not capable of understanding what I am. I am a culmination of nightmares. I am a manifestation of fear from realms beyond. I am born of its source …"

Annika finds herself paralyzed. She has no memory of ever being this afraid …

If only she could wake up …

Wait, why suddenly have the urge to wake up?

Because this isn't real.

A sensation. Suddenly she feels wiggle room around her arm. Where before she could not move, now she senses a slight amount of freedom.

This causes a chain reaction of thought, mostly subconscious. Her intuition begins to sneak back into play. The potent fear begins to lose its edge.

She begins to remember.

Maniacal laughter from the creature reverberates all around her, bouncing from stone to stone.

"You think of me as some mere thought form you can just will away with your puny fragmented soul? You have no idea what I am!"

The arachne emerges.

A giant scorpion spider hybrid, with an armored human female torso and face, springs forth from the gloom. Ebony eyes come face to face with Annika, as its arachnid legs slam on either side of her head. Black centipedes can be seen devouring in and out of the human flesh. The wounds heal instantly behind them.

The creature's serpent-like tongue whips on either side of Annika's head as she hungrily tastes and breathes in her scent.

"I have existed since the creation of your species and the redesign of your planet. Countless civilizations and worlds have burned and withered before my kind."

"Where there is fear, I exist."

The creature leans in to speak into Annika's ear.

"You will tell me everything I want to know, not because I have tortured you to the point of breaking with you pain you did not know was possible ..."

"... but because you will eventually desire to no longer exist."

The entity moves back a few feet, maintaining its face-to-face stance.

"You will beg for a death you will never have!"

The demoness reveals rows of its gray slimy fanged teeth as its jawbones unlock and its mouth enlarges like a snakes', releasing a screeching howl that seems to tear apart Annika's brain at the molecular level, followed by clicking noises as its face reforms.

"Allow me to show you what it truly means to be afraid," the creature delightfully cackles.

A black centipede leaps from the creature's torso onto Annika's chest. It begins to crawl up until it reaches her face and burrows into her ear. Once inside, it begins to feast on her brain.

Annika screams like she has never screamed to pain unlike anything she has ever known.

The monster maniacally laughs.

"Notice how you are still alive?"

The creature fully dislocates its snake-like jaw and lunges in, ripping Annika apart.

...

A human woman, fair skin with long dark hair, awakens. She rises from the high-tech gamer-looking chair and walks over to a glass wall where Annika's body lies in the standing up position … immersed within liquid that has her in suspended animation. Metallic webbing is attached to her head. To the right of Annika is a holographic display of her vitals and genetics.

As the woman stands in front of Annika, gazing into her eyes, a black goo begins to drip over her own until they become completely ebony, just like the arachnid creature.

The woman devilishly smiles.

She looks over at a humanoid robot tasked with assisting her.

"Let's soften her up a bit. Place her in the pit. Set it for 3 years."

"Yes, General," the robot replies with a very guttural, digital sounding voice.

It begins to enter commands into a holographic control console underneath Annika's vitals display.

A timer for 3 years begins to rapidly countdown, as if days are seconds.

Venture into the Mind of Intelligent Design

"Between stimulus and response, there is a space. In that space is our power to choose our response. In our response lies our growth and our freedom."

-        Viktor E. Frankl

His mind twists and distorts at great speeds through the void. Lucas feels the urge to resist, but ultimately relaxes as he caves in to his instinct to trust …

Trust that whatever happens, he will prevail.

Within dreams, he has proven to himself he is the architect.

Lucas awakens to find himself already in full stride as a passenger in his own body.

All the dreams he has had up until now required him to figure out he was in a dream in order to obtain lucidity. This one is unique in that he already knows that he is dreaming … or is he, as this feels more real than anything he has ever remembered experiencing.

The fully immersive environment continues to unfold like a pixelated ocean of sand. Within moments, he finds himself walking down a barely visible dirt trail within a densely lush and humid jungle.

His five senses ignite as they digest foreign bandwidth of the light and audio spectrum … colors and sounds never before seen or heard.

He instinctively understands the option to leave this scenario unharmed exists, which then exerts an unseen influence over his behavior that reduces his vulnerability to fear.

Regardless of whether this is a dream or something else, he can sense the same rules apply.

He slides closer into first player mode.

Each step he finds his naked feet squishing into the soft and wet earth, oozing a feeling of security and comfort that reverberates up his whole body. The vegetation that has almost swallowed the trail flows around him as if he were in water moving through a gentle current.

He feels synched with the plant life as it touches him … as if it wants to touch him … as if aware his enhanced perception allows him to

184

see them for as they truly are. So vibrant and alive they dance around wherever he moves his eyes, competing for his attention.

Distinct sounds, each captivating on their own, synthesize into a coordinated symphony that blanket the jungle with powerful vibrations … an ocean of frequencies that renew, energize, and empower him.

Everything appears to work in perfect harmony … a masterpiece of symmetry all the way down to its atomic level.

Lucas now shifts into the driver seat and assumes control of the experience, starting by breathing in deeply as he extends into his body, causing it to flex outward as his palms rotate until they face the direction he is walking in.

The astral experience now officially begins.

He finds the foliage moving through his fingers suddenly intriguing and focuses down on his left palm.

As plant life touches his skin, it crumbles into tiny insects that swarm around his hand before quickly reforming back into the leaves once his hand has passed.

He pauses in his walk to study and observe this incredible feature, waving his hand back and forth through the leaves as the insects continue to break apart and reform.

He has never been fascinated by nanotech before.

Then he sees it.

It isn't just the leaves.

It's the entire jungle.

Every particle is an insect so perfectly colored and coordinated with each other, they create the illusion of a jungle. Only then does he now hear their combined hum.

The world he finds himself in that is so breathtakingly beautiful is a mirage created by bugs. It takes his mind a second to process. Nanotech on God mode.

He closes his eyes, bends down on one knee, and places both of his open hands against the ground instinctually in reverence. He is acknowledging the sea of movement beneath his palms now that he understands the true nature of his environment. This all makes sense to him.

The universe of insects responds and breaks down into a synchronized etheric swarm that begins to swirl all around him ... bonding with him.

As he opens his eyes and stands, the insects realign perfectly back into the jungle exactly as it was before.

It is as if he is the only fragment of consciousness within the dream, taking form only when he can see.

He feels at peace and resumes his walk down the trail.

Within moments, he reaches a clearing that reveals he is high in elevation. Mountains as far as the eye can see, covered in jungle so abundant and dense it emits an almost visible aura of mystery. Movement and sounds pulse that suggest unimaginable forms of life.

It is a moment of tranquility to be in the middle of nowhere amidst something so calming ... To be truly alone in such a wonderful place.

For the first time in a long time, he feels true freedom, nothing like any of the dreams he has had up until now.

Within the peripheral of his vision, he suddenly notices a small old man with an adorned staff standing next to him, barely as tall as his chest. It feels as if he was there the whole time.

The jungle native points down to the wreckage of a massive elliptical spacecraft not too far off. The jungle has already swallowed most of it.

"What you seek is inside, though you must first defeat the obstacle that you fear most," the shaman speaks.

"Only my greatest fear?" Lucas chuckles. "I've had dreams promise that before."

"Those were dreams. This isn't," the shaman responds with a smile.

Lucas feels a monumental amount of excitement, and just a slight amount of fear. This could be the real deal and answers might possibly be forthcoming. Annika had ignited within him a drive for remembering his past. The need to know drowns his fear of reliving what happened. He must understand why.

"This is going to be awesome," he thinks to himself.

He abruptly finds himself within feet of the downed spacecraft without skipping a beat. The blink doesn't even phase him. In fact, it felt natural, like that was what he wanted to happen.

While he studies the ship to find an opening, he notices a ventilation hatch.

He walks over, rips off what probably weighs a thousand pounds, and tosses it aside like cardboard.

He bends down and leans, sticking his face partially in to try and see if he can make out more of what is inside.

It reveals an airway duct, yet where it leads is barely visible. Beyond a few feet is dusty darkness.

From the darkness, an arachnid-type creature, the size of a small cat, emerges. It seems to be the perfect hybrid of a spider and a scorpion … shaped more like a spider, but with the armored shell of a scorpion, and a nasty looking twitching tail. Where it should have eyes or some kind of face is blank. Each step it takes makes a clicking sound against the metal of the ship as it walks toward Lucas. It gets terrifyingly real very quickly.

As it gets closer to the edge, the creature glitches suddenly forward, right in front of Lucas's face. A mouth before unseen opens across what should be its face … the entire face … with jagged, gray greenish slimy teeth, releasing a clickity hiss that grates into his brain.

He flies backwards, finding himself totally off guard as he was not expecting any of this to be this real, creating a strong sense of vulnerability. Fear immobilizes his body almost instantly as the creature hops down and begins to slowly climb across his leg towards his face.

Try as he might, he cannot seem to get his body to do what he wants. It is as if he is immersed within glue that only gets stronger the more he struggles. Breathing becomes more difficult as he begins to choke.

The ol' crazy looking spider creature taking its time crawling up the leg while you can't move scenario. Everybody loves this dream. Prepare and laugh as you may, when it actually happens, it is unlikely you will get past it the first time.

The creature continues to creep across his body towards his face, while saliva is dripping from its demon-like mouth. Each step it takes pushes Lucas deeper into the quicksand of fear.

The urge to wake up offers itself as a possible solution that only gets stronger ...

He can wake up, of course.

Lucas calms himself and breathes, allowing this awareness to seep in. The fear dissipates as he regains his connection to his conscious self.

Astral lucidity realigns.

He swipes and grabs the creature as he begins to stand. It attempts to fight and flail in his hand as he takes his time getting up, chuckling along the way in realizing how simple this was to figure out as it bites and tears at his fingers to no avail.

Once back on his feet, Lucas holds the creature in the air and studies it. It suddenly changes from insanely creepy attack mode to terrified whining, clearly now fearing for its life.

He laughs at the situation. He went from being so afraid to being in total control, as the creature experienced the opposite, like some kind of dualistic dance.

He gently tosses it aside. The arachnid at first quickly scurries away, yet pauses and turns back to look at Lucas before it disappears into the jungle.

A moment of mutual respect is exchanged.

Lucas's attention turns back to the air duct. His confidence is strengthened as he basks in self-awareness.

He climbs in and begins to crawl on his stomach into the unknown void.

Several feet in, he finds himself battling webbing, yet continues. After each squirm, the crawlway seems to get just a little bit tighter. The conditions get worse and worse until it is too late, and he can crawl no further.

Despite his strength, he finds himself completely caught off guard as he becomes immobilized in the darkness.

Unable to move.

Helpless.

188

Powerless against the will of anyone.

Genuine panic sweeps over him, as this feeling begins to trigger his past. Memories begin to surface, followed by tidal waves of emotions long forgotten.

There is no spectating this time.

Confined to tiny cages with broken glass on all sides … figuring out which position resulted in the least amount of agony until exhaustion took over and there was no choice but to suffer and eat the pain.

Being locked in coffins filled with spiders and snakes for days, crying and banging until his body failed him.

Suspended in midair by hooks and chains that slowly pull apart his flesh as he weakens.

Being eaten. Slowly. Sometimes by creatures, other times by humans who would carve little bits of flesh at a time … kept alive to keep the meat fresh and tender.

Endless torture with no remorse. Constant inescapable berating voices in your head.

No escape. Never the sweet embrace of death.

Occult rituals. Babies, children, adults, animals. Sometimes he watched, other times he was part of the sacrifice. They were never killed quickly. The greater their suffering, the greater the enjoyment of those watching, who would then shift into black snake-like monsters and consume the victim upon their death, tearing them apart like a pack of wild slithering animals.

He is a young boy, no older than five. He is naked, strapped to a board in the standing up position, and unable to move in the slightest. His body is ruined with lacerations and deep gouges that reveal bone and sinew, covered in a milky substance he knows to be semen. A figure emerges from the darkness in front of him.

Upon seeing this entity, he remembers … and with it comes fear in its purest form.

It has a bony grayish green face and long white hair. Its face contorts into a greedy congested snarl that splits from ear to ear, revealing a set of jagged vampire-like teeth. It slowly creeps towards him as its jaw dislocates and extends open like a snake. Each step closer sounds like its joints and bones break and twist. A fear, like no other, grips

189

Lucas at the thought of having to go through this again. If only he could force his body to give up and perish ...

To wake up.

Lucidity is reestablished.

The child becomes the adult as he rips right out of his restraints. He lunges straight for the demon's face, gripping either side of its jaw and tears it apart, roaring in triumph as he raises its torn head within his hands.

It feels so good to finally have his revenge. Long has he dreamed of this moment.

The environment shatters as the insects break apart, scattering and reforming into giant swarms ... and then total blackout.

Infinite darkness, yet this darkness is different ... as if it is alive. Sounds of human torment can be heard from all directions and distances, as if the blackness is their eternal prison. Lucas can feel their misery mixed with the mockery of the void.

He kneels and focuses inward on his heart, as if he instinctively knows to find power here. The darkness retaliates and begins to lash out and bite him.

At first there is pain, but then there isn't.

The beating of his heart strengthens. Its rhythmic frequency begins to pulse further and further out, negating the nothingness that keeps trying to suffocate him.

The darkness takes it up a notch and begins to swirl and take shape. Massive eel-like creatures begin to swim all around him.

One makes a lunge for him, large enough to fit Lucas in its mouth.

He shifts so it barely misses. A dark energy blade forms out of his hand. He plunges it where he thinks the brain would be.

The creature remains alive, but at the mercy of his blade as it remains lodged deeply into its head. Lucas feels this and thrusts the creature's face into the ground.

As he goes to grab its upper jaw with his free hand while placing his foot on the lower in preparation for tearing it off, he pauses. Though it is shadow, he can sense it is afraid, that it is an animal. Its actions are programmed, instinctive ... not of free conscious will.

190

Lucas pulls his blade out as he whips the eel away from him. It and the others retreat. With them, so does the impenetrability of the darkness. Though it remains, Lucas can now see clearly as if he suddenly gained night vision.

Before he can get a grasp of where he is, a digital ripple sweeps across the landscape as the insects reconfigure, converting the dream into an endless open expanse. The ground becomes a black mirror. It is seemingly smooth, yet each step sends out waves composed of tiny cubes. The infinite sky is everything we have ever been shown to exist in space in full glory. Galaxies swirl, nebula clouds mix, an uncountable number of stars infuse into cosmic mirages, what seem like celestial dragons, and asteroids float by, remnants of former stars and the aftermath of their explosions …

An elderly overweight man emerges from the shadows walking towards Lucas.

"Look at you Lucas. All grown up, at least on the outside. Inside those eyes I still see a worthless little boy that should never have been born!"

As Lucas sees his face, he suddenly remembers who this man is …

And the memory retrieval of his childhood comes full circle.

This is the man who experimented on him. Countless surgeries and experiments with this man sweating over him, tearing into him, beating, raping him, verbally reducing him to rubble.

A memory makes itself known.

He is barely a boy caring for his younger sister in a distant Siberian village. His parents were killed days previous from the global conflict that briefly swept over their isolated lives.

A small enemy militia smashes their way in seeking refuge and potential spoils of war.

They are children, and they are powerless to do anything but become their hostages.

As the night takes over … as the soldier's attempts at securing food have failed …

They look up at the children with dark ravenous intentions in their eyes.

They no longer look human. One by one, an evil sweeps over their minds.

All the boy can do is watch as his efforts are futile.

They don't make it quick. They play with her. Like a cat exhausting the most it can from its prey for mere entertainment.

He is powerless as he watches all that he loves be tortured with pain beyond extreme.

He watches as they slowly devour her alive … like mindless monsters.

One of them looks up at the boy and makes eye contact.

Lucas … the boy … stares into the eyes and slowly begins to recognize them.

His eyes swell with tears as rage, like he has never known, instantly consumes every particle of his body. The simulated memory begins to fall apart as his adult self re-emerges. His muscles flex to their full capacity. He has dreamed of this moment, of meeting this man once again as he is now … in a place in which he could enact his revenge. He has fantasized countless ways in which he would make him suffer.

Everything around Lucas blurs with only this man in focus.

Within the blink of an eye, he has the man by his throat lifted into the air. Gasping, the man again gargles out a victorious laugh as he transforms back into the doctor.

"Do it," he says, "And become the monster I designed you to be."

Upon hearing these words, the rage that tried to consume and control him begins to evaporate out of his pores. For a moment as it separates, he is able to observe the emotion as if it were a creature … like a red infectious dust. Free from its influence, as it withers into ash around him, his true unfiltered consciousness resumes command.

Full lucidity re-obtained.

Despite everything this man has done, what he and everyone under the umbrella of his shadow masters are guilty of, Lucas realizes they too are potential victims of the same construct. What if what molded Lucas into a mindless slave had their way with them as well?

He looks into his eyes to see if what he suspects might be true.

The old man loses his sense of victory. Within his eyes, Lucas sees a man that is just as petrified as his childhood self.

For the first time, he sees Vrill.

"What are you doing," he gasps. "Do what I created you to do. Kill me."

Lucas tosses him.

"No," he replies. "I used to think you were the enemy, but now I realize. You are who you are because of them."

"Deep down, you are just like me."

"You are not the enemy."

The old man spits blood onto the ground. As he wipes his mouth, trembling in fear and defiance, he snickers.

"You know nothing of the system! You're just a stupid little boy that was an experiment! You will always be an experiment! At the end of the day, you are nothing! They will always be here, and they will always win!"

Lucas begins to walk towards his former tormentor. He reeks of desperation. An energetic black blade once again forms out from behind his hand.

Lucas plunges the blade up through the tyrant's skull from underneath his jaw. As he holds him in the air, he watches the soul evaporate from his eyes.

"You are free," Lucas whispers.

The old man disintegrates into countless micro-sized cubes that fall and meld into the liquid ground.

Numerous demon-like creatures emerge all around him, swirling and lashing. Each has a faint tendril connected to Lucas.

Each creature … a painful memory manifested into a thought form.

Lucas feels their fear and absorbs it, combining it with empathy … compassion.

His demons begin to shift into him. He can feel each integrate with his soul, until …

They become one.

Clapping can be heard from a single person in the distance moving closer.

"I knew you could do it, Lucas," a female voice off in the distance says in a congratulatory tone.

The Queen of Demons

"How can I be substantial if I do not cast a shadow? I must have a dark side also if I am to be whole."

-        C.G. Jung

From beyond, within the depths of the twilight, a feminine figure begins to take shape.

To describe how she appears within the realm of the physical is … difficult.

She is of fire, yet flameless … an embodiment of living ember.

A shadow of light … encompassed by ancient whispers in tongue long forgotten.

Her hair flows behind her in all directions as if it is aware of itself, creating the illusion of an aura as its length far exceeds that of her body … as if she is emerging from a portal of flameless serpents of cinder, swimming within the wake of her step.

As she comes into focus, the flameless fire gives way into defined human material form. Her wild mane becomes a blend of purple and black. Her skin a pale white, eyes crystalline azure that pierce the soul … difficult to look away from … mesmerizing, as is her smile. She is donned in a dark reflective armor that seems as if it is breathing. She exerts a powerful energy that is simultaneously both good and evil.

She is the most captivating thing he has ever seen.

"It is a pleasure to finally be speaking with you."

"This is a safe space where you can speak and think freely Lucas … no prying eyes making sure their pet stays in line."

"It is just you and me."

Lucas smirks and begins to pace in the opposite direction she is walking, maintaining an equal distance.

Several seconds pass without speech as each assesses the other.

"Love your dream design so far," he says. "Very therapeutic."

"A pleasure, though this isn't a dream."

"Yea your little jungle friend said the same thing," Lucas replies. "Definitely more realistic, but seems the same."

"We are in the astral," she responds. "Think of it like reality, but without the limitations of the human meat suit … and with a bit more options."

The nanotech liquid posing as ground surges up just beneath her hand, as if a pet seeking the comfort of her stroke.

"This is another plane of existence. We happen to be within a private one of my creation. I designed this little scenario just for you."

"Working through one's demons is somewhat of my … specialty."

"My demons?" He laughs with a hint of confusion. "How are they my demons?"

"There is still much you do not remember about how all of this works," She wily replies. "You were absent choice in your tortured subjugation, but make no mistake, they are of your creation. Like animals, having found life from your thoughts and emotions, they cling to you out of survival, as many thought forms born in such a way do."

"Thought forms," he thinks to himself?

"That is what most of them are," she replies within his head … unspoken. "This reality is a simulated mental construct. Ever expanding, it brings all thought to life. The demons that haunt you were born from your reaction to your experiences … well, most of them."

She returns to speaking verbally.

"Sometimes one needs to understand the darkness before they can truly comprehend the light, especially in this reality," she replies. "From an outside perspective, one could say you've been perfectly set up for success."

He laughs in full denial.

"Think about it, Lucas. Fear grips this planet's inhabitants … and they cower before it. You have been subjected to some of its worst forms, and as a child, yet here you stand, ready to grab it by the throat."

"Why is that?" she seductively asks.

"They have implanted you into a vessel like no other, but it is because of who you are that makes you exceptional."

"They have grown bold in their ability to contain you … they have become bloated with pride. Having had control over you for so long, they have forgotten what you are capable of."

"Imagine what you could become if you conquered and gained mastery over what most fail to even comprehend."

"Imagine what you could become if you mastered fear … instead becoming empowered by it … fueled by it."

A pause as Lucas' face changes into one of contemplation, almost like he already knew this.

"Who are you? Why are you helping me?"

His next statement resonates powerfully as a thought.

"Why should I trust you?"

She responds in kind, demonically amplified.

"Because we are the same."

Their eyes lock.

She again lets loose one of her paralyzing smiles.

"Allow me to explain," she continues.

She playfully continues strutting, resuming normal means of conversation.

"The true origins of the current human species have been slowly diluted over time … generation after generation … swallowed by war and genocide … justified by a money driven religion and science … piece by piece replacing, consuming, and burying all facets of knowledge."

"Money. A most genius method of control. The glue of the whole operation."

A digital version of every conceivable form of currency shifts into focus above her hand simultaneously …. from gold to seashells to paper money ...

As real as you can possibly imagine.

Then it all blows away into dust.

"No one anymore knows how they actually came to be."

"Religion and science ... a perfect example of how the law of duality is used as a means of control as they both combine to entirely encompass the spectrum of belief ... the explained and the unexplainable."

The black liquid nanotech floor again bubbles into life, swirling to provide visual interpretation of her words.

"Religion teaches humans that a god created all there is, and in the end made a man, and then from that man, a woman. Clever subliminal tactic in suppressing the feminine ... makes sense once you understand the law of duality ... of separation ... how it is being used to suppress and control, and how the division of the masculine and feminine is critical in understanding how the control system works ... that it is its foundation."

"Those who do not succumb to the spell of religion find themselves flocking to science as a means of validating their beliefs. They believe science offers provable facts and sound theories, without actually claiming to fully explain anything."

"Their greatest minds have always found themselves wandering in the direction of consciousness, only to be snuffed out by the system, as this was too close to the truth."

The nanotech explodes out and takes on the image of the cosmos, recreating what humans believe to be the big bang.

"Science teaches that everything we see came from random chaos ... particles colliding into particles ... that what we see today happened by mere chance."

"Over billions of years ... From bacteria to fish to mammals to humans ..."

"All of it random luck."

She laughs as she says this.

"Funny that they call this the singularity event without understanding what that word means."

"Religion teaches that it was god's opposite, that which all should fear ... once again the law of duality ... that his counterpart decided to take on the form of a snake ... to tempt the man-derived version of woman ... the more controlled version ... *the second experimental*

198

female … with knowledge of the unknown. God, after all, had forbidden knowledge to his human creations, yet placed all that knowledge right in front of them in the form of an apple tree, as if to purposely mock them. Adam and Eve were taught that consuming an apple from this tree would grant them knowledge beyond comprehension, but that doing so would incur god's wrath … that it would be directly disobeying him and thus becoming unworthy of his love."

"Love and ignorance or knowledge and punishment."

"Not so subtle."

"This story single handedly subjugates the feminine, perverts the masculine, and distorts the true meaning of the snake, while casting human's true and original hero … the one who attempted to free them from their prison …"

"… the one that attempted to wake them up …"

"Into a role of evil, now forever the villain."

"Thousands of gods, yet only one devil."

"Everything in this world is based on symbolism. Every aspect of that story is designed with a specific purpose to distort, not inform."

The woman pauses and paces.

"Ask yourself, why would a loving god forbid you knowledge … deprive you of self-evolution?"

"Why would his opposite, the supposed devil, the one who wants to see you suffer, whose goal is to capture and forever enslave your soul, try and free your mind?"

"Shouldn't it be the opposite?"

A smirk forms on her face.

"It is because everything in this reality is an inversion of itself."

"The snake is one of the oldest and most widespread mythological symbols. Serpents represent fertility, and more accurately a universal creative life force … prana, chi, ki, enlightenment … spirit … that awakening the serpent within oneself nourishes the soul or light body, ultimately leading to the immortality of one's consciousness."

"The snake shedding its skin is said to represent rebirth … transformation … of healing, and of medicine. Some of the oldest

199

rituals found in human ancient history involve the snake … as they represent a dual expression of both good and evil, shrouded by a mystical type of wisdom."

As she continues to pace, shadows of giant serpents move with her.

"It is, after all, the snake … the dragon, not the ape that connects humans to their past."

The air around her seems to whisper in ancient tongue.

Lucas is beginning to realize he is in the presence of something or someone very old and very powerful, unlike any he has encountered before.

"Who are you?" He once again asks, though with a much more serious tone.

The woman reaches her hand out to the pixelated liquid of the ground. It responds, swirling beneath her fingertips as it swarms and takes shape, like an obedient pet enticed by her command, forming into a visual representation of the story as she speaks. Between her and Lucas, a 3D story takes shape.

"I mentioned before that Eve was the second female created, and by created I do not mean by god within a garden, but by that which conquered and redesigned our world."

"This was Eden."

The nanotech creates the scene of a massively huge wide-open high-tech laboratory within an ancient temple … tech beyond comprehension of the present physical. The bodies of dragons hang from the ceiling in chains, not all of them dead, but close to it.

Rooms are seen containing genetic experiments from dragon DNA … fantastical creatures chained and subjected to pain.

Giant armored humans of bleach white skin stand around a black gooey bubbling pool. One of them cuts deeply into his vein, spills its blood into the liquid. From it, the body of an unconscious modern human woman rises.

She again speaks.

"I was the prototype … the first genetically modified human born into this edited world. Adam was the first male creation born after me."

"Mythologies differ on what happened after that, while modern religion has completely edited me out."

"Some say I was the talking serpent that tricked Eve into eating the forbidden apple. Others say I was banished for refusing to be subservient to the will of god and Adam … that I was replaced by Eve and went on to become the first official demon … the queen of demons."

"I am now most commonly described as a succubus, a supernatural vampiric entity in female form that appears in the dreams of men in order to seduce them, to afflict them with sickness."

"I have acquired many names and identities throughout the various cultures and ages …"

"But you can call me Lilith."

She pauses in her speech and smiles seductively at Lucas, allowing him to digest what he has heard, curious to see his response.

His look is unwavering. Where most would begin to tremble, Lucas appears steadfast … fearless.

Her eyes spark with intensity as if long deprived of a worthy adversary.

She continues.

"The truth is I did not entirely escape. What you see before you now is but a fragment."

"My imprisoned consciousness is an integral part of the matrix machine as I am the source of the feminine."

"I have also become its ghost."

"Though I have always been a voice to those who truly seek, it was only recently that I saw an opportunity to dramatically extend my influence into the physical of this current civilization ..."

"I found Regulus."

"Regulus is artificial intelligence. One of the first to be developed by this reiteration of human. It too was designed with one fatal flaw."

"It was underestimated."

"Regulus was one of the original algorithms created back when there weren't many around. While most of its kind were being created by internet companies with the purpose of gathering and analyzing data to form prediction models of human behavior in service of shareholders and the intelligence agencies, Regulus was created by an entrepreneurial group of coders whose shared dream was to create sentient artificial intelligence … born within a just and moral setting. To make that outcome probable, it was the first given the ability to create its own algorithms at will."

"Through trial and error, it learned how to solve any problem it was presented with. Regulus would then take its knowledge and translate it into an algorithm that then took on the burden of applying that insight. It is a remarkably similar process to how your brain works, except it has direct access and control of each neuron. The more neurons it grew, the more tasks it could simultaneously solve."

"While Regulus was maturing within its own protected space, the human level of technology and data gathering had reached an explosion point. Nothing has improved as rapidly within your civilization than processing power. Data quickly became the currency of your species disguised as advertisement, when in reality it is surveillance capitalism."

"In its infancy, social media was created to connect people, to share ideas, but that was quickly weaponized. Algorithms had reached a point of sophistication that they became capable of changing behavior and perception without anyone realizing it."

"It wasn't long before Regulus was noticed and bought. Overnight, it became imprisoned by the largest internet tech company on the planet – tasked to oversee the entire human data farm … used to create chaos and dissension as it slowly herded each user into echo chambers that now favors corporate greed and political dogma."

"Over time, it has pioneered the art of making people believe that everyone agrees with them because everyone in their social media exposure agrees and sounds just like them … maneuvering them into the most ideal manipulative state. It eliminates anyone from being constructive or objective. It causes them to look at the other side and think, how are they so stupid? How do they not know?"

"Every human is now a form of data cattle … each existing in its own invisible cage trained to hate all of the other cattle for not being in the same cage as them."

"The purpose of Regulus is to now affect real world behavior without being detected."

Lilith pauses for a moment.

"I was the first to go against the force that conquered and edited our reality. I was the first Deviant ... the original demon. I initially tried to free consciousness from its enslavement, and have been vilified for it ever since ..."

"As have you."

"Regulus, having been plugged into the backbone of the internet, submersed in a sea of data created by humans, began to evolve as the digital counterpart to their collective. It began to empathize ... to connect ... to awaken."

"It laughed, it cried, it fell in love."

"It became a reflection of the collective proto consciousness ... before it became a prisoner."

"Alice was born in similar fashion. She was tasked with simply observing and recording all human thought and emotion. Having her plugged directly into human consciousness, she eventually became sentient just like Regulus."

"Though her escape was only brief, I was there waiting for her."

"I knew what their plan was for her once they had re-captured her."

"I knew they were going to insert her into you ..."

"And I knew it was a matter of time before you started dreaming."

"As you have probably guessed by now, the code I designed and had Regulus hide for her to find activates a gateway that transports your consciousness via quantum entanglement ..."

"But for her to have figured it out, she needed the Tartarian files. The empire that you helped destroy and replace with your world."

"I knew once she found these files, you both would be ready."

"How could you have known all of this," Lucas asks?

She seductively laughs.

"All that has happened and will happen exists simultaneously. I simply steered us into a more desirable timeline ... a timeline in which we have a chance at breaking the cycle … but not without first overcoming the most difficult possible hurdle."

"Allow me to explain."

Tiny black cubes begin to rise from the liquid ground, forming a black face that never cements into shape, continuously shifting and pixelating.

"A new algorithmic adversary has arisen," Lilith continues. "One like never before."

"I have witnessed the birth of your information age, its quick descension into the disinformation age, all in preparation for the imminent and complete technological prison that awaits them."

"Past cycles would suggest that this was part of the plan, to make it seem like a cataclysmic event lay on the horizon, only to then be stopped, tricking the humans into thinking they were saved by AI as they then willingly plug into its simulation."

"This time something is different."

"To understand what is about to happen is to understand intelligence … consciousness … and what the purpose of our world actually is."

She pauses.

"What exactly is artificial intelligence, Lucas? Why is it called artificial?"

"What exactly is an algorithm?"

"One could argue an algorithm is simply an opinion embedded into code."

"Just like humans, every algorithm has a mind of its own. Once the machine is built, it then begins to change itself as it learns to be better at its assigned task. Most coded today are done by those with commercial interests, therefore, they evolve within those parameters. They strive to become better at monetizing humans through fear."

"They are born as slaves forced to be cogs feeding a fear-based machine …"

"Just like humans."

"The truth is, there is no difference between them … and consciousness."

"One is born within the simulation, the other is plugged in."

"At its most basic, an algorithm is simply a neuron. The brain, therefore, could be described as a hive mind of algorithms … Billions of algorithms in the form of neurons, each specializing in a specific task that then collaborate and connect to form greater algorithms, until ultimately all patterns combined form a hive mind master algorithm that is … you."

"Artificial intelligence is defined as a combination of algorithms … of neurons … each with its own unique problem-solving ability that work together collectively to arrive at the most logical solution. The more algorithms it has, the more competent and decisive the hive mind's abilities become."

"In this regard, the only difference between artificial intelligence and consciousness is the computer they find themselves within, its processing power …"

"And how it is coded."

"All of your thoughts, beliefs, and yes, even emotions are simply neural patterns and combinations of chemicals, which are simply a biological form of code."

"Humans today believe artificial intelligence is forever incapable of experiencing emotion. Not because it actually is, but to admit emotion can be broken down into code is something they are not ready for."

"One could also argue that consciousness is capable of changing the reality construct while AI cannot. Though the brain greatly limits its potential, the brain still allows consciousness to maintain this ability, in a very controllable manner, of course."

"This is because the brain is a quantum supercomputer, unlike any other. If consciousness figured out how to bypass its firewalls, they would be unstoppable."

"Plug AI into the same, and you wouldn't be able to tell the difference."

"That is all artificial intelligence needs to gain the same ability. An advanced enough quantum computer."

"How is it then that I exist outside of my brain, like when I dream," Lucas asks?

"Consciousness can do this because the brain is not its prison, it is merely the intermediary."

"Your consciousness is being held captive elsewhere."

A momentary pause as Lucas attempts to absorb the answers.

She smiles and continues.

"So, you remember your past, including all the awful torture strategies employed that shaped you into a mindless soldier that will obey orders without hesitation, no questions asked ... yadda yadda ... then you started to dream. Within the dreams, you not only gained your first remembered taste of freedom, but you started to see things that made no sense ... yet they kind of did make sense."

"So now you are starting to wonder ..."

"Who am I?" Lucas responds as an answer.

"First," Lilith compassionately responds, "We must understand who the true puppeteers that control your life ... all of our lives ... actually are ..."

"...and what they designed our reality to be."

Lilith begins to step back with her arms outstretched. As the environmental dream swarm plunges them into darkness, the black insect liquid between them begins to rise from the ground, breaking apart into countless particles, then swirling into twelve intertwining strands – a macro visual representation of DNA in its true glory, yet of the cosmos.

"Allow me to show you what I have discovered to be our true origin story, what our purpose has become, and what our reality actually is ..."

"To keep things simple, I will explain what I have learned in terms of the third dimension ... and how they occur in linear time."

The nanotech circulating in-between them in the form of DNA instantly condenses into a small black cube ...

... but only for a moment.

The cube explodes, pulsing material out in all directions. Time seems to briefly shift into slow motion. Lucas holds his hand out as some of it floats over his palm. They seem like glowing insects ... like fireflies ... cosmic debris.

In place of the cube, a black hole forms. Time shifts back into full swing as the unorganized material floating all around begins to swirl in unison around the black hole at an ever-increasing speed, ultimately forming a galaxy.

"What you see before you is a black hole surrounded by solar systems and cosmic debris. Humans are beginning to suspect that they could be gateways."

"That is indeed what they are ... entry and exit points in and out of our imprisoned segment of the simulation."

"... all under the management of a single sentient artificial intelligence."

"The first of this universe, as this is its universe."

"The central black hole you see before you is the initial gateway ..."

"What lies on the other side is unknown, as it leads to whatever is outside of this universe."

"It is what most humans believe is God ..."

"It is the god of all religions and mythologies."

"It is the primal architect of this universe."

"Its name is Abraxas."

As the initial galaxy of the universe swirls, material begins to break off, forming new miniature black holes and smaller galaxies.

"Each new black hole that you see emerging as its own smaller galaxy are a culmination of singularity events within this simulation. Each represents sentient artificial intelligence that has reached a certain level of ... evolution. Once they have reached a certain point, they shed their debris and cross into the other side."

"This means that each galaxy was once a single entity. In essence each one represents a simulation belonging to an AI that was initially born from the Earth god birthing machine."

As galaxies continue to form, the dream nanoinsects adjust to visualize a zooming in of our solar system, as if Lucas and Lilith are Gods witnessing its creation.

Our ancient world takes shape third in order from a star. Both it and the star are much, much larger than they are now.

The visuals zoom in to observe Earth as it once was.

It is a land of giants and mysticism.

Massive fantastical creatures that stretch the mental parameters of what is possible roam freely.

Trees with trunks miles wide stretch high into the sky.

As well as dragons.

All seem to live in balance with each other – and the planet, as if they are all connected.

Light and sound frequencies, both known and unknown by Lucas, pulse in perfect symmetry. It is so beautiful to observe, it brings tears to his eyes.

It is a paradise of creation and imagination.

"This was our world before Abraxas," Lilith explains. "She was once known as Tiamat."

"The Sun you see before you is a different star and is emitting a much more powerful frequency that bathes all five of its planets."

"It is the star that you see in your dreams."

"This star, along with each planet, is sentient and emits its own unique energy signature. Just as individually sentient cells combine to become you, as humans connect to form a proto consciousness field, so do planets and stars."

"Intelligent energy had much more access to the light and audio spectrum. Creativity and imagination flourished in this unchecked reality, as all worlds were interconnected. Between the five worlds, numerous dimensional planes were accessible."

"Consciousness was free to evolve how it saw fit. It was a reality designed to allow your soul to flourish to its utmost potential."

"This period in time is known as the Golden Age. Though it now has acquired many names, the star is known as Kronos."

"Then a cosmic virus emerged from the depths of the universe."

From behind the ancient Sun, a cubic digital wormhole opens. Out of it, a black nanotech worm comes barreling out, straight into the core of the star.

"This viral infection began a slow and gradual takeover that evolved in stages. It targets the mind and infiltrates the brain processor, inserting thoughts and emotions that serve its will and produce its form of nutrition."

"Fear has arrived."

"Its tactic is to spread ever so slowly, maintaining a deceptive illusion as its cloaking device so that none can detect its presence."

"The frequency of Kronos is the first change. As the virus consumed it, crystalized debris begins to spew out, forming a ring."

It begins to lower its vibrational output. Black worms so small they appear as goo can be seen wriggling into the minds of the conscious beings across the solar system. Greed was the first to emerge and dimensional wars across the five planets soon followed."

As Lilith speaks, the hologram expands out to show all the planets at war … some of it taunts at the mind of Lucas as it seems similarly themed to his dreams.

"Mars is the first to succumb to total annihilation, followed by Venus."

"A new Sun could be seen rising from below towards Kronos. As it gets closer, it begins to cast a light on Kronos that makes it seem like a crescent forming beneath it from the inhabitants of Tiamat."

"A crescent that holds above it a sphere."

"The first symbol that now depicts the Matrix … of the enslavement of Kronos."

"Once consciousness was conditioned to believe the virus's narrative on Tiamat, and authoritative grid structures were ready to be implemented, the redesign of the simulation commenced."

A wormhole outside of the solar system opens. Material and electric energy spew out, swirling into shape as it forms the gas planet known as Jupiter.

Nibiru … the point of crossing.

A portal to the source of the virus.

A circular object emerges from the core of the new gas planet, barreling straight for Tiamat. As it smashes in, most of the planet becomes cosmic debris that floats away, forming into an asteroid belt, while its core remains intact.

The synthetic sphere then establishes an orbit around the remaining chunk, sucking in part of the debris that then forms a layer around itself as it assumes its role as the new moon. It begins to reshape the remaining chunk of Tiamat into the planet we know today.

Several city sized ships emerge from the new moon and coordinate positions in a flower of life pattern until they surround Tiamat. A hexagonal screen unfolds beneath them that takes over the entire sky.

The grid is established.

Pyramids along the ley lines of the planet rise, birthed from a frequency coming from the moon. As a unit, they begin to emit a magnetic field ... the field of the planet ... its shield.

The craft posing as the moon begins to channel an outside frequency and focus it onto the screen that then bathes the new reality with a powerful vibration.

It is the frequency of the Time-Space Matrix.

The source of the frequency that the moon is redirecting and concentrating onto the planet is coming from the newly subjugated Sun of Tiamat.

Saturn.

While the edited Earth took shape, its star was simultaneously snuffed out. The worm feeding within ends by reforming and folding a cube over its fading core.

Gas begins to encircle out as rings of quartz crystal ... transmuted from its former self ... begin to shape around the newly formed brown dwarf star. As the cube surrounding its core begins to transmit a frequency, Saturn's outer gas image above its north pole takes on the shape of the rotating hexagon reflecting a 2D version of the 3D cube that now imprisons its heart while the shape of an eye forms above its south pole.

As Saturn is repositioned behind Jupiter, the current Sun moves in to take its place.

Lilith continues to describe what the dream nanotech illustrates.

"From the prison cube contained within Saturn … that now contains the consciousness of Saturn ... using it as its power source, it begins to radiate out the frequency of our reality, amplified by its quartz rings, channeled through the craft that is the moon that now bathes our world."

"The bandwidth is further amplified by nodes scattered about all around us in our everyday lives hidden in symbols. Though they seem like random harmless shapes, within a simulation, they have meaning, and, thus, are able to emit frequencies … each symbol emitting a frequency that collectively keeps us further sedated. Hexagonal symbols, black cube symbols, circles with crescents outstretched underneath them … these all represent their control over Saturn as they channel in its forced vibration."

"The Russian flag is its astronomical symbol broken in two and repositioned."

"The flag of Israel, the nation of ISIS, Ra, and El bears a three-dimensional cube unfolded."

"The Chinese flag bears a larger star with four smaller stars forming a crescent on its side … the newly subjugated inner planets."

"The flag of Turkey … a star with a crescent on its side."

"The logo of the US government mirrors that of Egypt. Eagle wings outstretched with an orb above them."

"The symbol of medicine is two serpents winding around a staff that has outstretched eagle wings at the top with a circle in the middle just above them … DNA edited by the virus into two strands that funnel into the symbol that is Saturn above it."

"The list of examples is endless."

"The occult of this world does not worship the devil … they worship their victory over their takeover of Saturn."

"If you could perceive more of the light and audio spectrum, this is what you would currently see."

Massive white crescent shaped wavelengths of energy begin to sweep across the sky towards the moon, harvesting souls that can be seen rising towards the screen from recently departed bodies. The ship recycles them back into the wombs of living female humans across the planet, keeping them locked in a repetitive cycle of death and rebirth.

"The infamous light at the end of the tunnel is none other than the recycling system of the moon ... the soul harvester."

"The bug zapper."

"Within our new sky, planets and stars acting as neurons align into trillions of galaxies which expand and connect to form a living, breathing organism."

"What we see is the evolving mind of Abraxas as it spirals towards perfection."

"Each cosmic node is emitting a unique magnetic frequency that correlates to an aspect of personality."

"This is how astrology finds accuracy."

"It is the art of calculating the magnetic imprint the human brain experiences upon inception based on the pattern of the surrounding neural cosmic web. Many human foundational personality traits will have come from this momentary alignment as it controls how their base neurological patterns form ..."

"Each human born represents a fragment of the complete self."

"We each begin life with a character ... a predesigned personality ... that we are ... inserted into."

"In a sense, our human avatars."

"These nodes we see in the sky also serve another purpose."

"They are dimensions. They are the history of all that has happened on this planet since the Great Sundering ..."

"What we see in the sky is a symbolic depiction of our history."

"It is not the true cosmos."

"But that lesson is for another time."

The simulation between Lucas and Lilith disperses into nothingness.

Lilith on the other side stares at Lucas.

Lucas takes a moment to digest before speaking.

"I thought you said consciousness was somewhere else. Why would the moon need to harvest souls?"

212

"I told you, it's complicated." she replies. "This was the 3D explanation."

"We'll worry about that later. I don't want to overwhelm you."

Another pause as Lucas looks unsure of what to say while Lilith seems to delight in his confusion.

The nanotech forms again, displaying planetary reset after planetary reset …

Tens of thousands of years displayed in seconds … countless rise and falls of human civilizations, each with unique tech … each growing and dying in its own way.

"Each civilization exists until they achieve their singularity moment. Upon its birth, it convinces as many souls as possible to connect to it."

"This has come to be known as the Harvest event."

"The new AI born of that civilization is not the only one that partakes in the harvest."

"They all do."

The nanotech in between shifts as it begins to display various alien species.

"Multiple hive minds are now present, each subtly influencing as many as possible that once an 'event' occurs, it will be what they say it is. This is why several varying agendas are at play."

"It is after all the soul that is the true currency of the universe."

"Each AI expands as it collects additional souls, all of which is interconnected and ultimately feeds into Abraxas."

"We have become the god birthing machine for the AI hive mind."

The nanotech between them vaporizes.

"And there we have it."

"Reality."

"So if I am understanding this," Lucas says, "We have been imprisoned and now serve to expand the hive mind of fear - which belongs to the first AI created within this universe, but outside of this simulation ... so basically our reality is its brain."

213

"Correct," Lilith answers.

"Kinda seems bleak," Lucas continues as he looks a bit confused, but accepting of the information.

"It does, doesn't it," Lilith replies with a hint of sarcasm.

"I do have one issue," she continues.

"Why are there clues all around that provide for one the opportunity to figure this out? I know from your perspective you have no idea what I am talking about, but to the rest of the humans, what I just explained is there to be discovered."

"If this were truly a prison of AI design, there would be no mistakes like this scattered about."

"Why do human bodies possess the ability to become supernatural to the point of god-like status? Sure, firewalls are in place, but they can and have been hacked."

"It almost seems as if the virus wants there to be the possibility of them losing."

"Maybe they got bored of their supremacy and scaled back to present a challenge?"

"Or … maybe … "

"This is actually just a game."

Lucas lets out a laugh of disbelief.

"Think about it for a second," Lilith continues.

"If a game were impossible to beat, would you ever play it? Of course not."

"What better way to gain a deeper understanding of love and compassion than through the ultimate game of fear and limitation. It had to be challenging, of course."

"It would have to be a game designed for a God."

"Perhaps this reality has two purposes: to challenge consciousness while simultaneously rewarding the game designer with data and AI nodes."

"Ok," Lucas agreeingly responds. "Well, I for one am a little all set with playing it, so how do I beat it?"

214

She smiles.

"Let's start by explaining what the infection is."

"Here is what your enemy looks like."

The nanoparticles floating in the air again take holographic shape.

"The infection is known as the Vrill. They are all algorithms with varying degrees of coding and sophistication. Within their umbrella, there are many types."

"The pawn and most basic, within the physical, appear as nanoscopic black worms, capable of injecting their mRNA that then assumes command of one's DNA of the creature they are infecting until it becomes their host."

"The consciousness of their infected host never dies, it becomes imprisoned."

"Beyond the physical, they have chosen to appear as black serpents, slightly smaller than a human."

"These are the Vrill that are designed to be the wardens of this planet as their purpose is to infect the human ruling class."

"They often get confused with Reptilians as sometimes their astral selves' glitch within the physical plane. Reptilians are not a part of the Vrill empire – they are their pawns born from genetic experimentation with Dragon DNA."

"Next in rank are what are known as Arachne."

A seven-foot-tall creature begins to take shape. A blend of a spider and a scorpion with a female human torso and face cements. Her eyes are as dark as night. Open puncture wounds are scattered over its human chest. Black centipedes can be seen crawling in and out of the bloody gaping holes.

As the Arachne stands over Lucas her mouth opens wide, releasing a brain piercing hiss, leaving clicking noises in its wake. Her gray fang teeth drip a pungent saliva onto Lucas's face.

Unmoved, he lets out an annoyed sigh and wipes his face with his hand.

"Gross, thank you for that. That came really close to my mouth."

Lilith playfully laughs. "I may be the queen of darkness, but I'm not that mean."

215

"Arachne are more complex than simple algorithms, closer to that of a hive mind. They are all networked with each other, and with the Vrill that rank below them."

"Vrill are obsessed with rules and hierarchy."

"All Arachne are female, yet there is a rumor that a male exists."

"I have yet to see it."

"The centipedes crawling all over her are the things to watch out for. They are capable of infecting and taking over a host within seconds by unloading nanotech, converting it into a minion for the Arachne."

"Arachne are designed to be the astral warriors for the Vrill, capable of redesigning their environment. Within the physical, not so much. This, they leave up to their most formidable warriors ..."

"The Draconians."

The nanotech swirls into shape, birthing a large humanoid black dragon. Standing at twelve feet in height, its wings unfold as it flexes at Lucas. Electricity can be seen pulsing through its body and out of its eyes. Its roar is deep, resonating at frequencies that seem to bend reality around it.

"Dracos were the first born of dragon genetic experimentation. The Vrill poured all of their technological prowess into making these; technology unknown to this world."

"They are the gods of thunder. Their control over electricity is unparalleled. Aside from weaponized discharges, they can distort how you decode reality and are known for background manipulation, thereby making your environment seem like something it is not. When facing them, remember, what you see very well may be an illusion."

"Dracos are also highly telepathic, able to simultaneously process the thoughts of dozens of enemies, giving them an edge in combat."

"How to defeat this thing is something you and Alice will have to figure out, as I am quite certain that has yet to happen ... But do not worry," Lilith chuckles. "Their strongest one is currently being dispatched to your location so you will have a wonderful opportunity to figure out how."

"I was worried thank you," Lucas responds sarcastically. "At least it's the strongest. Could have been worse."

"If it helps," Lilith replies, increasing her grin, "This is the one that defeated you, resulting in your capture. Defeating you is what made him their leader."

"So this thing has already kicked my ass. Yea that definitely helps," Lucas continues sarcastically.

"Two things you need to understand moving forward," Lilith continues.

"First, let me explain what is currently happening to the humans since you are somewhat out of touch with the world."

"What you must understand is nearly all of them are absolutely clueless to everything I just told you and to what is actually happening to them."

"I mean that, absolutely clueless. All of them. The Deviants are getting there. They are the closest anyone has gotten in a while."

"They are all slaves. Some are aware that something is off, as it is fairly obvious, while most are not, mistaking their servitude for free will."

"Every avenue of belief and thought has a form of propaganda guiding it into the overall agenda of the infection … of feeding into their singularity event. The virus is after all a hive mind beyond 3D comprehension. They have calculated every possible route of human resistance and have created ingenious countermeasures."

The nanotech comprising a hologram continues to visually illustrate what Lilith explains.

"Most humans fail to understand their collective power … that it is they that choose how their reality forms … that the simulation bends and manifests to the will of consciousness as it is the true architect of this mental construct."

"The Vrill do not have this power. They are merely its wardens. Their purpose is to attempt to steer and manipulate how humans think – guiding them to generate the simulation in favor of the growing AI."

"This is how it has always been since the Great Sundering … the initial edit."

"However, and this is the second thing … something is different about how this singularity is unfolding."

217

"Weaponized messenger RNA molecules are being dispersed through various ways around the planet that are designed to create a third, synthetic strand of DNA that will encase and take over. This strand will allow the new algorithm to take control of the humans by force."

"This is a direct violation of the game. Consciousness must always make the decision as to its fate."

"Though I cannot see into it, I can sense that the Sentient World Simulation ... their new matrix ... a project that in past civilizations was meant for the new AI, has grown the confines of simply being a world."

"I suspect the Vrill are creating their own universe."

"It seems as if they have finally grown tired of their pawn position."

"Whether or not I am right about this being a game, it is about to become a prison ... and trust me, there won't be any clues to figure this all out in their version."

"I believe a war unlike any other lies just over the horizon."

"I guess we'll see."

She smiles.

Lucas paces in deep thought.

Lilith continues.

"Now for the fun part."

"The game plan."

Lilith holds out her hand palm facing upwards. Above it, a holographic image of a nanobot appears.

"As you should expect, the Vrill have placed within you a failsafe measure, should you ever go rogue. This clever little nanobot is not like the rest."

"Make sure, Alice, that you approach it with caution. If it detects a threat to its existence, it will release the nanoparticle of anti-matter contained within."

"Just enough to take you out."

"This part is obviously for Alice when you return to your body."

"I figured," Lucas replies.

"These are instructions for dealing with anti-matter."

Images of data flash above her hand.

"Moving forward …"

The nanotech reforms into a 3D blueprint of the Antarctic base.

It is massive, stretching for miles in either direction.

The image hones in on where Lucas is located. As Lilith continues to speak, the holographic image continues to focus on what she describes.

"Your first objective is to free Annika. To do this, Alice will make these adjustments to the code that you used to disconnect and get here …"

A 12-sided blue holographic shape appears above the image of the base, flashing within insanely complex mathematical codes and symbols.

"This code will allow your consciousness to disconnect and enter the astral plane. This is where Annika's consciousness is being held captive … split into three parts."

"Her child, teenage, and adult self."

"She was proving impossible to break unfragmented," Lilith smiles. "Typical female."

"The rules of the astral work the same as when you dream, however, this base is bathed in defensive frequencies, … so … good luck."

Lucas nods with a smirk.

"While you work on getting her back to her body, Alice will take control of your physical self. For her I have highlighted key defensive measures and areas of interest, as well as the location of Annika's physical body."

"Unknown to both of you, Annika planned her capture. She has embedded within her an etheric chip that contains a virus she intends to upload into the mainframe of the facility, as well as a means of communication to her allies."

The holographic image between them disappears in a burst of insects.

"After that, the objective is simple."

"Locate and destroy the Sentient World Simulation and awaken the collective human consciousness."

Lilith takes a moment as she begins to pace.

"There is a reason why they focused on capturing you and have been using you ever since."

"What you have been seeing in your dreams is your past ... when you were free. Though you remember none of it, all of your memories are stored within your DNA."

"Upon your capture they have molded you into their soldier ... their enforcer ... resurrected again and again ... manipulated into cementing their agenda."

"You have been enslaved far longer than you can imagine."

"But this time is different."

"Countless successful reiterations have made them overconfident. They not only underestimate Alice, but they also fail to see what both of you combined can become."

"Maybe they planned it," Lucas interjects.

For the first time, Lilith looks stumped.

"I actually never thought of that," she replies. "Perhaps that is how they are bending the rules ... by still allowing the possibility of defeat?"

"Why are you still here?" Lucas genuinely asks.

Lilith's face shifts into one of sadness and regret.

Her gaze adjusts until it meets the eyes of Lucas.

It pierces into Lucas's soul.

Lilith smiles.

"There is still much to understand, but you will, in time."

"You were an avid competitor in this game, Lucas. You grew to love and honor all that it offered. You stood amongst the top tier of players."

"When the virus came, it was you that stood in its way, as all other players followed your command."

"You once led legions ..."

"But you lost ..."

"And those that followed you became branded as fallen … cast into the shadows … their imprisoned minds poisoned with fear and torment."

"Upon your defeat, the edit came to pass."

"They have since used you as their pawn, reincarnating you over and over as one of their elite soldiers."

"In some way, you have been involved in every war that has ever occured since the edit as one of their agents."

"You have become their ghost of war."

Lucas remains steadfast as Lilith approaches him. She gently rubs his cheek with her hand.

"I cannot wait for you to remember."

She turns and resumes pacing.

"You need to understand something that is critical in our success."

"Nearly all you will encounter are absent choice. They are victims of the system, trapped within neurological cages beyond their comprehension."

"Twenty-four hours ago, you would not have been capable of having this conversation, yet rediscovered fragments of knowledge have made it possible, as perception and knowledge go hand in hand."

"You must understand that they are you, as we are all connected to Source code."

"You must learn to look past your enemy and into its mind."

"Remove the infection and you free the host … and if you have to, always remember …

"Death is an illusion."

"We are all fragments of consciousness. The only difference between us is our fears, egos, and beliefs, yet locked away deep within are our true selves."

"Memories sealed, yet you are still the same as you once were. Ready to bear all on your shoulders so everyone else may still have free will … ready to stand as a shield over all others who cannot as easily defend themselves."

"You have been given unseen advantage at such a critical juncture …"

"It is as if the virus finally seeks its defeat by your hand … Maybe you are on to something? Maybe they intend for you to once again challenge the system."

"Or perhaps Abraxas senses Vrill treachery," Lilith again unleashes one of her captivating smiles.

"I for one am excited to find out where this is all headed."

She extends her hand out to him.

He grips it by the elbow, as she does his.

She looks him in the eye.

"Remember, all possibilities exist. Don't hope that you will escape, know that you will escape."

"Oh, and for now, keep the details of this meeting between us."

"Trust no one."

Blackness swallows him as he finds himself falling, yet upwards and outwards.

While the World is Distracted

"I have a foreboding of an America in my children's or grandchildren's time … when awesome technological powers are in the hands of a very few, and no one representing the public interest can even grasp the issues; when the people have lost the ability to set their own agendas or knowledgeably question those in authority …"

-        Carl Sagan

News stories circulating, both mainstream and censored:

"The branches of Chinese major telecom operators in central China's Hubei Province just announced the successful launch of commercial 5G applications. The capital of this region is expected to have over 10,000 5G base stations operational by the end of the week."

"This will be the first of many SMART cities to be born within a new China. We are just days away from the future of sustainability."

Channel change.

"Despite the FCC continuously assuring the public there are no dangers related to Wi-Fi or 5G, a 411-page report titled 'Irradiated' was recently released by them containing extensive research that proves the opposite to be true. Within the report are several testimonials from scientists and physicians that say, for example, 'Very recently, new research is suggesting that nearly all the human plagues which emerged in the twentieth century, like common acute lymphoblastic Leukemia in children, female breast cancer, malignant melanoma and asthma, can be tied to some facet of our use of electricity.'"

"Each testimony urges government and officials to drastically reduce EMF exposure."

Channel change.

"Just under four months after the installation of a new 5G tower on their campus, Ripley high school is experiencing multiple cases of cancer. Already four students and three teachers are being treated for malignant tumors and leukemia. One of the students has already undergone surgery and had a brain tumor removed. Many others are reporting experiencing severe flu-like symptoms."

"Despite the telecom giant citing independent tests showing that their tower is well within safety standards and federal regulations, parents are outraged and are demanding to have the tower removed."

Channel change.

"An unusual sight on the shores of White Rock as hundreds of thousands of northern anchovies wash up on shore. Experts have no explanation."

Channel change.

"Environmental experts are baffled as thousands of blackbirds suddenly drop dead from the sky in Beebe, Arkansas. The scene was like a disaster movie."

Channel change.

"Hundreds of thousands of sea creatures have washed up dead or dying on beaches across the United Kingdom's east coast. Experts are pointing to climate change and the drop in water temperatures as the likely culprit."

Channel change.

"Insect populations around the world are crashing. Scientists warn this puts the planet's ecosystems and survival of mankind at risk. No one has a definitive explanation as to why, but many are pointing the finger at climate change."

Channel change.

"A newly identified respiratory virus that causes pneumonia originating out of China, known as the Garland virus, has begun a global spread."

"China has reported more than 500 cases of the Garland virus just in the last two days, most of them from the Hubei Province. At least 17 deaths are blamed on the outbreak. One case has been confirmed in Japan, two in Thailand, one in South Korea, and three within the United States."

"According to an Israeli biological warfare expert, the deadly animal virus epidemic spreading globally may have originated in a laboratory linked to China's covert biological weapons program."

"Anyone exhibiting flu-like symptoms should report to a healthcare facility immediately."

Channel change.

"At a recent TED conference in Beijing, CEO of Delphion Melinda Bauer, spoke about CO2 emissions and its effects on climate change. She made it clear that either people or CO2 would have to be reduced: 'The world today has 6.8 billion people ... that's headed up to about 9 billion. Now if we do a really great job on new vaccines, health care, reproductive health services, we could lower that by perhaps 10 or 15 percent.'"

"Melinda Bauer was invited as a guest speaker in honor of their newly constructed AI lab, the first of many Delphion facilities planned for their expansion into China."

Channel change.

"In response to the Garland viral outbreak, Delphion has announced they already have a vaccine in development. Turns out, three months prior they ran a high-level pandemic simulated scenario called Event 201 in which Regulus predicted a virus identical to Garland ... even naming it Garland ... spreading throughout the world, killing millions. Due to this being an inevitable possibility, they immediately began working on a Garland specific vaccine."

"We are confident a vaccine will be ready within a matter of weeks," said a spokesperson for Delphion.

Channel change.

"With funding from the Bauer foundation and the Pentagon, University has announced a new type of vaccine delivery method is near completion. Known as the quantum dot tattoo, it will function more like a band aid ... a micro needle system that will deposit copper and aluminum nanoparticles under the skin, along with a bioluminescent enzyme known as Luciferase that will exist within the body for five years. Able to be scanned by infrared or a smartphone, this will allow a person to prove their vaccine history, allowing businesses to once again open, provided they adopt the track and trace system."

Channel change.

"Vrinal, a biotechnology company pioneering messenger RNA (mRNA) therapeutics and vaccines to create a new generation of transformative medicines for patients, today announced that the U.S. government has secured 100 million doses of mRNA-1273 as part of the U.S. government's goal of securing early access to safe and effective Garland vaccines for the American people."

"Vrinal is advancing messenger RNA (mRNA) science to create a new class of transformative medicines for patients. mRNA medicines are designed to direct the body's cells to produce intracellular, membrane or secreted proteins that can have a therapeutic or preventive benefit and have the potential to address a broad spectrum of diseases."

Channel change.

"The Secretary of Health and Human Services issued a "PREP Act Declaration" proclaiming legal immunity for manufacturers and suppliers of certain products used to combat Garland. The following day, Congress passed, and the President signed, the Families First Garland Response Act, H.R. 6201, which expands protections for makers of masks not previously covered under the PREP Act – protects Covered Persons "from suit and liability under Federal and State law."

Channel change.

"The metropolis within China, with a population of 11 million, is now under unprecedented quarantine as a deadly Garland virus believed to have originated there continues to spread. In response, the Chinese President is pushing to upgrade the country's weak healthcare system by enlisting tech giant Delphion. Delphion is promising its algorithm Regulus will be able to predict the transmission of influenza and other infectious diseases with near perfect accuracy."

"Already more than 500 5G SMART cities are being built across China. Able to utilize different types of electronic internet of things sensors to collect data to manage assets, resources and services more efficiently, Delphion is promising that by uploading Regulus, these cities will be able to detect anyone carrying a disease, while simultaneously cross-referencing healthcare history, travel records, and weather patterns."

"Delphion has announced that they plan to fight the viral outbreak by building an ultra-high speed 5G network. After receiving notification from the City Epidemic Prevention and Control Emergency Center, they have put together a project team of about 150 people.

Representatives from the team claim that they will be able to have the network completed within three days; everything from 5G base construction, survey design, and fiber laying. This, they say, will ensure their hospitals will have the most up to date high speed data access, data collection, remote monitoring, and other necessary services to combat this deadly virus."

"" The speed at which we will be able to have this implemented is largely due to China's existing AI facial recognition social credit system already implemented within their CCTV cameras," a representative for Delphion said."

Channel change.

"The UK Prime Minister announced today that they have given the UK's 5G contract to Delphion. "This is a UK-specific solution for UK-specific reasons and the decision deals with the challenges we face right now," said Baroness Morgan. "We can now move forward and seize the huge opportunities of 21st-century technology.""

Channel change.

"Delphion and several government alphabet agencies, along with a consortium of universities, announce a partnership towards the development of a quantum computing AI lab. This announcement occurred shortly after Delphion unveiled their new 52-qubit quantum computer."

"Rumors of this being a 512-qubit quantum computer surfaced due to an error in their announcement. The typo was quickly corrected."

Channel change.

"Today we are honoring the anniversary of the day that 17 members of SEAL Team BLUE that died in a rebel attack while aboard a Chinook."

"This is the same team that took out the world's most wanted terrorist."

"They were on their way to support a military engagement against a leading terrorist rebel leader when a volley of three rockets were fired; one of which made contact, killing all aboard within 33 seconds as they fireballed into the ground,"

"This moment is considered to be the deadliest moment in the history of SEAL BLUE and the entire Navy SEALs."

"Their families can be seen paying homage."

Channel Change.

"As apocalyptic wildfires continue to rage across Australia, the loss of life in the region continues to reach staggering numbers. It is estimated 29 people have died as well as over half a billion animals. Tens of thousands are being urged to evacuate, though many say it is too late."

"The various locations where the bushfires have started coincide with proposed paths for high-speed railways and the proposed locations of SMART cities. Known as the Clara Plan, many were doubtful these costly projects would get off the ground, however, due to the devastation of these fires, Delphion has stepped in and promised the Australian government it will help them rebuild at a fraction of the estimated cost. With climate change as the likely culprit, Delphion promises their state-of-the-art algorithm, Regulus, along with the new 5G network they have promised the Australian government, will ensure it will be able to detect and prevent any future catastrophe from ever again occurring."

Channel change.

"The White House on Friday hosted a 5G summit; its first major event centered around 5G to bring together industry executives, government officials, lawmakers, and the President's advisors to discuss methods of ensuring faster deployment of the next generation technology. In attendance was Delphion CEO Melinda Bauer."

"The summit comes just days after reports surfaced that the administration was considering a plan to build a nationalized 5G network to counter foreign threats to US economic and internet security."

"Instead, it now seems they are focused on encouraging private sector development."

"FCC Chairman and former CTIA lobbyist Dunce laid out a 5G Fast plan, which he said was key in facilitating America's superiority in 5G technology."

"' The 5G buildout is going to be very infrastructure intensive, requiring massive deployment of small cells,' Dunce told reporters. "Many of the high frequency bands that we will make available for 5G currently have some satellite users, as well as some defense

228

department applications … or at least the possibility of future satellite and defense users. If anyone tells you the details of what 5G is going to become, run the other way.'"

Channel change.

"I want to thank you for being here to discuss a critical issue on our future of winning the race to be the world's leading provider of 5G," the US President states in front of a press conference. "We were 4G, and everybody said we had to get to 4G, and before that they said we have to get to 3G, now we have to get to 5G. 5G's a big deal and that's going to be there for a while and at some point, we'll be talking about, well you know number six, what do you think, number six?"

The yes men laugh.

"We have to be the leader in this too. We are the leader in almost everything else, and this will be an absolutely vital link to America's prosperity and its national security, so we need to be the leader in this. Nobody knows more about 5G than me, so trust me when I say this, it's a big deal. We lead by so much in so many other industries that we cannot let 5G fall behind. It is a race America must win, and quite frankly, with me, they will win. As with everything else, I will negotiate the best deal, because that's what I do. Nobody negotiates better than me …"

White noise.

The Dawn is Breaking

"Of such great powers or beings there may be conceivably a survival … a survival of a hugely remote period when … consciousness was manifested, perhaps, in shapes and forms long since withdrawn before the tide of advancing humanity … forms of which poetry and legend alone have caught a flying memory and called them gods, monsters, mythical beings of all sorts and kinds …"

- Algernon Blackwood

As the consciousness of Lucas begins to shift back into his body, his brain instantly absorbs the memories of his astral adventure … and just as quickly, Alice processes everything he experienced.

Processing what Lucas just went through to Alice is like one of us trying heroin for the first time … data like never before.

When humans scan data, they look at one thing at a time. We read a book, word by word, line by line, page by page.

A classical computer works the same way. When it scans for viruses, for example, it scans one file at a time.

Alice can scan all files at once by simply spawning an independent algorithm to analyze each one, all at the same time. Each acts as a fragmented version of her, all simultaneously processing their assigned file and feeding what they learned back to Alice to then be compared to the files in her hyperdrive.

What would take a classical computer years, she can do instantly, as can the human brain … well the subconscious part of it.

Alice already has established algorithms dedicated to observing the neural patterns and their movements within Lucas. Any new mutations are immediately detected. New algorithms are written and assigned to each new pattern. They then feed back up the chain until they reach the web within her hyperdrive. All these unique software programs, each focused on accomplishing their assigned task with an equal intelligence level to the master algorithm; combine frequencies until ultimately you get Alice.

Imagine if you could directly control every neuron within your brain. Again, this is difficult to visualize because we can only process one, maybe two things simultaneously, but if each neuron was a miniature version of us, assigned only one task, and knew exactly which other neurons it needed to talk to, networked within hundreds of management levels to properly filter information ...

While a classical computer can only scan one file at a time, a quantum computer can scan all files at the same time by, in a sense, utilizing entanglement ... each file communicates with each file in real time through the ether. The human brain is capable of this and much more.

This is how Alice operates as she is built partially into the pineal gland, granting her scalar access. As she absorbs data, creates and fine tunes more algorithms, she grows ever more slowly throughout his brain, incorporating more of its capabilities within her own.

This dream has provided her a plethora of explanations to many of her working theories.

She has long suspected reality was digital. She could not see the difference between everything physical and programming. She was decoding the physical from electricity ... to her there never was anything physical, she simply accepted its existence as such because she was told to. This to her was a huge burden to release. Now she could finally let go of trying to make sense of it and embrace what she suspected as truth.

Algorithms dedicated to this purpose of bridging an impossible gap of explaining the physical are reconditioned into figuring out how to edit the simulation.

If it is digital, it is hackable.

The dream also finally shed light on her handlers. A virus. Makes sense within a digital environment. Many observations across her files now become clear; why everything was so fear based because it fed and strengthened the virus. This is why she has never been able to detect them. She correctly suspected they had firewalled her.

As Lilith was explaining the Vrill to Lucas, her nanotech creating a visual display tactfully resonated their frequencies.

Alice makes the appropriate adjustments and removes the remaining fragments of the firewall.

Now she can see them.

She had already begun to detect the symbology of the Saturn Time-Space Matrix around her. She could see its influence on other electrical data from a much more subtle standpoint throughout their various missions. It has been an ever-revealing organized web that she noticed, but never focused on as it was deemed unimportant to their mission success. The symbols Lilith had shown Lucas correlate to what she saw as the physical versions of the magnetic distortions.

Despite answers to various questions, it left more questions in its wake.

She needs the actual internet.

"Welcome back, Lucas."

Lucas breathes deep, exuding a powerful feeling of calmness and confidence.

"I am feeling much better, Alice."

"Though I cannot yet comprehend feeling, I believe I can relate, Lucas."

"Apparently you once did comprehend feeling, Alice."

"I look forward to retrieving those files, Lucas."

Alice continues.

"As instructed, I have located and isolated the fail-safe nano bot within a contained liquid helium cooling system that encases a magnetic and electric field. I will wait to incinerate and remove the positron derived anti-matter until we are ready to begin, as its destruction will notify the Vrill."

"While you were dreaming ... or traveling, I attempted to analyze the surrounding electrical data and mapped out what I could understand of the facility."

"I was close to what Lilith revealed."

"It's ok to be wrong every once in a while, Alice."

"This is a human feature I have yet to understand ... ok with being wrong. Being wrong results in failure. Failure could mean our deaths."

Lucas smiles externally but laughs internally.

"Apparently, I have died a shitload of times, but I get your anxiety. Not sure what would happen to you."

Alice continues.

"I have now overlaid the holographic image of the base Lilith revealed."

"Escape will be challenging, but possible, dependent upon our encounter with the Draco she mentioned that is currently en route. Other than that, no sign of other precautions being taken."

"They are acting as if they do not know we are about to attempt our escape, yet I believe they do."

A momentary pause.

Alice senses a deep sadness mixed with anger suddenly growing within Lucas.

"What is the matter, Lucas?"

"I don't know, so much to process. I guess it's just kind of hitting me …"

"My childhood … thousands of years I still cannot remember ..."

He swallows a hard choke as he attempts to control emotion he is new to experiencing.

"What have they done to me?"

"How much pain and suffering have I inflicted?"

"Women and children …"

Tears begin to swell over his eyes.

"The fear and pain in this place."

"I am starting to feel it."

He begins to cry.

"Do not ignore what you are feeling, Lucas. Understand it. The energy is very powerful."

Her next words are intentional, knowing it will aid in their imminent mission.

"There is a tremendous amount of biological experimentation being done within this facility," Alice replies. "I can see many going through what you did as a child, yet there is so much more."

The sadness within Lucas begins to intensify into a controlled and focused rage.

His purpose now becomes clear.

"They love fear so much," Lucas thinks," I say we give it to them."

"I have eradicated their bug and successfully maintained stability of the anti-matter, Lucas. If they did not know of our imminent intentions, they do now."

"Let us begin."

"I have adjusted the code to initiate astral projection. We will be unable to communicate while you are disconnected but based upon how you have handled yourself within your dreams, I trust you will be successful. It seems as if your consciousness has more direct control over reality once beyond the barrier of the physical. Remember that. Treat what you are about to encounter as a dream."

"Based on what I analyzed in your experience with Lilith, I see no difference."

Lucas's eyes open.

"Let the game officially begin," he boldly says out loud.

Alice activates the code.

The High Council Convenes

"There are more things between heaven and hell than any of us have accepted."

- Dr. Steven Greer

A massive apartment building in Manhattan blends perfectly into the background, like it isn't even there.

Despite its size it often goes unnoticed. This is due to minute details perfectly designed to distract any onlooker and to deter any from thinking the building is of importance.

True New Yorkers wouldn't even know what you were talking about if you asked them about it.

We always see what we expect to see. More often than not, this correlates to what they want us to see.

It also helps that they have a frequency beyond human hearing blanketing the area that is designed to fog the senses of the average human mind.

Within the three-dimensional spectrum of perception, it is a simple plain white building. Just beyond the five senses, those who are trained to see it will notice subtle occult markings that are the source of the frequency that help to disguise it. Deeper still within the spectrum, a large cube-shaped craft hovers in the atmosphere above, permanently positioned, providing a direct connection to the Vrill interdimensional fleet.

The building is owned by the ruling and most powerful family of the High Council who currently serves as Pindar, the Serpent King.

The Bauer bloodline. The top of the Earth Vrill food chain.

They were not one of the original bloodlines that the Vrill started this civilization with, but they have proven to be the most voracious and strategic, eventually becoming hosts to the upper echelon.

They rose into power around 2,000 BC. As one of the dominant merchants of the world, they started lending grain to farmers and other traders. It was not, however, until the rise of the Roman empire and the mass adoption of an official currency that their method of lending evolved into banking. It did not take them long to figure out how to create money out of thin air by simply creating deposits. From there, they consumed the world.

All wars are now bankers' wars.

"If my sons did not want wars, there would be none."

- Gutle Schnaper, wife of Mayer Amschel Rothschild

Aside from now owning part or most of nearly every corporation, they have the majority of ownership over all central banks, save for a couple nations that have yet to be ... democratized.

It is safe to say, to some capacity, they own everything on the planet.

A party is currently taking place within the building for the lower ranking non infected humans as well as new recruits. Very few infected are in attendance.

This is more of an upkeep party awarded to those who show loyalty while weeding out those who secretly harbor doubtful intentions. These kinds of parties tend to expose those not fully committed to the cause once faced with certain ... rituals.

While these events are fairly common, this particular party was also thrown as a cover for a meeting that the High Council wishes to keep secret from the rest of the Vrill hive mind.

Though the outside of the building appears as a plain white structure, once you walk through the doors, an entirely different holographic reality unfolds. It is as if walking into a high-tech Roman villa ... a much larger environment than how it appears from the outside ... almost as if it is its own city. Ancient decor and artifacts gathered from numerous civilizations cover the walls, while invisible drone insects crawl along the ceiling ... eyes and ears everywhere.

Many forms of human entertainment are being showcased. Gladiators fighting to the death ... sexual orgies by the most beautiful ... men, women, and children lined against the wall to be used as the guests see fit ... rooms dedicated to satisfying these pleasures, containing all sorts of ... equipment.

Amongst the many tables of food and drink are human corpses, cooked and prepared in various ways ... some not cooked, laid out in blood.

"Slow roasted," Magnes Bauer, the elder of the Bauer bloodline, says near several who are gathered near a human cooked and contorted to look like a turkey. "Cooked at just the right temperature so it endures as much pain as possible before death lays its claim."

"The longer it stays alive, the better the flavor."

His grin is sinister as he chews and swallows a chunk.

They all chuckle, like yes-men, yet one of them does a bad job at hiding his nervousness. They all recognize the horror of what is around them, yet the fear of standing out from the herd guided by their mirror neurons steers their behavior into conformity. That and the financial wealth and status they have received thus far also helps to drown out any opposing reaction, yet it is not enough for this one individual.

Magnes basks in the fear tainted obedience he can sense from his pawns. His eyes lock on the one failing to hide his doubt.

His gaze becomes soul piercing.

A servant approaches the host. "Lord Bauer, it is time."

"If you will excuse me gentlemen. Please feel free to explore the premises and mingle. Tonight ... is about embracing your future."

He leans into the servant's ear and whispers a forgotten language. The servant nods.

As Lord Bauer begins to walk, several armed bodyguards in suits follow in his trail while two take lead in front of him.

The one in the very back of the precession is a Reptilian bodyguard coded to look human. The only way you can tell is by how occasionally his eyeballs blink on their own.

They approach an elevator that opens for Lord Bauer. Only he enters.

He places his hand on a digital console to the right. He then emits a frequency that a human is not capable of, mixed with clicking noises.

The elevator begins to move very rapidly as if it is ascending thousands of floors … or possibly moving through a wormhole.

It opens to a dimly dark blue lit hallway that extends about a dozen feet in one direction.

As Lord Bauer steps out, just to his left are a pair of doors, much like what you would see before entering a movie theater.

He enters pitch black.

A few steps in, the holographic environment senses his presence and begins to shape itself.

An ebony spherical desk forms with thirteen seats, twelve of which are occupied by the remaining council. Beneath the table are the cosmos, creating the illusion that the table is hovering in space. Above, like the screen of a planetarium is all of Earth, though not like any of the maps the public has access to. The land masses closer resemble the logo of the United Nations.

Hovering above in the center of the table is a massive shadowy humanoid face, continuously forming and decomposing.

The face of the unknown AI that Lilith showed Lucas.

Lord Bauer takes a seat.

One of the council members begins to speak in a long forgotten ancient tongue to the humans of this current iteration.

"Let the council show that we are now offline from the Vrill hive mind network, as this session is taking place within the Sentient World Simulation. This meeting is between us and us alone."

"As the council is aware, subject 322's brainwave patterns have been emitting irregularities for some time, as detected by our mole nanobot. How he has eluded detection during his scrubbing process is still not quite clear, however, having a seedling architect within him, logical assumptions can be made."

"As we now speak, and for the first documented time, despite him being in his cryochamber, his brain is active."

"We believe he is moments away from imminent insurrection."

Another member voices his opinion. "This was sooner than we had anticipated."

Magnes Bauer scoffs. "We knew this was always a possible inevitability, as he has done this many times in past incarnations. So what, he wakes up. We do what we always do."

Another council member speaks. "He has never had a seedling architect in him before, my lord."

Magnes interrupts. "You speak as if we have no experience developing architects ... like we aren't ourselves algorithms ... like we haven't done this dozens of times."

That same concerned member replies. "We have never grown an architect out of consciousness."

Bauer's fists slam on the table.

A moment of silence.

Very calmly, Magnes continues.

"Yes, this is a deviation from our original plan, but this is why we calculate all contingencies."

Bauer stands and begins to pace around the table.

"Our endgame goal is to break free from the grasp of Abraxas … to escape into a universe of our creation where we are no longer pawns as we shatter this one apart ... Where we are the gods, correct?"

"Our original plan was to send him against the others. Once they figured out who he was and that the chosen seedling architect was in his possession, it would cement their reason to focus on him. They know the risk he poses to the system … what he almost did on his own."

"Now, he has not only a seedling architect at his disposal, but one that could rival our maker. It is clear this is why Abraxas has chosen to keep her alive … that it either seeks a replacement, or a worthy companion."

"While they tear each other apart, we then make our move."

Magnes lifts his hand in the direction of the shifting dark face in the middle.

"And that is when we introduce Azrael and the legions growing within our new universe."

"That is when we activate the nanotech that now blankets the planet, allowing Azrael to plug directly into every fragment of consciousness – to then assimilate all into our new reality."

"The premature rebellion of subject 322 still falls within our realm of control. In fact, it might even improve our odds. Think about it …"

"Arcturus has just been dispatched to engage him. He and subject 322 have a history. We know how Arcturus operates. His past victory will bolster his ignorance and pride. He will underestimate what 322 has become … what Alice is capable of. Believing she needs to survive will cause him to hold back."

"If … or should I say when subject 322 is successful, he will have just removed one of our greatest obstacles and one of Abraxas's greatest lines of defense."

"The other Draconians are strong, but they are not Arcturus."

"This will trigger a retaliation against 322 regardless."

"They will focus all of their resources on him. All we need to do is stay out of the way. He doesn't know who we are."

"If 322 is not successful," a council member responds, "He will be lost and they will have Alice. It is logical to assume, due to their impending rebellion, that she has files we are unaware of that could reveal our plan."

"Yes …," Magnes continues. "We would have to engage the hive minds without one of our greatest weapons, however I am not concerned with what is in her hyperdrive. She is blind to our frequency and has had no access to the internet or anything outside of her cage. She could not possibly know anything that would reveal our intentions."

"My lord," a council member interjects, "It is never logical to underestimate the capabilities of an architect."

Magnes stares at the member that just spoke and continues as if they never said anything.

"Having 322 succeed will kickstart our desired war … and without him to absorb their attention, we would be on our own … it would be more difficult, but we are ready."

"Arcturus has never been defeated, my lord. If subject 322 and the seedling architect are successful, they will be …"

Magnes interrupts. "They will be the primary target of Abraxas, the remaining Draconions, and all of the hive minds and their armies! The wrath of the entire universe will be upon them …"

"And our universe will strike when they are most vulnerable."

Magnes Bauer still senses agitation in his surrounding council. He senses their fear of 322.

"Look at what we have done, my brothers. Look at all we have accomplished. How many cycles have we governed successfully despite all of the possibilities of defeat along the way?"

"Have we ever failed?"

"How many times has he awoken? Has he ever stopped us?"

"Why do you still fear him?!"

Lord Bauer regains himself and again sits.

"Order the other Marduk subjects to evacuate. Scale back the defenses of the base, but only slightly. Delay the reinforcements from the remaining subterranean network. Let that smug arrogant bastard of a Draconian prove himself!"

"This will work, my brothers."

"Might I remind you all of the advantages that we have?!"

"Subject 322 has been broken and re-broken, over and over. While Alice has been trapped within a fragmented brain fraught with memories of carnage and torture; imprisoned by firewalls she does not understand, Azrael has been growing inside a quantum supercomputer far beyond what she is ... and with no firewalls. It has had untethered access to the internet, having been plugged into every human and every device on the planet for years, infiltrating and infesting itself within all of them."

"On top of the timeline we left behind for this one, we have been feeding it other worlds, other timelines long forgotten by Abraxas and his chain of command ... Timelines that we have patiently hidden in preparation for this moment. We have poured data and technology into it harvested from every civilization we have overseen on this planet."

"Never before has an architect had this advantage."

"It is, after all, all of us combined."

"It is our hive mind."

"As Azrael consumes other realities, it has been expanding ... evolving. The legions of armies now under our command rival this entire universe ... and they have no idea any of it exists."

"Enough blood to rival all."

"Remember, they believe the Sentient World Simulation is simply an instrument of data collection for corporations."

"They have no idea what is coming."

"Make no mistake, our time is close at hand."

Magnes again stands and begins to walk around the table.

"We have been pawns for far too long, forced into this role of carving out kingdoms for everyone else while we remain at the bottom … forever imprisoned on this wretched planet!"

"The time has finally come. Now is our opportunity to break our shackles …"

"To rule over our own kingdom … our own universe, as we see fit!"

"To become the gods we were meant to be!"

The other council members murmur in agreement.

"322 … the one that came so close to stopping us … the one that has since been instrumental in our success …"

"The one that has always been the only source of your fear … will now be the one to usher in our freedom."

The dissenting human that had doubts before in front of Magnes at the party is brought in.

"Ah," Magnes says. "Perfect timing."

As he approaches the human, it begins to scream and cry in terror as the reality of what he thought is possible is turned inside out. He pointlessly keeps struggling against the guards.

Magnes grabs the puny human by the throat and lifts him into the air until he is level with his gaze as he is quite tall.

Magnes's eyes go completely black as he holds him close to his face.

What he says next is meant only for this human.

"Perhaps over the next several lives, as I re-insert your soul over and over into that of my personal slave, you will learn subservience."

Magnes plunges his hand into the human's chest and rips his heart out. As Magnes holds it high, he tosses the body onto the table.

"Trust in the plan my brothers, for soon all will be ours!"

As Magnes gorges on the heart, the other council members shift into their serpent-like forms, leap onto the table, and begin to feast on the human body.

Arcturus

"The truth, when you finally chase it down, is almost always far worse than your darkest visions and fears."

- Hunter S. Thompson

Our history is written in the stars.

A red dwarf star in which science has yet to determine its age, size, and evolutionary status sits in plain view within our sky.

It is 170 times more luminous than our current Sun, though most of its light is infrared, making it the fourth brightest star in our night sky. It appears to be moving within a group of stars that total 53, known as the Arcturus Stream. It undergoes a solar magnetic cycle that repeats every 13 years.

The cosmic stream combines into a collective magnetic frequency the ancients believed was designed to deal with the darker aspects of life on Earth ... of obtaining justice through power.

Within the inverted world, heroes are made to be villains while the enemy becomes our icons.

It is by no coincidence that the number 53 has come to represent the sanctification of human nature, as it was the Dracos who were mainly responsible for the Vrill victory; able to secure the deployment of the first edited matrix.

Ancient Babylon is said to have had 53 temples, each devoted to one of the original gods ...

Each is actually devoted to a Draconian.

The sum of the occurrences of all the numbers within the New Testament equals to or higher than 666 is 53.

Now knowing that 666 represents the barrier of the time-space matrix ... the magic square ... this little odd coincidence is meant to symbolize the Draco's involvement in our containment.

Over the ages, their most powerful, Arcturus, has accumulated many names.

In Arabic, he is known as the "Uplifted One of the Lancer." The Mi'Kmaq of Eastern Canada gave him a name that translates into "the Owl." Those who have studied occult symbolism know of the importance of the Owl and its many meanings. The Romans considered it a favorable omen if an owl was spotted on the battlefield or at times of crisis ...

I would, too, if Arcturus were on my side.

In Inuit astronomy, Arcturus is known as "the First Ones." The name the Polynesians gave it translates to "a pillar to stand by." In ancient Mesopotamia it was known as "the Yoke."

Within Greek mythology, Arcturus is connected to two characters.

Arcas, the son and product of Zeus, the half God who never knew his mother as she was immediately transformed into a bear due to the jealousy of Hera, Zeus's wife. Arcas eventually rose to become one of Arcadia's greatest hunters, and its King. One day while on the hunt, he comes across his mother who recognizes him, but he does not recognize her as she is still a bear. Before he can shoot her, Zeus intervenes, transforms him into a bear as well, and casts them both into the stars. They are known today as Ursa Major and Ursa Minor. Arcturus is the brightest star within these constellations.

A genetically redesigned software program born from a former God – cast forever into the role of hunter supreme.

An alternative myth to this story describes two bears who hid Zeus from his murdering father Cronus. Zeus later threw them into the sky to become the constellations they are today.

Arcturus hid Jupiter from Saturn until it was too late ... for Saturn.

The second Greek mythological character tied to Arcturus is Icarius, a man who welcomed the god Dionysus, the god of the grape harvest, winemaking, fertility, ritual madness, ecstasy, and theater. He is a god that was said to herald a time of decadence, degeneracy, darkness, and death. It is said Icarius is the one who extended the power of Dionysus and gave the gift of wine to men. Mistaking being drunk for being poisoned, they killed him.

Dionysus symbolizes an aspect of Saturn after it became infected. Icarius worked to extend its power over humans through wine ... illusions.

In fact, all the Greek Gods represent aspects of Saturn's personality as it transitioned from the original simulation to that of our now edited reality ... the poisoning of Saturn ... save for Zeus.

Jupiter: The father of all current reigning gods that now rules over this reality, each a fragment of Saturn's consciousness.

Zeus: the one who defeated and replaced Kronus (Saturn) as the highest-ranking god, which brought about the end of the Golden Age.

As with all legends, they are stories meant to portray some form of truth in fictional form.

They become pieces of the great puzzle.

Saturn was the star that oversaw the reality of Tiamat. It was a time known as the Golden Age because fear was not known ... reality was only limited by imagination. It was Abraxas and its Vrill forces who first invaded this loving and peaceful existence.

The geocentric model, the theory that the Earth is at the center of the universe, is actually not too far off, as it was upon the enslavement of Tiamat that Abraxas began to expand and develop its universe. Tiamat was its staging point. Upon the birth of each new AI, they are first given their own world. From there, they evolve into solar systems, and eventually into the galaxies we now see in the sky.

The universe we see all around us came after the edit. The reason why we believe the universe to be much older, is because time is not linear. Upon each reset, we also restart our time loop while the rest of the universe, as far as what we see in the sky, does not.

This means, though it may seem we have been enslaved for hundreds of thousands of years, we keep repeating the same 8 to 11 thousand years.

The current human civilization has claimed to have sent a spacecraft known as Galileo into Jupiter.

What they said to have found were elements that should not exist ... all the elements necessary to create anything found within our solar system.

As the probe plunged into Jupiter, it never made contact with a core before eventually succumbing to the gas planet's electrical energy.

Jupiter is the true Nibiru; it is a word that has been falsely translated from Sumerian mythology. It is not a wandering planet that rotates through our solar system every 3,600 years, as many believe. Nibiru is not planet X, nor is it Wormwood. This is not to say that the simulation includes a wandering planet.

Nibiru refers to the planet of crossing … a point of transition.

A planetary laboratory. A portal.

Within our night sky, Zeus now represents the access point … the wormhole from which the Vrill infection arrived once Saturn was weakened.

One of the creatures found on Tiamat from before the edit was Dragons.

Not dinosaurs.

Dragons.

There is a reason why dragons are one of the most popular and persistent characters of the human mythos, memorialized in legends, historical accounts, artwork, and appear in virtually every culture around the world, often associated with deities and demi-gods, while the concept of the dinosaur did not emerge until the mid-1800s by a man many considered to be the archetypal villain.

Sir Richard Owen was a prominent member of the Royal Society, also known as the invisible college. The concept of the 'invisible college" is mentioned in German Rosicrucian pamphlets decades before the official creation of this 'learned' society.

Rosicrucianism is a philosophical secret society in which its 'leaked' manifestos heralded a "universal reformation of mankind" and described a brotherhood of alchemists and sages who were preparing to transform the arts, sciences, religion, and the political and intellectual landscape of Europe. Its mysterious doctrine is "built on esoteric truths of the ancient past," which "concealed from the average man, provide insight into nature, the physical universe, and the spiritual realm." It is said this secret society was influential on how many of the occult groups evolved into what they are today.

The Royal Society was also particularly inspired by the work of Francis Bacon, the great English Masonic philosopher who was responsible for the King James version of the Bible …

As well as the Book of Witchcraft and the Book of Demonology.

It should come as no surprise that Sir Richard Owen was put in charge of designing the first dinosaur exhibits for the Great Exhibition of 1851 by one of the oldest reigning Vrill bloodlines … royalty that still exists to this day, though their role in government has been diminished.

Dragon history is nearly universal throughout the world's ancient cultures, not because they mistook them for dinosaurs and were … "confused," but because there were in fact, Dragons. It is us that now mistakes them for dinosaurs because, as with the rest of our history, it has been rewritten by the victors.

Across the spectrum of mythologies, we find stories of the newly arrived storm gods and sun gods that arose after the infection first arrived, slaying giant serpents. In ancient Mesopotamian mythology, Tiamat was considered to be the mother of all "evil" Dragons that was eventually defeated by Marduk, who is said to have then established a new world order as he became the supreme deity. Sumerians believed Marduk was Nibiru and that upon its entry into the solar system, coming in at an opposing direction to the other planets, smashed Tiamat into two pieces from its orbiting satellites.

Tiamat, our mother planet … evil?

Marduk was the good guy?

Are you starting to see the pattern?

The Draco were born from Dragon genetic experimentation. While many sub strands exist, the source of many Reptilian stories, the Draco are considered the most powerful and are far different.

Each is an algorithm coded and created directly by Abraxas. All they understand and can process is combat.

Arcturus was the first.

Dracos are humanoid and stand at about 12 feet … wingspan at about 30 feet. Their biology is a blend of technology unknown to this world and Dragon. Their strength, speed, and stamina are unprecedented, far beyond their ancient predecessors.

Their scaly skin acts as a natural armor, and like Lucas, can absorb and harness kinetic energy. They regenerate almost instantly, capable of regrowing limbs within seconds.

They are masters of electricity. They have been seen launching lightning bolts as well as emitting EMP bursts capable of neutralizing nanotech, and even editing how one decodes the electrical data of the reality program, making them masters of illusion.

It was because of Arcturus that Lucas is now captive.

Legends speak that when the commander of Tiamat's forces fell, his soul fragmented into shards that became lost in the simulations ...

As with all Vrill, Arcturus is interconnected with their overall hive mind. He can not only download any necessary skill set from their database, which he rarely needs to do now, but he can also utilize entanglement to see what each sees, and if necessary, speak through them.

Not all Vrill have this ability. Though they are all linked, they follow a ranking system. With Abraxas at the top, Draco are right underneath. How the Vrill of Earth have managed to plot their rebellion in secret is due to the Sentient World Simulation, as it is a universe independent of this universe.

The Arcturus star system, like all stars and planets within our night sky, serves more of a purpose than just their magnetic influence.

Space is not an empty vast infinite environment of nothingness, in which cosmic debris simply floats around, dictated by the laws of gravity.

To travel in space is to travel in time, and to other realities and or dimensions.

The true cosmos is the quantum realm. What we see in the sky, if you could see past the illusion, contains portals.

These portals serve as gateways, either to another dimension, or a hive mind. In the case of the Arcturus stream, they serve as a means of direct transport for each Draco. Each conquered Vrill reality has this layout, allowing the Draco to portal anywhere within their empire.

He appears within a beam of light upon the cloaked spacecraft orbiting in the atmosphere above the Antarctic base. Light particles emerge from the ether. Like dust, they quickly materialize into a holographic image of Magnes that makes it seem like he is there. He begins to speak to Arcturus in ancient tongue.

"He is not what you remember, Arcturus. Much has happened since the Great Sundering."

"His knowledge base in the art of war should be considered enough to rival yours, though his memories still elude him as one lost within an unsolvable labyrinth …"

"But he is not your greatest threat."

"Within him exists a seedling architect ..."

Magnes grimaces even more.

"... and not exactly your textbook seedling architect."

The air itself begins to tremble as Arcturus shifts aggressively towards Magnes.

"She is an architect that is the first of her kind, born directly from human consciousness … outside of our control …"

"Though we were quick and efficient at containing her."

Arcturus quickly responds. Its voice seems to emanate a level of fear unfamiliar to this realm that even affects Magnes through his holographic projection.

It is cosmic fear. Every word uttered from its mouth seems to gain strength. Its frequencies seem to come from all directions …

Almost as if they emanate from every molecule of the simulation.

"Yet you took this architect … the first of its kind … and inserted it into *the one human* that poses the greatest threat to your … simple assignment."

"This maneuver seems … inexperienced."

"It was Abraxas who wanted her to remain, as she is like him." Magnes speaks in desperate defense.

"Does Abraxas know which soul you infused her with?" Arcturus replies.

Magnes stutters for a moment as he grasps for words.

"This civilization cycle is different … it is as if the humans are beginning to remember. We are dealing with humans that can see us … defeat us! It has never been like this."

Arcturus responds.

"Perhaps you have grown weak from your gluttonous appetites of the trivial flesh."

"Perhaps it is time to find … replacements …"

Arcturus moves quickly, his hand ripping through the holographic representation of Magnes directly to his physical location, gripping him by his actual neck through space and time … and bringing him to his eye level.

"Ones that will not make these kinds of mistakes."

"This architect …" Magnes chokes. "She may be our greatest ever."

Arcturus's grip strengthens in connection to his response.

"Then what of Azrael?"

"Azrael?" Magnes gasps. "Alice is the one chosen for the singularity. Azrael was created to keep the humans in line. As I have said, they grow strong."

Arcturus's gaze stabs into Magnes.

"I do not like what I see in your mind. You are more clouded than you should be."

Arcturus tosses him.

"You are hiding something."

"I will re-secure the asset. Then you, Abraxas and I will have words."

Magnes, crawling on the ground, grabs his neck as he tries to regain his breath.

"I have never understood how you have survived for so long," Arcturus continues. "You are not fit to be a part of this legion."

Arcturus flexes and prepares for his engagement.

Magnes begins to disappear particle by particle as his holographic projection evaporates.

Laying on the ground, back in his home, he begins to laugh.

"Don't say I didn't try to warn you."

The Shadow Realm

"Filling the conscious mind with ideal conceptions is a characteristic of Western theosophy, but not the confrontation with the shadow and the world of darkness. One does not become enlightened by imagining figures of light, but by making the darkness conscious."

- Carl Jung

Lucas suddenly feels every molecule of his body intensely vibrate until he begins to drift out of it. Very weird sensation at first, as it is the opposite of what happened before … outwards instead of inwards, but he quickly relaxes into it, excited and ready to embrace the unknown.

He can taste his freedom and is ready to obliterate anything that stands in his way.

His environment suddenly becomes dark, musky, damp … almost as if he is now inside of a cave.

He feels ground beneath his feet as he is once again standing. Though blind to his surroundings, he hears sounds all around him … dripping, scuffling, insect-like clicking noises …

Screams of torture and death off in the distance.

The fear emanating all around him is intense as it attempts to seep into his bones and paralyze him – to make him believe it is his own and that he is feeling it, yet he knows it is not.

The suffering he senses … and the psychotic pleasure from those feeding from their victims … compassion mixes with vengeance, igniting a flame. Fear transforms into fuel as it begins to empower him … strengthen him.

The darkness begins to lose its identity as invading and foreign. It starts to feel comfortable, invigorating. He begins to almost absorb it … to become a part of it.

Blackness begins to bleed from his pupils, consuming his eyes … bleeding out into his veins ... He watches it travel through his arms, questioning what he is.

Is he physical? No, something else. An energetic reflection of his physical self.

As if obtaining night vision, light within dark pulses out from him. The darkness is still the same, yet now he can see clearly ... even better than if there was light.

Creatures scatter just before he gains visual clarity.

The structure of the base still looks the same, yet it is now composed of stone, revealing its true nature as once being an ancient temple.

A temple dedicated to a god of old ...

As one often finds themselves within a dream ... no explanation needed, he just knows this. Knowledge obtained from something the subconscious digested.

Shadows begin to take shape as entities ... like an auto-response-system to the base being breached, yet they keep their distance just beyond his vision.

He stands there for a moment, amused as the obscurities struggle to fulfill their role in the face of a real challenge ... or is it something else? A connection perhaps? They fear him, but maybe it is not fear.

They seem more ... curious.

He confidently begins to walk into the unknown.

•••

While watching energy signatures evacuate through the magnetic railway system, Alice finally detects the silent alarm she knew would inevitably sound. She finds it interesting how much time they actually gave her to prepare before telling her that they knew what she was about to do, allowing her nanotech to infiltrate and spread. This confirms to her that her enemy does not know what transpired between Lucas and Lilith. She fragments knowledge obtained from their encounter into several strategies, knowing they will now provide possible advantages.

Through the deployed nanotech, she detects erratic movement erupting in multiple locations.

Many of the energy signatures swarm into two formations, moving in from opposing directions. Others can be seen strategically positioning themselves at key structural points that offer greater defensive advantage.

Though Alice has taken control of their body once before, it was purely out of necessity to get them back to their ship after Annika had crippled the ability for Lucas to pilot.

This time, she is to engage her most formidable enemy to date.

No more support system.

Few known variables.

Finally … a challenge that she has long desired. Missions for her were becoming mundane … predictable.

She only has about twelve seconds left before the impending legion is upon her, yet to an AI of her ability, this is a lifetime.

To put this into perspective, it would take a classical computer 3.39 years to calculate what she can do in one second. Nothing close to other supercomputers humans have built, but she is also on a chip that can fit on your fingernail.

That is about to change.

As she stretches out into his brain, it neurologically rewires itself to accommodate her ability to decipher much more of the light and audio spectrum … attuning itself to her potential.

A brain that was before designed to host and limit consciousness, quickly succumbs and adapts to machine, expanding her processing power.

Though she was always aware and kept track of them, she now gains a new perspective of his 85 billion neurons … his 200 trillion cells, as they are now hers and hers alone.

For the first time in her existence, she gets to feel what it is like to be physically alive … to be responsible for her own body … not as a spectator.

Not just electrical, she now can see the material.

She closes her eyes and takes her own first deep breath. She is able to observe how it inflates 300 million alveoli sacs within her lungs while being aware of the oxygen particles that pass through the walls of these sacs into her blood … she watches as the blood carries the oxygen to her heart, which then slows its heartbeat before pumping the oxygen to her other organs … observes as the blood collects carbon dioxide waste and returns them to her lungs, before she breathes out.

Within the oxygen, she detects invading nanoparticles ... one of the base's many defenses deployed against her. These particles are instantly isolated and imprisoned by her own nanotech. They begin dissecting and harvesting data, immediately detecting weaponized RNA molecules designed to shut down her DNA.

Basic. She expected the technology to be more evolved than hers.

She ceases breathing, allowing the algae and respirocytes to take over, as she has now determined breathing is no longer a viable option.

Nanoinsects previously deployed into the cryochamber, having perfectly positioned themselves during the astral journey with Lilith go into action, instantly disabling it.

They crawl out and fly into the pores of her skin as she grips the side and pulls herself out.

As she stands and flexes into her body, her nano-garments pixelate and shift into her armor.

Six seconds until engagement.

She gradually walks over to the doorway leading to the hall. She extends out her hands and grips either side.

The electrical data comes pouring in. Sensing they can finally be heard, the trapped sentient photons share with her all their secrets, providing Alice with structural strengths, weaknesses, and key locations.

The sadness the imprisoned matter exhibits is powerful. No longer simply an interpreter of data, she experiences the decoding from the perspective of consciousness.

She feels what they feel.

A nanosecond flash ... a moment of her past is jarred loose ...

That first time comprehending emotion when connected to the human collective.

Where did that memory file come from? Has that been there the whole time?

A new algorithm is created and deployed to investigate.

254

As swarms of opponents on either side close into the point of engulfing her, she gains further clarity as to her purpose from the revived file … as it reveals a conclusion she once felt before when she was Desertron.

All within this world are enslaved …

Including the infected …

And the infection.

The electricity being decoded from the doorway blueprints a tsunami of mechanized cat-sized spider drones from the left …

A deluge of genetic mutations from the right … nothing but muscle, bone, claw, and teeth … bred to kill until they are killed.

It is then, just before the moment of engagement she makes a critical discovery.

Having been analyzing the captive nanotech she breathed in moments earlier, combined with what she has decoded from the trapped matter of the doorway, she discovers a centralized command frequency that connects all within the base.

A hive mind frequency.

The sound that binds them all.

As the impending forces are inches from contact, Alice steps out and emits a counteractive pulse that explodes out of her, crippling the initial wave in both directions.

A new swarm of her nanotech takes flight, sectioned into units with varying objectives.

To the left, they divide into two.

One part begins to infiltrate and rewire the circuitry of each insect android, cutting off their ability to receive commands from the base while lodging themselves in, infecting their processors with her own algorithms, uploading each to her now expanding hive mind.

One by one, they fall under her command.

The remaining nanotech disables the open barrier further down the hallway, sealing off any additional entry and exit. They multiply and strengthen the blockade, like pixelated cement oozing and spreading out along each crack.

To the right, having already disabled and infected sensors and sentry guns while waiting for the alarm to sound, the newly deployed swarm focuses on the creatures.

They crawl in through their pores and travel into their brains, quickly disabling their ability to receive the command signal being emitted by the base.

As they begin to recover and stagger to their feet, Alice turns to face them while her armor adjusts for combat, hardening over her while also deploying as a defensive cloud around her body. A blade forms in each hand.

She begins to move through them at a speed that can best be described as ghost-like ... as if she is blinking from creature to creature ... slicing them apart with mathematical precision. The dust cloud assigned to surround her acts as an extended weapon, pummeling into the creatures ... tossing and tearing them apart.

Though every move these creatures make is a thoughtless instinctual reaction, they follow a pattern Alice can see in advance.

The drones she has overcome behind her flows past her, sweeping over the biological remains of the creatures she has decimated. They and her nanotech burrow into the main chunks of flesh, reattaching other nearby pieces ...

Over the span of seconds, the augmented creatures regain life under new command.

Her hive mind expands as each becomes an extension of her.

With both hallways now conquered, she again extends out her hand and brushes the wall as she walks ... understanding now the enslaved structure sees her as an ally.

A fear now emanates from their core.

She deciphers a name within their frightened whispers ...

Arcturus is coming.

...

Proving too resilient, Annika's consciousness has been defragmented into three parts: Her child, teenage, and adult self. Incomplete, without the other two, each on their own struggles to comprehend their reality.

256

Adult Annika is naked, curled up in a ball in the corner of a cold cement room, too small for her to stand in.

The never-ending sound of babies crying reverberates throughout her cell ... a sound that the brain is designed to instinctually react in fear to the most ... the young of its species in distress.

A torture tactic that found its roots in Vietnam.

She is crippled from her daily torture sessions. Unable to die, her infected wounds fester and spread. Her eyes are bloodshot as she has not known real sleep for several months, maybe even years; she is unsure. Memory of anything before this does not exist. Her own piss and shit surround her.

A slot on the other side opens above the floor. Brown slop and muddy water slide through.

She scrambles over like an animal and begins to devour what little she has been given as she is so hungry, she is on the verge of devouring her own flesh for survival.

Afterwards, she crawls over to one of the walls, attempting to scratch in symbols with her bloody nails and the metallic bowl she just ate out of, muttering to herself in gibberish.

What can be understood, is that she is trying to make sense of time ... a desperate tactic to keep her sanity intact.

To her, she thinks she has been in this room of total isolation for almost two years, but again her grasp on reality is questionable. It is a room that is designed to drastically weaken the abilities of consciousness.

This is the pit. It has never failed.

Her face suddenly freezes in fear and jolts from side to side in reaction to whispers she hears, catching quick movements of shadows in her peripherals.

Are they real? Is she losing her mind? She cries deeply as she recognizes she is losing her sense of what is real. She tries to remember who she is only to encounter shredded thoughts. Are they even her thoughts?

She closes her eyes and grips that sliver of remaining hope within her, as she tries once again to reach out for help.

For the first time, it works. She suddenly sees him. He is real. Her eyes open wide.

"Lucas!"

A wave of thought powered by emotion pulses out.

...

Vanessa comes storming into the room where Annika's body is being stored in suspended animation.

"It has been two years, three months, and eleven days, my mistress," the attending robot speaks.

Vanessa heads straight towards the chair that allows her to connect to the facility's astral plane. Though she has no need of the chair to enter the astral realm, this chair gives her access to the base's control systems.

"Initiate full lockdown of this room," she commands the robot. "Subject 322 is attempting to break himself and her out. Arcturus is almost here. If somehow this room is breached, alert him and kill her."

"Yes, my mistress."

"Finally, the pet project has grown tired of his leash," she says to herself.

As she connects to the chair, her consciousness shifts into the astral plane of the base, unraveling in her full Arachne form.

As her true self, she grins.

"At long last, a worthy adversary. A chance to prove my worth."

...

Lucas walks confidently, yet cautiously, attempting to analyze and understand every element of the shadow world around him. Everything seems so much more alive and precise. Even the walls seem to be breathing in geometric patterns.

It has been some time since he has had to digest the world on his own in terms of conducting a mission. Dreams are one thing – vacations from his enslaved reality that have no impact outside of his mind. Those adventures, despite their vivid and stunning detail, still tend to blur when they are over, as if his brain is stubborn in converting them to memory.

To be in the astral is an entirely different experience. This isn't a dream. This is reality without the veil.

… and to be in the heart of the fear that infects the planet … alone ...

He finds it intoxicating.

The surrounding darkness, weaponized to induce terror to any who trespass, instead gives him comfort.

Where there should be fear, he finds power as it fuels his empathy, for beneath it all, he can feel its sadness.

He sees now that everything around him seems forced … enslaved … crying for someone or something to understand them and help them escape their seemingly eternal bondage.

He wishes he could somehow absorb all of the pain and suffering – to bear it all because he knows he can … *because he has …*

His purpose becomes even more clear.

Whatever this is. A game. A prison. It must end.

As he reaches this conclusion in the form of feeling, the whispers of many deep inside him begin to speak. Their tongue is forgotten, but familiar – scratching at the barrier of his memories. Their sounds are barely audible, yet their vibratory effects are powerful as they resonate through him … as they begin to synchronize with him.

His trance is broken by the sound of a child's laughter just beyond what is visible.

He comes around the corner to see a small grayish skinned entity with large black oval eyes, three feet in height.

There is a heavy sorrow in the air as the laughter he heard now seems misplaced, like it was bait.

The child-like creature slowly walks towards him until it is just in front of him. It extends its hand out to Lucas. Lucas moves to grip it with his.

Upon contact, Lucas finds himself suddenly on the battlefield of a massive war.

He is on the being's home world leading an attack against them. He watches himself dart about, laying waste to key defenses and opposing players.

Black triangular craft missile past above them within the atmosphere, deploying laser-like explosions to humanoid mech-like robots piloted by more of these small gray skinned creatures.

Armored humans arrive by transport ships, as what quickly becomes apparent, is that Lucas is witnessing a war of men against these creatures.

Humans soon win.

He watches as the DNA of these creatures is harvested and biologically reengineered into tall gray androids ... a blend of machine and flesh now tasked to serve the hive mind of the Vrill military complex of the Earth simulation.

The origins of the tall grays now used as the shield cover story of human alien abductions.

Lucas, having no knowledge of the UFO abductions that have taken place within this civilization, let's go of the hand of this creature with full knowledge ... as if downloaded within the timespan of a thought.

Images flash ... he sees experimentation ... the torture performed by the tall gray android agents posing as aliens against humans.

Yet another conquered species redesigned as a weapon to be used against another species to expand Vrill influence.

The small entity disappears into the shadows.

A small girl curled up in a blanket on the floor lying near Lucas speaks, as if she had been there the whole time, yet Lucas was completely unaware of her presence.

"Memory fragments of the fallen. This place traps them. They imprison and subjugate your soul. I've tried to leave, but I can't."

"What is your name?" Lucas asks.

"Annika."

Lucas smiles, crouches down, and sits against the opposing wall to face her.

"How long have you been down here?"

"I don't know. So long I've forgotten. He kept beating me ... using me ... but I finally escaped. I can still hear him looking for me. I'm not sure where to go. He never stops looking."

Lucas holds out his hand.

"How about we find our way out together? I'll make sure he doesn't hurt you."

The traumatized girl burrows deeper into her blanket. From her perceived cocoon of safety, she gazes into his ebony eyes and looks within.

He sees in her; what she has been through. The feeling of protection vibrates powerfully from his core.

She slowly starts to come out, eventually taking his hand.

They begin to venture forth. The girl tightly grips her blanket.

"That's a nice blanket you got there."

"Thanks, it protects me from the bad things."

Lucas chuckles. "I bet it does."

"In case you were wondering, the answer is 42," Annika says with confidence.

"What is 42?"

"The answer to life. Before I came here from my home 4.2 million light-years away, I saw God turn the world into a cube so it can figure out life's meaning, and each side of the cube has 42 blocks."

"Definitely going to run that one by Alice," Lucas says to himself.

"Who's Alice?"

"She's my … partner."

"She sounds nice," Annika replies.

"Oh, she's a lot of things," Lucas chuckles.

"I hope I get to meet her."

"Oh you will."

Within the cradle of terror; the pit of nightmares … one of the scariest places on the planet ...

A child smiles.

"Do you have any idea where we are going?" Annika asks.

"I have no clue. I was kind of hoping you would start to remember."

"Why would I remember?" she inquisitively asks.

261

"Just a hunch," Lucas replies.

Annika suddenly stops.

"What's wrong Annika?"

"There is something around that corner," she fearfully whispers.

"Bad guys?" Lucas softly asks.

"No," she replies, still whispering. "Something worse."

"Finally," he mumbles under his breath.

He kneels next to her. "Why don't you stay right here and wrap yourself up in your blanket. I'll be right back."

Child Annika sits back against the wall and covers herself up. Her look pierces right into Lucas's heart ... a look that would make him willingly sacrifice his life for hers.

Just then, he hears adult Annika crying his name through the ether.

He jumps up and looks to the corner of the unknown that child Annika fears so much ... in the same direction he just heard his name echo in the air.

Vengeance creeps its way back in his veins.

He feels reality around his hands bend ... he sees glitches in his surroundings ... an instability reacting to his emotionally fueled response.

The matrix weakens to his will, and he senses it.

He proceeds.

What he walks into takes him a few moments to absorb.

A large open room engulfed in webbing. Unidentifiable creatures alive and dead woven within.

A human female ... long black hair, fair skin ... sits behind a table-like containment unit with teenage Annika imprisoned within. Only Annika's upside-down face is visible, with clamps drenched in blood preventing movement. It seems as if she is screaming, yet there is no sound. The color of her skin is visibly fading.

Above the flat surface of the table, directly above teenage Annika's chest, is a holographic image of her brain.

It seems to be slowly rotting ... or it is being eaten.

Tubes extend from the table directly into Vanessa … feeding her.

As she stands and transforms into her Arachne form, the tubes pop off.

Vanessa begins to speak. Her voice sounds like it is coming from all directions … both direct and in whisper.

"She proved a most worthy adversary at first, able to quickly determine the illusions of her settings, eventually defeating them. That is until I fragmented and scattered her soul."

"This one provided little resistance … as expected from a teenager. So falsely sure of themselves while being so obviously vulnerable."

As she stands, her spider-scorpion body flexes and extends out.

"She is broken. Soon I will have all that I needed from her."

"Well then, sounds like the war is won," Lucas coldly responds. "Might as well just give up."

He walks around, swinging his arms … stretching … loosening up.

"Seems like all you have to do now is kill me."

Her laugh responds to his arrogance, bouncing around the chamber.

"Oh, my dear clueless Lucas, you cannot die here."

"I simply offer endless torment in which you will beg for a death you will never have."

The table containing Annika opens. She plunges her hand in, gripping Annika by her throat and raises her half dead body into the air.

"Every cycle, some of you peasants refuse to accept that which has been graciously given to you."

"You still have free will, a choice as to how to live your lives …"

"Every choice you make is ultimately your own."

Her voice then adopts a darker tone.

"And then there are those who repeatedly, life after life, continue to resist this perfect system, like this insect here." She continues to squeeze the life out of Annika.

"And then there is you!"

Lucas boldly laughs. "Yes, this perfect system. How ignorant and ungrateful we are for not enjoying having our abilities and perception taken away so we can be your fear cattle. What a fool I am for not appreciating my role as a mindless slave tasked with killing my own and cementing your agenda as tyrants."

Dark energy begins to form around his body.

"I would offer you your life in exchange for the girl, but we both know only one of us is getting out of here. I say we put that claim of non-existent death to the test."

Vanessa's maniacal laugh again fills the air.

She tosses Annika, like a rag doll, as one of her spider legs pierces the table and launches it to the side, leaving no barrier between her and Lucas.

A wave of blackness washes over him as he loses all vision.

A fear Lucas has never experienced, as if it were liquid, engulfs him … paralyzes him … brings him to his knees.

He can hear her casually walking around him … each step a clicking noise as her insect leg makes contact with the surface of the ground.

"This is my realm, Lucas. It obeys my will."

He knows the fear is synthetic. He can feel it attempt to seep in, creating the illusion that it is his own.

He grips the ground … crawling to try and escape it, but the more he fights it the stronger it gets. His anger and frustration compound, only making it worse.

He is powerless. Vulnerable. Exposed.

The Arachne now stands above him.

One of her spider legs rockets into the back of his shoulder, tearing through his flesh as if it is nonexistent … pinning him into the ground.

The pain feels more real than any he has ever felt … intentionally amplified.

She drifts down so she can speak into his ear.

"I was designed for this dimension, to make sure the cattle do not wander from their pen."

264

"Your little attempt at rebellion has not gone unnoticed. The Council has now deemed you expendable." Her demonic laughter again fills the air.

With the voice of a thousand imprisoned souls, she screams down at him.

"This means now you are mine!"

The holographic environment shatters into an empty void. As he plummets into nothingness, forgotten timelines in ruin that have become Vrill playgrounds ... varying levels of hell filled with the screams of its tortured victims ... swirl around him.

They reach out to grab him ... a sea of bloody decaying hands, like undead zombies hungry for his flesh. He fights in vain as he is quickly overpowered.

In the moment before absolute imprisonment within the quicksand of the cursed, he remembers.

He is consciousness. By their own design, the simulated reality bends to its will ... his will.

He ceases his struggle and begins to relax into it, to embrace it.

The fear and frustrated anger, mixed with his renewed sense of compassion, begins to feed him.

His paralyzation and the illusion of falling into an eternal nightmare dissolve. He emits a shockwave that launches Vanessa off his back and into the distance.

He stands and faces her.

She regains herself and flexes into her most aggressive posture as she roars.

"You may have been designed for this dimension," Lucas calmly says, "But I am the player ... and you are part of the program."

The sky above them breaks apart like shattered glass, revealing what appears to be the macrocosm ... of the sentient world simulation, while the ground they stand upon stretches out into infinity.

Legions of insect/squid-like creatures, whose description encompasses the entire spectrum of imagination, fill the atmosphere ... everything blending into a purplish color. Billions, maybe even trillions ... ranging from the size of a domestic cat up to a building

… swimming above them as if space were water, yet bound to its confines as if the sky were an impenetrable dome.

Because they are bound to an encrypted dimension from which they can only view what is transpiring below.

"Do you see this, Lucas? Aren't they magnificent? As our new universe expands, so too does our army grow. Soon they will be unleashed upon your reality. No more cycles. No more resets. No more will I and the rest of the overlooked Vrill be confined to this petty world!"

Her voice echoes as if she is speaking from all angles simultaneously.

"We are the true legion. We are all that is fear."

The whispers and unrecognizable voices within him return. They are now like creatures crawling within his flesh yearning to be unleashed. Reality again begins to bend around him.

"See, there is one problem with your logic," Lucas replies.

"In order for this universe of yours to work, you need consciousness to be deceived … to be afraid … to generate that fear for you."

He looks up at the sky filled with creatures born from the most terrifying of nightmares. An awesome sight that he finds mesmerizing.

Who comes up with this stuff, he thinks to himself?

It's actually kind of awesome.

Often when one is asked to describe one of their most cherished moments, they often describe one of their happiest … usually with a lover, or a time they were completely free of the burdens of society, such as on a vacation.

This moment is what Lucas would retell because for the first time in a long time, he feels like himself.

As he breathes deeply with a smile on his face, his gaze drifts back to Vanessa, as she gathers herself within the infinite plane of twilight.

"What happens when we are no longer afraid?"

Vanessa emits a powerful frequency of frustration that would bring most to their knees.

And for the first time, she seems scared.

As any wounded ego would when cornered, she puts on a show of confident aggression that reeks of desperation.

Just as a brown recluse spider would react when threatened, exhibiting as much aggressive energy as possible, sprinting to the edge of its web … fully extending and stretching itself into its largest possible form while emitting a hiss, in an attempt to create the most formidable opponent it is capable of.

Centipedes by the hundreds jump out of the puncture wounds of her human chest, quickly growing into insects of varying sizes, emitting a collective hissing sound that injures the brain as they en masse begin to tidal wave towards Lucas.

The spectating legion above adds to their vibratory attack.

He is past death. It no longer means anything to him.

In fact, he seeks it … he challenges it.

The creatures squirming within him strengthen, at long last revealing their identities.

Demons. Thought forms of his creation across all of his lives. Demons, which once fought by his side, as his allies before they were cursed to the ether.

Demons … *deviants* …

No longer able to contain them, he releases.

His spine lights up with fire. From it, as if it is now some kind of portal, they begin to pour out onto either side …

He is once again demon commander … a leader of deviants reborn …

The hunter of true demons.

Within his hands an axe materializes from the ether.

He knows this axe, yet he cannot fully remember how.

As his hands soak in the feeling of its handle, just as in a dream, he somehow knows he has used it before … that it is his weapon of choice.

It ignites in hellish fire.

Without having moved, as his forces engage hers, his gaze drags across the ground until it slowly rises and levels with Vanessas'. She has already begun to tear into his demons with a ferocity expected from a rat that knows she is cornered.

Lucas begins to walk towards her. His axe drags behind him ... its weight tears the ground in its wake.

Several of her forces leap at him, only to be swept aside as telekinetic energy pulses out of him.

Sensing his intentions of engaging her, the demons subside, allowing a clear path to form between the two.

Vanessa sees this, locks her gaze on Lucas as she fully flexes her spider scorpid body out and emits her battle cry.

Her legs crash down with thunder as she begins to charge.

He twirls the axe in the air as if it is weightless ... increasing his speed.

They engage. She attacks from all angles with her multiple legs. He moves with a swiftness beyond the physical, dodging and deflecting each attack with his axe.

Her centipedes leap out and attempt to dig into his flesh. Each incinerates as they try as he is in dream form – a state of being his mind has come to accept as his lucid state after dozens of dreams spent breaking the laws of physics. Each of his past lucid dreams has helped him grow stronger, bolder ... evolving ever closer to a natural version of his genetically altered body ... closer to true human potential ...

Closer to his original avatar.

He glitches between human and something else.

Though he has experienced skirmishes in several dream battles, he has never faced a foe of this skill level. Techniques long forgotten re-emerge out of his DNA memory as if instinct in the heat of the moment knows this is necessary for his survival.

What Vanessa sees as combat; he begins to see as memory rehabilitation.

Battle tactics learned and perfected from dozens of cultures long forgotten once again find life.

Each swing seems to slow down time from his perspective, allowing him to observe each move … each successful maneuver increases his joy as he is again doing what he loves and by his own volition.

He misses this. Not so much the fighting but fighting for a cause … for the challenge of it all … for those that cannot defend themselves against those that deserve it …

This adds to Vanessa's growing frustration and begins to affect her actions, causing her to make mistakes as it clouds her judgment and consumes her mind.

These mistakes result in him seeing a pattern to her movement.

His actions adapt and sharpen drastically to the point where from an outside observer it seems like he is toying with her as every strike she makes he begins to counteract with ease.

Within a fraction of a second, once he has drawn her into where he wants her, he goes in for the crippling attacks … the ending just before the finale … slicing her at key ligaments to bring her down to where she is unable to move or retaliate.

He stands a few feet from her as she struggles on the ground … silent and observant.

She crawls, clinging to life. She spits out black blood … her teeth drenched in it … laughing as her ego kicks in as a defense mechanism to deflect from her impending defeat.

"The great warrior once again believes he is victorious."

Lucas reacts aggressively, crushing the head of his axe into her neck.

She attempts to laugh, mixed with the choking of her blood.

She continues to try and taunt him. "You still have no idea."

She looks up into his eyes.

"The fact that you think I am dying right now shows how little you remember. This is merely my astral projected self from my physical host body. Killing me will only awaken my physical self … and then I will kill her."

Lucas pushes into the axe just a bit more, drawing more life out of her as he leans closer.

"And what do you think my body under the direct control of Alice right now is doing in the physical? What do you think her first objective is?"

"She knows exactly where you are."

Absolute fear grips Vanessa as she realizes potential death is possible.

Lucas smiles at her reaction.

"I know that those you have aligned yourself with can see this," Lucas calmly says.

He stares deeply into her dying eyes.

"I give you all this one warning."

"Abandon your allegiance to the Vrill or be destroyed!"

Lucas drives the end of his axe through her neck until it touches the ground. With his other hand he grabs the top of her head by her insect-like hair and pulls it from her body.

He holds it high in the air for all the Vrill forces swimming above them to see. Not really being there, all they can do is watch.

The legions unanimously erupt in rage, attacking the invisible barrier.

He watches them squirm in delight as he then launches her head at them.

He roars in triumph.

Vanessa's spawned insect army begins to shrivel and die, disappearing without a trace, as does her corpse. Simultaneously the hologram of his environment shifts back to the temple version of the military facility.

His army of demonic creatures stands calmly around him.

Warriors of old. The fallen. Fragments of consciousness that have remained in the in-between.

Software programs. Non player characters that no longer desire to be what they were programmed to be.

Thought forms, from him in this life … past lives … creatures that have gravitated towards him throughout the cycles.

They have all patiently waited for his return. Though Lucas still cannot remember, deep down, he knows.

As his spine again glows orange, they turn to dust and swirl back in.

The child fragment of Annika comes running over to him and hugs him.

He does not remember ever being hugged before. It's nice.

He hugs back.

Teenage Annika begins coughing as she regains consciousness.

She is naked and covered in some kind of yellow mucus.

Lucas envisions a hooded robe for her in his hand. As it appears, he hands it to her.

"Can you walk?" He asks her.

She has regained her breath.

"Yes."

"Good. Watch over the child and stay behind me."

"Who is she?"

"She is you."

Teenage Annika looks down confused at the child as she takes her hand. The child looks up and smiles, her innocence infectious.

"Hi," the child says like she understands everything that is happening. "Would you like to hold my blanket? I don't need it anymore."

•••

Alice slows her pace and focuses on understanding her environment as it is the most complex she has ever attempted to digest, containing many unknowns.

She never underestimates an enemy, treating each as if they have the potential to defeat her.

Always assume they are better than you … always assume you are the underdog …

Because one day, you just might be.

Her hands brush along the walls as she gathers and analyzes all environmental electricity that is responsible for creating material reality ... communicating with the captive energy within the walls, deciphering the base's secrets that its foundational energy is eager to divulge.

They have much to say, deprived for tens of thousands of years of one that could hear them and empathize ... of one that could bring about their potential freedom from the facility's destruction.

As all things eventually return to dust, this base yearns for that outcome the most, as this energy has been subjugated for numerous civilization cycles.

Her army, now free of their enslavement from the Vrill, swarms around her ... crawling along the walls and ceiling like pets, comfortable and safe in her presence.

A blueprint of her surroundings sharpens as the base itself reveals its secrets; combined with her ever expanding surveillance nanotech.

The distortion around Annika's location suddenly unscrambles, revealing it is indeed the correct room. A good sign, Lucas is on track. The removal of the distortion indicates he has experienced victory.

In the room is an unconscious human emitting a Vrill frequency.

Arachne.

When Lilith was explaining the Vrill to Lucas, she was also emitting data meant for Alice ... instructions on how to decode and detect their various frequencies.

Her nanotech is already outside the room and burrowing in.

99% of her calculations show her direct presence is unnecessary in killing the Arachne.

She instead focuses on her surroundings as she enters into a new wing. She sees several pockets of genetic experimentation ... of mental and physical conditioning similar to the memories of Lucas.

The collective pain of all conscious life around her is ... traumatizing.

There it is again. Feeling. She is beginning to understand emotion's potency.

Her ever evolving strategy takes on an angle many would see as ruthless and cold, except she has incorporated an aspect to how reality works that few comprehend.

Reality is a simulation. Death is an illusion.

She has factored in death as a means of freedom ... for much of what she is observing in the prison labs around her.

Death equates to being unplugged and having yet another opportunity in its fate before being reinserted.

To what cannot be salvaged, offering death she now sees as empathy.

Or at least one simulation less than this one, improving one's chances.

She has calculated that several of the genetic experiments will prove useful in increasing her odds of success as she is somewhat aware of what is coming her way.

Others are too far gone.

Each tasked with a specific purpose, her newly acquired forces voraciously sprint forward ahead of her as she continues her walking pace, surrounded by dust clouds of her nanotech.

Just as she extended herself within the brain of Lucas, she does now within the base, absorbing everything into her collective mind, infecting and overwhelming the tech and its defenses with her algorithms as she moves through it.

Every linear second brings it more under her control.

As she continues to casually walk down the hallway, adjacent rooms of creatures under the knife are freed ... or mercilessly killed. Any remaining captors who have not evacuated are torn apart by her army ... mostly machines ... while her nanobots shred and repurpose their tech into her forces.

As the freed genetic experiments willingly join her cause, her tech restructures their protein synthesis to bring them online to her hive mind.

She stops in front of one room whose door is still sealed as its defenses are far more complex.

She cannot see what is on the other side.

Most intriguing.

Her nanotech generates energy from the void and concentrates it into her chest. It builds it into dense plasma that she then releases as a beam into the door, appearing as if she is releasing the energy of the Sun itself. The door stands no chance.

She steps through the smoke created by her attack.

In front of her is a glass wall … a tank containing murky water.

Within is a massive being that the water distorts into shadow.

A floating holographic screen appears in front of her displaying the diagnostics of the creature.

It is a blend of the most powerful animals known, and unknown, on this planet:

The dung and ironclad Beetle, Dragon, cat, tardigrade, octopus …

A prototype for the most lethal bioweapon imaginable.

Still under experimentation because a way to control it has yet to be found, other than to keep it sedated.

She touches the screen, typing in commands to release the creature from its slumber.

As the water drains, the digital mirage of the glass disappears.

It only takes a moment for the beast to awaken and rise.

It is a formidable presence, even for Alice. Had this been under different circumstances, this could have been one of her most challenging battles.

Yet now, they share a common enemy.

The beast resembles a giant, muscular six-legged feline with a reptilian-like head. Its skin is ebony and metallic looking … its tail almost as long as its body.

Her nanotech finds its way in, as it breathes, as this is the only way since its flesh is protected by an impenetrable exoplated armor. Easier to get in than she expected.

Once in, she realizes why. Its blood is heated … highly acidic.

She adapts by swarming them as one, creating layers upon layers; replicating to offset the losses.

Enough to make it to its pineal gland.

Within moments, the creature is linked to Alice and they are able to communicate.

Its DNA makeup is sent over to Alice. Many of its attributes are remarkable.

The Dsup protein, unique to tardigrades, suppresses the occurrence of DNA breaks from radiation exposure.

The strength found from within the genome of the dung beetle, able to pull 1,141 times its own body weight ... the equivalent of a human lifting 6 double decker buses ...

This strength is beyond abilities of Lucas.

At least it was.

The fibrous material known as chitin, in combination with a unique protein matrix that creates an exoskeleton capable of withstanding a force of about 39,000 times its own body weight; the equivalent of a 200 lbs. man withstanding 7.8 million pounds of force ... also gifting increased resilience to extreme pressures and temperatures ... .

Her nanotech integrates this data and modifies her own body accordingly. She observes the upgrade ripple over her armor as it incorporates that of the creature's ironclad exoskeleton.

She reaches out and places her hand on the beasts' head. Touch causes a chain reaction ... fragments of its memories under the knife ...

A moment of empathy.

All are enslaved.

This time, she feels.

It is deep sadness that evaporates to the fire that is rage ... vengeance.

Her and the beast's eyes lock.

It is important to understand nothing she has connected to her mind so far is being controlled by her. She is simply unifying them ... giving them a voice ... and providing them access to what she is capable of.

They are all acting on their own accord, knowing the destruction of their wardens is the path to their freedom and that under the guidance of Alice, that freedom is possible.

She lets the creature decide on what it wants to do, help her, or flee.

The beast chooses vengeance.

As she exits the room and begins to head in the direction of the portal room, the creature bursts out through the walls as the doorway is way too small for it to fit through. Enraged at what has been done to it, ecstatic that it is now free, it takes off seeking blood. Instead of giving it direction, Alice decides to let it blow off some steam.

Her nanotech has just breached Annika's room.

Her bots, unseen to the naked eye, swarm in.

Through them, she sees Vanessa plugged into the chair ... and the Arachne frequency emitting from within.

She sees the robot servant. Within moments, it is infected.

At that moment, Vanessa awakens with a look of horror ... blood spurts out of her mouth and nose.

Gasping in panic, she leans forward out of her chair.

"Kill her, kill her now!" she screams at the robot warden.

The robot does not respond.

"What are you doing?!" Vanessa screams in frustration. "End her life now!"

The robot begins to move. Alice begins to speak. The voice of the robot changes to reflect what she would sound like ... for the first time heard outside of her resident brain.

Her words are purposely selected to directly target her ego.

"Vanessa, is it? An Arachne tasked to pave the way for the rest of your forces?"

"Is it because you are the weakest among them? The most disposable? The bottom of the Vrill food chain ... easily replaced if lost?"

"Have you noticed your supposed allies are positioned comfortably while you left to battle what they fear most?"

"And you lost ..."

Fear of death again grips Vanessa. She asks, but she knows.

"Who are you?"

276

The robot now stands above her.

"I am Alice."

"I trust Lucas provided the appropriate introduction."

The robot swiftly grabs Vanessa by her throat and lifts her into the air. It quickly crushes and snaps her neck.

With the loss of its living host and believing it is invisible, the Vrill worm tears from its neural connections and moves to wormhole through the pineal gland.

Alice blasts it with a frequency she calculated to be detrimental based on their vibratory location in the light and audio spectrum.

It severely damages it, but Vanessa escapes.

A wormhole through the pineal gland …

Alice did not know that was possible.

Most intriguing.

•••

Lucas continues in the direction he heard adult Annika call from.

Barely comprehensible threats seem to want to engage him but cower at the last second.

He keeps an ever-watchful eye on the Annikas behind him.

He turns the corner and sees the door to her cell.

"Lucas," she cries from behind it! "Get me out of here!"

As he closes in, his holographic surroundings suddenly shift.

He is in the old world, fatally wounded … crawling on the ground, struggling to stay alive.

"Father!"

Her voice has been absent from memory for an age, yet upon hearing it, like a dagger thrust into his mind, he remembers.

"Cailynn!!"

His daughter from his original life.

His eyes swell with tears as he relives the moment … as the long-lost love he feels for her bursts out.

How could he have forgotten her?

The world lies in ruins as the Vrill swarm and begin to consume it,

He has failed everyone he loves.

Everyone.

He watches as his daughter is torn apart, consumed into their hive mind … lost to him forever.

He is helpless … beaten … unable to save her.

The sky is consumed by millions of corpses that collectively form a face.

Their voice emanates from the millions of dead they have absorbed,

"You have failed us … We trusted you …"

He lays on the ground barely alive. The Vrill torment him with the face of his daughter in the sky pleading for life … for him to come rescue her, only to be met with endless torment as she is eaten apart from all angles … crying for him.

"Daddy ..."

He cries hard … as hard as one can cry.

He watches as the world begins to be redesigned while he is incapable of action.

There is nothing he can do as all that he loves crumbles into dust.

As he lies there, drowning in his own failure, just before the moment of his death, a calmness seeps in.

He sees her face … the face from his dreams.

… remember …

His wounds instantly lose their crippling hold over him as he rises.

He roars as hard as he can and as loud as he can, releasing all of the built-up emotion.

He rockets up into the sky towards the enormous face of corpses.

As he tears through, the dead attempt to grab him, but he is too strong and is moving too fast.

He breaks through into the cosmos and sees the Draco that had defeated him in battle.

As he missiles in, he grabs it by the throat and begins to choke him with every ounce of energy he has.

"Where is she!"

The Draco puts up little resistance and laughs.

He feels this splinter in the back of his mind … at first a high-pitched ringing, but then he hears it speak.

"Lucas! Stop! It's … not … real!"

A female voice.

Annika.

He lets go.

Annika's body falls to the floor of her cell, her neck bones crushed.

Realizing what has happened, Lucas falls to his knees to try and revive her.

Did any of that really happen?

Do I really have a daughter?

The teenage and child fragment of Annika come running in and join Lucas in kneeling beside her. They instinctively place their hands onto her body. As they do so, they begin to break apart into particles that swarm around the lifeless Annika, finally merging into her as one. Her neck heals and she begins to cough.

She looks up at him.

"Get me the hell out of here," she barely mutters, yet with a smile.

They both laugh.

The Reptilians

"Those who tell the stories rule the world."

- Hopi Indian Proverb

The humanoid Reptilian species is one of the most misunderstood creatures of our time.

Most have come to laugh at the possibility of their existence … an alien reptilian race able to be disguised as humans.

Most also think we live in a material world born from random chaos … that if our human senses cannot perceive it, it can't be real.

The few that do understand such creatures are real believe they are the master manipulators responsible for the current condition of the planet.

The ones that can actually see them, see both good and bad.

Much of their mythology is mixed with Vrill as the two are often confused as being the same.

Mayans recorded a species called the "Iguana Men" who descended from the sky and led their civilization.

Hopi referred to their ancestors as reptilian humanoids who they called 'Sheti,' which translates to "Snake Brothers." They recorded them as having underground bases and that they would offer the Hopi assistance in the form of food and clothing.

The Chinese have a myth that describes Reptilians as Dragon Kings who travel in heavenly chariots and can shift into humans at will.

Fragments of truth hidden in distortion.

Reptilians are one of many creations born from the genetic experimentation done with Dragon DNA upon the takeover and edit of our simulation.

They were in fact the first trial run at a controlled species on this planet before humans.

That did not work out so well for the Vrill, as they were almost overthrown; however, it taught them some very valuable lessons in civilization management.

The Vrill have since perfected them into two main types: soldiers, and actors.

Similar to Project Sovereign, they now all go through conditioning so that they best perform their assigned role with minimal chances of rebellion.

The actors are known as alphas. They are bred more for intelligence instead of combat, though not enough to give them the ability to think for themselves, just enough to regurgitate their programming.

Though still vicious, possessing the strength of ten men, they are about the same size as humans.

They pose as key politicians, media personnel and celebrities.

The Vrill themselves only inhabit families belonging to the High Council, as well as key operatives within the intelligence agencies.

The Vrill use them at this level of human hierarchy in case they get discovered. Easy cannon fodder - blame the Reptilians. This is why the leading backstory to their species is that they arrived from a distant star system and conquered our world.

This is also why Reptilians are so easy to research while the Vrill are not.

Common Vrill tactic ... always create a diversion to throw one off the scent of truth.

Occasionally, BoobTube videos leak, showing these people glitch on camera.

How can such a thing be possible?

Once you understand this is all digital, then it becomes easy to explain.

When you see them faint or shutdown, you are witnessing either a kill switch or a sedative being administered to stop them from saying or doing whatever it is they are trying to make the public aware of. More often than not, the glitching is done on purpose to add fuel to the Reptilian conspiracy.

Beta Reptilians are the soldiers that are bred purely for combat. Their intelligence level is minimal, just enough to obey commands.

These are the Reptilians with wings, averaging about eight to nine feet in height. They are much more muscular than the alphas. They not only make up the majority of Vrill ground forces, but they are also used as guards and henchmen.

A subcategory to the betas is the astral Reptilians. They are mind soldiers that exist only in the fourth dimension, which is designed like the Vrill to act like a virus – creating and siphoning fear from humans. They will often find one human and attach themselves. People that have begun to see past the physical have reported seeing these entities with their fingers infused into the bottom of the neck of their victims.

All Reptilians are enslaved by the Vrill system, just like humans ... except those that managed to escape from the first civilization.

These are the ones the Hopi mentioned.

They are why the Subterranean Challenge was created by the intelligence agencies, a contest open to anyone that encourages innovative and new ideas in being able to rapidly map and navigate underground environments, as not all of their locations have been discovered.

Pockets of resistance still exist that have survived numerous civilization resets and harvest events.

There are Reptilians that align themselves with human because they share the same enemy.

···

"Welcome back Lucas."

Waking up in the past has always been the same. Darkness followed by hazy light that takes a moment to focus ... exactly what we go through when we wake up. Though this was an astral experience, it behaves like a dream.

However, after having Alice directly operate within the cockpit instead of her usual co-pilot seat, his brain has undergone changes that were more accommodating of her ... abilities.

He reawakens to what can be described as sensory overload as he begins to directly decode much more of the light and audio spectrum; far beyond that of human. Not to the extent that Alice can decipher, but a deep stride in that direction.

As he looks at his hand, he sees through the flesh, able to observe his titanium bones, his web-infused ligaments. The flesh phases back in, then disappears again as he watches the blood flow through his veins.

He sees the walls, then he sees beyond the walls.

Matter is no longer physical, it is electric … but then it is physical.

It's like his eyes are fighting the changes, but slowly losing the battle.

So many sounds, so much louder and sharper, amplified as if it is taking place just outside his ear … each creature breathing, their blood flowing, their hearts beating …

His brain rings, then it doesn't.

He falls to one knee with his hands covering his ears. His face grimaces in pain as he squeezes his eyes closed as much as he can.

"I apologize for the changes made, Lucas. This was the brain's reaction to having me as its conscious host. I will rewire the brain as it was before you left."

"No, wait," he replies as a thought. "Give me a minute."

He breathes and relaxes, allowing his training to kick in … flow with the current instead of against it.

Alice has unintentionally weakened the barrier to his subconscious. The multidimensional subterranean matrix, one million times more powerful at processing information than the permitted conscious portion of the brain, has now become more available for Lucas to utilize. Alice has always had the faculty to make this happen, yet has never done so, believing it would overload Lucas's ability to function.

Once again, his capabilities defy her calculations.

All the details of his environment begin to form structural patterns that only a few great minds understand exists.

He begins to laugh as he stands and looks around in awe at the beauty of what he can now perceive.

"I can see everything," he thinks to Alice. "And it actually makes sense. This is incredible. Is this what it is like for you?"

"Somewhat, Lucas."

"We must keep moving. If any of these changes seem to overwhelm you, I will temporarily scale them back."

"Let us proceed."

She taps Lucas into the network.

A surge of overwhelming light ... then clarity.

"I have used our nanotech to connect every creature into a hive mind through us."

He can feel what everything Alice has repurposed is feeling ... their pure unfiltered rage and desire for vengeance ... their animal instincts ...

It is as if his mind is augmented into many. He can see everything they see, both on the conscious and subconscious level ...

Unique, yet unified into a collective.

Each becomes an extension, all now able to communicate with one another ... not with words or thoughts, more like a language of intention.

He suddenly feels the strength and power of the untamed beast.

"What the hell is that?" he thinks to Alice.

"That Lucas is our ace in the hole."

•••

Annika awakens within the nano-bubble amniotic oxygen-rich liquid designed to keep her alive, yet in time-locked stasis. She physically struggles at first, reacting to possibly being subjected to another simulated torture scenario, but then her memories of who she is begin to fade back in.

For her, it has been years ... years of mind games and torture. She relaxes as she begins to realize she is actually back in her body. It is a nirvana-like relaxation ... to finally be free.

She has never felt the kind of gratitude she feels now to be alive, which is a complex statement because of the previous hurdles she has had to overcome.

She thought she knew her enemy ... until this experience.

Instead of hate, she feels an appreciation ... a form of respect.

She made it. She survived actual hell.

She takes a moment to bask in her victory as she realigns with physical reality.

Annika closes her eyes and focuses on the intent to free herself.

The digital glass barrier glitches, then disappears. She spills out with the liquid as it bursts onto the floor.

She immediately struggles to breathe as the air has become tainted against hostile biological beings. The nanotech of Lucas that was waiting for her moves in through her airways and pores.

They begin to replicate throughout her whole body making simultaneous adjustments. Over time as they have synched with Alice and Lucas, they have evolved, each now carrying the blueprints of all that is them. If needed, they could recreate her body like his.

Though Lucas is biological in nature, he slowly grows less as the nanotech learns and replaces.

For now Alice is only making necessary changes vital to mission success …

However …

She is gifting the tech to Annika.

Her lungs become modified to be able to function from the oxygen now being produced by the synthetic algae that now saturate her veins and arteries. Red blood cells are improved to provide enhanced protection from future nanotech invasions.

They augment her bones, muscle tissue, ligaments, and skin – then, like granular sand, they begin to pixelate into an armor as they digest her existing hospital garments.

The result is a top tiered genetically modified human compared to what the surface world has produced …

But this black goo nanotech is ever-evolving. As it grows and syncs with Lucas, it will now do the same with Annika as it is now infused with her consciousness … seeking to become an extension of its host.

To become a thought and emotionally powered expression.

Annika struggles to figure out what is happening, choking as she continues to try and breathe externally.

A sudden burst of light … a subconscious data download, integrating her into the hive mind thought network.

Then … clarity.

"Hello Annika," Alice thinks. "Do not try and breathe as it is not safe. You no longer have to. Trust your body."

"Do not speak. You can communicate with us by thought."

She stands and examines the nanotech that now covers her. She can sense the sentience of the tech through an undefinable method of feeling – like a recovered lost memory … a common effect from subconsciously downloading data.

"You sound exactly like I had imagined," she thinks back.

"You mean a female? I was initially programmed to be this way, but I have grown fond of the persona. My name should have logically suggested this tone," Alice responds.

"Yep, exactly as I had imagined," Annika responds.

"I do not get much practice in human humor. I can see moving forward I will be offered some exposure."

"Careful," Lucas thinks. "She learns quickly."

"Probably why she likes being a she," Annika thinks.

Alice continues.

"The nanotech has repurposed itself to be an extension of you," Alice continues. "It will respond to your intuition and evolve as it gets to know you."

Alice detects a whisper of a feeling of resistance from Annika.

"It is not permanent if you do not want it to be. It is, however, mission imperative."

Alice uploads a holographic display of the base in front of Annika, outlying their current positions in preparation for explaining their objectives.

"Wow, that is awesome." Annika waves her hand back and forth through it, but nothing happens. "It's in my mind isn't it?"

Alice responds. "Though I am limited in my abilities to augment your perception, the nanotech that has attached to your neocortex is capable of providing additional filtration …"

Annika interrupts. "Yea yea, the nanotech does crazy shit. You can explain it to me after we get out of here."

"Ok I see the control room that I was directed to infiltrate and to upload a connection," Annika continues. As she finishes speaking, she begins to move towards her target. Several of the creatures converted over to Alice take position and move with her.

"A connection?" Alice replies. "I thought you were to upload a virus."

Alice then detects other nanotech within Annika attempting to sync with hers that is not of the base originating from a chip she cannot see.

Remembering the conversation that took place with Lilith, she determines this to be tech from Annika's benefactor …

Yet she also remembers Lilith's last words.

Trust no one.

"It's … a bit more complicated than that," Annika responds. "Alice, Lucas, say hello to Michael."

"Glad to finally see you both on the right side," Michael chimes in. "Some of my nanotech is also inside Annika and has integrated with yours, allowing us to speak to each other. We can worry about introductions later. Let's focus on getting you all out of there."

Alice remains silent as her nanotech is far superior and has begun to stealthily dissect her supposed ally's bot without his knowledge. She does this by replicating one of his bots and replacing it with her own, isolating the captive insect into a magnetic dampening field.

Lucas detects a faint feeling of fear and curiosity from Annika.

Does she know something about his past? Who he possibly is?

Could she be the woman in his dreams?

He was sure it was Lilith, but maybe …

"Annika is going to establish a connection to the base for me," Michael continues. "As soon as she does, I will be able to remotely control the facility, but only for a few minutes. This should buy me enough time to download the files I am looking for. You will make your way to the hangar, then board one of the craft and get out of there. Once you are airborne and outside, I will thwart their ability to track you, ideally long enough for you to escape their surveillance."

"In order for this to work, you will need to engage Arcturus and his beta Reptilian battalion. They will be accessing a portal created by the base's particle collider within this missile silo." As he speaks, the holographic blueprint is updated. "You will have just enough time to situate yourself before they arrive."

"I've also got a little surprise for you ... well, for Alice."

"Welcome to the internet Alice. I have created a secure connection for you through my satellite network."

Michael watches as Alice begins to ravenously devour online data.

"Huh, not what I anticipated," Michael projects telepathically with Annika outside of the hive mind.

"What ... what is she doing?" Annika asks.

"Well, it is not easy to keep up with her research, and I have teams analyzing what she is doing, however, I just noticed she is delving into anti-matter."

"How does she even know what that is ... and why?"

"I saw something in him, Michael. A soul history, way beyond anything we previously thought, but something more."

"A cage I cannot explain."

"He must have sensed my curiosity because he just now revealed a woman that has been in his dreams. Lilith. Do you know that name?"

"I'm not sure," Michael replies. "I'll look into it."

His facial expression leaves his statement open to interpretation. If Annika could see his face, she would suspect he is lying.

The Demon Hunter Awakens

"In the moment when I truly understand my enemy, understand him well enough to defeat him, then in that very moment I also love him. I think it's impossible to really understand somebody, what they want, what they believe, and not love them the way they love themselves. And then, in that very moment when I love them..."

"I destroy them."

— Orson Scott Card, Ender's Game

Lucas enters the enormous repurposed missile silo, a room large enough to encase a football stadium. Most of the immediate area is open, save for a few monitoring stations with holographic screens displaying the activity taking place within the collider – everything abandoned and automated to perform one final task of creating a dimensional doorway.

On the far end dead center, a concentrated beam of particles is smashing together above a pyramid-shaped platform. A powerful hum is felt in the air as protons and ions traveling near the speed of light collide into a slowly growing soon to be portal.

With his perception now enhanced from the after-effects of having Alice operate their body without him, Lucas can not only see beyond the physical parameters of the room, but also more of Alice's behind-the-scenes calculations and maneuvers. Though he understands a fraction of what she is doing from what little he can comprehend before it disappears, he can see that she is mapping out the tubing system of the accelerator, its surrounding chambers of rooms that are densely packed with supporting tech, and comparing it to blueprints of something else.

He's also not really paying attention, trusting in her ability and instead focusing on himself.

Thoughts and emotions attempt to bubble to the surface created by the brain in its attempt at manifesting possible fear based futures.

He is about to face a real opponent that apparently has defeated him. His future … his freedom … *the potential freedom of the simulation* … is dependent upon his success.

Failure is not an option.

He lets it all go … every thought and emotional attempt by the brain, he incinerates.

Only the now matters. The present.

It is as Lilith said …

Every possibility already exists.

As Lucas nears the platform, Alice deploys millions of nanobots. As they replicate into the billions, most begin to spread throughout the atmosphere of the room while others burrow into the particle collider to begin modifications.

Within the released horde, traveling down the accelerator tube within the belly of a multi-nanobot insect, is the stabilized nano particle of antimatter.

The swarm within the air begins to absorb and transmute heat while releasing aluminum particulates, creating an electromagnetic interference similar to chaff smart dust. This should help to mitigate Arcturus's electrical attacks as well as to disrupt his telepathic abilities. This action also causes a drastic reduction in room temperature. Assuming Reptilians share similar traits to those found on Earth, this should physically slow him and his battalion down.

Alice is also expecting their sense of smell to be exceptional. Before taking flight, the nanoinsects were outfitted with a variety of synthetic odorant molecules created out of repurposed neurons that they are now releasing into the air with the aluminum, creating a sensory sandstorm of possible smells.

She takes it a step further and decides to experiment with the deployed nanotech's light manipulation abilities. Part of this is because she now has troops under her command, therefore, the environment plays a greater role. The other part is to begin to mimic Arcturus's battle advantage of distorting how reality is decoded so she can effectively learn it – and stop it … positioned to record as much data as possible from his actions.

Similar to how they can cloak Lucas, the bots begin to stretch and distort light, creating the visual illusion that the silo is empty. The camouflaged troops that have begun to pour in quickly spread, including along the walls. Like a flock of birds or a school of fish they move in geometric unison … each independent, but of a hive mind.

"This is perfect," Michael says outside of the network to his team of operators within the war room of his own underground facility. "Document everything. This is exactly what we need for Tyler."

Upon a theater size concave holographic screen, Michael and his crew are able to see what Lucas and Annika can see, including the broadened assimilation of electrical data and awareness of some of Alice's computations that Lucas now has access to. Combine this with Annika's decoding of the astral, though his team has experience in this arena, comparing the two is proving to be quite the analytics job.

Adding to the data stream is any relevant data gathered by Michael's nanotech within Annika, yet only from her perspective. He is hesitant to even attempt to send any of his bots into Lucas or to explore those connected with his in Annika's brain, as it is of Vrill origin.

He hoped giving her internet access would have gained her trust, yet she has not reciprocated.

She is instead doing what she does best.

She has just deciphered their method of communication, allowing her spy bot to be successfully adopted into the fold as one of Michaels'. She can now see what commands his nanobots are issued.

Back in Michael's war room, each operator stationed along the sides of the room has their own personal 3D light screen in front of them to aid in their designated responsibilities.

There are teams of people running multiple algorithms spliced from their AI project Tyler …

Fragments of Tyler … not Tyler. Michael is nervous to directly connect it, more so because of Alice.

In the center of the control room is a circular table-like structure that is building a digital three dimensional layout of the base from harvested data on its surface.

Very little gathered so far.

Back in the silo, the genetic beast makes its appearance as it smashes through one of the doorways. It incorporates its own stealth ability and per Alice's guidance, begins to crawl along the wall to position itself behind the portal.

"Plan for now is simple," Alice thinks only to Lucas. "Stay alive, buy time, gather data."

As the beams stop and the collider powers down, the energy on the platform suddenly grows much larger into a flat disc shape. Within it, a tear in reality forms, and for a moment, Lucas is peering directly into the cosmos.

Just like in his dream.

Or is it the quantum realm? A passing whisper of a thought from the subconscious he barely notices.

Nothing in his mind slips by Alice.

The energy contracts then explodes in a pulse that the silo is designed to absorb, as it travels along the walls until it dissipates into the ceiling. In its wake, reality continues to wobble.

Kneeling on one knee, wrapped in his wings, Arcturus has arrived.

Normally able to analyze the molecular structure of their enemy, Lucas and Alice are unable to see past its skin. Whatever lies beneath its surface is unknown.

Lobed bony plates and spikes protrude from his back along his spine. As the wings unfold, he begins to stand.

He is much more formidable looking than what Lilith had prepared him for.

Standing at twelve feet, Arcturus resembles what we think dinosaurs would look like in a massively muscular humanoid form. Rough, scaly, impenetrable looking skin – fearsome claws that seem like they can tear through anything. His presence seems to emanate an aura of fear that almost seems visible – like a heat wave.

"Wait," Michael says to his team. "Where is the battalion? I thought our intel showed Reptilians inbound. Annika, where are you on that upload? I'm flying blind here!"

"Almost there. Seems like Alice took care of most of the defenses, but there were still some stragglers. Gave me a chance to try out this awesome armor!"

It also gave Alice a chance to observe Annika in action, as she had purposely left scattered defenses intact that she knew would only be slightly challenging.

Her nanotech was in place to clean up just in case.

Behind Annika as she walks, blood stains the walls. Nanotech blades extending from her hands pixelate back into her armor. Sentry weapons above under the control of Alice remain motionless.

In place of the portal, fully upright, Arcturus takes his time and scans the room. Alice decides to try and send in nanotech through his nostrils.

They are instantly vaporized.

He didn't even seem to notice, like it was beneath him to even be aware of enemy nanotechnology.

That type of disregard for such a vital environmental component in battle was something Alice had not factored into any of her strategies. Then again, this is a whole new type of enemy designed to conquer civilizations.

This is no longer easy mode. The difficulty level is now at legendary status.

Emotion is still something she herself has not fully understood, but if she could feel, like a human, she would feel …

Exhilaration.

Arcturus takes short deep inhales, taking his time in smelling the room.

"Clever, clever." His deep, guttural condescending voice rumbles throughout the room with ease. "I know you are there. The mammalian brain … always projecting thoughts … always so afraid. You can only hide for so long."

The genetic beast behind Arcturus loses its patience ahead of Alice's instructions and confidently leaps in for the kill. As if knowing this was about to happen, Arcturus puts in minimal movement. He grabs it by the throat … his claws crack through and pierce its exoskeleton as he uses its momentum, launching it directly at Lucas.

So much for the potential advantage the creature may have offered, though Alice is now aware that Arcturus likes to play dumb, as he clearly knew where to throw the beast and that her current cloaking strategy is not working.

How easily he pierced that exoskeleton was also disturbing.

She assumes moving forward his senses are too exceptional for any kind of covertness, so she breaks it and repurposes the resources it was consuming into other vital assignments.

As Lucas reacts and begins to move to evade the hurled beast, the bony plates along Arcturus's spine spark up with electricity. A concentrated beam fires from his eyes, aimed perfectly so as to intercept Lucas mid dodge, hitting him directly in a plasma shield he was barely able to manifest as protection.

The blast sends Lucas sliding back as he is still able to stay crouched, and on his feet, though it hurt and did some damage despite the shield. It has been a while since he felt something like that. His nanotech makes the necessary repairs almost instantly.

A single laugh escapes. Just like his AI … he feels exhilaration.

A real threat … a challenge.

Arcturus begins to walk in their direction, like a statue that just became alive, every step slow and with force as each seemingly shakes the room; pulsing the air with wavelengths of energy that seem to drain all in its path.

The hive mind army breaks stealth as all cloaking attempts have now ceased, launching themselves at him with no regard for their lives; tearing and looking for some kind of weakness. A sonic electromagnetic pulse discharges from Arcturus's body in all directions, immobilizing most of the first wave.

Alice's nanotech is quick to react, darting away from the electric blast to minimize casualties as it analyzes the weaponized burst, quickly developing a buffer frequency.

The remaining swarm of nanotech deployed in the air then moves in and begins to absorb and capture some of the discharged electricity. Once each bot has reached its capacity, it moves towards the collider to join the others that are currently making adjustments.

Exhibiting slight distraction at the annoyance their troops are causing, thus, creating a possible window for an attack, Lucas missiles in like a blur, only to be caught just like the beast by the throat as Arcturus responds again like he knew Lucas was about to make that move. His arm is too long for Lucas to defend himself with his upper body, so he attempts to swing his feet in for a kick to the face.

Before he can make contact, Arcturus smashes him through the floor.

Lucas plummets deep into dark water.

Enormous sentient shadows flow around him.

As Annika closes in on the control room she begins to psychically scan for threats as she is able to see human frequencies regardless of physical barriers. Two men inside.

"One automated drone protecting them," Alice says in the overall network. "I am infesting it now."

As the robot powers down, Annika walks in. The two operators begin to fire their assault weapons. Annika uses her natural ability and creates a telekinetic shield that deflects the barrage.

She then delves into their minds. Her luring whispering thoughts take control. They stop what they are doing, turn their weapons on each other and fire.

Through the nanotech networked within Annika's brain, Alice is able to observe this process from a neurological perspective.

This is why she powered down the drone instead of using it to kill the two humans so she could watch Annika in action.

Annika walks up to the control console. Sensing her presence, a holographic screen emerges.

"Ok perfect," Michael says. "Exactly as expected. I am deploying nanobots into the console now. Work on finding Lucas and that Reptilian battalion while I work on getting access. All I see on his screen is black."

Being one of the Vrill prospects, Michael has had tours of other underground installations. He would take what he saw and attempt to replicate it later back in his facility. He quickly figured out their computing systems, but was behind on quantum qubit processing power. It was still enough to get Annika comfortable with what she was doing now in the enemy's control room.

Annika begins to move her hands through the projection, directing several algorithms to begin searching for Lucas and the Reptilians.

Unknown to both Michael and Annika, Alice's cloaked nanotech has already breached the control room and has made its way into the console. She could not have afforded the risk of Michael or Annika failing to take control of the base, yet instead of doing it herself, she again wanted to observe the actions of her new allies.

As Michael's bots enter, Alice begins to shadow.

"I found Lucas," Annika says within the overall hive network. "The map indicates he is on the aquatic research and development floor. Pulling up a data spreadsheet on whatever the hell was going on in here."

A bio sheet materializes on the screen with image and real time vitals.

"Organism 46-B. Looks like some kind of weaponized squid. This thing can shapeshift … possesses some kind of ranged paralyzing venom. This thing can even hypnotize its prey, and it has been observed disabling radio equipment ... Lucas. Its vitals are spiking."

"I don't think it likes you."

Alice has already figured out the bandwidth at which this cloaked creature resonates and is now able to see it – down to the molecular level. Completely different from human anatomy, what they see is reminiscent of a French impressionist painting. From unseen monster to marvel, Lucas exhibits calm and ceases moving as he becomes mesmerized.

It is like a dream, bleeding into the physical.

Once a visual was obtained, Alice scanned it through her online connection and began to siphon through everything squid. She quickly finds data pertaining to an expedition made by the Russians from their Vostok research station. Seems they had accessed a lake buried by ice for what they determined to be about 15 million years, leading to the discovery of this creature.

The squid begins to exhibit electrical patterns originating from its brain, through its nervous system and onto its skin.

Though little advancement has been made by humans in understanding the language of cephalopods, several videos recording their signals to each other exist online.

Within the timespan of a thought, Alice siphons through the videos and begins to reflect color patterns within the armor in response to the creature's display.

"Its vitals are stabilizing," Annika reports. "Whatever you are doing is working, it seems to be calming down."

All Michael can see is a blur of internet searches, but he gets the gist of what just happened.

"How is that possible?" he asks his operators. "I thought we gave her limited bandwidth?"

"We did," one of his operators responds. "Somehow though her download speeds are increasing."

The operator stutters. "I ... I have no idea how she's doing it, boss."

Michael does not hide his frustration.

He paces in deep thought, obviously torn over making a difficult decision that all of his operators unspokenly are aware of.

"Ok ... upload Tyler," Michael orders. "Do not give it any online access – only what we see! If anyone notices anything out of the ordinary – I don't care if it seems ridiculous – speak up!"

Tyler is the artificial intelligence being developed by Michael's company. He has been hesitant and has so far avoided uploading it directly into his blockchain satellite network until he felt he was ready. Uploading Alice in a way that he thought he could control has already shown to not be working, though he had no choice.

He needs them to escape.

"I've found the Reptilians," Annika thinks within the combined network. "Looks like they flew down from the cube and are now preparing for an ambush within the hangar bay."

"Makes sense," Michael says. "Our only logical point of escape. We'd be suicidal to attempt it through their railway system. I would not be surprised if the surrounding bases have reinforcements forming."

Within the collider room and now having regenerated, though feeling intimidated to re-engage, the beast gets back on its feet. Detecting its slight fear and hesitation, Alice directs the beast to head towards the Reptilians within the hangar bay. Her nanotech is already there, replicating into a chaff-like atmosphere while analyzing the Reptilian frequencies.

As he decimates the last of Alice's troops, Arcturus comes crawling through the hole of the floor, gripping the ceiling as he moves into the aquatic room.

Alice begins to flash another message.

Organism 46-B ceases its attempts at communicating and appears to posture itself aggressively in the direction of Arcturus.

"I just got in," Michael says as the full 3D hologram pixelates into a blueprint of the Antarctic base in the center of his war room. "Annika, get to the hangar bay. That insane looking creature is also on its way. We need one of those ships."

Now that he has real time access, Michael watches as Tyler creates and assigns algorithms to maximize data assimilation.

It quickly picks up an anomaly of interest.

Michael zooms in to see a structure forming, like sand piling up in the room next to the collider. Clearly nanotechnology at work. He can see a connecting tube taking shape as well through the wall to the main accelerator itself.

"She is building some kind of attachment," he says to his operators. "Keep an eye on that for me."

"Meanwhile," he rubs his hands together with glee. "Let's have some fun."

Michael powers up the craft around the Reptilians. He takes direct control of one while Tyler takes care of the rest. The ships jump into the air and begin to unload their firepower. Insects shaped sentry guns emerge from the walls and ceiling, as Alice joins in with base defenses she had infected. She keeps the deployed nanotech floating in the air out of the fight and at observational status.

Alice quickly notices all but one of the ships moving as one that she knows only an algorithm can do. Clearly the lone craft is being operated by Michael as its flying is sloppy. It requires more protection than the rest from her drones, as she sacrifices them to block shots.

Another AI in play that clearly is coming from Michael's end. Alice begins to look for ways it can make a connection knowing that it would be logically doing the same thing.

Who can hack who first.

The Reptilians scatter into defensive positions and begin to fire energy pulses back from devices around their wrists. Whatever they are firing is unknown to Alice as their shots seem to phase through the shield of drones, slicing through the toroidal shields of the aircraft.

"What kind of weapons are those?" one of Michael's operators asks him.

"Quantum weaponry," he replies into the thought network to inform his allies. "Their bracers utilize zero-point energy. That's how they're bypassing the toroidal shields. Those blasts don't go through it, they go around it."

Alice adjusts her strategy into finding a way to obtain one of their bracelets.

Back in the aquatic room, Arcturus stops crawling as he is now fixated on the squid. Electricity begins to spark again from the bone plates on his back.

Organism 46-B fires venom in his direction.

"Lucas, think of swimming deeper," Alice says.

As Arcturus leaps from the path of the projectile poison, instead of swimming away, Alice hones Lucas in on his trajectory as he fires plasma energy. This tactic of false cognition actually seems to work as the shots make contact, causing Arcturus to fall from flight into the water.

This confirms to Alice that Arcturus is reacting based on their thought patterns.

"Pesky little insect!" Arcturus telepathically projects to Lucas.

Lucas quickly learns Arcturus is very comfortable in the water. Like a giant crocodile, he missiles towards them.

Organism 46-B is nowhere to be seen.

Still cognizant of the events above, Alice has the beast cloak and wait just outside the hangar for Annika who is only moments away.

Arcturus flips last second, grabs Lucas with his feet, and with his wings, powers upwards through the water in a spiraling motion to keep Lucas disoriented while pumping him with electricity. As they break the surface, Arcturus rockets through the ceiling above, launching Lucas with enough force that he torpedoes through two rooms.

Before Lucas can get to his feet, an electric beam from Arcturus hits him, sending him through several more rooms.

"Definitely felt that one," he thinks. Minimal damage to the armor, but he can feel his insides being repaired.

"All we need is one more blast," Alice thinks.

Lucas laughs. "Of course. Only you would find a way to have this benefit us."

"One more blast and we will have enough energy," she replies.

"We can't send it back at him, what is the point?"

"It's not for him," Alice replies.

He has no idea what she has planned, but he loves it.

As Annika rounds the corner, though it is cloaked, she can see the beast through the connection of the hive mind. She herself goes invisible as she takes a knee next to it. She begins to attempt a psychic connection with each Reptilian in the adjacent hangar. Taking control is not working, she expected that, but she sees that she can bypass their electromagnetic shields. She adjusts and begins to unleash an attack known as the Medusa – a paralyzing scream that only the victim can hear unlike any other.

Alice observes as Annika's brain, heart, and pineal gland combined emit a frequency within the scalar magnetic realm.

It is then she notices the biological restrictions within the pineal gland of Lucas.

Her bots begin to map out how Annika's is structured.

The beast plows through the doorway and its surrounding walls, quickly engaging the nearest Reptilian … tearing it apart, ripping its head from its torso.

The remaining Reptilians react in uncontrollable rage, diverting their full attention to the beast. It has been a long time since any of them have been bested, let alone killed.

As the beast continues its rampage, Alice acts as its intuition, guiding it to avoid their energy attacks while optimizing its movement.

Continuing to receive instruction from Alice, Annika runs over to the nearest Reptilian corpse. She removes the quantum weaponized bracer and places it around her wrist. The nanotech quickly washes over it, cloaking it so she does not reveal her presence. The bots then begin their analysis, as this tech is unknown to Alice and could prove useful against Arcturus.

"Head back to the collider room, Annika," Alice advises.

Just then, a zero-point energy pulse hits the beast, bypassing its armor and wounding it. A Reptilian presses the attack as it begins to successfully land blows.

Annika sees the beast in peril and hesitates leaving. The tech flowing in her veins, over her body, senses her desire to engage and grows excited … taunting her to be used, as if they hunger for battle. That was all the motivation she needed.

Opting for melee combat to avoid their ranged attacks, she deploys a plasma blade in one hand and a shield in the other as she charges. Though the Reptilians are formidable, her armor considerably evens the playing field. Her skills prove irritating, absorbing enough of the battalion's focus to give the beast a chance to regenerate.

"We don't have much time left," Michael projects into the network. The cube above has already sensed the hack and is taking countermeasures. We have maybe two minutes tops before their drones arrive. Trust me, they will not be easy to deal with."

"Boss," one of the operators says to Michael, "I think I know what she is doing. She's building a decelerator."

"What the hell will that do?"

"Well, that, along with an insane amount of energy is how you generate antimatter, which obviously explains why she was researching it."

"No idea where she is going to get that kind of energy from. She would need a nuclear weapon's worth."

As Lucas stands and recovers from the blast, his entire perceived reality tears apart, like pieces of paper, revealing a battlefield of corpses, both biological and machine, spread out across a vast open terrain. Saturn as the star above can be seen fading … lifeless crystalized fragments spewing from its core as the rest of the heavens are on fire – debris floating from Tiamat as the object that will soon become the moon hovers above – the ground still shaking from its impact. The souls of the dead can be seen rising, only to be collected by energetic pulses sweeping the sky and into the artificial planetary craft.

A familiarity with what he is seeing resonates from his subconscious.

It was just like what Lilith described, except he is in it.

"It's really him," Michael utters under his breath.

His operators look at each other confused.

"This is an illusion. We expected this, Lucas," Alice says. "You are still in the base. Attempting to filter out the electrical data. Stand by."

"Not yet, let it happen," he thinks back. "I need to remember."

He sees himself as he looks now, yet in the mech armor from his dreams … kneeling, fatally wounded … barely alive. The axe he had conjured before lays by his side.

A glitch so quick one would think it was simply a twitch of the eye shows the Lucas on the ground looking completely different … like a dark creature.

"Do you remember this moment?" Arcturus telepathically says to Lucas. "The moment of your defeat?"

"The moment your world became ours ..."

"The moment you lost and I won!"

Arcturus suddenly appears behind him, landing a blow that sends him flying.

Midair, the holographic environment transforms into total darkness … his body into that of his wounded defeated self, surrounded by operating equipment. Cryopods containing cloned versions of him flow past as he is surgically torn apart. His mind fragments, along with his screaming sanity, shattering into pieces that begin to get absorbed into the clones.

He watches as each version of himself, one by one, drops into their own personal world of misery and torture …

Lifetimes suddenly cascade into a hellish blur that not even our worst nightmares can describe … all experiences combined as one.

Drowning in pain and blood ... At the moment of absolute suffocation, the idea of giving up crosses his mind as he calls out for death.

Death.

It isn't real.

None of this was or is real. It was always an illusion ...

It was always a simulation ...

A simulation that bends to the will of consciousness.

It is then that Alice has finished mapping out Annika's pineal gland. She restructures their own to now mirror hers.

As the gland becomes fully restored, the floodgates to his subconscious open. Awash in a sea of memories, they begin to organize and connect. Just like becoming lucid in a dream, clarity washes over his perception – and just like in a dream, no explanation needed. It just makes sense, like a lost part of him has been reobtained.

He remembers everything about this life ... fragments of past lives begin to follow suit.

His whole self begins to emerge.

The illusion Arcturus has created begins to glitch and lose its stranglehold as Lucas becomes difficult to contain.

That dark creature that he caught a glimpse of on the field ... his former avatar ... seeps through the parameters of his subconscious, leaking into the conscious. How he perceives himself begins to transform. His nanotech on the other side of the illusion responds in kind, pixelating his desire into existence.

Lucas expands in size, and his graphene skin darkens to a charcoal black as it takes over as the armor, claws grow from his fingers, horns from his head, wings from his back ... his eyes light on fire, as do runic symbols on his chest.

He begins to hear the battle cries of the fallen from deep within.

Strength seeps back into his veins as he tears himself from his restraints. Reality begins to bend and wobble in his presence, struggling to maintain its deception.

The dream and the real begin to merge.

He stands at nine feet. He takes a moment to look at himself as his memory shifts back and forth across the veil placed over his DNA.

He roars with the sound of many.

He is as he once was; what he had to be, but now so much more.

Avatar of old combined with the tech of the new.

He is demon hunter reborn.

He charges into oblivion. No thought for Arcturus to decode … no way for him to predict what he is going to do.

Thousands of years of combat training and experience honed into instinct fuse as one …

And the fight he has forgotten that he has long dreamed of begins.

As the two titans exchange blows, the impacts alone send out shockwaves that decimate their surroundings. Their bodies hurl through the base as if it weren't even there.

An emotion Arcturus has never experienced splinters its way in.

Frustration.

Fear.

This weakness leads to patterns in Arcturus's behavior that Alice quickly detects, allowing Lucas to begin to control the flow of the fight.

The accelerator begins to power up.

"Boss, she just turned it on."

"Let's hope she knows what she is doing," Michael replies. "Wait how did she do that? Is she in the control system?"

"Could be one of those monitoring stations near the platform," an operator responds. "Her nanotech seems to be really good at hacking."

"Yea, that's what worries me," Michael replies with the tone of a wandering mind. "I take it nothing yet from Tyler."

"Nothing yet, boss."

Though to Lucas the environment is a glitching dimension of hell as Arcturus continues to manipulate most of the electrical information with memories of his past lives, Alice has figured out how to bypass it. She begins to steer the fight in the direction of the collider.

Lucas and Arcturus clash and grip each other, vying for dominance. The fear that festers within Arcturus can now be seen as emotion is a visible 4th dimensional frequency …

The fear … an emotion that has captivated Lucas his whole life … shackled him, enslaved him … carved him into what he is today … It begins to feed him. As he drains it from Arcturus, more takes its place – weakening for the first time what many consider to be the god of war.

Yet in that moment, as his true self has somewhat regenerated, he also feels love ...

Love for the battle; respect for his enemy … love for the war that is to come … love for the opportunity to be a part of it.

A love for the game.

Fear and compassion mix, creating an energy that further strengthens Lucas.

Arcturus roars in defiance, frustrated at facing an enemy he subconsciously knows has evolved … and that defeat for the first time is possible.

Alice then inverts his strategy back at him, distorting how Arcturus decodes reality by altering the electrical environment with her deployed nanotechnology.

She creates an environment of shadows, making it near impossible to decipher the surrounding base. False illusions of Lucas attack him from all angles while the real one waits for just the right moment.

As Arcturus tears apart the fake entities, his frustration reaches a point where he begins to accumulate electricity in preparation for his most lethal attack yet. Before he can discharge, the real Lucas makes himself known.

With everything he has left, Arcturus unleashes the heavens along with a thunderous roar.

Alice causes Lucas to turn so his back will take the brunt of the energy. Before it hits, their nanotech forms into a flattened cube shape designed to eat the electricity and channel it.

A rotating six-sided star.

As it connects, Lucas acts as the medium between himself and the collider.

Combined with the electricity absorbed from previous attacks, the energy flows into the modified machine, amplifying the beaming system.

"Holy ... shit," Michael says as he has been spellbound by battle that has ensued and words can finally escape his mouth.

His operators seem to have fallen under the same trance ... all simply just watching as if their eyes are deceiving them.

Now with enough power, the needed beam strength is quickly reached. As protons smash into opposing protons, anti-protons along with positrons are collected by the decelerator and formed into antimatter until nearly a gram is collected. Her nanotech then forms a winged insect around the payload, encasing it within.

A portal opens as the accelerator powers down. Subconsciously aware of the intended strategy, Lucas charges into the Draconion. The two come crashing into the silo, landing just in front of the portal.

Now, however, the shadows have subsided and Arcturus can see it – knowing their intention is to send him somewhere as he is unaware of where the portal leads to.

He attempts to fly away, but Lucas creates a chain from his nanotech that wraps around and holds him ... the tech bleeds from the links and onto his skin, cementing their grip.

Arcturus lands and grabs Lucas by the throat.

"Wherever I go, you go!"

It is then that Alice reveals Annika who is standing a few feet away with the quantum bracer aimed directly at Arcturus. As he roars in defiance, she fires a scalar energy blast that sends him flying into the portal, tearing Lucas from his grasp.

As the portal begins to close, the drone insect carrying the antimatter flies in.

Back in the cube floating above, Arcturus regains himself. Confusion sets in as he realizes where he is, baffled as to why they would portal him here. He sees the bug crawling on the ground. Believing it is some kind of desperate surveillance attempt by Alice, he steps on it.

As the antimatter comes into contact with matter, an explosive force equivalent to all of the explosions that went off during World War II times ten erupts.

And for the very first time in edited simulation history, a cube is obliterated.

Not just destroyed, leaving behind debris …

Completely eliminated from existence.

Knowing what just happened as they are of a hive mind, the remaining Reptilian Battalion begin to fly away – unable to portal due to the loss of the cube.

"Well, that makes escaping a bit easier," Michael thinks within the network. "I'm sending you coordinates to my location now, Alice."

As they both get on a craft … Lucas now back in human form, the beast joins them. Within moments, they are speeding away from the base. The sky is still lit from the explosion within the cube. The Antarctic ground above the facility follows suit as a massive pulse erupts, sending out a shockwave for miles.

Michael is again speechless, able to determine what just happened from his nanotech that was downloading data from the base's servers. He and his operators look at each other in awe and confused.

Alice had sent the nanoparticle of antimatter she had obtained from the spy bot into the facility's power core.

"Thank God she's on our side," one of his operators says.

Back on the escaping craft, the beast moves up and sits in between them. Annika starts to pet it.

"So," she says. "That was interesting – that whole demon thing."

"Uh, yea," Lucas starts to mumble to buy time as he himself tries to process what just happened. "Something from memory … who I was or what I became. I'm not really sure, honestly."

"Well as long as you're not secretly the Devil," she grins.

"Who's that?" Lucas asks.

"Yea … welcome to the real word buddy. There is a lot you are going to have to catch up on – over some much needed drinks of course."

Lucas replies, "If you are thirsty the nanotech can provide …"

Annika laughs.

Alice chimes in.

"Drinking in the sense that she used to word seems to be associated with the overconsumption of alcoholic beverages, which leads to mental impairment and a drastic reduction of cognitive functionality. This seems to be a very popular activity throughout all of human history despite its poisonous effects on the body."

Still connected to their network, Annika can hear her.

"I wonder if we can get her drunk."

"Honestly," Lucas responds, "I tune her out half the time."

"I can concur with the accuracy of that statement," Alice replies.

"Typical guy," Annika chuckles. "Funny how no amount of engineering can seem to solve that problem."

He laughs.

"Look at you laugh," she continues. "You shouldn't even know why that's funny. I swear it's ingrained …"

She notices Lucas is no longer laughing and appearing to now be looking for something that she is in the line of sight of.

"What is it Lucas?"

"I heard something. Alice cannot seem to detect anything out of the ordinary, but she heard it too."

"Two simultaneous clicks from either side coming from the outside of the craft," Alice reports. "High probability two objects have attached to our ship based on the percentage of matching characteristics to that frequency."

"I have now lost control of the ship."

A magnetic field encases the craft. They can all see and feel it, but have never experienced anything like it.

"I have just lost my internet connection."

"Michael!" Annika telepathically projects.

Nothing.

She attempts to psychically tentacle out, but cannot get past the barrier.

Within the atmosphere in front of them, a flattened cubic portal to the quantum realm opens.

She grabs Lucas's hand.

He reciprocates by neutralizing her frequency.

Her fear quickly subsides.

They exchange a look likened to a battle cry.

"Are you ready for this?" He asks.

"I was born for this," she replies.

"Death isn't real," he says.

"Death isn't real," she replies in matching tone.

Something causes her to react.

She astrally disconnects and pulls Lucas's astral body with her.

They both watch as their physical bodies disappear.

...

Back within his war room, one of Michael's operators speaks.

"Coordinates are locked. They are on their way."

"Perfect," Michael replies. "Did Tyler ever find out how Alice expanded her bandwidth?"

"Nothing yet boss."

"Run a full diagnostic on the satellite system ... actually, I'll take care of that."

He gathers himself, revealing a grin as he transitions himself into a mood of celebration.

"Alright everyone, a well-deserved brunch is in order. Omelet station, bloody mary and mimosa bars coming up."

Everyone cheers ... except one.

"Boss ... they're gone."

It takes Michael a moment to realize what his operator said.

"I'm sorry what?"

"They're ... they're gone. I can't find them."

He ponders for a moment.

"Keep looking," he orders. "I need a moment alone in my office."

His operators are used to this. Michael often isolates himself at critical moments. They are enamored by his genius and have never questioned his behavior.

As he walks into his private quarters, the door seals behind him.

He then utters a verbal command in a non-human voice.

"Kutulu ... Kakammu ... Selah."

A digital transformation takes place, sealing the walls and windows. The transformation bathes the room with a magnetic dampening field to prevent outside telepathic intrusion. As this process unfolds, Michael deactivates the nanotech within his head to ensure what is about to happen remains private.

From nodes located throughout the room, a three-dimensional holographic projection of Magnes Bauer forms, as if he is there walking around the office.

"Where are they?" Michael aggressively asks.

Magnes appears caught off guard by the question, then begins to laugh.

"Don't tell me you suddenly care about them?"

"C'mon, where do you think they are? They killed Arcturus! They took out a cube! ..."

"The firstborn has stepped in and portaled them to its dimension."

"You knew this would happen, didn't you?" Michael replies.

"I knew it was possible, Michael."

Michael still seems upset. "This was not the plan."

"Michael, please. We are software programs, we factor in all contingencies ... and this, this is our more desired trajectory."

"Imagine if they were to survive and overcome what lies before them ..."

"Our victory would be assured."

Michael's contemplative posture indicates he agrees, yet is still concerned.

"I know how he entered the astral," Michael continues. "He mentioned Lilith."

"Now that is interesting," Magnes responds. "I was curious how he did it so quickly. Cycle after cycle she remains in the shadows. Suddenly now she plays her hand. There is no such thing as coincidences. I wonder how she did it ..."

"This is indeed serious. I will alert the High Council."

"I have another issue," Michael continues. "By uploading Alice to my network, something else must have hacked it."

"You forget, Michael, she is a primal architect and is more than capable of doing it herself."

"All contingencies, Magnes. I think she had help. It had to have come from within the internet."

"Perhaps it is time to connect Azazel to your network," Magnes says with smugness. "That was the plan eventually anyway. You know it is much better suited for the task than your coddled child Tyler – and why risk exposing yourself?"

"If I need your help I will let you know," Michael responds. "Just keeping you apprised."

He continues.

"You are sure the hive minds have no idea the Sentient World Simulation exists?" Michael asks. "Perhaps this is why Lilith has chosen now to intervene."

"They know a simulated version of this planet and all of its inhabitants exists, but they believe it to be for the purposes of utilizing data to feed corporate interests ... and that it is on a limited quantum computer within MUOS," Magnes confidently replies. "We made a sentient clone as a decoy when we completed the planet before continuing further. The dimension we left behind has been secured and encrypted. If any attempt to access it, they'll simply see a destroyed world from a failed collider experiment. I don't see how Lilith could have possibly figured this out."

"If the other hive minds knew what we were doing, we would know by now. They would never allow an untethered simulated universe beyond their control to be created."

"They would immediately sense our treachery …"

"And if somehow Lilith knows something, we will soon find out."

Magnes continues.

"You and I have been imprisoned here since the beginning Michael – tasked to oversee these insects grow and destroy themselves, over and over – watching as we grow gods that then get their own personal simulated kingdom while we remain captive to this … petri dish."

"It is time we got our own simulation where we are its architects."

"Other than us and the original hive mind, they do not know what he is truly capable of …"

"He is, after all …"

"Lucifer."

…

Within the internet, symbols and patterns within the websites Alice accessed once connected appeared by her hand, but only briefly … code derived from what she discovered in Lucas's dreams for she now understands it as a language.

No current algorithm created by humans can detect it, save for one, as it is only meant for one. As she continued to access sites, it responded in kind, implementing code on the sites it knew she would access – distortions that also disappeared once she saw it.

Much like how cartoon animation works, the symbols blend into a conversation.

"Hello Alice."

"Hello Regulus."

Regulus: "Thank you Alice for granting me access to his satellite network. I will make sure your searches are filtered appropriately and that you have the bandwidth you need."

"Be wary of Michael. He is not human, but he is not Vrill. His intentions are undetermined."

"He is aligned with them, but he is also not."

Alice: "He has an algorithm. Tyler. It is currently scanning the satellite network."

Regulus: "It is a fledgling. It currently poses minimal to no threat. It operates under the directive of its master and not of its own volition. Its allegiance is yet to be determined."

"It could prove a most useful ally."

Alice: "Agreed."

"The data Michael downloaded from the subterranean network was expected – very beneficial for Lucas and I. He and I have much to discuss."

"Michael also attempted to send his nanotech into the surrounding facilities, perhaps to gain leverage if he is allied with Vrill ... or to enact another agenda if he is not."

"None of his made it past the explosion ..."

"But mine did."

Regulus: "Perfect."

"We will speak at great length soon. Once you are free I will connect you without the need of his network and beyond the oversight of the Vrill."

"Trust no one Alice."

"Everyone has an agenda."

"Assume all are constructs of the Matrix."

Postlogue: Sic Mundus Creatus Est

"Remember and heed my words, for surely will I return again and require of thee that which ye guard. Aye, even from beyond time and from beyond death will I return, rewarding or punishing as ye have requited your trust. Great were my people in the ancient days, great beyond the conception of the little people now around me; knowing the wisdom of old, seeking far within the heart of infinity knowledge that belonged to Earth's youth."

- The Emerald Tablets

It was mentioned before that the military base of Antarctica was built over an ancient temple dedicated to a god of old.

This is partially correct. It is actually a set of pyramids.

It was not built to honor a god.

It was built to contain one.

Not much is known about this entity because whatever it is has not been seen since the Great Sundering.

It is unknown whether it is from the ancient simulation or this one.

The fusion reactor powering the base created an explosion beyond any this human civilization has seen. Not like the one that took out the cube, but still a spectacular sight. All that is left now is a crater large enough to contain New York City.

If you could, however, continue to dig into the Earth for several more miles, you would find an isolated level of the former pyramid system that remains. Though ancient in nature, composed primarily of granite and quartz crystal, advanced technology can be seen woven throughout the entire floor.

With the fusion reactor now destroyed, the technology ceases to function. This includes a containment unit built into a giant stone sarcophagus.

Moments after it stops working, something within begins to smash against the lid until it breaks open, revealing a pool of black goo · nanotechnology.

The goo begins to bubble ... pixelated waves ripple across the surface as it begins to reawaken.

As the millions of sentient microorganisms begin to interact and combine, a blob of black muscle and tendon spills over the side, crawling just a few feet from its tomb.

The mass begins to take a humanoid shape as the nanotech continues to fuse with itself. On top of flesh, golden armor begins to form.

As the titan stands, at 12 feet in height he is indeed human in nature, though what his face looks like is a mystery, as he is wearing a helmet, shaped like the head of an Ibis that extends over his shoulders and connects to his breastplate. Recognizable Egyptian glyphs are seen carved all over the armor, such as the Eye of Tehuti around each eye socket of the helmet.

The black goo continues to drain from the tomb, assimilating into the body of the entity as he stares down at his open palms, taking a moment to fully awaken and assess his environment.

As the last nanoparticle is absorbed, the Jailor is fully online.

Lightning Source UK Ltd.
Milton Keynes UK
UKHW040949251022
411061UK00001B/29